LADY OF ASHES

Books by Christine Trent

Lady of Ashes

By the King's Design

A Royal Likeness

The Queen's Dollmaker

LADY OF ASHES

CHRISTINE TRENT

KENSINGTON BOOKS
www.kensingtonbooks.com

KENSINGTON BOOKS are published by

Kensington Publishing Corp.
119 West 40th Street
New York, NY 10018

All Kensington titles, imprints, and distributed lines are available at special quantity discounts for bulk purchases for sales promotion, premiums, fund-raising, and educational or institutional use.

Special book excerpts or customized printings can also be created to fit specific needs. For details, write or phone the office of the Kensington Special Sales Manager: Kensington Publishing Corp., 119 West 40th Street, New York, NY 10018. Attn. Special Sales Department. Phone: 1-800-221-2647.

Kensington and the K logo Reg. U.S. Pat. & TM Off.

ISBN-13: 978-0-7582-6591-3
ISBN-10: 0-7582-6591-3

First Kensington Trade Paperback Printing: March 2013
10 9 8 7 6 5 4 3 2 1

Printed in the United States of America

For my mother, Georgia Carpenter

A mother is the truest friend we have, when trials heavy and sudden, fall upon us; when adversity takes the place of prosperity; when friends who rejoice with us in our sunshine desert us; when trouble thickens around us, still will she cling to us, and endeavor by her kind precepts and counsels to dissipate the clouds of darkness, and cause peace to return to our hearts.

—Washington Irving (1783–1859)

ACKNOWLEDGMENTS

The idea for this novel came from Mary Oldham, a fellow writer who casually said to me at a writers' conference, "I've always wanted to read a story about a Victorian undertaker." From that offhand comment a book was born.

I had the great fortune of talking to many experts in the course of researching this book. In particular, I extend thanks to the following: Doug Lyle, MD, for his timeline of forensic science during the Victorian period; Trevor May, historian, for his research on embalming; Shirley Nicholson, a guide at the Linley-Sambourne House in London and author of *A Victorian Household*, for her kindness toward an American visitor with endless questions about Victorian life; Rosemarie Wood, Chapel Steward at St. George's Chapel, Windsor Castle, for her assistance in understanding how a funeral procession would work inside the chapel; Ms. Eleanor Cracknell from the St. George's Chapel Archives for her quick response to questions about Prince Albert's funeral; and Ned Brinsfield, funeral director of Brinsfield Funeral Home, for graciously answering probably the strangest questions of his career.

My editor, Audrey LaFehr, gives me the freedom to write whatever I want, no matter how odd the subject material, and my agent, Helen Breitwieser, always encourages me to think "off the shelf." It is a pleasure to work with them.

Good friends keep a writer going. My thanks to Mary Russell for spending countless hours driving me to book signings and to Petra Utara for listening over numerous steak and pasta dinners. I am also indebted to Carolyn McHugh and Marian Wheeler for rummaging through used bookstores on their own time to find research books for me.

My brother, Tony Papadakis, is a Civil War enthusiast and provided me with lots of details I would have never thought to look for elsewhere.

Thanks are essential to my beta readers, Georgia Carpenter and Diane Townsend, for reading my manuscript in record time and providing feedback to ensure I made my deadline.

Finally, I thank God for giving me my Jon, who is the best husband I could have ever been granted.

Ecce Agnus Dei.

PROLOGUE

I killed a man today, and although I didn't mean to do it, I must confess that it wasn't unpleasant at all.

I suppose some might call it murder, but is it really murder if the victim deserved it? If he was especially irritating?

Unfortunately, most societies frown upon this thing called murder, so I suppose I shall have to reinvent myself. Again. If only one could declare the deceased an obnoxious bore or an unrepentant fool and be done with it, there wouldn't be quite so much fuss.

Fuss should be left to the undertakers, who sweep in with their tall hats swathed in black crape and nod solemnly at the family as they charge their exorbitant fees for the funereal spectacles that people love.

I wonder what it must be like to live the life of an undertaker, never actually getting to do away with the less desirable members of society, but at least having the satisfaction of seeing them all sealed away forever.

But, my dearest diary, let's return to more important concerns. Where should I go? Another town far away? Or perhaps another country, where no one will have heard of my nefarious deed. My possibilities are quite limitless.

I must think carefully.

⇾ 1 ⇽

In the midst of life we are in death.

—The Book of Common Prayer (1662)

London
May 1861

Violet Morgan often wondered why she was so skilled at dressing a corpse, yet was embarrassingly incompetent in the simplest household task, such as selecting draperies or hiring housemaids.

If only they hadn't moved to fancier lodgings in a more elegant section of London, she wouldn't be burdened with having to learn a myriad of rules for keeping a proper home. Surely her domestic mismanagement was the source of her husband's current displeasure. How else could Graham have become so morose and embittered these past few months? Surely it wasn't the hot weather, which had never before made him so bilious.

Violet picked through her tray of mourning brooches, organizing them neatly for the next customer who wished to make a purchase. She slid the tray of pins into the display case and reached for the pile of papers Graham must have carelessly thrown on top of it. She sorted through the mix of invoices, newspapers, and advertising leaflets. A recent copy of *The Illustrated London News* caught her eye. Graham had circled headlines regarding events in the United States and scribbled in his own comments beside them. Her husband was avidly following current events transpiring across the Atlantic, hoping for destruction on both sides of the U.S. conflict.

One article opined on the expected duration of the conflict raging there. The Americans had recently engaged in hostilities, after years of Southern states bickering with those in the North. Since last month's first firing of shots at Fort Sumter, South Carolina, much taunting and posturing had occurred. How the citizens of the United States enjoyed fighting. Each side boasted the skirmish would last just a few months, and self-proclaimed experts declared that all the blood to be spilled in the contest could be contained in a single thimble, or wiped up by one handkerchief.

The newspaper agreed, but Violet felt that was foolish optimism. England's own civil war had gone on for almost a decade and nearly destroyed the country.

And to what end? The Roundheads eliminated the monarchy with the beheading of Charles I in 1649, and by 1660 the monarchy was back with his son, Charles II. Nothing changed, but thousands of lives lost and a king beheaded. Surely the Americans would end up with a fallen leader, too.

Another article, which Graham had not only circled, but drawn brackets around, focused on the South's hunger for recognition. During the past couple of months, the Southern states had pressed Britain to recognize their burgeoning nation. The poor fools thought they had Britain in a state of helplessness because they controlled much of the world's cotton, so necessary for England's cloth mills. They didn't realize that England had been storing cotton for some time and was flush with it. What the country did need was wheat.

Wheat was produced by the Northern states.

The crafty British politicians, though, were willing to host a confederate delegation in London and let it press its suit for diplomatic recognition, thus not publicly rejecting the South in case it should win the war.

Violet sighed as she separated the pile of papers into related stacks before removing another tray to straighten, this one full of glass-domed mourning brooches. Buyers could weave the hair of the deceased into a fanciful pattern and place it under the glass to create an everlasting keepsake to be pinned to one's breast.

To think of all those American soldiers who would die ignominious deaths, heaped into mass graves, without the distinction of a proper funeral and burial. How could her husband, a man whose profession was to bring dignity to death, wish for mass slaughter?

She replaced the second tray. The display case looked much better now that it was tidied up inside and out. She moved over to the linen closet, its door discreetly hidden in the wallpaper at the back of the room. Inside were shelves stacked with bolts of black crape for draping over windows, black Chantilly lace for mourning shawls, and fine cambric cotton for winding sheets. Except the cambric had all tumbled to the ground in a heap. How had that happened?

"Graham?" she called out. "Did you let our cambric fall to the floor?" Only when there were no customers at Morgan Undertaking would she dare raise her voice above the gentlest of tones.

"For what reason would I have done that? Maybe Will was the sloppy one going through it," he replied from the shop's reception area.

Perhaps, but Will was usually as careful as Violet.

Violet glanced at the mantel clock over the fireplace. Nearly ten o'clock in the morning, time to visit the Stanley family. She gathered up her cavernous undertaker's bag, filled with embalming fluids, tinted skin creams, cutting tools, syringes, fabric swatches, and her book of compiled drawings of coffins, mourning fashions, flowers, and memorial stones. Going to the display case, she pulled out a selection of mourning jewelry and added the pieces to her bag.

Violet lifted her undertaker's hat from its stand and tied the sash under her chin. The extra-long, flowing tails of black crape wrapped around the hat's crown were a symbol of her trade. Graham wore his own hat adorned with black crape when meeting with customers, as well. She peered into a mirror she kept next to the hat stand, pinched her cheeks to bring some color into them, and tucked an errant strand of hair under the brim of her hat before putting on black gloves. In his more jovial days, Graham used to tease her that one day he'd be rich because he'd cut off and sell her long hair, which he deemed the color of newly minted bronze ha'pennies and of even more value in its beauty.

With a quick farewell to her husband, she left the premises and boarded a horse-drawn green omnibus for Belgravia. Graham always insisted that they hire private cabs for transport to meetings with grieving families, contending it was more representative of the Morgans' socially elevated state, but Violet was still uncomfortable with their new entry into higher circles and usually ignored his demand. She wasn't quite sure their income supported the luxuries Graham contended were their due. The omnibus, London's horse-drawn public transport, cost a mere threepence to travel to most places through central London, and only sixpence to travel farther out.

She exited the omnibus a few blocks from the address she had been given, and walked the rest of the way.

The Stanleys lived in an up-and-coming neighborhood on the outer edges of Belgravia, an area known for its wealthy—and usually aristocratic—residents. The Stanleys' townhome wasn't quite as stately as the residences nearby, being situated in a long row of recently built units that reflected the current construction craze in London.

Nevertheless, this district was a few steps up from the London locale where she and Graham had settled after inheriting his father's undertaking shop. Graham's ambition was eventually to move to Mayfair, maybe even Park Lane, yet Violet was just as happy in their Grafton Terrace townhome in Kentish Town, a very respectable area north of Regent's Park.

Mostly respectable, anyway. They did have odd neighbors, Karl and Jenny Marx, who named all of their daughters after Jenny. Mr. Marx seemed to have no occupation other than writing letters and essays every day, sometimes under the name "A. Williams." There was also neighborhood gossip that Mr. Marx, or Williams, had fathered a child with his housekeeper, but Violet stayed out of such tittle-tattle. She lived in a pleasant area and had no desire to stir up anything ugly.

There was no black crape festooned under the windows and above the doors of the Stanley residence. Violet made a mental note of it as she pressed the "Visitors" bell. Some debate existed as to whether or not an undertaker should be using the "Servants" bell, but in Violet's opinion, anyone assisting the family with a proper departure from their earthly existence was certainly entitled the rank of Visitor.

A maid with swollen eyes and dressed in black opened the door. Immediately recognizing who Violet must be by her garb and large black bag, the young woman silently led Violet to the front parlor and closed the door before going to seek out her mistress.

The Stanleys were far wealthier than she and Graham were. A new grand piano, polished within an inch of its ivory-keyed life, stood prominently in one corner as a testament to fashion. The windows were draped in three separate layers of material, a sign that the Stanleys took current trends very seriously. Multiple linings were expensive, but kept out the dirt, heat, and noise from the street. The papered walls proudly displayed paintings and bric-a-brac, while the wood floors were covered with bright, intricately designed carpets. Violet's own attempts at interior decoration fell far short of the Stanleys' remarkable expressions of taste.

Here was a family that would demand a funeral of nearly aristocratic proportions.

The same maid opened the door to the room again, and a middle-aged woman, haggard beyond her years and dressed head-to-toe in black, entered. Violet nodded solemnly.

The other woman spoke first. "Mrs. Morgan? I'm Adelaide Stanley. Thank you for coming to attend to my Edward." The woman brought an extravagantly laced handkerchief to her eyes. "I can hardly believe he's gone. Such a good husband he was. I don't know how we'll manage." Mrs. Stanley twisted the soaked handkerchief in her hands.

"God finds a way to help us manage," Violet said, pulling a spare cloth from her sleeve and discreetly handing it to the woman, who accepted it with a fresh flow of tears. "Where is Mr. Stanley?"

"Upstairs in his bedroom. So calm and peaceful he was when he passed. Like an angel, despite the torture he endured from pneumonia. Do you wish to see him now?"

Violet considered. Mrs. Stanley was truly grieving, but was relatively composed, unlike some of the hysterical relatives Violet usually encountered, so it might be best to address practical matters first in case her customer should later collapse.

"Why don't we discuss Mr. Stanley's ceremony first?" she suggested.

"Of course, as you wish." Mrs. Stanley rang a bell and gave instructions for tea to another maid who appeared, dressed much like the first one. Violet and her customer sat in deeply plushed, heavily carved chairs and chatted innocuously until the maid returned. After steaming cups had been poured, the maid withdrew, and Violet pressed into the delicacy of arranging a proper funeral.

"I saw immediately upon approaching your elegant front door that Mr. Stanley was a man of some importance, is that not so?"

"Indeed. Edward made us quite comfortable through investment in the London and Birmingham rail line back in the forties. Once it merged with Grand Junction and the Manchester and Birmingham Railways, well, Edward had proven himself to be a very astute investor. He had many influential friends."

"Quite so. And this parlor tells me you are a woman of impeccable taste. Your extensive blue-and-white china collection is to be commended."

Mrs. Stanley was no longer crying. "You are kind to notice, Mrs. Morgan. Mr. Stanley and I strove to present the right sort of furnishings befitting our station. The china is all antique, you know, none of those newly manufactured pieces that have become so popular with the masses."

Violet shifted uncomfortably in her chair. Graham had ordered several new imported blue-and-white vases and jardinières to ornament their home.

"Of course," she replied, removing her gloves and opening her bag, which lay at her feet. "Mr. Stanley wasn't part of a burial club, was he?" Violet withdrew her undertaker's book.

"My, no. We never expected him to go so soon. We never had any thought of it."

"Actually, I applaud the fact that you never did this. Many burial clubs are operated by unscrupulous undertakers who tell grieving widows that they cannot pay out the money until the club's committee meets in three months' time. Naturally, since the burial must be completed quickly, she cannot wait, and the undertaker offers to loan her the money, and charges an exorbitant sum for the funeral.

"My husband and I would never engage in such a practice. I'm simply relieved that we don't have to try to wrest your money from such a club. You and Mr. Stanley were very wise not to have been deceived by one of these dishonest groups."

Violet reached over and patted Mrs. Stanley's hand, and received a grateful smile in return. She continued. "There is much you can do to ensure Mr. Stanley's status is properly recognized at his funeral. Let me show you." Laying the book open in her lap so that Mrs. Stanley could see it, Violet flipped through sections marked "Poor," "Working Class," and "Tradesman," stopping just short of "Titled" to the section marked "Society."

"Most people of your position opt for a hearse with two pairs of horses, two mourning coaches each with pairs, nineteen plumes of ostrich feathers as well as velvet coverings for the horses, eleven men as pages, coachmen with truncheons and wands, and an attendant wearing a silk hatband."

Mrs. Stanley's eyes grew wide. "Oh my. Is all of that necessary?"

Violet flipped backward in the book to the section marked "Tradesman." "Please be assured, we can assist you at a variety of levels. We could pare down to a hearse with a pair and just one mourning coach, and reduce the mourning company to just eight pages and coachmen."

"And that is the standard for what those in the trades do?"

"Yes, madam. For a tradesman such as a railway officer or a solicitor. The cost of such a funeral is around fourteen pounds sterling."

Mrs. Stanley frowned. "And for the other one? With all of the horses and mourners?"

"A bit more, at twenty-three pounds, ten shillings."

"I see. That is certainly well within our abilities. It wouldn't do for my husband to have a funeral that wasn't worthy of him."

"No, madam."

"Tell me, what sort of cof—resting place—would my husband have?"

"An exceptional one, made of inch-thick elm, covered in black and lined with fine, ruffled cambric; a wool bed mattress; and the finest brass and lead fittings on the coffin. Its quality would be nearly that of an aristocrat's. See here." Violet flipped to a page containing a line drawing representing the coffin she was suggesting.

Mrs. Stanley nodded. "A beautiful resting place for my Edward."

"Very elegant, I agree. Now, Mrs. Stanley, do the Stanleys have a plot or mausoleum?"

"His family is at Kensal Green."

"Perfect. A lovely garden cemetery." It truly was. It had attracted many prestigious families and even some royalty. Augustus Frederick, the Duke of Sussex, as well as Princess Sophia, uncle and aunt to Queen Victoria, were both buried there. The princess rested in a magnificent sarcophagus.

"But they're in the crypt under the chapel. We never thought about purchasing a mausoleum in a better section. We never imagined anything would happen to him," Mrs. Stanley said in explanation for why the newly wealthy Stanleys were not in a more exclusive part of the cemetery.

"Please don't fret over it, Mrs. Stanley. Take your time purchasing a location and we can move your husband later."

Violet steeled herself for the next question she must ask. "Mrs. Stanley, tell me, do you wish to have your husband embalmed?"

The look of horror that passed over Mrs. Stanley's face was a familiar sight. "Heavens me, no! What an un-Christian-like thing to suggest," the widow said, a hand across her heart.

"My apologies, I have no wish to offend. It's just that Mr. Stanley would be . . . available . . . longer if he was embalmed, and you could therefore have more visitors."

Violet hardly had the words out of her mouth before Mrs. Stanley was emphatically shaking her head. "Absolutely not. My husband will be buried naturally, as all respectable people are."

Embalming was a new concept in England. Although the practice had been around for centuries, with the ancient Egyptians routinely employing it as one of their many types of funeral practices, it had been mostly limited to royalty in Europe, and even then not frequently. The Americans whom Graham despised so much were already making use of it for their battlefield dead, and the French had written extensively on the merits of the practice, but, thus far, Morgan Undertaking had only performed it on a handful of corpses. Most people were still suspicious of doing something so unnatural to a body that would shortly be committed to the ground.

Violet, in particular, ran into difficulties with families who found it unseemly that a woman would be desecrating a newly deceased person by making cuts, draining blood, and injecting fluids to prolong the freshness of the corpse. Putrefaction typically started within twenty-four hours of death, requiring profusions of flowers and candles around the coffin during visitation, as well as a quick interment.

Violet jotted notes in a small ledger tucked at the rear of the book. "Very good, madam. We have a cooling table that we can place under the coffin to keep him comfortably set during visitation. I'll arrange for your husband's placement and will direct the procession to the cemetery personally. And may I make a few suggestions regarding other accoutrements that might aid you during this difficult time?"

For the next hour, the women discussed further purchases, including black crape for draping across the front of the house, photography of Mr. Stanley in repose, memorial cards, and mourning stationery.

Finally, Violet pulled out her tray of mourning jewelry, made mostly from jet, a popular material derived from driftwood that had been subjected to heat, pressure, and chemical action while resting on the ocean floor. "These pieces are made in one of the finest workshops in Whitby, Yorkshire, Mrs. Stanley. You'll find no better than what I have here."

The new widow picked out a glittering necklace and earrings for herself, both intricately carved, as well as simpler pieces for her two adult daughters, who would be arriving from Surrey in time for the funeral. Violet noted the purchases in her ledger.

Shutting the ledger and putting everything away, Violet addressed their final matter. "I would like to see Mr. Stanley now."

Fresh tears welled up in his wife's eyes. "Yes, of course, this way, please. Two of my maids have already washed him."

Family members or servants frequently handled the initial preparation of the deceased, and in poorer families they might handle all details regarding attendance on the body to save money.

Clutching her bag, Violet followed Mrs. Stanley up a wide staircase in the center hall of their townhome to the next floor of the four-story home. From the top of the landing they walked to the rear of the townhome to a shut door. Mrs. Stanley took a deep breath before opening it and entering, with Violet at her heels.

The room did not yet even have a musty odor to it, despite the heat. Given Mr. Stanley's large figure prone on the bed, she guessed he must have only been dead less than a day. The more corpulent the deceased, the quicker the decay. She glanced at a mantel clock in the room, which was stopped at four twenty-three, confirming that he had just died the previous afternoon. Clocks were traditionally stopped at the time of death to mark the deceased's departure from this current life and into the next. Tradition held that to permit time to continue was to invite the deceased's spirit to remain in the home instead of moving on.

Violet waited near a window while Mrs. Stanley went to her husband, who appeared to be sleeping quite peacefully under a coverlet, kissed his brow, and said, "My dear, the lady undertaker is here. I called for her because I thought she would be most tender with you. I hope you aren't angry with me for not hiring a gentleman undertaker."

She kissed her husband on the cheek this time and patted his chest, then nodded silently to Violet as she slipped out of the room, still teary-eyed, and let the door gently click shut behind her.

This was the part Violet both revered and dreaded, for her almost indescribably heavy responsibility toward both the deceased and his family.

She approached the body and set her bag down on a large table along the wall across from the bed. "Good afternoon, Mr. Stanley, it is a pleasure to make your acquaintance," she said, opening the bag once again and pulling out an array of bottles and a wooden box containing her tools. She arranged her bottles in the order they would be used.

Transferring the box of tools to the bed, she pressed the latch to open it. In what would have been seen as a bizarre gesture by the outside world, Graham had given her this set of Sheffield-made tools to celebrate their fifth wedding anniversary three years ago. Each time she opened the box now, she was reminded of how glorious their married life had initially been.

Graham and his brother, Fletcher, had been trained by their father, known as old Mr. Morgan, to take over the family undertaking business, which had been established by their grandfather in 1816. But Fletcher had a taste for the sea and eventually set himself up as a trader, taking tea to Jamaica, picking up sugar from that country, selling it in Boston to be made into rum, and returning with barrels of finished rum for sale to the Englishmen who craved it.

When old Mr. Morgan died, therefore, Fletcher was happy to let Graham buy out his share of the business. Soon after, Violet met Graham at a church social and was immediately fascinated by the work he did.

For his part, Graham seemed fascinated by a woman who was not repulsed by an undertaker.

Violet reached over and gently squeezed the deceased's hand. Rigor mortis, the chemical change in the muscles that caused the limbs to become temporarily stiff and immovable, had not yet set in, much to her relief, else she'd need to return the following day to finish her preparations, creating undue anxiety for his widow.

Her and Graham's relationship developed amid explanations of coffin ornaments, funeral hospitality, and the care of the dead. Within a year, twenty-year-old Violet Sinclair and twenty-three-year-old Graham Morgan were married, and took up residence with his mother, who remained in her own home after her son and daughter-in-law eventually moved to their more upscale lodgings. Together Graham and Violet rode in each day to their working premises on Queen's Road in Paddington, joyful in their death profession as only two young people in love could possibly be.

Violet sighed as she took out several jars of Kalon Cream. If only her life had remained so happy.

"Now, Mr. Stanley, this might look a bit frightening, but let me assure you that it won't hurt a bit. I promise to be gentle and to fix everything so that your wife will hardly notice that I have had to muddle about with you." Graham had taught her that talking to the deceased helped wash away the dread of working with a dead body. Many customers also talked to the deceased, and those who did, like Mrs. Stanley, seemed to adjust better to their losses.

She examined the contents of each jar, finally deciding that "light flesh" was the right shade. She scooped out some of the cosmetic, a dense covering cream that she rubbed into Mr. Stanley's face and hands. A corpse naturally paled as blood pooled downward, so cosmetic massage creams helped bring a more lifelike appearance back to the body.

After wiping her hands on a cloth, she used a paintbrush to apply a pale rouge to the man's cheeks and lips, thus further enhancing a living appearance. Once she was satisfied with his visage, she unrolled a length of narrow tan cloth and snipped off about a foot of it. She threaded a special needle, then sewed one end of the cloth to the skin behind one ear. Next, she pulled the cloth tightly under his chin, then sewed the other end behind his other ear.

The cloth would prevent Mr. Stanley's mouth from dropping open accidentally during his visitation and frightening dear Aunt Mollie or Grandma Jane as she was bent over whispering last words to him. Sometimes, instead of this method, she used a small prop under the chin, later covered by the deceased's burial clothes.

Every undertaker had his own methods for preparing a body, and those methods were trade secrets.

"All finished, Mr. Stanley. I trust it wasn't too uncomfortable for you. We'll need to get you arranged in the parlor for visitation, then you'll have a journey of great fanfare to the cemetery. But first we must get you properly attired."

She'd forgotten to ask Mrs. Stanley to provide her with burial clothes. Well, there was no help for it, she couldn't possibly ask the woman back in here now, with her husband in such condition. Violet went to the enormous mahogany armoire that loomed in one corner of the room and searched until she found what she assumed was Mr. Stanley's finest set of clothes. She selected a shirt with the highest collar possible to cover the jaw cloth.

Dressing a dead body was exceedingly difficult to do alone, making Violet wish she had Will or Harry, the shop's muscular young assistants, with her. However, Graham had them busy on other assignments, so it couldn't be helped.

Trying not to grunt aloud, Violet pushed and pulled Mr. Stanley's limbs and torso as she struggled to undress him and place him in his finery. Once he was dressed and his hands positioned decorously on his chest, Violet packed up her bag and straightened out the bedclothes, ensuring no evidence of her work was left behind. That was something else Graham had taught her. An undertaker must be like a housemaid: all work performed invisibly and with as little inconvenience to the family as possible.

She returned to the parlor, where Mrs. Stanley was pacing back and forth, worrying the handkerchief Violet had given her between her fingers. "How is my Edward?"

"Resting quite comfortably, Mrs. Stanley. I think he would be quite pleased with how you've provided for him."

Violet assured Mrs. Stanley that she would accompany the coffin, along with a bier, for setup in the parlor the following day. "May I recommend that you perhaps go visit a close friend tomorrow and allow me to escort Mr. Stanley to the parlor privately with one of our assistants?"

"Yes, yes, of course. Whatever you say. You'll be careful with my husband, won't you?"

"Madam, I will treat him as if he were my own husband."

Perhaps she should quit using that turn of phrase, since lately Graham's behavior would have made her more than happy to see him trade places with Mr. Stanley.

Violet dropped her *carte-de-visite*, or calling card, which offered her compliments on one side and the Morgan Undertaking address on the other, on the silver salver in the hallway on her way out, pleased with how this customer visit had transpired and anxious over what mood Graham might be in when she returned.

≫ 2 ≪

Of all those acquirements, which more particularly belong to the feminine character, there are none which take a higher rank, in our estimation, than such as enter into a knowledge of household duties; for on these are perpetually dependent the happiness, comfort, and well-being of a family.

—Beeton's Book of Household Management

"Where have you been?" Graham asked as she untied her hat, combed out the tails with her fingers, and hung it on its stand in the back room. She tossed her black gloves on a nearby shelf.

"At the Stanley residence near Belgravia. Our commission from Mr. Edward Stanley's funeral should enable you to buy a marble bust or two for your collection."

"Belgravia, you say? Not bad, although I don't think it's that much more prestigious an address than ours."

"Their blue-and-white collection is antique."

Graham was momentarily silenced. He didn't pursue that line of thought. "You didn't tell me you were leaving. I was worried."

"I've returned, so there's no more need for worry. What did you do while I was out?" Violet heaved her laden bag onto the counter and removed her paintbrush, setting it aside for cleaning later.

Graham picked up the paintbrush. "I'll take care of this. No customers called. Fletcher stopped in for a visit."

"Back again with a shipment of rum?" She stowed her bag behind the display counter, making a mental note to refill her bottles of embalming fluid ingredients before her next appointment, in case a customer should actually request the service.

"Yes, he thinks his profits will soon exceed ours."

Violet laughed. "People may or may not always drink themselves insensible. They will certainly always die. It isn't a contest between you two, is it?"

She immediately regretted her words. Graham and Fletcher were close, and it wasn't fair to taunt him this way.

Something else must have been on his mind, for he ignored her comment.

"He showed me this." Graham proffered her Fletcher's *carte-de-visite*, a tinted ambrotype of his brother standing next to a crate marked "Felton's New England Rum" and holding a conical sugar loaf wrapped in paper. Beneath it were these words:

Fletcher Morgan
Quality Imports and Exports
Specializing in Chinese Tea, Caribbean Sugars, Fine Rums

On the rear of the card was his ship's docking location at St. Katharine Docks, as well as assurance that his ship, *Lillian Rose*, was insured by Lloyd's. In smaller type was the name of the image maker, "Martin Laroche, Daguerreotype Artist, Oxford Street."

"What do you think?" Graham asked.

Violet returned the card to him. "Impressive. It makes Fletcher appear much more serious about his business."

"I agree. It elevates him above others. Which is why I think we should have one done."

She laughed again. "Will you stare into the camera holding a bottle of embalming fluid and a syringe? I believe that will drive away our customers."

"I'm serious about this. We'll appear in the picture together, wearing our undertaker's garb and standing behind a wreath of lilies. It will elevate our standing."

Violet had to agree. "Shall I call on Mr. Laroche to arrange the sitting?"

"Yes, do that. Very good." He kissed her cheek, but she felt that it implied approval, not affection.

Graham had more to discuss. "I also want to talk about Annie.

I'm most displeased with her cleaning work, and what she calls roasted lamb is no better than boiled leather. Really, Violet, we should have a separate housemaid and cook. I'd like you to terminate her and find someone more suitable. I was also most unhappy with the new rug you had put down in my study—"

Ah, the same exhausting tirade was commencing anew. Graham was perpetually unhappy with Violet's household management, from her selection of servants—they'd been through five maids in two years—to the shade of wallpaper in each room ("too green," "not red enough," "all-around ghastly").

When they were first married, Graham adored Violet for being consumed with their undertaking business and considering everything else a distraction. With her efforts unburdening his time, he had the luxury of becoming fixated on his increasing social status. His passion was with their new townhome, recently theirs on a seven-year lease at fifty pounds per year. She had to admit that their home did reflect their prosperous status. Not only was there both a large dining room and a spacious drawing room—appropriate masculine and feminine spaces—on the first floor, but such separation was evident on the second floor, with Graham having his own study and Violet possessing a dressing room off their bedroom.

Even more impressive was their lavatory, installed with one of Mr. Crapper's brand-new water closet mechanisms that promised "a certain flush with every pull." Graham was almost as proud of this contraption as he was of his profession. The only concern Violet had was that the basement had a strange odor to it, which she attributed to the water closet's pipes somehow leaking fumes down into the walls.

Nevertheless, it was a fine home and she enjoyed living there. She just didn't particularly care for managing it. She pushed aside the nagging thought that Graham might eventually demand that she focus all of her energies there and leave undertaking to him and their assistants. Surely Graham still remembered the contented days of their marriage when they worked together so closely.

Violet knew she was a mediocre mistress of her own household, but she was a faultless undertaker. Clean coal grates and chintz bed hangings simply held no interest as compared to the care of the dead and their grieving families. Graham used to think the same way, but his attitude was changing. Whereas he once gave her a box of embalming tools as a gift, his most recent offering was a copy of Mrs. Beeton's *Book of Household Management,* a tiresome volume full of domestic instruction for good Englishwomen, from cookery to management of servants to proper visiting etiquette.

Violet had tried many times to absorb the thousand pages of detailed lessons, but, honestly, who cared what kind of tea leaves should be strewn on a carpet to absorb dust and odors before sweeping it? Was it important to know the recipe for furniture polish—linseed oil, turpentine, vinegar, and wine spirits—when one could simply buy a jar of Stephenson's furniture cream? Although she had to admit the section offering treatments for burns, congestion, and other medical problems offered some interest.

Violet nodded noncommittally at her husband concerning Annie and went about other duties, taking care of details for Mr. Stanley's funeral. She also headed out again later in the day, this time to pay a visit to the director of Kensal Green Cemetery. He showed her the Stanley family crypt beneath the Anglican chapel. The chapel was a magnificent structure in the center of the cemetery. With its imposing Doric columns and white stone façade, it resembled a Roman temple more than a building of the Church of England.

Beneath the chapel lay a series of crypts, at least part of which was dedicated to the Stanley family. Most wealthy families had stone mausoleums above ground for their families, as large as they could afford as testaments to the value of their loved ones. Once Mrs. Stanley had selected a plot and erected a suitable mausoleum, generations of Stanleys could be interred together for all to see. The poor, however, were consigned to common graves that usually lay at least four deep.

After concluding arrangements at Kensal Green, Violet took an omnibus to Oxford Street to visit Mr. Laroche's studio. She was greeted by the photographer's assistant, who assured her that his employer could come to Morgan Undertaking with his portable developing tent in two weeks' time.

Exhausted from the day's activities, she headed home, where a tearful Annie struggled past her in the street, lugging an old leather portmanteau, and Graham waited for her in his study . . . with an astonishing declaration.

❧ 3 ❧

Good temper should be cultivated by every mistress, as upon it the welfare of the household may be said to turn; indeed, its influence can hardly be over-estimated, as it has the effect of moulding the characters of those around her, and of acting most beneficially on the happiness of the domestic circle.

—*Beeton's Book of Household Management*

Graham sat behind his ebonized desk, one detailed in a floral pattern that he had purchased because he thought it blended well with their Chinese porcelain collection. He ran an impatient hand through his shock of unruly black hair, a feature Violet once considered charming, and now thought made her husband look unbalanced. His cloudy green eyes did not help dispel the notion.

"I'm sorry, Violet, but I went ahead and fired Annie. You simply *must* hire appropriate staff for our home. What sort of *maîtresse de maison* cannot manage her own servants? If you cannot do so adequately, I'll . . . I'll send you to Brighton to your parents." Graham shifted his eyes downward as he said this.

How dare he suggest such a thing? Violet took a deep breath, quickly sorting through the multitude of retorts in her mind and focusing on what was most important.

"I think your sense of reason has left you, Graham. I'll not return to my parents' house any sooner than you would bake an apple tart and serve it to the inmates at Newgate. Besides, you know perfectly well how much you need me at the shop."

He exhaled. "Darling, you don't know how hard I work to keep you insulated from world events. In return, I ask that you keep a decent home for me, one that reflects our standing and makes me proud when I come home each night."

"I've never asked to be insulated from world events. Besides, I don't even understand what you're talking about."

"Violet, if you understood the insidious forces at work against our kingdom, you'd beg me to let you return to Brighton."

"What insidious forces? Who is working against Great Britain?"

"This is what I mean. You don't understand how the United States is attempting for the third time to break Great Britain's back. It can't be tolerated."

"I cannot for the life of me understand why the Americans have made you so angry, Graham. What have they to do with you?"

He slammed his fist down on the desk, causing Violet to jump. She'd never seen Graham so passionate about politics before. "They nearly destroyed my family is what they have to do with me! My grandfather was a shattered man because of the United States. We should have smashed and annihilated them the moment they had the audacity to dump good British tea into their harbors. We would have saved generations of trouble."

Violet sat down in a chair across the wide expanse of desk. Its top was carefully arranged with decorative painted boxes, porcelain bird statues, a piece of elephant tusk, and a letter opener carved from black ash.

"Graham, please tell me the truth. What bothers you so?"

He ran his hand through his curly mop of hair again before rubbing his eyes and looking at her bleakly.

"You never met my grandfather, Philip Morgan. He died probably three or four years before we met. He was a brave and honorable man, and was revered not only by my father, but by Fletcher and me."

"I know you respected him."

"Pap fought under Major General Ross during the second war with the Americans. They landed in Benedict, Maryland, and marched through that pestilent state before horsewhipping the Americans at the Battle of Bladensburg. Pap was particularly proud that they were able to burn the U.S. Capitol afterward. However, after that he was separated from his unit when it was sent on to Baltimore, but he successfully made it through American lines, throwing on a disgusting hide coat he lifted from a dead

American in order to cover his own uniform. Pap was not only brave, but resourceful. I've seen the coat. It was a patchworked thing made from weasels and dogs. Even years later, it was absolutely hideous and stank worse than a four-day-old corpse.

"But he made it out of there safely wearing it, walking miles through woods while trying to find the British line. He collapsed from exhaustion, and while he was sleeping, a group of Yanks found him, thought he was dead, and tried to lift the coat from him.

"When they realized he was still alive, they carried him off to their camp and held him prisoner for weeks, treating him abominably. He wasn't sure whether he would die from exposure to heat or if they would starve him to death first."

Violet had never heard this story before. "How did he escape?"

"By pretending to be even more injured than he really was. They quit paying attention to him after a time, thinking he was too lame to get very far. One night while the Americans sat around drinking whiskey and playing cards, he quietly slipped away and found his unit, still wearing that awful coat. Can you imagine? He nearly died at their hands—and for what? So some cursed American could parade around looking like a dead animal hodgepodge?"

Violet stood and went around to where her husband sat, putting an arm around his shoulder and her cheek against the top of his head. "I'm sorry for your grandfather's suffering, Graham."

He clutched her free hand with his own. "My grandfather always told me that the worst thing about the Americans was their sense of privilege. Their horses eat better than the average British soldier, yet they have carped and complained for decades about all of their deprivations and English oppression. Pap witnessed it all firsthand while in their camp.

"He told endless stories about the cruelty the British troops suffered at the hands of the overfed American bullies. I've never forgotten any of them, although none are fit for a woman's ears. Suffice to say that the United States doesn't deserve to exist as a nation, in my opinion. It's a wilderness full of heathens and barbaric Indians and greedy speculators. Their arrogant posturing always leads to tragedy for others. Just think how Fletcher's business will be affected by this brainless war. It makes my head throb to the point of distraction."

She kissed the top of his head. "I wish I'd known of this before."

"I wish you had no need to know of it at all."

That night, husband and wife found a truce in each other's arms. Violet remained uneasy and apprehensive of her husband, yet desperate to reclaim the peace they once knew.

The next morning, she gazed down at her husband as he still slept. The lines of anger on his face were less noticeable, softening his expression and reminding her again of the sweet and enthusiastic man she'd married seven years ago.

She assured herself that all would be well once time passed and Graham forgot about his furor over the Americans. She rose, dressed, and prepared for another day at Morgan Undertaking, not realizing just how dreadfully wrong she was.

⇒ 4 ⇐

The Cemetery is an open space among the ruins, covered in Winter with violets and daisies. It might make one in love with death, to think that one should be buried in so sweet a place.

—Percy Bysshe Shelley (1792–1822)
Adonaïs (1821)

Washington City, D.C.
May 1861

Charles Francis Adams offered his son a cigar to celebrate his new appointment as Minister Plenipotentiary to the Court of St. James, with St. James referring to the palace of that name and ultimately referring to the British monarch. He did not have the formal title of Ambassador, but was designated authority to represent the United States in Great Britain.

Henry accepted the cigar, took an appreciative sniff, and bit off one end before lighting it and offering the safety match to his father as the two men sat in comfortable old leather chairs inside the family townhome. "So, Father, or should I say, 'Your Excellency,' how was your meeting with the president?"

Charles shrugged. "Lincoln is indifferent to me. Hardly looked me in the eye the entire time, despite our support of his presidential campaign."

"Abominable way to treat the son and grandson of presidents, I should think."

"I suppose I don't blame him. I wasn't his first choice, but he deferred to what William Seward wanted, now that Seward is secretary of state. Regardless of the president's personal feelings over my nomination, I've discussed it with your mother, and she, Mary, and Brooks will be accompanying me to London." Mary and Brooks were two of their six children. Charles Francis saw the uncertain look in Henry's eyes. After spending two years on the Grand Tour, Henry had come to live with the family in their Washington City quarters, where Charles Francis was serving out a term in the U.S. House of Representatives. Although an intelligent, grown man, Henry was still floundering to find his place in the world.

Charles Francis understood too well how difficult it was in a family that had produced his own father, John Quincy Adams, as well as his grandfather, John Adams. Charles Francis's own career had prospered, too, perhaps due to his own raw talents, but he thought it more likely due to his family name. Certainly it wasn't due to a voracious political appetite. In fact, he doubted his own diplomatic skills in what might prove to be a delicate situation with Britain. Lincoln's reservation over his appointment didn't reassure him.

He put his own cigar down in an ash stand and leaned forward.

"I'd like you to come to London with your mother and me, son, as my personal secretary. You've been on the Grand Tour, so you will easily understand English sensibilities, and you've made quite a journalistic mark already with your writings. I plan to send your brother, John Quincy, up to the old house in Massachusetts to look after financial affairs from there. Charles Francis Junior is, I suspect, an army man through and through and won't wish to give up his commission—"

"Father, the answer is yes. No need to convince me. What would I do otherwise? Return to Beacon Hill and rattle around up there while you're gone?"

"I just want you to know that I value your company. I'm also thinking of revising your great-grandfather's biography and could use your help on it, in addition to assisting me with some foul offal I intend to have removed while in London."

That piqued his son's interest. "What sort of foul offal?"

"I have seen certain communications that indicate British shipyards are already secretly building commerce raiders on the South's behalf so the rebels can best us that way rather than in open combat."

"Commerce raiders?"

"Ships sent to attack its enemy's merchant ships on the open seas. As opposed to the blockade runners, who are trying to get their ships through our blockade in Virginia."

Henry nodded. "I see. What do you plan to do about it?"

"We'll have to ensure that ships returning home from Great Britain sail in convoys, preferably protected by naval escorts, provided we can do so without raising the ire of Parliament. I don't trust Britain to support us in it, since we don't know yet whose side they will take, but I do intend to keep U.S. ships safe."

No need to tell his son yet of his plan to actually ferret out rebels positioned in London who were not only contracting with shipbuilders for commerce raiders, but were encouraging merchants to break the blockades set up at locations like Hampton Roads. That part of things could get . . . messy. He hadn't even told his wife, Abigail, yet of his real intentions in London, nor did he intend to do so. She would flutter about him with wifely concern and worry herself—and him—to distraction.

He would eventually tell Henry, just not yet. There was time enough once they got settled inside their new residence in London.

A mild twinge of headache announced itself quietly behind his eyebrows. Charles Francis passed a hand across his brow and was reminded once again of the Adams affliction. Why did all the men in this family have such confoundedly bald heads long before their time? Even poor Henry, just twenty-three, had the receding hairline that marked—nay, cursed—the Adams men. Soon he would join his father in a completely bare pate, save curly tufts above each ear.

Henry tamped out his own cigar. "I look forward to joining you and Mother in England. When do we depart?"

"Soon. A few weeks from now at the most. As soon as I get my affairs in order."

As soon as my contacts in London send me more information.

Violet was gratified to receive a note from a customer thanking the undertaker for giving the family's mother such a beautiful farewell. The thanks of a happy family member meant far more to her than moving in society ever could. She shuddered to think what she might be doing this day if she were a member of the society Graham was so anxious to enter. She would probably be making weekly calls on other ladies at the precise moment she knew they would *not* be home so that she could have credit for visiting while not actually having to talk to Mrs. Whatever-her-name-was. Meanwhile, Mrs. Whatever-her-name-was would be doing the same thing. Was there anything more ridiculous?

Violet folded the note and slipped it into a drawer for rereading later as a reminder that her work was valuable and worthy. It was time now to focus on the Stanley funeral.

One of their assistants, William Swift, had recently scrubbed spotless the glass of their funeral carriages so they sparkled anew for bystanders craning their necks to catch a glimpse of the coffins within. London soot and fog were constant irritants to maintaining the necessary elegant look of a funeral procession, and the Morgans were constantly freshening their equipage.

Although Graham had hired Will without consulting Violet, resulting in quite a row between them, she had to admit that he was a hard and dedicated young worker, and took pride in any task, even that of sweeping dust from corners behind doors. She'd not complained when he later hired Harry Blundell, whose brawn made easy work of moving the fleshiest of corpses.

Unlike most undertakers, who merely rented funeral horses and carriages from stables specifically set up for such business, the Morgans kept three different types of funeral carriages at a mews nearby, as well as several Clarence coaches used for transporting family members to the grave site. One funeral carriage, a black lacquered, open carriage, looking more like an elegant cart than anything, was specifically meant for those who could not afford the costlier glass carriages, of which they owned two.

Their largest glass carriage, decorated with silver and gold trim and topped by three posts plumed with ostrich feathers, had enough window space to easily display a coffin to onlookers. This stately funeral car, intended for the wealthiest of society, was tall, and the ceiling loomed several feet above the coffin as it rested inside. Fancy dark green draperies adorned this carriage both inside and out. Paired with four plumed horses, it was an impressive sight as it slowly but proudly made its way to whatever resting place for which the deceased inside was intended.

Unfortunately, this magnificent car wasn't called into use as often as their small glass carriage, lined with fringed black velvet drapes. It was the one that now carried Mr. Stanley to Kensal Green. Mrs. Stanley and her daughter followed behind the funeral carriage in one of the Morgans' black Clarence coaches with its blinds drawn and the driver riding up high atop a lavishly embroidered velvet seat cloth. The women wore dresses of black crape, black veils and gloves, and were adorned with the jet jewelry purchased from Violet. The second mourning coach behind the funeral carriage contained Mr. Stanley's brother and sister. Other mourners followed behind in their own carriages.

The entire cortege was surrounded by pages, attendants, and professional mourners walking alongside the carriages dressed in black and looking suitably somber. The Morgans were fortunate to know a bevy of reliable men happy to earn extra pocket money this way.

Graham rode on the funeral car, driven by Harry, while Violet stayed back at a discreet distance in their own simple horse and carriage with folding top, a conveyance the undertakers used strictly for following funerals.

The procession made its way at a walking pace for the four-mile ride from Belgravia to the cemetery, with a detour around the circumference of Hyde Park to ensure maximum display to London's citizens. As they neared Kensal Green, more rightly known as the General Cemetery of All Souls, Graham motioned to the pages and attendants, who all climbed onto the various coaches, and the drivers increased the tempo along Harrow Road to a brisk trot. Once a procession was beyond the view of onlookers, it made no sense to continue at a walking pace.

At the cemetery's entrance lodge, an imposing structure of arches and Doric columns, the foot attendants climbed down from the coaches, and once again the procession returned to its slow amble. The thirty-year-old Kensal Green Cemetery was one of

London's first public burial grounds, a response to the grossly overcrowded church grounds that could no longer cope with London's exploding population. Violet loved the design of this cemetery, which reminded her of a pleasant retreat, with its long vista of sloping grounds and dense plantings of oaks, evergreens, shrubs, and flowers.

The procession rolled its way down the tree-lined road that cut the cemetery in half. The cortege moved slowly and in complete silence except for the creaking of wheels and carriages, and the occasional snuffle of a horse. The Anglican chapel loomed large before them in the middle of Kensal Green. Dissenters, those who separated from the Church of England, such as the Baptists, Presbyterians, and Quakers, were buried in a remote part of the cemetery.

Once the funeral carriage pulled up to the chapel entrance, the entire procession stopped. Graham jumped down from the funeral carriage and directed the pallbearers to remove the coffin from inside its glassed-in location and carry it gently inside the chapel. Six pallbearers had been selected from among Mr. Stanley's friends, and could only serve in this duty if they were near Mr. Stanley's age. Even at children's funerals the pallbearers had to be selected from other children close to the deceased's age.

While the pallbearers did their work, wearing black gloves and crape armbands, Graham somberly opened up the door to Mrs. Stanley's carriage, put down the steps, and helped her and her daughter out, tipping his black crape–wrapped hat at them.

Graham was always the perfect blend of humility and boulder strength during funerals. Widows always responded with a smile beneath their tears or by holding on to his proffered arm just a moment too long. Violet wished it weren't considered unseemly for her, as a woman, to be in as much attendance on things as Graham was. After all, hadn't she performed all of the indelicate work on Mr. Stanley?

She continued to wait outside while the carriages emptied out their passengers and everyone trudged into the chapel for the service. A short while later, the women exited from the chapel, with Mrs. Stanley once again on Graham's arm for comfort. Graham deposited Mrs. Stanley back into her carriage and returned to the chapel.

Everything was almost over. Once it was time for the coffin to be lowered down into one of the underground vaults inside the chapel, women were generally dismissed from the scene so that they wouldn't be subjected to the unsettling vision of a loved one, whose coffin now rested on a mechanical bier, being lowered down into the depths of the crypt.

It did rather resemble being sent to the gates of hell.

Such a process also prevented mourners from the temptation of throwing themselves in after the coffin.

Men usually stayed behind until the coffin was in its final resting place. Ah, they were all coming out now and joining their womenfolk. Graham popped out one more time to signal to the driver of Mrs. Stanley's carriage to move in front of the funeral carriage and get the procession moving again. The cortege's pace went quickly to a trot, for everyone would now be heading either back home or to the Stanley residence to hear Mr. Stanley's will read.

Violet and Graham were, of course, not invited to such an occasion. Their business was with the dead, not frolicking with the living.

Once everyone was out of view, she climbed out of her own carriage to join Graham inside the chapel. The interior was filled to overflowing with arrangements of lilies. Their cloying fragrance never ceased to overwhelm Violet. They were the flower of choice for funerals because they smelled so strongly that they overpowered any unfortunate odor arising from the deceased. Yet no matter how many pots of them she picked up from the florist or arranged inside a chapel or the home of a grieving family, she was always a little nauseous afterward.

Graham had no such problem with the fragrance of the lily, which was, admittedly, a strikingly beautiful bloom. In response to her grumbling about them, he always smiled and said that God made lilies beautiful to compensate for their sickly-sweet aroma.

Violet wished again for her husband of old, who could make such clever statements to lift her spirits and who was not alternately sad and incensed.

Graham wasn't on the main floor of the chapel, and the floor opening in the center of the sanctuary—through which a coffin was lowered—was closed. He must be down in the crypt. She went to the hidden door at one side of the chapel and made her way down the narrow, cramped staircase to the vast crypt below. Her black skirts were filthy from brushing along the stone walls.

Burial in a crypt was certainly respectable, as long as one was not unfortunate enough to be of so few resources as to be buried in the poor section of it. Coffins were stacked four deep there, almost as if they represented geologic layers of dirt. Perhaps they were really a testament to the history of London's people.

It was better than some church graveyards, though, where the poor were reduced to complete ignominy, buried in countless stacks of coffins. She swept away the thought, which was an anathema to any decent undertaker.

Graham was shaking hands with the director, and turned to leave. He frowned at seeing Violet there.

"Why are you here? Why didn't you wait outside?" His voice was gentle for the director's benefit, but Violet knew he was unhappy.

Right. Why *hadn't* she waited for him in their carriage?

The director saved her from having to answer by greeting her. "Mrs. Morgan, a delight to see you again."

With pleasantries exchanged, she and Graham departed, her husband still concentrating on his scowl. By the time they returned to the mews to ensure Harry had properly returned the funeral carriage, the storm had broken and he was affable once more.

"When does Mr. Laroche arrive to make the calling card?" he asked.

"In a little over a week," Violet said.

"Very good. You'll have a replacement for Annie before then, won't you? I'd like my best suit cleaned and pressed for the sitting. Hopefully the new maid will be more competent than she was."

Violet sighed. She saw little hope of it.

The bell tied to the knob rattled in protest as Violet pushed against the door to the dressmaker's shop on nearby Bayswater

Road. Apparently Mary still hadn't found the time to repair the lopsided door frame.

Looking about the shop, Violet could see why there had been no opportunity to hire a man to see to the door. Her friend's shop, which specialized in mourning clothes, was cramped even more than usual. Mannequins wearing half-completed shawls, mourning coats, and black-sashed bonnets were nearly obscured by heaps of folded fabrics and laces, stacks of silk top hats, and a revolving rack stuffed with threads, boxes of buttons, and other trims. The area surrounding Mary's sewing machine, an Isaac Singer model powered by a foot treadle instead of the old hand-crank type, was lit by candle sconces protected by drip trays along the wall behind it.

A longtime dressmaker, Mary Overfelt had never quite adjusted to gas lighting, fearful of its effect on her fabrics. She worried more about a fire from a gas leak than from the open flame of candles.

Mary emerged from a door at the back of the shop. She picked up a rack of fluttering scarves and hatbands that fell over from the breeze of the opening door. As she rose and patted the impossibly large puff of hair coiled at the back of her head to ensure it hadn't fallen out of place, she realized that it wasn't a typical customer who had entered.

"Violet, my dear! What brings you here today?"

"I have the final installment of Mr. Dickens's *Great Expectations* story from *All the Year Round*, and thought you might like to read it." Violet offered her friend the periodical, already battered from being toted around and read in snatches of time.

"Ah, so we can finally discover Pip's fate. What will finally happen between him and Estella? I'll look forward to this tonight over my bedtime tea. I imagine you enjoyed this far more than *Oliver Twist*, given its unfavorable view of undertakers."

Mary looked around for a free space to put the magazine. Giving up, she placed it on top of her sewing chair, which must have made for an interesting work experience, since it, too, was heaped with materials and patterns.

"I'd invite you to sit down, but . . ." She held her hands out helplessly.

"Not to worry. I also wanted to see if you've received new plates for next year's mourning fashions."

"Not yet. Well, perhaps they've come by post, who knows?" Mary pointed to a stack of mail on a table in a corner. London's mail was delivered efficiently two or three times each day, and it was obviously overwhelming the dressmaker.

Poor Mary; her story was a moving one and had brought tears to Violet's eyes when she heard it one evening over cups of chocolate. Involved in dressmaking from the time she could wield a needle, Mary enjoyed a twenty-two-year bond of love with her husband and their dressmaking shop until Matthew's untimely death from a malignant growth in his brain.

When her own mourning threatened to consume the forty-five-year-old widow, she moved to London from Cornwall to escape her memories and focus her energies on constructing clothing for others who were suffering as deeply as she. London also had wealthier customers.

Five years later, Mary's grief had mellowed into a poignant wistfulness, but her reputation for mourning clothing had increased beyond all expectations, making her the most sought-after mourning dressmaker in Paddington. However, Mary's hair had gone an unusual shade of gray in her grief and was so thick and unmanageable despite her attempts to control it that it seemed as though she was wearing a thundercloud atop her head.

Violet heard of Mary's growing renown and made it a point to become acquainted with the shop owner two streets away. Surprisingly, the two women discovered many common interests—including books—and a friendship developed between them, despite the twenty-year difference in age. Nowadays their conversation on any given day might be about the latest novel by Mr. Wilkie Collins, or the trouble between the prime minister and his ambitious chancellor of the exchequer over the Reform Act, or even the increasing price of British-produced crape.

Mary picked up a crumpled piece of white crape being sewn as a border for a widow's bonnet, which was lying across her sewing machine. She folded it neatly, placing it atop another tottering pile of folded squares nearby.

"How was the Stanley funeral?" Mary asked.

"Elegant, I think." Violet picked up another carelessly tossed piece of fabric, folded it, and added it atop the white crape. She and Mary wordlessly began folding, straightening, and organizing the shop together in companionable silence.

"I entered the chapel after the mourners left," Violet said, breaking the quiet.

Mary stopped what she was doing to look at her friend with concern. "You did? Was Mr. Morgan inside?"

"He was."

"Did he see you? Why did you go in?"

"Honestly, I don't know what possessed me to go in. My husband has been so . . . odd . . . as of late, and I felt somehow compelled to check on things."

"What happened?"

"Nothing, really. Graham wasn't happy about it, but he didn't chastise me as much as usual. Not like he did over Annie."

"What about Annie?"

Violet picked up a spool of gray thread that had rolled under the sewing table and tossed it onto the revolving rack that Mary was organizing by color and type of trim.

"Graham dismissed her without consulting me. He was displeased with her work, and by extension displeased with me."

"Hmm. How many maids does this make?"

"Annie was the third in the past year."

"What will you do now?"

"I don't know. He expects me to replace her within a week so that his finest suit can be pressed before we sit for a new calling card. Recommendations of nieces and distant family members from our employees and from hired mourners have not proven successful, so I must devise a better way to hire a servant." Violet shook her head. "I despise handling these household matters, yet it's so important to Graham. Perhaps he would have been better off with a more domesticated wife."

"I hardly think he is the one who would be better off, Violet."

"Sorry?"

"Never mind. Have you placed an advertisement in *The Times?*"

"No. Graham thinks a servant might be put off to know in advance that we're undertakers."

"Foolishness! It's the method Mrs. Beeton recommends."

"Yes, the indomitable Mrs. Beeton."

"I'm sure I have *The Times* here somewhere." Mary approached her stack of mail with determination, managing to rummage through it without toppling it.

"Ah, here we are." She opened it up and searched for several moments before finding what she wanted and showing it to Violet. "Look, here are not only advertisements placed by employers, but situations wanted by girls willing to work. If Mr. Morgan doesn't want you to place your own solicitation, surely he won't object to answering one of these."

With Mary looking over her shoulder, Violet studied the page, which included a multitude of "situations wanted" running down a single column. Several caught her eye.

> AS COMPANION, or Nursery Governess.—
> A young lady, age 20, who wishes to obtain
> a SITUATION in either of the above ca-
> pacities. She is acquainted with the rudi-
> ments of an English education, and is a good
> needlewoman. No objection to travel. Ad-
> dress to E. Hendricks, Dendridge Close,
> Enfield.

"That sounds promising," Violet said.

Mary shook her head. "Too young. She'll be flighty. She's too far away, as well."

"The railway runs from Enfield Lock to the city center, doesn't it?"

"Yes, but that just means she'll want to live at home and ride in each day. Or else she'll be homesick every day and you'll have her suffering the pangs of nostalgia."

Violet continued scanning the list and read another advertisement aloud.

> AS HOUSEKEEPER, or to Superintend
> the Kitchen in a nobleman's family, or as
> professed Cook and Housekeeper in a
> quiet family, a person who understands her
> business in all its branches, with several
> years' high character from a nobleman's
> family. Address L.L., Mr. Bentley's, 63 and
> 64, Piccadilly.

"I rather like this one," Violet said, "except that her expectations might be too high for a pair of undertakers recently moved up a bit in society. Graham would be pleased with her for certain. What else is there?"

> AS good COOK, a middle-aged person.
> She understands the duty of a kitchen. Or
> to a single gentleman, where there are one
> or two more servants kept. She can have a
> good character reference from the place
> she has just left. No objection to a short
> distance out of town. Direct to E. Scrope,
> Mr. Browning's, post-office, Conduit-street,
> Westbourne-terrace, Hyde-park.

Mary cut her off before she could make comment. "She's seeking a husband. No sense in it being yours."

Indeed not.

In the end, though, Violet decided to answer the ad for the middle-aged cook. Within a couple of days of posting a reply, she received a visit from Edith Scrope, a stout woman who wheezed when nodding or shaking her head, and wheezed herself nearly into a fit when Violet told her that the Morgans were undertakers. A strange habit, but not so odd that it would interfere with her duties. Contrary to Mary's opinion, there was nothing about Edith Scrope that remotely suggested she was on the hunt for a new husband.

Violet hired her on the spot at eighteen pounds per year with an extra allowance for tea, sugar, and beer. She explained the rules of the Morgan household—what few she could remember—and prayed Mrs. Scrope would be a success.

"Graham, be still," Violet said, squeezing his shoulder to stop his fidgeting as she stood behind him inside their shop.

"My collar is scratching me intolerably," he said. "What did Mrs. Scrope use on it?"

"I don't know. Shh, Mr. Laroche will never be able to get a proper exposure if you keep moving about."

The photographer stood hunched over his camera box, which rested on a wood tripod. It had taken an hour for their scene to be posed to Mr. Laroche's satisfaction. In the end, Graham was seated with his legs crossed and Violet stood behind him with her right hand on his left shoulder. Both wore full undertaker's garb, and a wreath of lilies hung on a stand to their left.

They'd argued all morning about whether to put a child's coffin in the scene, with Violet opposed to it on the grounds of it being too ghoulish, whereas Graham thought it more accurately portrayed their profession than just a floral spray. Mr. Laroche put the matter to rest by telling them he wouldn't be able to fit it properly into the portrait.

It was a hollow victory for Violet, because now Graham was grumpy and dissatisfied with how their photography session was proceeding.

"All done," Mr. Laroche said, hurriedly gathering up his supplies so he could take his wet plates to the portable darkroom studio parked outside. He had only about ten minutes for the entire developing process before the plates dried.

When he was finished, the photographer returned to the shop, triumphantly brandishing their ambrotype. It was indeed a good likeness of them. A series of pictures from this one ambrotype would be developed onto sheets of paper, each cut into eight individual cards. At a price of less than two shillings per card, it was inexpensive advertisement.

"May I suggest having the image tinted?" Mr. Laroche asked. "I have an excellent colorist who can bring a bit of blush to your cheeks and emphasize the white of the flowers. It will cost just a bit more."

After agreeing to his price and concluding their transaction, Violet left Graham at the shop while she went home to discuss menus with Mrs. Scrope. Thus far, the woman was proving invaluable. With Mrs. Scrope minding all of their domestic matters, Violet could concentrate fully on their undertaking business. Even Graham was pleased with her work, and except for this morning's tussle over their portrait sitting, he'd been cheerful and loving for days. Violet could only hope he would remain this contented.

Mrs. Scrope was, indeed, a domestic triumph, if just a bit intimidating.

Her first accomplishment was a thorough scrubbing of all four stories of the Morgan home, which took nearly two weeks in order to, in Mrs. Scrope's words, "bring the place to decent standards."

Thank goodness Graham wasn't around to hear that.

Almost like a miracle, the smuts and blacks, those nuisance particles of soot and coal dust that continuously swirled around the London air, vanished from atop the mantel, the carpets, and the furniture.

Mrs. Scrope then completely organized their pantry, making a list of all the vegetables and fresh food on hand and compiling a list of what more was needed in order to bring the pantry up to an adequate condition. She did the same with the dry and tinned foodstuffs in the storeroom.

Violet happily gave Mrs. Scrope the money she requested to obtain more flour, sugar loaves, salt, spices, dried milk, beans, onions, potatoes, and other staples she deemed necessary.

Mrs. Scrope wheezed mightily in agreement when Violet asked her if there were improvements that could be made to the kitchen, located in the low-ceilinged basement along with the larder, the storeroom, the pantry that stored china and glass, the scullery for food washing and preparation, and Mrs. Scrope's own quarters. Violet knew instinctively that the kitchen, even though it was new, needed updating, but had no idea in what way. Mrs. Scrope provided the answer.

"Yes, ma'am, it needs more light. Dark as the devil's playground in there. And I'd appreciate gas lighting downstairs, too, just like upstairs, so's I don't have to tend to dozens of candles a day. I could also use a roasting jack for the fireplace. Your closed oven is just fine for boiling water and baking, but no joint of mutton is going to be tasty coming from an oven. I should say not. It needs to be roasted over a proper open fire."

Violet was mentally calculating the expense of what Mrs. Scrope wanted. "Do you need anything else?"

"Well, in fact, ma'am, yes. I certainly could use a clotheshorse installed over the kitchen fireplace, one of those retractable types that can be pulled out of the way when I'm cooking. It sure would keep the laundry damp off me and get your clothes and bedding dry much quicker. Most nice homes have one."

"Of course, of course." Being fashionable was all Graham needed to hear in order to approve the clotheshorse, no matter what the expense. In order to be truly fashionable they should be sending out their laundry to be done, but Mrs. Scrope insisted that she was far better at caring for it.

Mrs. Scrope was saving Violet's tattered female sensibilities by taking the home well in hand, so she couldn't care less what the woman wanted. Whatever it was, Violet would see that she had it. In fact, the Morgans were saving money with their new servant around.

For, without Mrs. Scrope, Violet would have never realized that the butcher was sometimes trying to pawn off an old joint of mutton, or that the coal man was shortchanging his delivery, or even that the local tea merchant was adulterating his tea leaves with "smouch," a substance made from dried ash leaves and difficult to distinguish from genuine tea leaves. Mrs. Scrope ferreted out their deeds and didn't hesitate to use her sharp tongue on them.

In fact, Violet was just a bit intimidated by her new servant. When Violet proposed preparing an inventory of china and silver, she was dismissed by Mrs. Scrope's simple "Not ready for that yet." Violet was too fearful of losing her heaven-sent housekeeper-cook to insist, as was her due as mistress of the household.

Any attempt to plan a weekly menu would more than likely

amount to Violet nodding in agreement with whatever Mrs. Scrope wanted. Yet none of that mattered. Among Mrs. Scrope's considerable talents was her thrifty use of leftovers. A roast on Sunday might reappear in tasty chunks inside a baked crust Monday, sliced with potatoes on Tuesday, and mashed up into fried cutlets on Wednesday.

There was no aspect of Violet's household that Mrs. Scrope didn't see a way to improve on. She even cleaned out all of the Morgan linens and bedding, sending the ones she felt not worthy of "a respectable household" out to the rag-and-bone man. This scavenger took up worn fabrics, meat bones, and other household discards and sold his wares to paper mills, gluemakers, and fertilizer manufacturers.

Yes, Mrs. Scrope was a blessing. A blunt-edged, sharp-tongued blessing.

Fletcher Morgan held the card up to the light of the window of his new office near St. Katharine Docks. St. Katharine wasn't able to accommodate the larger merchant ships, and was therefore a cheaper alternative for Fletcher's narrow old clipper than the West India Docks. "Not a bad likeness of you, Graham. Of course, Violet is quite fetching and dominates the whole scene, doesn't she?"

"Mind your manners, Fletcher. You wear your jealousy of me too openly."

"Ah, so true. Yet you preen like a stuffed peacock when I talk about your wife. But back to your calling card. Let's see, what does it say underneath the picture? 'Morgan Undertaking, Purveyors of Funerals, all levels of society, embalming on request.' Embalming, what a thought. I should have stopped after admiring Violet's breathtaking visage."

"Violet shares my view that embalming is the future of undertaking. Monsieur Jean Gannal has written extensively on it in France, and the Americans are already beginning to embalm their dead soldiers."

"True, but their soldiers have to be preserved for transport by train back to their families for burial, sometimes hundreds of miles away. Most people in England die where they live and can be buried a few days later." Fletcher handed the *carte-de-visite* back to his brother, who slipped it back into its protective cover and tucked it in his brown tweed frock coat pocket. "And when did you ever become a supporter of anything the Americans do?"

Graham scowled, an expression Fletcher always found amusing.

"My agreement with certain funerary practices has no bearing on my overall distaste for them," Graham said. "The Americans have done little to commend themselves to me."

"Yes, it would seem they have made a concerted effort to disappoint you for many years." Fletcher's sarcasm was lost on Graham, but at least now the conversation was where Fletcher wanted it. "What do you hear of the war? Is it likely to last much longer?"

"It would appear to have just started, now that the fool Americans have finally figured out that civil wars are never resolved promptly, being fought in endless skirmishes and big battles by neighbor against neighbor. They just had their first battle at someplace in Virginia called Manassas. The South routed the North, and now President Lincoln is scrambling to recover and has replaced his commander over the federal army with General George McClellan. No doubt the South's president, Jefferson Davis, will have an opportunity to do the same thing when he's routed in battle, as each side attempts to prove moral superiority. Both sides consist of dogs." Graham shook his head in disgust.

"You still think about Pap, don't you?"

"Of course. I never forget. You remember, too, don't you?"

Fletcher shrugged. "I thought I read that the North is importing and distilling thousands of barrels of liquor as a standard ration for their army's men."

"Wouldn't surprise me. Is the South doing the same?"

"Not that I could see. Seems a shame to miss such an opportunity, doesn't it?"

Graham was no longer scowling. "What do you mean?"

Fletcher nodded toward the window, which overlooked Limehouse Reach, the western bend of the Thames around Isle of Dogs. "A man with a fast ship and a knowledge of Southern trading routes could do quite well for himself while the Americans are beating each other's brains out."

"But you already run rum through Boston back to England."
Fletcher dropped his voice for effect. "Everyone plies the
liquor trade. I'm talking about something far more valuable."

"Not slaves!" Graham put out a hand as if to physically distance
himself from his brother.

Fletcher chuckled softly. "No, brother, something far more to
your liking. What I propose is this. . . ."

> *Reinventing myself has been more interesting than I'd
> ever thought possible. A new name, a new profession, even
> new clothing tailored to my new station in life. I risked
> running out of money, but have discovered that, among my
> many other talents, I have a gift for committing robberies
> among the unsuspecting. I practiced petty thievery at first,
> just to see how successful I could be, but it wasn't nearly as
> satisfying as a thorough swindling. Or hornswoggling, as
> my dear grandmother used to say.*
>
> *After all, why lift change from a man's pockets when,
> for a small investment in careful planning, you can divest
> him of everything he owns?*
>
> *I do believe I am enjoying this new life I have created
> for myself. Sometimes I lift my hands before my face
> and can only gaze in wonder at what they are able to
> accomplish. Dare I to think that I am brilliant? Yet not a
> single soul around me knows who I really am.*
>
> *Only you know me, my dearest diary.*

⇒ 5 ⇐

The half-hour before dinner has always been considered as the great ordeal through which the mistress, in giving a dinner-party, will either pass with flying colors, or, lose many of her laurels.

—*Beeton's Book of Household Management*

London
June 1861

Samuel Harper exited the hackney in front of the Langham Hotel. Egad, his back hurt. From the treacherous sea voyage across the Atlantic to Bristol, then the train to Paddington, where he found it nearly impossible to hire a private hack in all of the chaos of that location, and finally a ride through the densest fog he'd ever encountered.

What in the world caused such copious amounts of swirling mist and particles on the streets of London?

He paid the driver his fare, quickly checked in to his hotel room to drop off his meager belongings, and was back out on the street again in less than an hour.

It was time to find an enterprising businessman willing to help a patriot make a purchase to defend his way of life.

First, though, he needed to set himself up properly. Samuel passed a hand over his developing auburn beard, an asset for covering his features while serving on this assignment. It was grown enough to look natural for a photography sitting, he thought. Probably needed a haircut, though. And his suit was not only rumpled, it practically shouted out to passersby that he wasn't a gentleman, not by a jug's full.

Fortunately, he'd been provided enough gold and silver to rectify any such problems. He inquired at a newsstand where he might find a barber, a tailor, and a photographer, and proceeded to visit them in that order, with the goal of creating a very respectable visiting card for Mr. Samuel Harper of the Confederate States of America, Buyer of Special Goods.

Abigail Adams graciously excused herself from the reception rooms by pre-arrangement, leaving her husband, Charles Francis, with Lord Russell. The look of disapproval on his guest's face told him he'd probably committed a social disgrace by having his wife excused before dinner, but it was too late now.

"My congratulations, sir, on your elevation," Charles Francis said, grasping Lord Russell's hand before escorting him to the dining room. Henry joined them, poised with his notebook, pen, and ink to take notes.

John Russell, the third son of the sixth Duke of Bedford and not in line to inherit the family estates, had just been elevated to the peerage himself as the first Earl Russell.

Charles Francis had to give a nod to this mighty achievement of ability, especially in the heavily stratified British society. He and Henry had studied the backgrounds of all of Queen Victoria's important ministers prior to their sailing, and Lord Russell was an obvious paragon among his peers. In just thirty years, the man had served in a variety of important posts: leader of the House of Commons, home secretary, secretary of state, prime minister, lord president of the council, and now foreign secretary. Charles Francis mused that with his boundless energy and drive, despite his advancing age, the earl would have enjoyed great success in America, as well.

Not only that, he was a member of the Whigs, the party that believed in the supremacy of Parliament over monarch, and had supported American independence nearly a hundred years ago. In other circumstances, Charles Francis might even admire the man, despite his being a Briton and by definition untrustworthy.

Hopefully, Lord Russell would be sympathetic to American interests once again.

The foreign secretary sat down across from Charles Francis and Henry. Lord Russell had the girth of someone who had lived well, and the face of someone who had worried much, over the years. Even his side whiskers were a bit tangled, as if they were too troubled with more important concerns to bother lying neatly against his face.

"My thanks to you, Your Excellency. My wife, Lady Frances, is already planning to redecorate Pembroke Lodge, our country estate, to make it fit for human inhabitation, as she says." The Adams men laughed politely at Lord Russell's unsuccessful attempt to clothe himself in modesty.

"Your wife has every right to express her contentment with her husband's success. Alas, Peacefield, our family home south of Boston, is in the hands of my son, John Quincy the Second, while the rest of the family is here. He's just gotten married, so I expect that when we return, his wife, Fanny, will have completely torn the place apart to suit herself."

Russell nodded. "No sense in arguing with a wife's desires, whether your own or your son's. You have another son, don't you?"

"Yes, two others. We lost another boy when he was but five years old. My youngest, Brooks, is thirteen but chafes to be a man." The men laughed. "Charles Francis Junior has an army commission and is busy fighting the rebels in the South."

"Ah. So you—" Lord Russell stopped what he was saying as a servant arrived to present them with the evening's menu, which Abigail had taken great care in developing. They were to have fried cod with fried oysters, mutton chops, savory rice, potatoes, fried broccoli, and brandy bread pudding. Charles Francis asked their guest to select a libation from his wine cellar list, and the foreign secretary chose a Cabernet Franc from Adams's expansive collection. The bottle was presented with a flourish, and Lord Russell was offered the opportunity to sample and approve the selection.

"Where was I?" Russell asked. "Oh yes, so you Adamses are devoted to the North's cause, even to the point of sending your sons into the thick of fighting?"

"We don't send our sons, they elect to go. I believe this will all wrap up soon and Charles Francis Junior will be returned to Peacefield long before I am."

Lord Russell took a long sip from his glass. "So you feel confident in the North's prospects in this conflict?"

"Of course, why wouldn't we?"

The earl rubbed the stem of his goblet between his hands, violently swirling the remaining liquid inside. "I sympathize with your position, truly I do—slavery is an abomination and the states' rights argument is a bit specious to me—but I admit I'm not entirely convinced of the North's ability to gain the upper hand, especially after your defeat at Bull Run. There are many who believe the Southern secession is an accomplished fact." Lord Russell drained the glass. "I count myself among them."

Charles Francis was too stunned to respond. By the furious scratching of pen to paper going on next to him, his son was in no such state of surprise. As a good journalist, Henry surely recognized that Lord Russell had just thrown a mortar of information into the center of the table.

At that moment, their conversation was interrupted by the arrival of dinner. Their food was elegantly served on white plates edged in alternating bands of gold and cobalt, with an intricate pattern of gold swirls next to the innermost blue band.

The bone china here in England was much finer than anything they had in the States. Charles Francis surreptitiously glanced at the underside of his empty teacup to see the maker's mark. *Royal Worcester*. He made a mental note to have Abigail visit Harrods to order several sets and ship them home for use at Peacefield.

Which reminded Charles Francis, it was time to make peace in this conversation before it became a heated discussion over the North's chances against a belligerent South.

"So tell me, Lord Russell, what of Lord Palmerston? I hear he is most unusual. What can we expect when we meet him?"

Charles Francis had discovered a good diversion point. The foreign secretary smiled, all other thoughts forgotten as he delved into the topic of the notorious Viscount Palmerston, prime minister of Great Britain.

"That old reprobate." He said it with more affection than revulsion. "Palmerston and I have had many differences over the years in our struggle for supremacy over one another. In fact, back in the late forties, I was prime minister and it was Palmerston who was foreign secretary. We've continuously ousted one another from various offices.

"He and I have never seen eye to eye on much of anything. I dismissed him as foreign secretary in 1851 for recognizing Louis-Napoleon Bonaparte's regime in France. What was the man thinking? Last year I introduced a bill to reduce the qualification for the franchise to ten pounds in counties and six pounds in towns in order to offer more people suffrage. Palmerston didn't support it, of course, so it died. He's supposed to be a good Whig, but has never cared much for our principles. He treated his tenants in Ireland abominably during the famine and has never seen a relief bill he couldn't block." Lord Russell poured himself another glass of Cabernet Franc.

"But we've patched up our differences now that Palmerston has formed a truly liberal cabinet. I must tell you that we are in agreement that Great Britain will remain neutral in your country's affairs."

They were wandering back into uncomfortable territory again. But Charles Francis had not been a lawyer for years without knowing how to maneuver through a murky, polluted river and emerge as clean as a hound's tooth.

"Speaking of affairs, are the rumors about Lord Palmerston true?"

Lord Russell's face lit up in amusement. "Beyond your wildest imaginings. Another way in which he and I are quite different. They call him 'Lord Cupid' for all of his wanderings with other men's wives, and he's seventy-six years old. 'Lord Lecher' is more like it."

Father and son respectfully laughed again at Russell's joke. "How does the queen view Lord Palmerston's . . . activities?" Charles Francis asked.

"Despises him. Early in her reign, he attempted to seduce by force one of the queen's ladies-in-waiting by entering the lady's bedroom while staying as a guest at Windsor Castle. She fought him off and her screams woke the household and brought everyone running.

"The queen is a very strict observer of morals, as you know. He was nearly removed from office then, but it was his support for the French emperor, an autocrat just like his uncle, Napoleon Bonaparte, that did him in. Queen Victoria abhors his foreign policy as much as his loose morals, but finds him admirable in domestic matters. I do not entirely find him admirable in such matters, but nonetheless we are getting on well enough now."

"Does the queen agree with your—and Lord Palmerston's—assessment that Southern secession is an accomplished fact?"

Lord Russell paused before replying. "Prince Albert does not condone the acts of a slave-holding nation, and the queen is in full agreement with the prince's viewpoint, although it is not a matter of great moment at Windsor," he said evenly.

Ah, Lord Russell was also demonstrating his credentials as a politician. Charles Francis fought the urge to clap the man on the shoulder and say, "Well done!" for his deftly worded statement.

Instead, he pretended Lord Russell had just made a statement implying that the queen fully supported the North's case. He leaned forward and dropped his voice. "May I ask, then, Lord Russell, if the queen sees a problem with a slave-holding nation breaking a blockade?"

Russell pursed his lips as he considered this. "Does such blockade breaking impact Her Majesty's people?"

Charles Francis sat back again. "Perhaps. It depends on whether the building of commerce raiders in English shipyards is cause for impact to Her Majesty's people."

Charles Francis watched as Henry's furious motions of dipping his pen and scrawling across the page became a blur. His son poised his pen in midair as they both waited to hear Lord Russell's reply.

Lord Russell smiled. "Do you seek an intervention in such practices, if they exist?"

"Actually, I seek far less than that. I would like free license to make discoveries for myself about whether or not Southern representatives are contracting with English shipbuilders and traders, and I will take care of them myself."

"Without calling out any British subjects, of course, who I am certain would have no knowledge of their activity being unlawful."

"Naturally, the U.S. has no interest in accusing innocent British citizens of any wrongdoing when in fact it is entirely the fault of American subversives."

Lord Russell nodded. "Then consider yourself so authorized. Lord Palmerston will wish to know about this, of course, so I will arrange a meeting for you at the earliest opportunity."

With both dinner and their official business concluded, Charles Francis signaled for cigars to be brought to all three men as they retired to the smoking lounge, where they spent the remainder of the evening discussing the proliferation of railroad building in both the U.S. and England.

In Kentish Town, north of the Adams residence, Violet and Graham hosted their families for dinner: Fletcher; Graham's mother, Ida Morgan; and Arthur and Eliza Sinclair, Violet's parents.

The Sinclairs had moved to Brighton not long after Violet's marriage, Eliza having always desired to live near the sea. King George IV had made the seaside resort fashionable in the early part of the century, and even Violet could remember her mother talking about it during her childhood. Her parents were now nestled in a cottage in Preston Village, on the outskirts of Brighton.

Violet had made a few train trips down to see her parents in Brighton, but until now they had not left their comfortable environs for a visit. However, her parents were off to visit an old boyhood friend of Arthur's who now lived up in Leicester, and so decided to spend a night in London before proceeding north.

When Violet told Graham of their impending arrival, he suggested a large family dinner to enable both sides to spend time together. She immediately agreed. Mother and Father had not yet seen their new home, and Violet was anxious that they approve.

She should have rested easy, knowing that Mrs. Scrope had the meal well in hand, but for once, she was more concerned with laying place settings than in laying out a corpse.

Even Mrs. Scrope's extra-loud wheezing as she bobbed her head up and down in pretended agreement with Violet's ideas and suggestions didn't deter her from being consumed with the idea of creating a perfect dinner for her parents.

For the very first time, she sat down and went over the menu in detail with her housekeeper. Violet changed her mind repeatedly over how many courses to serve and what should be included in each one. Finally, in frustration over her mistress's indecision, Mrs. Scrope suggested that they see what Mrs. Beeton might recommend.

That dratted busybody Mrs. Beeton again. Realizing, though, that she couldn't afford to lose the invaluable Mrs. Scrope, Violet agreed, and a menu was planned to include three courses, each comprising several dishes, plus an entrée course that would include braised beef, spring chicken, roast quarter of lamb, beef tongue, and roast saddle of mutton.

But that was just the beginning. Violet was concerned with how napkins would be folded. "The miter design is the best look," Mrs. Scrope said patiently.

What of the tablecloth? What color? "Always white and crisply ironed," Mrs. Scrope said.

Right. And should the service be *à la française*, or *à la russe?* Mrs. Beeton didn't seem to think much of *à la russe*, but wasn't it becoming the more popular serving style?

"We'll serve *à la française*, as is proper," Mrs. Scrope said, a tad less patient now.

Violet carried on with her worries until Mrs. Scrope threatened to burn the first-course soup if her mistress didn't stop fretting and let the housekeeper do her job.

Violet stopped fretting in front of Mrs. Scrope, but continued to do so in private, marveling that she must be the only wife in London whose servant spoke down to her like this.

Is this what a mistress of the house is supposed to do every day? Worry about menus and the number of candles on hand and whether or not the smuts are scrubbed off the front stoop? It was agonizing, and she resolved to immerse herself back inside her shop the moment her parents left.

On the day of her parents' arrival, Mrs. Scrope forbade Violet from coming near the dining room, assuring her that everything would be perfect and telling her to concentrate on her toilette. *Really, I should reprimand her for talking to me thus, but what would I do if she left?*

So Violet concentrated on dressing in her new russet pelerine jacket and matching skirt over her widest crinoline. The sleeves of the jacket were gathered at the elbows and then flared open, permitting her snowy white sleeves to show through. The jacket's entire edge was trimmed in a black loop fringe. She pulled her hair back in a loose knot and topped it with a cap that matched her white sleeves. Violet Morgan would never be a society woman with a lady's maid to dress her hair in elaborate styles.

As she prepared to go downstairs, she met Graham on the landing. His black trousers were tight fitting, accentuating his thighs and calves, and the chocolate brown cravat surrounding his raised shirt collar emphasized his piercing green eyes. He pulled a watch from his checked waistcoat and nodded, as if verifying they were on time.

"You look dashing," she blurted, instantly regretting her unreserved tone.

His eyes raked over her. "And you, dear Violet, are a vision. Perhaps we should conclude this little dinner party early, eh?" He raised an eyebrow suggestively and she blushed, unused to her husband's teasing advances, which had all but disappeared over the past couple of years.

"By the way, I have something for you." Graham reached into a pocket and pulled out a small box secured with a burgundy satin bow. Inside lay a magnificent pair of pearl ear bobs.

"They're lovely," Violet said.

Graham removed the bobs from their velvet resting place and clipped them onto Violet's earlobes, doing so with a tenderness that swept away her earlier misgivings about her husband. *The man I love is still there.*

He cupped her ears as if making sure the bobs were placed correctly and kissed her forehead. "Now you look utterly perfect, sweetheart."

She took his arm and they went together to greet their guests. Violet's heart was the lightest that she could recall in months.

Although the dinner was a success from a meal perspective, Violet was left unsettled by the final events of the evening.

Everyone arrived promptly at seven o'clock. The dining hour in London was becoming later and later because of changes in people's work habits. The railway system in England was improving to the point that many families had moved out to the suburbs of London where the air was cleaner, and the men simply commuted into the city each day for work. However, by not living above, or at least near, their shops and employers, they returned home later in the day, thus postponing the family's evening meal.

Violet was glad she and Graham remained close to the city. If they had chosen a home in one of the fast-growing outer suburbs, like Richmond, it would have been too easy for her husband to leave her behind each day to manage the house while he rode into the city center to manage their business.

What a dreadful thought.

Greetings were passed all around, with Violet restraining herself from launching into her mother's arms after such a long absence. Mrs. Scrope tinkled a bell from somewhere outside the room, signaling Graham to take Violet's hand on his arm and lead everyone into the dining room.

At Graham's insistence, their dining room was decorated in a fashionable red motif. Crimson flocked wallpaper, heavy red draperies puddled on the floor to prevent drafts, a bright red Turkish carpet, and red chair cushions were equally weighed down by a mahogany dining table, sideboard, and fireplace surround. Even the glass over the sideboard was framed in an ornate mahogany frame.

Their imported blue-and-white collection sat on individual shelves above the fireplace for admiration by guests. Graham preened as Violet's parents proceeded to do so.

In all, Violet felt as though she were being choked to death inside this room, but Graham loved it for the message it sent about the Morgans' increasing status.

Mrs. Scrope had done an admirable job setting the table. A variety of steaming side and corner dishes were strategically placed around the table atop containers of hot water, while a tureen of soup was placed in front of Violet's place and a platter of fish sat on Graham's end.

They all sat down and Graham said grace, then Violet and Graham stood to serve soup and fish to everyone, with Mrs. Scrope on hand to pass plates. After they had eaten that, Mrs. Scrope removed the soup tureen and fish platter, replacing them with the braised beef in front of Graham and the spring chicken for Violet to serve. Mrs. Scrope also ensured that the side and corner dishes, none of which required carving or ladling, were passed around to each guest.

The entire meal took hours serving *à la française*, but the conversation and wine were plentiful, and Mrs. Scrope was a miracle in the manner in which she guided Violet along, such that it appeared to their guests as though Violet was in complete control of things.

Discussion started pleasantly enough, with the Sinclairs telling amusing stories about their neighbors in Brighton, and Fletcher doing the same about his ship's crew members, who he said were as difficult to train as a school of dead haddock.

"With no offense meant to our earlier delectable dish, which would have no doubt been easier to teach the mechanics of pumping bilge than my own crew."

Fletcher could always be relied on for brash humor. Soon he was openly flirting with both Violet and her mother, but managed to do so in such a way that Graham and her father didn't notice, or at least didn't take insult.

Ida Morgan laughed at appropriate times and responded when directly addressed, but was mostly interested in devouring whatever meat, vegetable, or bread made an appearance on her plate. Violet had once thought her mother-in-law rude, but came to realize that for Ida Morgan, there were only two important things in life: food and her two sons, neither of which could ever fail her. Unfortunately, Violet felt she was a frequent disappointment to Ida.

Ida's adoration for Graham meant she'd keep her opinion to herself, but Violet sensed that the older woman disapproved of Graham's marital choice. Whether she viewed Violet as an interloper in the family business or despised Violet for not being a rung on the social ladder was unclear. The woman was the least of Violet's worries, though.

Ida Morgan somehow remained thin and tiny as a tree sparrow, unlike Eliza Sinclair, who, Violet thought fondly, was enjoying her relaxed life in Brighton too much. Mother's cheeks were filling out, and she was struggling inside her corset while seated.

Father still maintained his tall, angular build, although his hair was thinning a bit on the sides.

Suddenly, Violet felt sharp pangs of homesickness. She'd hardly missed her parents at all since marrying Graham, but sitting together to dinner like this made her long for them, long for a time before she was responsible for home and hearth and her husband's mercurial disposition. Yet how could she wish to return to a time before she had her life's passion in undertaking? She dragged herself back to the conversation.

Violet's father was interested in Fletcher's work. "How many sailings to America do you make each year?"

"As many as I can, sir. The Jamaicans want their tea, and the British need their rum."

Violet's father chuckled. "Quite. Although I never understood the propensity for rum. I much prefer port or claret, which I hope we will partake in tonight?"

"Of course, sir," Graham said. "I've saved my finest for you."

"This is quite fine, too, brother," Fletcher said, lifting the red wine bottle and offering it around the table. "Violet, did Graham tell you he is joining me in a new venture?" Fletcher asked.

"No, he didn't—"

"No need to burden Violet with our little enterprise," Graham said.

"It's no burden. What venture is this?"

Graham tried to interrupt again, but Fletcher cut him off. "We're going to make the Morgan name known across the Atlantic. Because of their war, there is quite a demand for funerary supplies in America, so we're going to ship them the superior goods provided by Morgan Undertaking."

"Graham, you haven't mentioned this to me."

"It's nothing, really. We're developing certain contracts that will allow us to ship coffins, shrouds, wreath cases, and the like over to help families bury their sons, brothers, and fathers."

"How much is this costing us? How will it affect our own inventory? Graham, you should have told me."

"Now, darling, that's why I didn't tell you about it, lest you worry over nothing. I have everything under control."

Ida looked up from her plate. "Violet, a good wife trusts her husband. I'm sure Graham knows best."

Violet ignored her mother-in-law. "They don't have their own cabinetmakers who can build coffins? Wouldn't that be cheaper than importing coffins from us? And aren't there undertakers over there?"

"You see, Violet, that's why I didn't share this with you. You don't have a head for international business transactions."

"I have as much head as you for all of our business dealings."

"But this is much more sophisticated and complex. You see, you're already hysterical and you know nothing of it."

"I'm not—" Violet swallowed her retort. Her parents looked stricken at the argument taking place between husband and wife. Ida had returned to her food, but could not disguise a self-satisfied look.

Her brother-in-law attempted to repair the situation he'd caused.

"Mr. and Mrs. Sinclair, you probably don't realize how the Morgan reputation has grown under Graham's leadership. I never had any interest in the family business and it would have undoubtedly failed if I'd remained in it. Graham was always the one with a mind for the hereafter, so to speak.

"When he met your breathtaking daughter, well, the match was secured by the Almighty for the two of them to work side by side on dressing, cosmetically altering, and otherwise preparing their, er, clients, for their final meeting with their divine destiny. I've often wondered if those you know are bound for Hades receive less attention than those bound to sit at the right hand of the eternal throne. Perhaps you don't dress them in their finest?" He winked at Violet.

"Honestly, Fletcher, you're going to frighten my parents into thinking I'm somehow influential in those destinies. Mother, Father, pay my brother-in-law no mind. He's had too much sea water to drink and it's made him dizzy."

Ida Morgan managed to put down her fork long enough to say, "Violet, really, it's rather vulgar to speak in such a manner to your brother-in-law."

Fletcher laughed. "I'm not offended, Mother. But, Violet, you would admit that you do alter your subjects' appearances at times, wouldn't you?"

She didn't like speaking of the deceased as though they were dolls she casually dressed and posed. "When the circumstances call for it. We strive to help families give their loved ones decent Christian burials, no matter their status."

He pressed further. "What happens when you receive someone who has been drastically injured, or has perhaps lost an arm or something? Do you just pin up his sleeve, or do you wrap the sleeve around something arm-like?"

Violet's mother put a hand to her mouth. Leave it to Fletcher to guide the conversation from an unseemly spousal argument into completely uncivilized territory.

Violet treated the question as though it were perfectly normal dinnertime conversation. "It depends. The family might not have the money to do much more than minimal cover-up, in which case, depending on the injury, we might use a closed coffin, with just a window to the view the face. A well-to-do family, however, might want to see their dearly beloved in as close a state to living as possible. In that case, the options are more . . . flexible. I can use a bit of clay and wax to perfect a nose or ear that has been mangled. I might go so far as to purchase a wax prosthetic from Madame Tussauds in the case of a missing limb."

Fletcher sat back like a solicitor who had just delivered an irrefutable argument to a jury. "Fascinating."

By this point, the diners were finishing up their third-course selections from dishes of strawberries, cherry compote, and Neapolitan cake, and were washing it all down with glasses of Madeira.

At the blessed conclusion of the meal, Violet rose and invited her mother and Ida to join her in the drawing room, pulling closed the heavy, sound-blocking draperies that divided the two rooms behind her. The men would remain in the dining room to drink port. She and Graham had agreed in advance that tonight there would be an exception to the no-cigars rule.

Violet had outlawed cigars in the house the moment they moved in. The smoke could never be aired out because the windows always had to remain shut to prevent smuts from drifting into the house. With their difficulties in keeping servants, Violet needed no further strain on maintaining the cleanliness of their household. Especially since that peculiar smell was still wafting periodically through the house. One day she would have to hire a man to check the pipes.

The three women sat down, with Violet almost sighing in relief to be gone from the inquisition and contention of the dining room.

"So, my love," her mother said. "Your new housekeeper seems very efficient. How did you discover her?"

"Mrs. Scrope placed a situation wanted advertisement in *The Times*, which I answered. She was looking for a place with a single gentleman, but had no objection to a married couple."

Violet's mother frowned. "What did her references say about her?"

"I didn't actually bother with her references, given that she seemed so competent—and has proved to be so—and Graham gave me so little time to find a replacement for Annie."

"Hmm. Do you keep your tea and sugar locked away?"

"Well, no. I'm so busy at the shop that I can't be here every time she needs to scrape some from a block for that evening's dinner."

Ida interrupted. "A good mistress makes her home her first priority."

"Yes, Mother Morgan." Violet shifted uncomfortably. "But Morgan Undertaking requires so much of me. . . ."

Ida sniffed. "It seems unladylike to me that a woman would place dirty hands above her husband's comfort. I certainly never did so while my husband was alive."

"Graham is not uncomfort—"

Violet's mother broke in and steered the conversation back to Mrs. Scrope. "Well, the woman does appear to have your home well in hand, and I know you were never much for learning the finer points of managing a home yourself, so I suppose all is well for you. At least tell me you keep your silver under lock and key."

"Of course. You can take comfort that one of the lessons you tried to instill in me found its mark."

"If I was able to teach you just one thing, I consider your youth a great success."

Eliza Sinclair had taught her daughter at home as much as she could: reading, handwriting, arithmetic, and religion. Mother had also attempted to teach her the graceful arts of music and dancing, but Violet had been hopeless at them. Violet smiled. "I must have been a terribly difficult child."

Ida sniffed again. Violet resisted the temptation to give her a handkerchief and ask her if she was suffering from an ague.

"Not difficult, just single-mindedly determined and more interested in asking the butcher, the physician, the train porter, and everyone else you met questions about their job duties, rather than learning the duties you should take on as a young woman. Your poor father, he was mortified by it." Eliza Sinclair's eyes crinkled at the corners, and Violet knew that, contrary to her father's chagrin, her mother found it all amusing.

Perceptively realizing that Ida wasn't particularly interested in musing about her daughter-in-law's childhood, Eliza Sinclair went to the heavy upright piano Graham had ordered from Monington and Weston. It wasn't as majestic as the Stanleys' grand piano, but served not only its functional purpose, but was decorative as well, with its appropriate fringe-edged lace runner on top and a variety of china pieces lining it.

Violet's mother culled through a nearby cupboard containing several pieces of sheet music that came with the instrument, found something she liked, and sat down to play. The sounds of "Come into the Garden, Maud" soon filled the air. After tapping her foot for several moments, Ida joined Eliza at the piano and sang along, completely out of tune to the music but with utter abandon, leaving Violet alone with her thoughts.

What was going on between her husband and brother-in-law? She didn't like it one bit, and a knot of worry in her stomach urged her to confront Graham over it.

At nearly midnight, their guests finally left, with the men having exhausted three bottles of port and Violet's mother having played every piece of sheet music they had, twice.

Violet went upstairs ahead of Graham, who wanted to speak to Mrs. Scrope about replenishing their wine stock. Relieved of her corset and wearing a comfortable nightgown and wrapper, Violet sat at the chintz-covered vanity table in her dressing room, brushing out her long hair after so many hours pinned tightly to her head, as she continued to ruminate on the evening's events. It was so comforting to see Mother and Father again, even if that comfort was tempered by Ida Morgan's disapproving glances and snorts. Fletcher was charmingly exasperating and seemed to have stolen Graham's portion of charisma.

She didn't even realize Graham had entered her dressing room until he was bent over behind her, circling his arms around her waist and burying his face in her neck.

"You did a wonderful job, sweetheart," he said. "The meal was prepared to perfection. That Mrs. Scrope is a gem, isn't she? And I think your father was impressed with our new home." He pushed aside the right shoulder of her robe, placing tiny kisses along the exposed skin.

Violet put down her brush and tilted her head to give her husband better access to her neck and shoulders. She sighed in contentment at his gentle touch.

"In fact, I think we should host more dinner parties," he said, continuing to kiss her and now stroking her arms. "I'm thinking we can invite Fletcher and some of his business associates and their wives one evening. You could invite Mrs. Overfelt over to pair with Fletcher so there would be an even number."

Mary and Fletcher were acquainted, and although neither would have the least romantic interest in the other, especially given their age difference, they would be amenable dinner partners.

"I'd like to give Mrs. Scrope a rest after last night's venture, but we could certainly do it again soon," she said.

"Good. Some of these men may be my own business partners one day, so I may as well start courting them now. They can see how prosperous we already are."

"What is the nature of these 'future business partners,' Graham? Are they involved in shipping funerary supplies to America, too?"

Graham offered his arm and gently lifted her from her chair to face him. "Among other things. As I said, it's nothing for you to worry over. We have more pressing matters to discuss."

He leaned down for a kiss, but Violet pulled away.

"I'll not be spoken to like a child. I work just as hard as you in our shop, and I deserve to know what you are planning to do with our supplies and money."

"This is a private matter between Fletcher and me. All you need to know is that it is guaranteed profitable, which will one day have you in silk dresses and feathered hats, with perhaps even a move to Mayfair."

"It is *not* private between you and your brother. The mere fact that you won't tell me means it's something immoral or illegal, and I won't have you using our shop for it."

"*Our* shop? Mrs. Morgan, I daresay you forget your place in this marriage. You are an adequate undertaker, and a great help to me in the shop, but it is my shop to do with as I please. And it pleases me to do a little trading with America."

"An adequate undertaker? I've contracted for twice as many bodies so far this year than you have, and have attended every single one of their funerals. I make sure our supply closet is maintained and our employees are paid and our fees are collected."

Graham took two steps away from Violet. "Yes, you are merely adequate, because all of the marvelous work you do is always at the expense of our home, which is your wifely duty and the clearest sign of our prosperity. My mother has commented to me more than once that our home is not kept to a high standard. God clearly favors you, for we now have Mrs. Scrope, but with all the servants previous to her, this place teetered on disaster. You've neglected me far too long. You hold a cold, white corpse in higher regard than you do me."

"If I hold a corpse in higher regard, it is because it is more respectful of me than my own husband, and doesn't see fit to criticize everything I do. I also find that our deceased customers keep fewer secrets than you do."

Graham looked sideways through the dressing room door. "Lower your voice, Mrs. Scrope might hear us."

"Yes, and you are far more concerned about offending Mrs. Scrope than your wife, are you not? After all, she is far more than *adequate* in taking care of you and your needs. Perhaps Mrs. Scrope would even suit you better as a wife."

"Don't be ridiculous, Violet. She's servant class."

"Ah, her lower status being your only impediment?"

"Of course not, she's thoroughly unattractive and makes that annoying wheezing sound—wait, why am I even justifying myself? This conversation has gone completely around the bend."

"Not as far around the bend as you seem to have done, between your obsession over my competence as your wife, your volatile mood changes, and now your secret dealings with your brother."

"Violet, you don't—"

"I'm finished." She headed through the doorway into the bedroom, yanked down the tester bed's coverlet, and slid in, staying turned away from Graham's side.

As he followed in behind her, she reached up and extinguished the gas lamp on the wall above her, then sank back down on the pillow. Violet felt him standing next to the bed, staring at her. His bullish exhalations were the only signal of his fury. She clenched her eyes shut, willing him to go away.

He complied, muttering "Blast it all," as he left the room, slamming the door behind him.

* * *

Full of anguish and regret after a sleepless night, Violet arose even before Mrs. Scrope would be up to draw open the drapes in the dining and drawing rooms. She searched for Graham, intent on making amends with him.

The sight of disarrayed pillows on the sofa in his study told her where he'd spent the night. A square envelope with her name scrawled across the front sat propped up against an inkwell on his desk. Inside was a hastily written message.

> *I won't be home for dinner this evening. Please inform Mrs. Scrope.*

Not even a signature, much less an endearment.
Blast it all.

Samuel was pleased with his visiting cards, which showed him seated next to a table with a globe on it, the photographer's best idea for representing him as an important man of the world. Underneath the picture were the words "Samuel Harper, Buyer of Quality Goods, Confederate States of America."

Samuel purchased ninety-six copies of the untinted ambrotype and headed off to Isle of Dogs to make some inquiries.

Isle of Dogs lay on a low, marshy tract of land on the left bank of the Thames about five miles below London Bridge, facing Deptford and Greenwich. It comprised a great colony of shipbuilders' yards, ironworks, chemical works, tar manufacturers, and other similar establishments. Their by-products filled the air with noxious smells, rendering the atmosphere nearly fatal to a newcomer. Samuel grimaced at what he was willing to endure for his homeland.

He spent time walking past the shipyards and examining their names, who they employed, and how prosperous they seemed to be. Only a very specific sort of shipbuilder would do. There seemed to be about a dozen shipbuilders in all, each its own busy hive of activity. Samuel estimated that there were thousands of men at work on this little peninsula. The clanging of riveting hammers was interspersed with the lilting sound of Scotsmen. The occasional worker who noticed Samuel passing by greeted him with a "How are ye?" in that distinctive Scottish accent.

Public houses abounded on the island, and so, now sweating from the heat of a sun having risen high in the sky, Samuel stopped inside the cool, dark Highland Mary for a meal and to see if he could meet anyone . . . helpful. The smell was only marginally better here.

Samuel ordered ginger beer and a dish of fried cod slices with anchovy sauce before sitting down at a rickety pine table next to a window facing one of the shipyards. He glanced at his pocket watch and saw that it was now exactly one o'clock in the afternoon. Almost as if a bell had rung, workers dropped their hammers and other tools and either retrieved lunch pails from inside a locker or began pouring into the Highland Mary and other nearby public houses, chattering loudly as they ordered food and found places to sit down.

Could my timing have been any better planned?

With one foot, he pushed out the chair opposite him, an invitation for any of the workers to join him. Most ignored him, except for the owner, who had been eyeing Samuel warily from behind the counter as he served whisky and ale to the workers.

Soon the owner emerged from where he had been pouring refreshment for the shipyard workers and approached Samuel's table, wiping his hands on his dirty apron.

"Don't ken ye, do I?" the man asked.

"No, I am a visitor here. I'm hoping to find someone who will help me with a shipping endeavor."

The owner's eyes narrowed. "Dinna like the sound of your accent. Where're ye from?"

"America. Specifically, Virginia."

The Highland Mary's proprietor wasn't impressed. "Ye sound foolish. An ill-faur'd limmer, are ye?"

Samuel had no idea what the man was talking about, but he was probably Samuel's best hope of finding a contact. Using his best

American negotiating technique, he offered the man a gold sovereign to tell him where he could find a ship owner willing to take on a special project.

As it turned out, the American negotiating technique was understood in Great Britain, even if Samuel's accent wasn't.

Violet hadn't spoken to Graham in days. He slept on his sofa each night and left before she arose each morning. He ignored her in the shop—no easy feat inside their small quarters—and in the evenings he disappeared for destinations unknown.

Mrs. Scrope, bless her heart, pretended nothing was amiss, although she was no longer asking what the master might like for dessert.

Tired of the chilly atmosphere at the shop and the even more frigid temperature at home, Violet made a visit to Mary Overfelt for some cheerful company.

The Overfelt Mourning Dressmakers shop was as much a catastrophe as it was when Violet had helped to clean it up just a few weeks ago. She swept a hand around the room. "Mary, what happened?"

The older woman shook her head. "I know, dearest. I don't seem to be able to stay on top of things. I'm just so busy with new commissions—not that I'm complaining, mind you—that the condition of this place simply gets away from me."

"You need a maid to help you." Violet could only imagine what Mary's quarters above the shop looked like.

"I'm not sure there's enough to do here on a daily basis for a live-in."

"Why not day help? Better yet, I could probably spare Mrs. Scrope for a few hours each week. She's been a marvel at our home. She'd have you set to rights in no time."

"A generous offer, Violet. Perhaps I'll take you up on it. But enough about my appalling condition. Come to the back room, and if we can actually find a place to sit, we'll have tea and get caught up with one another."

Violet told her friend about her parents' visit and about all of the improvements Mrs. Scrope had made to their townhome. She avoided discussion of Graham, and for a brief hour, she nearly forgot that her husband was ignoring her as though she were a street urchin tugging at his jacket, seeking a penny.

It was only after she left that she realized Mary hadn't even asked her about Graham, almost as if she instinctively knew something was wrong.

Do I wear my feelings on my sleeve?

When she returned home, there was a note from Mrs. Scrope, stating that she had gone to see about a chimney sweep and to run other errands. She would return in plenty of time to make dinner.

At least Mrs. Scrope signed her note.

Violet trudged upstairs to take a nap and resolved to herself before drifting off that she would attempt to make amends with Graham the next time she saw him.

She'd hardly gone to sleep when the letter carrier's distinctive double rap on the door with his baton told her that mail had been delivered through the door slot. Awake once again, she decided to pick it up herself rather than waiting for Mrs. Scrope to do so.

Ah, a letter from Mother. Tossing aside the other envelopes and periodicals, she read the correspondence from her mother, who was back in Brighton once again. She chatted gaily about their visit to Leicester, inquired about Graham, then came to the point. Who was the manufacturer of her silver cutlery?

Violet smiled. Mother had admired Violet's simple but elegant fiddle and thread patterned set while she was at dinner, but thought it would be in poor taste to ask for purchase details in front of the Morgans. Mother knew everything about social etiquette and managing a home. She was the perfect wife and mother.

I should have paid more attention when I was a girl.

Although Mrs. Scrope probably knew the answer without having to look at the silver, Violet decided not to wait for Mrs. Scrope to return to answer the question, but to instead take on this task for her mother herself. She went back to her room and removed the key ring that was kept hidden beneath a drawer in her dressing room table and went back downstairs to the dining room to open the silver chest. Forks, knives, and the like were kept in a mahogany chest specially designed to hold them, whereas larger serving pieces were locked behind a large serving cabinet. She lifted her skirts and knelt before the chest, inserting the key and lifting the lid to view its contents.

Something wasn't right.

There were stacks of lobster forks, round bowl soup spoons, and luncheon knives in their correct slots, yet . . .

She picked up a stack of salad forks and counted them. There were nine. Shouldn't there be twelve of everything? She lifted the dinner forks. Ten of them. Eight consommé spoons. Nine butter knives.

How had she not noticed this before?

Because before you always just opened the chest and let Mrs. Scrope rummage around as she pleased.

Please, God, no, it just couldn't be.

She rose and went to the serving cabinet. With dread, she opened both doors, and her fears were confirmed. The ice pitcher, usually wrapped in felt on the lower shelf, was gone, as were one of the fruit stands and a pickle caster. Graham had been so proud when they were able to afford these elegant silver serving pieces.

How am I ever going to explain this to him?

She heard a noise outside. Parting the layers of dining room draperies, she saw Mrs. Scrope descending the stairs to the basement entrance, carrying a bundle of goods, including a wrapped package of fish.

How Violet would miss the woman's fish pie.

She went to the top of the servants' staircase and called down, "Mrs. Scrope, can you come up to the dining room, please?"

The assembly of packages went down with a thud on the kitchen worktable as Mrs. Scrope loudly sighed to do her mistress's bidding.

This was why the dead were so much more pleasant to work with than the living.

Violet stepped back into the dining room and waited, the key dangling on its tasseled ring before her. Mrs. Scrope entered with a "Mrs. Morgan, I have to—" and stopped.

Violet had to give the woman credit. It took Mrs. Scrope a mere second to ascertain everything. "So you noticed some of the plate is not there? Yes, there were some tarnished spots I couldn't get out on my own, so I sent it all out to—"

"Mrs. Scrope, I may be an absentminded mistress, but I am not a foolish one. It's not just to the rag-and-bone man that you're giving our goods, is it? If I begin opening other drawers around my home, what else will I find missing? Is my tea caddy empty?"

"Mrs. Morgan, you impugn my integrity—" The housekeeper was wheezing now.

"You impugn your own integrity by treating this household as your own personal trading shop. You are dismissed, Mrs. Scrope."

"You can't do this to me. Madam, I meant no harm. I was just supplementing my meager wages with a little extra. I have an ailing cousin down in Exeter and I was saving for a train fare back home and—"

"Meager!" Violet exploded. "You demanded eighteen pounds per year in wages, nearly double what I paid the last girl considering your extra allowances, which I gladly gave because I had such high hopes in you."

"She was a young chit and shouldn't have earned as much as me. Anyway, 'tweren't enough for all the duties I had to do. A house this size should have a cook, a parlor maid, and a housemaid. I was doing everything myself, wasn't I? Most mistresses at least help with turning mattresses, or hanging laundry to dry, but you've no care for the place. A little pinch and a nick here and there wouldn't hurt you and the master none, and made it so I could improve my own status."

"I didn't hire you to improve your status. I needed you to improve my home so my husband wouldn't—" Now it was Violet's turn to stop. "I needed you to keep our home to a good standard. That standard includes not thieving me into destitution."

"Instead, *I'll* be the one who's destitute."

"Your own doing, Mrs. Scrope. Be off the premises within the hour."

The housekeeper's eyes narrowed. "I'll need a good character from you."

"You'll get no reference from me. Good day, Mrs. Scrope."

"Good riddance to you as well, madam. The stink downstairs is intolerable anyway, and you've not seen fit to do anything about it." Mrs. Scrope stomped back down the stairs. Violet stood at the dining room window, waiting until she finally saw the woman who she'd thought was a godsend exit from the basement door, a worn tapestry bag in each hand, containing all of her belongings. Were the bags gifts from a previous mistress, or items Mrs. Scrope thought her employer could do without? Violet knew she should insist on searching the bags, but was anxious for the whole sordid mess to be finished.

Mrs. Scrope paused outside, unsure where to go, then finally marched down Grafton Terrace, out of Violet's life forever.

Violet put her forehead to the windowpane. Not again. Not another round of referrals, advertisements, and interviews to find an honest servant. She'd have to try something different this time. She had no idea what to do about her servant problem, although one thing was certain: Violet wouldn't be sending Edith Scrope to Mary Overfelt.

She turned to more immediate matters in the kitchen. Everything Mrs. Scrope had purchased had to be put away. Well, at least the woman had thoroughly organized everything, making it easy to figure out where it all went. Violet stored the purchases away, except for one last item that sat on the table. There was nowhere to put it; it had to be prepared and eaten right away, for it would spoil quickly.

Good Lord, would she have to prepare the fish herself?

Luckily for her, Graham was in more of a mood for reconciliation than she was and came home that evening with a gift, a cameo pin surrounded by tiny seed pearls. He apologized for his boorish behavior and begged Violet's forgiveness.

She in turn kissed him, apologized herself, then told him the sorry news of Mrs. Scrope's departure.

Graham merely shook his head and smiled. "My wife has the worst luck with domestics. I'll miss her stewed veal, but it's not worth having the place cleaned out, is it?"

"You're not angry with me for making such a poor hiring choice?"

"Servants are difficult in the best of circumstances. I leave it to your care how to hire the next one."

He didn't even complain that the turbot fillets were still raw in the center and that the peas hadn't soaked nearly long enough to be cooked properly, merely raising his glass of wine to her in a salute and forcing down his inedible meal.

How mercurial Graham had become, but she liked this side of his twin-sided temperament. If only she could figure out what mischief he and Fletcher were up to behind her back, for surely there was more to his new trading arrangements than mere funerary supplies.

This time, Violet placed an advertisement herself and was rewarded with several applicants. After weeding through them all, including one woman whom she rejected for simply looking too much like Mrs. Scrope, Violet settled on an unusual choice: an older couple named Walter and Hazel Porter.

Graham raised an eyebrow at the thought of having a male servant, since typically only the largest homes had them, and even then in the form of personal valets or footmen, neither of which they needed in their stylish, yet still middle-class, home.

But he shrugged and told her to do whatever she wished.

Having learned too many lessons over the past few years, Violet did a thorough interview of the couple, asking them detailed questions about their knowledge and experience in managing a household.

Mrs. Porter usually did cooking and laundry, while Mr. Porter performed household repairs and heavy cleaning jobs, such as hauling carpets outdoors so his wife could beat them. The pair had been together since working together in a country estate in Berkshire. In his youth, Walter burned to be his own man, and so convinced a young Hazel to elope with him to London, where he then opened a barber's shop. It failed miserably within two years, and together they returned to service, working in various homes and ending up in the household of an eccentric widowed woman who kept a menagerie of parakeets, spaniels, and even rabbits inside her home.

The widow had recently died, bequeathing them a small inheritance, but not enough to allow them to retire. The Porters vowed to stay together in service and sought a home with a bit less chaos than the screeching, barking, and dander cleanup that went on twenty-four hours a day at their previous location.

Violet's heart wanted to soar over the Porters, but she knew better than to get too excited yet. While Graham managed the shop by himself, she visited as many of the Porters' previous employers as she could, including the menagerie woman's grown daughter, who knew the couple and gave them a glowing reference.

When there was no investigation left to do, Violet took a deep breath and offered them employment, promising that she would have the attic converted into a small apartment for them, since the small bedroom off the kitchen would never do for two people. Along with their quarters, she offered them forty pounds per year with no extra allowances.

The bargain thus struck, Violet prayed the Porters would be a success and that they would stay until the day she or they died, so she would never have to go through the torment of hiring another servant again.

She was glad to get this all behind her so she could return to the comfortable world of crypts and coffins. Her comfort was not to last, though, for word soon came that Ida Morgan had had an accident and was not expected to survive.

> *Dearest diary, I had a most uncomfortable encounter with the law today. I boarded an omnibus, intent on implementing a minor swindle on an unsuspecting passenger. I didn't have quite enough to make my rent this month. I know you understand.*
>
> *I sat next to a kindly-looking woman who also seemed to be the richest aboard the carriage, given her richly dyed silk dress and the gold bobs dangling from her ears. Showing her the worthless ring I'd picked up from a street*

vendor, I explained that it had passed through my family—one with French aristocratic roots that had been destroyed during the Revolution. Hard times were upon the family; would she care to purchase the family's signet ring for a very fair price?

Naturally, she was most eager for the ring, but I wasn't aware of a constable watching our transaction. At the following stop, he made his way to our bench and began asking questions.

Fortunately, my mark proclaimed herself quite happy and in no need of assistance, so the officer removed himself and I made sure to depart the omnibus as soon as I could.

Sometimes I wonder how the rich get that way, they're so bumbling and stupid. I pocketed several gold coins, and she is undoubtedly off waving her pudgy, beringed finger in her friends' faces, telling them of her connection to the fictitious Lefronteau family.

I was able to pay my rent and can now concentrate on more important things.

⋟ 6 ⋞

Spare me the whispering, crowded room, the friends who come and gape and go, the ceremonious air of gloom—all, which makes death a hideous show.

—Matthew Arnold (1822–1888), English poet and critic

June 1861

Violet and Graham flew to his mother's bedside, where Fletcher was already posted, his eyes bloodshot and his clothing crumpled.

"I took Mother on an outing to Regent's Park. She wanted to see the zoo's aquatic vivarium. Afterward, we were visiting the Rhino House, where a young child began taunting the beasts in their cage. A black rhino, smaller than the others but with two devilishly sharp horns, charged at the boy. Mother jumped out of the way and walked farther down along the cage bars, and I'm not sure what happened next. I suppose the beast mistook Mother's movement for that of the boy, and he charged her, managing to slip his horn through the cage and gore her. God, why did I agree to escort her to such a dangerous place?"

Graham was silent as he stood at the foot of the bed, staring at his mother's sleeping face. Knowing his silence could only serve to make Fletcher feel worse, Violet said, "How could you possibly have known what would happen, Fletcher? You were a good son doing a nice thing for his mother."

She glanced at her mother-in-law, who lay under piles of blankets. She wondered what pulling back the covers would reveal. Probably a wound too awful to contemplate.

"I suppose," Fletcher said. "You can't imagine the noise the thing made, grunting and snorting. It actually managed to work it-self up to a gallop inside its small confines. Poor Mother, she never saw him coming. The zookeeper said they have poor eyesight and that tends to make them volatile." He turned back to the prone figure. "Mother, I am so sorry."

Still Graham said nothing, although he did reach out a hand to clap his brother on the shoulder.

"Fletcher, what did the doctor say?" Violet asked.

Fletcher let out a single great sob and shook his head. "He tended to her chest wound, and said it was very deep and jagged. She had blood everywhere, it was terrible. She runs a great risk of infection, and the doctor said we can only wait and see."

Within a day, though, it was apparent that Ida was not going to survive her injuries. She woke for brief periods and expressed delight to have her two sons nearby, although Violet detected a faint scowl on the woman's face whenever she entered the room.

Very well, let her be with her boys. Violet busied herself by bringing in sprays of flowers that she picked from Ida's small garden and ensuring Ida had the tastiest of foods to eat, most of which were ignored.

Ida refusing food was the surest sign that the woman was not long for the world.

Violet brought in a recording journal, but when the men showed little interest in using it, Violet spent as much time as she could tucked discreetly in a corner of her mother-in-law's bedroom, in order to record Ida's final days. To the best of her ability, Violet captured the days and times that Ida was awake and sleeping, what her countenance was like, and every word she uttered. She also recorded the prayers that both men said over their mother, and what actions they took, whether to hold her hands, dab her face with cool water, or change out a blanket.

The important moment would come when Ida told them that she accepted her fate and had made peace with God. This was also a moment when family members expected their loved one to make final wishes or commands. Even better was if the dying one had any sort of visions of the great beyond to share with the family. It was vital that Violet be there to record exactly what Ida said.

Every devoted family created such a journal for family members who died of illness, old age, or for other reasons that did not result in instantaneous death. The journal would be passed down through the family, so that future generations could know their ancestor, although the future existence of the Morgan family seemed relatively bleak.

Despite Violet's long vigil at Ida Morgan's bedside with Graham and Fletcher, her mother-in-law slipped away in the middle of the night about two weeks after her goring without ever giving her sons a final message or exhortation.

After Ida's great "whoosh," the distinctive noisy breath that indicated a passing, Graham looked at Violet and said simply, "I can't."

"I understand." Violet arranged to have another undertaking company make all arrangements for her mother-in-law, working closely with them without ever sharing the details with Graham, who holed himself up in their dining room with Fletcher, coming out only for new bottles of port.

The funeral procession was a magnificent affair, if a little above Ida Morgan's station. Afterward, Fletcher thanked Violet profusely, whereas her husband merely gave her a solemn nod of thanks. Fletcher went back to his ship, and Graham went back to his port.

Violet hardly saw Graham after that. His mother's death did nothing to draw husband and wife together, and Violet felt as adrift as ever from him.

July 1861

Violet could hardly believe their good fortune, albeit at the expense of someone else's earthly existence. Morgan Undertaking had just received its most prestigious commission ever with the funeral of Thomas Herbert, a Vice-Admiral of the White who fought in the War of 1812, was decorated by Queen Victoria with the Order of the Bath, and had served as Member of Parliament for Dartmouth up until 1857.

Never before had they been approached with such a distinguished client. Even Graham was ecstatic that they were able to honor a hero of the previous war with the Americans.

More importantly for Violet, Herbert's widow had agreed to embalm her husband so that admirers could have plenty of time to pay their respects to her husband prior to interment, which would be private and not a state ceremonial funeral.

Graham had finally come out of his stupor over his mother's death and was once again active in planning funerals. That day, they had two separate families to visit in the same area, so Graham agreed to let Violet handle the Herbert arrangements, while he would attend to the other family and pick her up later.

They drove together in their carriage the nearly six miles from their own house to Admiral Herbert's residence at Cadogan Place in Belgravia, a few streets away from the Stanley home.

London's street congestion, which grew denser by the day, became nearly impassable at times. The more track was laid to shuffle people between towns quickly and efficiently, the more traffic there was on average streets. By the time they arrived at the Herbert home, they were dirty and sweating from an unusually warm day. Violet had to remove her hat to brush off the smuts. Graham did the same, as well as swatting a handkerchief across his neck to remove the dirt that was already accumulating on his collar.

Violet adjusted her black gloves on her arms, grabbed her laden undertaker's bag from the floor, and hopped down as gracefully as she could from the carriage, given the extra weight of her bag from her embalming supplies. She put up a hand in farewell to Graham, who urged the horse on to his next destination.

The street was full of large, elegant townhomes. If she wasn't mistaken, the strident abolitionist William Wilberforce had died in a home somewhere along this row, back in the early thirties, before Violet was even born. What would he think of America's troubles now?

The Herbert home was recognizable by its doorknob, which already had a length of black crape tied with a white ribbon to it. This symbol indicated that the "dread visitor" had entered the home, and visitors were now requested to avoid ringing the bell with its noisy reminder of active life. The Herberts' door was slightly ajar, a sign that visitors could go ahead and enter quietly.

The widow Herbert, with porcelain skin unravaged by age and crowned with luxuriant, snowy hair, was calm and composed. Wives of soldiers and jack-tars usually were, since they lived in perpetual terror of their men being felled by disease, discipline, or danger on any given day. In fact, Mrs. Herbert was so self-possessed that Violet almost didn't believe her own ears at the widow's first words to her. "His Royal Highness, Prince Albert, will be here shortly to pay his respects. I was just informed of his impending arrival only two hours ago. Please make yourself as discreet as possible while he is here."

The widow spoke the words as though she were merely informing the cook to set an extra place at the dinner table.

The prince consort was coming here? *Now?* Violet looked down at her garb. Serviceable, but meant for the messy work of undertaking. She wouldn't dare show her face to a member of the royal household even if Mrs. Herbert invited her to do so.

"Would you prefer that I return later, madam?" She would have to take a hack to where Graham was; then they could return here together after the prince was gone.

"No, no, the admiral needs your attentions. I merely request that you stay in his room with him for the duration of the prince's visit."

Violet could hardly breathe. First the commission for Admiral Herbert, now to be in the same premises as a member of the royal family.

The prince, a German cousin of the queen, was initially viewed by the British with the same suspicion that every foreign royal spouse is. However, Albert had greatly endeared himself in many ways, from guiding his young wife into making more mature political decisions, to taking a more prominent position in Britain's foreign affairs, and even to implementing reforms in the areas of education and welfare. He'd proven himself not only a capable administrator, but a man curious about science and the natural world around him.

The prince's most notable accomplishment was the successful Crystal Palace Exhibition of 1851. Not quite an adult yet, Violet had taken the train into London with her parents to visit the exposition, intended to showcase Great Britain's superior technological and manufacturing achievements. Including the Sinclair family, the exhibition attracted over six million people. Violet remembered gaping in amazement, not only at the magnificent glass pavilion that held the event, but at the impossibility of seeing the more than thirteen thousand various exhibits. Her favorite sights were the Koh-i-Noor diamond, the largest known diamond in the world, and Mr. Colt's frightening but thrilling demonstration of his revolvers.

The royal couple was renowned for their devotion to one another, even though it was rumored that the prince was initially less than enthused about his prospective bride. Clearly he had overcome his disdain, for they now had nine children together, and not a breath of extramarital scandal had ever wafted out of Buckingham Palace or Windsor.

For now, though, Violet needed to focus on what might be wafting from the prone Admiral Herbert. A maid escorted her up to the admiral's expansive room. He and his wife had separate bedrooms entirely, a popular trend but one that Violet and Graham could never countenance, despite their ever-growing number of disagreements and Graham's periodic stays in his study when angered. The draperies in the admiral's room were pulled tightly across the windows, preventing almost all light from penetrating into it. A crisp uniform and related body linens were laid out across the back of a settee. The brass buttons running down the front of the dark blue jacket gleamed from a recent polishing. The gold shoulder epaulettes were accented by gold trim at the neck and wrists of the jacket, as well as down the outer legs of the trousers. Also nearby was a sword belt, and Violet was sure the sword in its casing gleamed as brightly as the uniform's buttons.

She took a deep breath. Musty, but not extreme yet. The only other distinguishable scent came from a ribbon-tied sprig of fresh lavender artfully arranged atop a lace doily on a nearby occasional table.

The maid lit two lamps and departed as quickly as most servants did with a dead body nearby.

Now in silence with her client, Violet began her ritual. Speaking in soft tones, she set her bag on the floor next to him, removed her gloves and set them aside, and examined his arms. Rigor mortis was thankfully complete.

She dragged the occasional table as close to the side of the bed as possible, removing the lavender, lace, and other decorations and putting them on a chair. She hefted the bag onto the table. "Admiral, thank you for allowing me to take care of you today. I promise that this will be quick and will enable all of your friends and admirers to have an opportunity to see you and pay their respects before you are buried. Don't be alarmed by this large metal pump I'm pulling out of my bag; it's necessary for preserving you."

Violet placed the pump on the table and reached into her bag again for a large jar and some tubing. She searched in the bag for a small nozzle and inserted it into one end of the tube, while placing the other end inside the jar and putting the apparatus on the floor next to Admiral Herbert.

She then produced a small knife with a slanted blade and used it to make a small cut in the crook of his right elbow. She picked up the nozzle and placed it into the slit she'd just made.

"Halfway done, admiral."

Violet picked up the pump canister, a cylindrical can about six inches in diameter and two feet tall, and unscrewed the lid. The bottom of the unit housed a long hose, finished off with a narrow nozzle on the end, whereas the lid held a pump handle mechanism.

"Now I need to prepare your special solution. Let's see, a half ounce of chloride of zinc, and a quart of alcohol, plus this bottle of water . . ." She added the ingredients to the canister as she spoke. "Some embalmers like to add creosote as an additional anti-putrefaction agent, Admiral, but I think not in this case. I should hate to run the risk of creosote's highly objectionable odor coming from you. It would be unseemly for a man in your exalted position."

She searched through her bag again and pulled out a small bottle of red liquid.

"I'm going to add a bit of red dye to your solution, sir, which will give you a bluff, hearty complexion, much as I'm sure you enjoyed while sailing the high seas for England."

She screwed the top back on the pump canister and swirled the contents together.

"I'm afraid I have to be a bit, er, invasive now, Admiral, but I promise to be as quick about my business as possible."

Violet rolled the covers down from the body. The man was so emaciated he was nearly engulfed by his sleeping gown. He must have suffered a protracted illness.

"Sir, please forgive my wandering hands. This is quite necessary, I assure you." She pushed his gown up over his knees and bunched it over his pelvis. Picking up the knife, she felt for a good location along his inner thigh, as close to the groin as possible.

"Here we are, Admiral. Just a quick slice across, nothing too drastic. Well done, sir. Now that I have access to your femoral artery, we can give you some preservative."

Violet gave the pump canister one last swirl and inserted the syringe end into Admiral Herbert's leg. With one hand holding the syringe in place, she pumped the handle up and down to force her concoction to flow through the hose and into his artery. Once the flow started, she held the canister aloft to allow gravity to maintain the pressure of the fluid moving into the artery. As the pressure of the embalming fluid forced its way into the admiral, it also flushed his blood out through the other tube, draining into the jar on the floor.

"You're doing well, sir. We'll be finished in no time. Just be patient."

Soon there was a light tinge of pink under the admiral's skin. When she'd pumped all of the fluid into him, she gently withdrew the syringe from his leg and put the entire apparatus away. She also removed the tubing from the vein and the jar, tightly screwing the lid on the jar, now heavy with blood. She would drain it later in a specially dug, discreet trench behind their shop.

Violet examined the incision site. "Hardly noticeable, and once we have you dressed in your burial finery, you'll never know the difference. Time now to—"

She was distracted by shouts from downstairs and a commotion outside.

It must be the prince consort.

Violet still had plenty to keep her occupied in this room, for the admiral still needed to be dressed and have his features touched up. She decided to dress him first, since his uniform might prove to be form-fitting even on his wasted figure, therefore requiring more than normal jostling of the body. His thin frame meant he wasn't as heavy as most men, such as Mr. Stanley.

She reclothed the admiral deftly but carefully in his dress uniform, taking care to keep her eyes averted to the extent possible. Violet always imagined what the deceased's reaction to her ministrations would be if he were still alive, which kept her respectful of the dead. Some undertakers were careless with bodies, treating them as no more than a dead cat. It wasn't right.

With his clothing complete, she draped a white cloth around his chest, over his neckband, and up behind his head to prevent any ingredients from mussing up his jacket. Violet took out her jars of creams, powders, and colorants, plus her box of various-sized brushes.

Hmm, the good admiral could use a trim on his whiskers.

Out came scissors and a razor.

As she began the cosmetic work on Admiral Herbert, Violet listened as the commotion from outside transferred into the house. She heard the heavily accented voice of Prince Albert of Saxe-Coburg and Gotha, but couldn't make out the words. Mrs. Herbert must have then issued an order to the servants, because there was the sound of feet scurrying throughout the stairs and hallways and they presumably vanished to do her bidding.

She glanced up at a clock on the wall. Graham would return in about an hour. If the prince's entourage was still here, for certain her husband would wait a short distance away. She had plenty of time to finish.

Tempted as she was to peer through the closed draperies to see the prince's conveyance and what liveried servants might be standing around, she stayed focused on the admiral. Willing herself to forget that Queen Victoria's husband sat below her, probably having tea and cakes as he expressed royal condolences on the loss of such an able commander who had served his country well, she remained true to her task. She groomed the admiral's wispy hair and whiskers, artfully applied further color to his skin with a combination of creams and paints, and gently brushed away the residue that fell down to the cloth covering his chest and shoulders.

Violet stood back and surveyed her work. "What do you say, Admiral? I think it's as close to life as we'll get."

She removed the cloth from his body and used it to wrap up her used brushes, putting them back in their box before re-sealing her jars and bottles. She accidentally tipped over a container of talcum powder, creating a dusty trail on the table and sending a cloud of the powder clinging to the front of her dress.

Lovely.

Well, there was no help for it, she'd have to seek a whisk broom and dust pan, as well as some wet cloths, in order to clean up her mess. Might as well take the brushes to the kitchens for rinsing now rather than wait until she got home and risk their hardening.

Violet crossed the room and quietly opened the door. The voices of the prince and Mrs. Herbert were lower now, but he was obviously still here.

Deciding that the widow's instruction to stay locked away was obviated by the need to tidy up the mess she'd made, Violet ventured into the hallway.

No servants in sight. Now what?

Traversing to the back of the house, she found the servant stairs leading down. She took these stairs, knowing there was little chance of encountering a family member here. She reached the ground floor, where the prince and Mrs. Herbert were in conversation somewhere nearby. Their voices were louder now, and she could hear Mrs. Herbert telling the prince about all of the admiral's adventures during the Napoleonic Wars, the War of 1812, and the First Opium War twenty years ago. The prince was murmuring some kind of appreciation.

Drat, the servant stairs ended here. There must be another set somewhere down to the kitchens. She padded down the endless hallway as quietly as possible, but couldn't find the telltale narrow servant stairs. She backtracked to her original point and nearly ran into the most elegantly attired gentleman she'd ever seen in her entire life.

Despite his balding head—evidence of his creeping middle age—and a wan complexion, he still had a commanding presence. His elegant clothing only completed the look of total assurance. Surely this was Prince Albert.

"I am looking for the necessary room if you can kindly show it to me," he said, the German-accented words short and crisp, as though life was too brief to waste time on speech. To ask such a personal question of her meant he thought she was a servant, for no one ever asked a house's occupants such an embarrassing question.

Violet reddened. "Pardon me, sir, I'm so sorry—" She dropped into a curtsy, unsure if she was executing it properly. "I'm afraid I'm not a member of the staff here."

The prince frowned. "Surely you are not a guest of the Herbert family?" He rolled out the "r's" in "Herbert" so that Violet could almost imagine herself riding the word like a wave.

Violet looked down at her disheveled clothing and dared look the prince directly in the eye. "I suppose I do look like the pastry cook, don't I, Your Highness? However, I am Mrs. Morgan, the undertaker, here to take care of the admiral, except that I managed to spill some powder and have need to clean it up."

"You, madam, are the undertaker?"

"Yes, Your Highness. My husband and I own a shop in Paddington."

"Rather unseemly for you to do this work, isn't it?"

"Some think so, sir, but women have been preparing bodies for burial since biblical times. This is no different, except that I have more tools." She looked down again at the dusty front of her dress. "I also make more disasters."

The prince was still regarding her curiously. "How did you come into such a trade?"

"I suppose I married into it. My husband's family has owned the shop for decades, and when I expressed interest in it, well, my husband began training me."

Albert rubbed his chin. "Fascinating. I can't say that I've ever been in the presence of someone in your profession before. I should like to watch you at work."

"I'm sorry?"

"Are you finished with Admiral Herbert yet? No? Then I will accompany you back to him to observe what you do." The necessary room was forgotten, and the next thing Violet knew, she was going back upstairs with Great Britain's prince consort at her side.

The unreality of it was tempered only by the recognition of what Mrs. Herbert's fury would be when she realized that not only had Violet not stayed behind closed doors, she had seemingly lured her royal guest into her dead husband's bedroom.

However, one did not willingly disobey a royal request.

She showed the prince the contents of her bag and explained how she applied cosmetics, as well as how she concocted her embalming formula for injection into Admiral Herbert.

"You're saying you fill the body with alcohol and zinc chloride?"

"And water."

"This preserves the body so it doesn't have to be interred as quickly?"

"Yes, Your Highness. The practice has been used for centuries, in different ways, of course, but is not popular here. The Americans are embalming their dead soldiers, enabling their bodies to make long train journeys back home without the normal putrefaction that sets in within a short time."

The prince bent over Admiral Herbert's body and gently sniffed, as though he expected to receive a message directly from the deceased's spirit that way. He quickly stood erect again. "Fascinating. I should not have thought a woman would have the temperament for this sort of thing."

"My husband would say my choleric temperament suits this work very well," she blurted without thinking.

Albert's eyes opened wide in shock, but settled into crinkles as he smiled, then laughed at her unintentional joke. "Marriage requires heroic effort by both parties, does it not, Frau Morgan? Well, then, I'll take my leave of you. I think I've probably stretched Frau Herbert's hospitality to its bounds by now, given that I told her I would be gone just a moment."

Violet reached into a side pocket of her undertaker's bag and pulled out one of her new cards. "Your Highness, Morgan Undertaking is at your disposal at any time."

The prince slipped the card into his trouser pocket without glancing at it. "Ahem, yes, thank you for a most interesting demonstration, Frau Morgan."

Violet curtsied again. "It was my honor, Your Highness. About Mrs. Herbert—"

"Never fear. She'll need never know that her undertaker deterred me from accomplishing my task."

Graham was alternately delighted and distressed over Violet's unexpected meeting with the prince. He peppered her with questions during the entire ride home, during their dinner over Mrs. Porter's beef brisket, and even while she prepared to retire.

His primary concern was whether or not Violet might have secured them even more prestigious work from the crown itself.

She climbed into bed with a sigh. "Highly doubtful. He hardly looked at my *carte-de-visite*."

He sat on the edge of the bed and pulled the covers up, tucking them around her, a romantic gesture he'd always used in the early days of their marriage.

"He knows of Admiral Herbert's service, correct? That he served on HMS *Euryalus* against the Americans in the War of 1812? That he was specially recognized for his exertions along the Potomac River, such as the raid on Alexandria?"

"Yes, Graham, he's fully aware of these things. I hardly think the good admiral's widow would merit a royal visit unless his exploits were well known."

Graham went to his side of the bed and extinguished the lamp before sliding in next to her. "Just think what a boon it would be to our business if the prince recommended us. I wonder if there is a royal warrant for undertaking."

On that hopeful note, Graham turned over, probably to dream further on his vision of the royal warrant hanging in their shop window.

≫ 7 ≪

Friendships should not be hastily formed, nor the heart given, at once, to every new-comer.

—*Beeton's Book of Household Management*

Windsor Castle
July 1861

The queen handed the card back to her husband with a sniff. "You say this woman was actually *embalming* a man? How horrifying for you, my love."

Albert tucked the card inside the top desk drawer of the Blue Room at Windsor Castle, originally built as a fortress and now the longest-occupied palace in Europe. The present residents enjoyed luxurious state apartments, renovated early in the century by George IV. Victoria brought further improvements to the castle, including running water, but had refused the installation of gas lights, preferring candles as so many Britons did.

"Quite the opposite. I was enthralled. Curious that we aren't doing it here. It seems a worthy endeavor to me."

"Hardly!" Victoria wrinkled her nose. "It sounds like a disgusting practice to me. And being performed by a woman, no less."

"I thought so at first, too, but she was very competent, *liebchen*." He tapped the desk drawer. "Remember Frau Morgan when my time comes."

"Your time? You're just forty-two years old. Your 'time' won't occur for at least another forty-two years. Or never, if I have anything to say about things."

Albert smiled gently at his wife. "I've no doubt that the Almighty would be the loser in a confrontation with you over the matter. Nevertheless—"

"You're still just gripped by your carriage accident last year while we were visiting Vicky in Coburg, which was outdone by your illness at Christmas. It's making you obsessed about death-related things."

"Hardly," he responded, imitating her wrinkled nose. "I do not cling to life. You do, but I set no store by it. If I knew that those I love were well cared for, I should be quite ready to die tomorrow."

"Such wild talk. You cannot wish for your own death."

"You're right, of course. Sometimes I think it's that boy of ours who must wish for his own death, so outrageous is his behavior. My only hope is that once we finally arrange a meeting with the Princess Alexandra, he will fall madly in love and forsake all of his other peccadilloes. He's nineteen years old already, and it's past time that he mature and settle down."

"Vicky has already met the girl and says she's delightful, full of loveliness and charm."

"Our daughter's assessment is undoubtedly astute. Unfortunately, Bertie finds that all young ladies have the same qualities. He has no discernment and has never known a filled chemise he could resist. He'll either send me to my grave or go to one early himself."

"Albert! Please, let's not talk of this any longer. It reminds me of my own dear mother's passing back in March, and I feel a shiver across my back when you say such things. Besides, you look a little peaked. Do you feel unwell?"

"No more so than whenever we discuss unpleasant subjects. However, I am sure that if I had a severe illness, I should give up at once. I should not struggle for life. I have no tenacity for it."

He stood. "Perhaps I am maudlin because I haven't had tea with my wife yet today. Let's do so now, shall we?" He held out his hand to his wife, who grasped it as eagerly as she had the day they were married two decades ago. Albert pulled Victoria close as they left the room, whispering *"Ich liebe dich"* in her ear as together they went to find someone to serve them a tray. She blushed. It still thrilled her when her husband told her he loved her.

* * *

Graham drew up next to *Lillian Rose* with a wagon bearing a coffin. It had been no easy task to escape Violet's watchful eye. As part of the business venture, Graham dressed in full undertaker regalia, yet put a minimum of decoration on the funeral carriage and horses. To the untrained eye, the undertaker was planning to load a loved one onto a ship for burial elsewhere out of London.

Violet would have realized in an instant that Graham was up to something suspicious.

St. Katharine Docks was humming with activity. He put a handkerchief to his nose, wishing he had one of those old-fashioned pomanders people used to carry. How did naval people stand this? The stench was worse than anything he had to deal with in his daily business. Even from his distance he could see animal offal and trash sloshing in the water.

The smell was intensified by the tension of what he was about to do, causing Graham to sweat profusely inside his black suit. This was best accomplished quickly so he could return home, bathe, and get back to the shop before Violet wondered where he was.

To Graham's great irritation, Fletcher was lounging outside one of the dock's many seedy taverns, flirting with a barmaid and paying no attention whatsoever to his brother's arrival. After ten minutes of this, Graham snapped his whip in the air, garnering the attention of not only his brother, but every worker nearby.

He waved apologetically to the people around him as Fletcher sauntered over and jumped onto the driver's seat next to him.

Graham was furious. "We have important work to do and you're preoccupied with pretty misses. If you can't manage to stay focused for more than ten seconds at a time, then clearly my time in this enterprise is wasted. You said you had something important to discuss. Kindly do so."

"Can I help it if Miss Turnbull finds me irresistible? I think it's my new whiskers. What do you think?" Fletcher stroked a side of his face.

"Wispy. Sparse. Limp. Hardly worth a mention."

"Well, I certainly don't have your capacity for sprouting foliage—a talent you keep regrettably hidden behind your razor—but I didn't think it was too unattractive. Ah, but what I do have a great capacity for is growing money."

"Finally, we are coming to the point."

Fletcher ignored him. "As you know, we've had some difficulty getting launched, as startup for our little endeavor has been more expensive than anticipated, and you have only been able to provide me with limited funds."

"I thought you knew bankers who were standing by to help us."

"Right. Well, many of those contacts didn't pan out. However, I believe our monetary worries are over, as I've found a backer. An enthusiastic one, at that, since he will directly benefit from our enterprise."

Graham frowned. "Benefit in what way?"

Fletcher leaned close, his galling way of dramatically emphasizing his next point. "By being the recipient of our goods." Fletcher leaned casually back against the seat, his other irksome habit of giving the hearer an opportunity to absorb the magnificence of whatever he had just uttered.

Although Graham had to admit to being impressed.

"Are you saying you've made contact with a buyer *here*, in London?"

"I have indeed. A man named Harper, from Virginia. He's a perfect businessman, too. He asks few questions, has plenty of money, and is eager to part with it. Now, let's get this box on board *Lillian Rose* and see how well it fits in my hold."

The brothers climbed down from the carriage and struggled the coffin up the gangplank and onto the ship, carefully maneuvering it into the hold. It was the sort of hot, grimy work that Graham imagined Fletcher was accustomed to doing, but Graham was flagging.

What a terrible sailor I'd make.

Once they finished with the coffin, which was stuffed with goods, it would be sent on a maiden voyage to the colonies to see if Fletcher's theory that no one would want to inspect a coffin would hold true. For now, Fletcher recommended that they head over to the Three Hulls for refreshment.

"I'll not even look in Miss Turnbull's direction, I promise."

After ordering brandies, the brothers sat down near an open window. Graham removed his undertaker's hat and pulled at his collar to loosen it. He finally gave in and removed his jacket. He was drenched.

Fletcher grinned. "What a coddled life you lead, brother. Speaking of your coddled life, how is our dear Mrs. Morgan?"

"She's well. She had to fire Mrs. Scrope for theft, but now we have an older couple working out nicely. Did I tell you Violet met the prince consort while tending to Admiral Herbert?"

"At least twice now."

"She showed him a little bit about what we do. She even demonstrated the embalming pump."

"I don't know how the man contained himself for the joy of it." Fletcher drained his glass.

"During the admiral's funeral, his widow, who had been very well composed until that moment, made a terrible scene because there was no finger bell for her husband to pull in the event he wasn't really deceased. Violet told her—within the prince's earshot—that the admiral was so full of embalming fluid that only the immediate return of Christ would rouse him from the dead. I was mortified, but the prince found it uproarious. His good humor over it mollified the widow's fears. Sometimes Violet truly amazes me by what she manages to pull off without offending anyone."

"Violet attended the funeral openly?"

"She wasn't planning to, but the prince asked after her—did I mention that I spoke with him, too—and it didn't seem right not to bring her forward."

"Does this mean you love your wife once more?"

Graham looked at Fletcher sharply. "What are you insinuating?"

"Nothing, nothing at all. You are the consummate husband. Now, back to more practical matters. I want to introduce you to Mr. Samuel Harper. Do you think you can have Violet put on another dinner party?"

"Yes, she'll do it. I'm sure that we—Fletcher, quit winking at the barmaid."

"How can I help myself? She's delectable. Besides, isn't every British citizen's example set by Lord Palmerston and his bevy of love interests? It is my patriotic duty to imitate him well into my dotage."

For God's sake, Fletcher could be irritating. He was lucky he was so clever.

Charles Francis was pleased as he read over his son's notes. His investigations had already borne fruit, and it looked as though they had already uncovered a possible smuggling operation.

What fools men could be where money was concerned, he thought. Weren't greed and pride two of the seven deadly sins? And what was war but an expression of pride, sometimes righteous, but usually just arrogance-laden. The North was struggling to maintain its virtuous principles while the South beat its breast and howled in defense of its corrupt policies.

Yes, a trap would be laid for all of the participants working against the interests of the United States, and when the time was right, Charles Francis would pull the cord, yanking them all up in his net.

The president would then have to recognize the wisdom of making Charles Francis Adams his Minister Plenipotentiary to the Court of St. James.

Hmm, he'd have to be careful not to succumb to that worst of vices himself.

Charles Francis picked up a pen and wrote some names on a scrap of paper. He rang a bell, summoning Henry, who, as always, had ink-stained fingers and carried a notebook.

"Son, these people will need further inquiry."

Henry scanned the list and looked up at his father curiously. "You think a woman is among the smugglers? Are you sure?"

"Not entirely, but no guilty party will escape the noose I am knotting, woman or not."

Dear diary, today I find myself most dyspeptic. There is much to disturb me in London and beyond. Grandmother always told me never to worry beyond what was within my means to control, but she never understood what a vast territory of events I need to command. Hah! I sound like a dedicated army general, do I not?

But back to my immediate concerns. I wonder if I'm not on the verge of detection. Despite my brilliant planning and painstaking arrangements, I believe there are some who are sniffing the air around me and are generally displeased with my odor.

What if I am discovered? What shall I do then? Move away? Don't worry, dearest diary, I'll always keep you with me.

Hmm. I know there are other methods for ridding myself of unwanted annoyances. Methods that don't involve the great inconvenience of moving away, provided I plan things out properly.

The situation bears watching. In the meantime, I shall watch what happens on both sides of the Atlantic, in case an opportunity arises for someone of my substantial aptitude.

⭐ 8 ⭐

The choice of acquaintances is very important to the happiness of a mistress and her family.

—*Beeton's Book of Household Management*

"Certainly, I don't mind being Fletcher's dinner partner," Mary said, pouring Violet another cup of tea. "You say he and Graham are entering a new business proposition with this Mr. Harper?"

"Yes, to ship funerary supplies to America, to serve the accumulating war dead there."

"So their war won't be ending anytime soon?"

Violet lifted the steaming cup to her lips and gently blew on it. "Not likely. I read that the Confederacy's president, Jefferson Davis, is sending a delegation to Europe to represent their interests. They hope to buy war supplies from Britain, France, and Spain."

"Perhaps they have need of my ready-mades, too?"

"Perhaps. You can ask Mr. Harper yourself during dinner."

"Will he be bringing his wife?"

"I don't know. Graham tells me so little and gets irritated when I ask for these details. The table balance will be upset if Mr. Harper is by himself, and then Graham will be cross yet again. I suppose Mrs. Porter will just have to be prepared to make an extra place setting at the last moment."

Mary shook her head sympathetically and changed the subject. "I finished the last installment of *Great Expectations*. I must say, I enjoyed *A Tale of Two Cities* much more. It really made one think about how we are sometimes no better here than the French revolutionaries."

Violet nodded. "Yes. At least Mr. Dickens is no longer slighting undertakers, as he did in *Oliver Twist*. It's a wonder I'm not spat upon in the streets, what with the ongoing popularity of that novel. Which reminds me, I need to order a new top hat from you for one of my mourners to replace one that was trampled on by a horse during a particularly windy funeral procession."

The women discussed a variety of funerary orders while they finished their tea, then Violet headed back to the shop.

She opened the door of Morgan Undertaking and was struck by the stillness. Will and Harry were out grooming the horses, but where was Graham? He knew she'd be gone a couple of hours to visit Mary; why in heaven's name would he stroll off, leaving the shop open and unattended?

She sighed. She would never understand her husband.

She heard a rustling coming from the coffin display area. What was it? Pray God they didn't have mice chewing and nesting inside the muslin lining of their coffins. She lit an additional gas lamp. Even at noon it was shadowy in the shop, usually a preferable situation when dealing with the grieving, who were calmed by the low lighting.

Violet carried the lamp with her to inspect which coffin had acquired furry new tenants. Some coffins were displayed open and some with their lids down to better exhibit the brass plates that could be affixed to them.

She heard the rustling again, coming from an open coffin to her left. She nearly dropped the lamp. Was that a flash of an elbow?

"Who's there?" she asked, her voice sharp in her own ears as she struggled against rising fear.

Receiving no response, she cleared her throat and tried again. "I can see you, you know."

Gripping the lamp as a weapon that might somehow save her from whatever was burrowed in the coffin, she walked the walk of the damned toward it and cautiously peered inside, hoping she wasn't about to be strangled by some madman lying in wait for her.

Unbelievable.

A waif of a girl, probably not yet a teenager although it was impossible to tell because she was so emaciated, lay curled up inside, both hands tucked under one cheek. She'd look almost angelically asleep with her halo of blond curls, were it not for the filth that covered her body and the rag of a dress she was wearing. Her bare feet were nearly black from dirt.

Still holding the lamp, Violet reached in and put a hand to the child's shoulder, gently shaking her. The girl's eyes flew open and she scrambled into a seated position on the wool mattress, panting heavily in fear as she stared at Violet. She looked like a corpse springing to life, reminding Violet of Mrs. Herbert's greatest fear for her husband.

Violet stepped back and put the lamp down atop another nearby coffin. She held up both hands. "Be calm, little one. I won't hurt you. Who *are* you?"

The girl knotted her fists and refused to answer. Blue eyes sparked in defiance like fireworks underneath the grime that covered her face.

"Are you going to bite me if I come closer?" Violet asked. "Scratch me? Kick me?"

The girl shook her head. Was that a hint of a smile on her lips?

"Will you tell me what you're doing in my shop?"

No response.

"How about at least telling me your name? I'm Mrs. Morgan, and it's my shop you have trespassed."

The girl crossed her knotted fists in front of her.

"Child, do I not have enough troubles of my own? How am I supposed to return you to your home if you won't speak to me?" Violet rubbed her eyes. What would Graham say if he walked in on this little scene?

This seemed to strengthen the girl's resolve not to say anything.

"Right then. How about a biscuit? You look like you haven't eaten in days."

The girl's eyes widened and she bit her lip.

"Don't move. I'll get you something to eat."

When Violet returned with the contents of the lunch box Mrs. Porter had prepared that day for her and Graham, the girl had, indeed, not moved. Not a single inch. Violet rummaged inside the box and pulled out a plum, which the child devoured in three bites, juices shooting out all over her face and tattered old dress.

As well as on the inside of the coffin lining. If it wasn't ruined before, it certainly was now. Well, she'd contend with that later.

Violet produced a cheddar scone and a potato pasty, which were also gobbled up in quick order, crumbs and gravy going everywhere. In all her days, she'd never witnessed someone eat a meal from inside a coffin. She laughed aloud, wishing Mr. Laroche were here to capture the scene. A fine *carte-de-visite* it would make.

The girl reached out a sticky hand and patted Violet on the shoulder. Violet's heart swelled at the gesture, but she wasn't sure why it would do so for this grubby mute who had somehow gotten lost or been abandoned.

"All right, little miss. You've had a nap and your tummy is full at my expense, so now it's time for you to do something for me. I want you to let me inspect your clothing and body for lice or other little crawling beasts."

The girl frowned, but reluctantly climbed out of the coffin to stand before Violet with sorrowful eyes, like a lamb waiting its turn in line, resigned to its fate before the blade.

Violet laughed again, earning another frown of disapproval. "Now, since you won't—or can't—talk to me, let's see what we can find out about you from your dress. I'd say the first thing we can determine is that you've never had the privilege of an Overfelt-made dress. This thing is a rag. Why, one sleeve is noticeably larger than the other. In fact, it's a different fabric altogether. What kind of foolish alteration is this?"

Violet visually inspected the girl's body as she spoke. There appeared to be no signs of lice, nor the telltale red bumps of fleas. Just a couple of bites here and there that anyone might have.

She slowly reached out a hand to the girl's collar. The child cut her eyes over to watch Violet, but did not resist. Lifting the knotted mass of hair from the girl's neck, she examined the interior of the dress for some kind of identification. Nothing.

Violet lifted her own skirts and knelt before the girl. "I'm going to lift your hem," she said, and began examining the threadbare cloth for something—anything—that would give her a clue as to where this girl was from.

Ah, there was a label stitched inside the back of the dress, behind the child's thighs.

Susanna Sweeney
St. Giles-in-the-Fields and St. George Workhouse

"Good Lord! You escaped from a workhouse!" Destitute people went to workhouses voluntarily to work in exchange for rations and accommodations until they could find their own jobs and living quarters. Life in a workhouse was intended to be bleak, so as not to encourage its residents to stay long, but Violet had no idea how bleak that life must be.

The girl shook her head violently. *No.*

Violet cocked her head to one side. "Is your name Susanna?"

The girl slowly nodded.

"And do you belong to St. Giles?"

The violent head shaking again.

Violet sat back and considered the girl. She really was filthy. A good scrubbing couldn't hurt while she figured out where the workhouse was located and how to get the child back there without a struggle.

Doubtful that it could be accomplished without a struggle, though. Maybe Mrs. Porter would have an idea.

"You win for now, Susanna. How about if I take you home for a bath, some fresh clothing, and dinner, while I figure out what to do with you?"

Violet was rewarded with a winsome smile, revealing teeth that were a tad overcrowded, but white with no sign of decay. Miraculous.

"You say she was in one o'yer coffins, Mrs. Morgan?" asked Mrs. Porter, who worked without question to help feed, bathe, and dress Susanna in one of Violet's nightgowns by tearing off the hem and rolling up the sleeves on the girl's painfully thin arms. Susanna was now asleep on the bed in Mrs. Scrope's old room off the kitchen.

"Yes. Sleeping like the dead, so to speak. Her name is Susanna Sweeney, and I think she fled St. Giles for some reason. Looking at her condition, I can assume her situation there was less than ideal."

"She can't possibly weigh more than five stone. She needs plumping up. Why would a young girl be at a workhouse by herself, without her mother?"

"I don't know. Perhaps the mother abandoned her there. Or maybe the mother is in residence there, too. She might be looking for Susanna as we speak. What if she's sought help and the constables are looking for her right now? I could be charged with kidnapping. Or worse—training her up to be a pickpocket!"

Mrs. Porter shook her head. "Tsk, Mrs. Morgan, you're reading too much o'that *Oliver Twist*. Let's not get a flight o'fancy."

"You're right. I need a good night of sleep myself, then in the morning I'll simply have to take her back, no matter how she protests. I don't want to risk being arrested for a crime. Besides, what am I to do with a child?"

"Don't tell me you don't know the answer to that, Mrs. Morgan! Every woman knows what to do with a child."

"No child should be surrounded by the dead, especially not a young girl. Good night, Mrs. Porter."

Mrs. Porter had already taken Susanna well in hand. By the time Violet was up and dressed, she found the girl seated at the dining room table eating a breakfast of pork cheese, fried rashers of bacon, and poached eggs. Her hair was smartly combed up in a bow, and she wore appropriate girls' clothing.

Leaving her to her meal, Violet went to the kitchen to find Mrs. Porter.

"How did you manage to find clothing to fit her overnight?"

"I gave Mr. Porter some measurements and sent him out last night to visit the servants in some of the grand households we know. He came back with discards that were going to go to servants of the children, but they willingly donated them for a child in worse straits than they were."

"You mean she's wearing cast-off clothing?"

"They fit her proper, don't they? And it's just until you deliver her back to the workhouse. That moth-eaten sack she had wasn't fit for a mule saddle. I burned it last night."

"You're right, of course. The workhouse will appreciate it that I brought her back in better condition than I found her. Did she say anything to you this morning, perchance?"

"Not a word. Expressive face this one has, though. You can read her thoughts without her uttering a thing."

"What of Mr. Morgan? Did he see Susanna this morning?"

"No, madam. I heard the front door shut just as I was getting up myself. He has no idea she's here."

"It's just as well that he continues to have no idea. Why stir a pot that has yet to be placed over a fire? Which reminds me, Mr. Morgan and I are planning for three guests Thursday evening next. Perhaps you could make your roasted duck for us?"

Violet discovered that the joint parishes of St. Giles-in-the-Fields and St. George had erected a parish workhouse in Holton, at the junction of Endell Street and Short's Gardens, quite a distance from Paddington. How had the child ever traveled such a long distance?

Without lying outright to Susanna about their destination, Violet managed to get her to the entrance of St. Giles without the girl going into hysterics. However, once Susanna realized where they were, she fought wildly like Boudicca against the Romans, as if content to go to her death to avoid capture.

Violet reasoned, cajoled, and threatened, to no avail. Susanna was determined not to enter the workhouse.

Finally, Violet struck a bargain with her. "Listen to me. I *must* take you in there, lest I be arrested for stealing you. It would hardly be of benefit to either of us if I'm imprisoned. If, as you insist, you don't belong there, I'll find somewhere else to take you. Are we agreed?"

Susanna considered this. Violet could practically see the girl rolling it around in her mind. Finally, Susanna nodded once and took Violet's hand, clutching it like a life preserver.

St. Giles looked as though it had begun its life as one building, and then slowly started incorporating whatever house, tavern, and shop lay in its path in all directions.

A porter stood guard outside a nearby building, presumably some sort of administration offices, and asked Violet's business. When she explained that she needed to see whoever was in charge of women and children in the workhouse, he pointed to a forbidding brick building across the street that resembled nothing less than a flat-faced fortress. She couldn't tell what the building's origins may have once been. Surely no one had ever lived here before it was a workhouse building.

Susanna began tugging on Violet's hand, but Violet refused to stop. "Susanna, we have a bargain, remember?"

The inside of the female quarters was even more unwelcoming than the outside, if such a thing were possible.

Dark and low-ceilinged, the building was a rabbit's warren of hastily—and poorly—constructed wards, hallways, and individual cells. Water seeped down the walls in endless moldy streams. Turning a corner, she entered a cavernous hall. At least it had a towering ceiling with windows at the top to permit plenty of light. But seated shoulder to shoulder at row after row of rickety tables were the women of the workhouse, slurping up a thin soup from bowls Violet suspected were none too clean. The women had an air of defeat, as though chatting among themselves would require too much energy and an admission that it was worth doing. The hall reeked of disinfectant, a noxious odor to contend with while trying to eat, although perhaps the smell of cleaners was preferable to what they were eating.

Violet quickly left the dining room. She was aghast as she pulled Susanna along in her investigation of the workhouse. How did such a place remain in existence? Surely the parish did not knowingly permit such appalling conditions to exist. No wonder Susanna acted as though she was being forcibly sent into Roman slavery.

She was.

She stopped and touched the shoulder of a seated woman, who was bent over and offering milk to her baby. "Please, can you tell me where I might find the matron?"

The mother looked up, wan and devoid of hope. As inexperienced as Violet was with babies, it was obvious that this child was not going to survive. The mother pulled a hand from around her child and pointed down another hallway.

"Thank you," Violet said, pressing a coin into the mother's hand. The workhouse resident offered her a silent, gummy smile.

Picking up Susanna's hand again, Violet hurried down the hallway the mother had indicated. At the end was a closed door marked "Private. No residents beyond this door." She knocked twice and entered, too sickened to consider whatever etiquette might apply to a workhouse.

A ruddy, stern-looking woman sat behind a desk heaped high with papers. She wore a plain gray dress with no decoration, no jewelry or feminine touches whatsoever. A frilled cap provided the only relief in the severity of her fashion. She was busy making entries in a log book, and looked up in surprise at the interruption.

"You are?" she asked without preamble.

"Mrs. Violet Morgan. This," she said, "is Susanna Sweeney."

The woman's face was blank. "Yes?"

"Does she not look familiar to you?"

"Should she?"

"Yes. She ran away from here recently and into my care."

"A runaway, eh? Happens all the time. There'll be no supper for you today, little miss, and you'll be stuck with scrubbing privies for the next week."

Susanna shrank back around Violet.

"You must be joking. This child is hardly nourished as it is, and you intend to starve her further?"

"We have rules, Mrs. Morgan. Running away from duties comes with consequences for our pauper residents, whether they be eight or eighty. If there is no punishment, what prevents anyone from running into the streets during the day and returning each night for a meal and warm bed without making a contribution here?"

"It must be difficult to make a contribution when you're half-starved." Violet's sarcasm was lost on the matron, who was busy studying Susanna as though trying to place her.

"What's the child's name again?"

"Susanna Sweeney."

The matron looked through her log book, running a chipped fingernail down the columns of several pages and stopping at one entry. "Here she is. Susanna Sweeney, aged twelve."

The matron looked up at Violet. "You're obviously not her mother come to claim her. Says here Ellen Sweeney died shortly before the girl's arrival. Let's see—" She studied the log book again. "An intestinal disorder. Father died sometime in the past. Who are you?"

Susanna must have witnessed her mother's death. What happened to her mother's body? Was there a funeral? Was it just thrown in a pauper's grave? Violet felt bile rising up in the back of her throat, not only for the appalling conditions of the place, but for the matron's indifference to Susanna. Mary would be horrified when she learned how accurate Mr. Dickens had been in *Oliver Twist*.

Violet squinted at the name badge sewn onto the matron's dress. "Mrs. Baker, is it? I believe I have several questions far more important than my own identity. First, who is in charge of this pestilent place? Second, how do you come in here every day and look this horror in the eye? I am an undertaker, and the corpses I prepare for burial are healthier than the poor women and children I see here. I can only imagine what the men's ward looks like."

Mrs. Baker leaned forward and folded her arms on the desk. "Let me guess who you really are, shall I? You live in a nice townhome in one of the new, fashionable neighborhoods of London. You have plenty of coal to get you through the winter and a pantry full of dry goods and staples. I bet if I saw the hem of your skirt, there would be only a single day's worth of dirt on the edge.

"This little girl was your first real encounter with poverty except to perhaps toss a coin to a beggar before completely dismissing him from your mind."

Violet winced at the woman's description.

"Yet you march in here with your outrage and presume to tell me exactly how a workhouse should be run. Do you think you're the first high-handed lady to do so?"

Seeing Violet's chagrin, Mrs. Baker relented. "This is a workhouse, madam. The poor come here as a last resort to *work*, as the name implies. They are given a clean roof over their heads, hot meals, and a small wage to sustain them until they can find outside work. In return, our buildings stay maintained, laundry is washed, and gardens are tended by the residents while they stay here, so as not to put too much of a tax burden on the rest of England's citizenry. It is a helping hand to most of the men and women here."

"Surely there must be a way to do this that doesn't pain the citizenry but provides conditions that are better than those of the zoo. Susanna is a child, not a chimpanzee. Don't our poor laws prevent workhouses from being prisons?" At the sound of her name, Susanna popped back out from behind Violet and leaned against Violet's side. Violet instinctively wrapped an arm around the girl's shoulders.

"Quite the opposite. Clearly, madam, you have no idea how the poor laws have completely hampered our ability to serve the destitute among us, who are expanding at a great rate. Church parishes and relief societies can hardly keep up."

"You're correct, Mrs. Baker, I have no knowledge of a workhouse's operations and I am not experienced with the poor. But here's what I do know, which is that I can at least make a difference in this one child's life. You can send every constable in London after me; I'm not leaving Susanna here with you."

Mrs. Baker shrugged. "One less orphaned mouth to feed and find placement for. I'll just need you to sign her out."

Violet did so, practically tearing through the page with the pen point in her haste.

She grabbed Susanna's hand and marched out of the administration building with Mrs. Baker calling out after her, "She's old enough for service. Place her now and it will save her from prostitution later."

Violet didn't look back, and in fact maintained a long stride until they were physically out of sight of the building. Susanna ran to keep up with her hand securely lodged inside Violet's. When they were a quarter mile away, Violet stopped next to a music seller's shop and knelt once again before a now-breathless Susanna.

"I promise I will never bring you back here again. Never." Violet felt tears pricking her eyes.

Susanna sniffed and threw her arms around Violet's shoulders, nearly toppling her over backward. Violet responded by hugging the girl around the waist and whispering to her.

"I'm sorry, Susanna, I'm sorry. I had no idea how terrible it really was there. Please forgive me. You're safe now with me."

Susanna pulled back, with both hands on Violet's shoulders, searching Violet's moist eyes as if to determine whether or not she meant it. In a rush she threw herself against Violet again and placed a kiss on the undertaker's cheek.

There's that tingly feeling in my heart again.

What am I supposed to do with you, Susanna? And how will Graham erupt when I tell him I've brought an orphaned juvenile into our home to live?

It didn't bear thinking about.

"I have an idea. How about if we visit my friend, Mrs. Overfelt, who I bet could make you a perfectly lovely dress of blue to match your eyes? With buttons up the front and grosgrain ribbon around the hem? I imagine she might even have a crinoline just the right size for you."

Still clinging to Violet, Susanna nodded her head up and down.

"Perhaps then you might speak to me?"

No response.

Arranging a trousseau for a girl, even one as small as Susanna, was expensive, even with Mary offering as attractive a price as she could and throwing in a shawl for free. What did Violet expect, since the girl had nothing, not even her own chemise? It was comical to watch Susanna's pained expression as she was fitted for her first corset.

They tramped around London buying boots, bonnets, and a couple of children's books. Violet hoped that even without speaking, Susanna might be able to learn to read.

Violet sent Susanna downstairs with Mrs. Porter before Graham arrived home, telling the housekeeper to delay dinner for a half hour while she spoke to the master about the girl. Mrs. Porter nodded and took Susanna by the hand, promising to show her a kitten that had been hanging about at the basement door.

"Please, Mrs. Porter, no animals in the house." Violet suspected her instruction would be completely ignored.

Graham's eruption was as volcanic as anticipated.

"You *what?* You brought some other woman's daughter into our home? Have you lost your senses?"

"Hush, Graham, our neighbors will hear you."

"Perhaps they need to know that I'm married to a Bedlamite. For just how long do you intend to keep her here?"

It's the same question I keep asking myself.

"I don't know. Until I can figure out where to place her."

"How long is that? Where can you possibly place her other than an orphanage? Unless you're going to put her in service. If she's twelve years old, she's old enough."

He sounded like Mrs. Baker.

"I'm not putting her into service."

"Why the hell not? You're not getting attached to the child, are you? For heaven's sake, Violet, she just woke up inside one of our coffins not twenty-four hours ago. She'll have to work off that damage, let me assure you."

"I'm not putting her into service, and she will not be our slave for accidentally soiling some coffin padding."

Graham looked at her incredulously. "You've never been able to produce a child born of our union, yet all of a sudden you're defending this fawn like a mama red deer. What has happened to you?"

"Nothing has happened. I simply feel responsible for her. She would never have even gotten into the shop if you hadn't disappeared, leaving the door wide open for her—or any other sleepy Londoner—to wander in for a nap."

"I don't understand you. I give up." Graham threw up his hands. "Do what you will; I have more vital things to think about. We have a guest coming on Thursday, in case you've forgotten."

"I haven't forgotten. Mrs. Porter has things well in hand with the menu, and Mr. Porter has been shaking out every curtain in the house."

"Mmm, and hopefully none of it goes missing. This meeting is the most important one of my life, Violet. Fletcher believes he has secured an investment banker for our new enterprise."

"The enterprise I'm too simple to understand?"

"The enterprise that doesn't concern you yet. Honestly, as much as I have to worry over, and here I am arguing with my wife about lost, flea-infested orphans—"

"She doesn't have fleas, she's perfectly clean."

"—and whether or not she can have a suitable dinner party prepared in a few days' time. I'm finished with this discussion, wife. I'll see you again on Thursday."

True to his word, Graham managed to avoid Violet completely until the all-important dinner party featuring Mr. Samuel Harper.

The all-important Mr. Harper wasn't what Violet expected. She assumed that he would be rough-hewn, illiterate, and bad-mannered, given that he was from Virginia.

Instead, he was well-dressed, well-mannered, and, well, strikingly handsome, with intelligent dark eyes and fashionably long side whiskers. Even Mary, supposedly long beyond any desire for men, fluttered and flirted amusingly during dinner. Unfortunately, Mr. Harper had no wife, so the table balance was upset, but Graham didn't seem to mind.

For his part, Mr. Harper was unfailingly gracious, although his strange speech was drawn out slow and sweet, like molasses from a spoon. His lilt was full of self-assurance and good humor. Did all Americans talk this way, or was his a special dialect?

He said that he was a lawyer by training, but now served the new Confederate government in special acquisitions. Graham shifted uneasily in his chair when Mr. Harper said that.

" 'Special acquisitions,' Mr. Harper?" Violet said. "I suppose funerary supplies are indeed special, although I don't understand why—"

Graham cut her off. "Mr. Harper, Fletcher here trades rum with

Boston. It's a fine job they do with it, meaning no disrespect to your side."

"None taken, sir."

"Have any of the Southern states considered dealings in spirits with England? Surely your soldiers would appreciate some good British ale. Or we could take care of bringing round some rum through the blockade for you."

"Perhaps, perhaps. I know doctors are already prescribing spirits for melancholia. The men miss their families, and a dram or two helps take the edge off their pain." Mr. Harper held his fork in his left hand, cut with the knife in his right hand, then laid the knife down and switched the fork to his right hand to pick up the morsel he'd just cut.

How inefficient it all was, Violet thought, as she maintained her fork in her left hand the entire time, as was proper English etiquette.

The conversation was interrupted by a thin, childish wail piercing through the dining room wall from the basement at the back of the house.

Mr. Harper cocked his head to one side. "Sounds like your daughter is unhappy, ma'am."

"She's not our daughter, just a visitor," Graham said.

Why did Graham have to behave as though Susanna were some criminal invader in their home?

"Mr. Harper," Violet said, "Susanna is an orphaned child in my care. I'm afraid I'm not used to having a child around, and she doesn't have the ability—or perhaps the will—to speak, so it is difficult to know what's bothering her."

"It sounds like she's suffering a digestive upset."

"Possibly. She's not eaten well in who knows how long, so we're finding that she doesn't always react well to what Mrs. Porter prepares."

"If I'm not intruding too far into your domain, Mrs. Morgan, may I make a recommendation? When I was a boy, my grandmother used a remedy of a spoonful of ashes stirred in cider. It always calmed my intestinal woes. May I recommend it for your Susanna?"

He said it without a hint of malice over the child's crying. For a brief moment, Violet didn't resent the presence of a man who was surely involved in something questionable with her husband.

"Thank you, Mr. Harper. I will indeed see to the preparation right away, if you would be so kind as to excuse me."

Mr. Harper nodded as Violet moved her chair away from the table, but she was frozen by Graham's stare.

"Darling," he said quietly. "Perhaps you would be so kind as to wait until our meal is concluded."

"But Susanna . . . I should at least give the recipe to Mrs. Porter."

"It can wait." Graham stabbed at his asparagus spears and lifted one young stalk to his mouth.

Violet pulled back to the table, angry and humiliated. Blood roared in her ears.

She kept her head down for the remainder of the meal to hide her resentment while Graham discussed the current events of the war in America, asking for Mr. Harper's valuable opinion every minute or so.

Violet looked up at her husband through hooded eyes, ignoring Mary's sympathetic gaze and Fletcher's forced laughter.

Husband, I do believe my heart just splintered a little over you. Please don't give me a reason to hate you.

The moment she was released so the men could have their business discussion over stronger libations, Violet fled to the kitchens, with Mary right behind her, to tell Mrs. Porter the ingredients for Mr. Harper's tonic. The housekeeper quickly assembled the curative while Violet and Mary went to see Susanna in her room, the one once occupied by Mrs. Scrope.

The forbidden kitten lay curled up on the bed, while Susanna sat next to it, tears streaming down her face. Violet felt another slash in her heart, but this one was longer, and accompanied by a twinge of fear and protectiveness.

Mary tried to coax words out of the girl, mostly by praising the little black-and-white ball of fluff that Susanna was petting. Mary was no more successful than Violet or Mr. and Mrs. Porter had been.

After Susanna willingly drank down the potion, they waited anxiously to see what would happen. In just a few minutes, the girl was smiling happily again.

What a relief.

Violet put her hands on her hips, assuming a sternness she did not feel. "You know the kitten will have to have a name, don't you? Let's see." Violet reached out and stroked the kitten's fur, which was already luxurious despite the animal's youth. The kitten rolled over and reached a paw up to Violet, who clasped it in her own hand. "How about Mrs. Softpaws?"

Susanna smiled and picked up the kitten, burying her face in its fur while nodding.

"Then that's settled. Good evening, Susanna and Mrs. Softpaws." It would be far from settled when Graham realized there was a cat living in the household. Maybe she'd prove to be a good mouser.

Violet and Mary returned to the drawing room to converse quietly and wait for the men to conclude. After a light conversation about the latest books in Mr. Hatchard's window and Susanna's condition, the subject turned back to their earlier dinner.

"What do you think of Mr. Harper?" Mary asked.

"He understands medicinal preparations, and for that I'm grateful. I needn't ask what you think, Mary Overfelt, what with all of your simpering and eye-batting."

"I've never batted an eye in my life. I just appreciate his well-formed looks, is all."

Violet smiled. "You've never appreciated Fletcher's well-formed looks as much."

"Ah, Fletcher. A sweet boy but flighty." Mary shook her head. "What am I saying? Both must be fifteen years younger than me, and neither could live up to the memory of Matthew."

"Maybe you're simply opening yourself up to the idea of love once more. A man would be proud to call you his wife, Mary."

"No, there's no one on this side of heaven for me except Matthew.

He was my dearest heart, my friend, and my business partner. I wouldn't even try to replace him."

Graham was Violet's business partner, too. She supposed they were still friends, as well, but was he really her dearest heart anymore?

Mary interrupted her reverie. "Susanna is a lovely child, although painfully thin. With this new tonic, hopefully she'll be able to eat more and fill out. What are your plans for her?"

"I don't know. It seems heartless to turn her over to an orphanage, which would be no better than the workhouse, yet Graham is less than enthused about her presence here."

"A solution will present itself, I'm sure of it." Violet could always rely on Mary for a word of encouragement.

Soon Mary was trying to disguise her yawns, so Violet told her friend that she herself was exhausted and wanted to retire if Mary had no objections.

Her friend didn't seem to mind, so after Mary's departure, Violet settled back down in the drawing room with a copy of *Silas Marner* by George Eliot, which had just come by post the previous day. Her attention to the words flagged and she dozed, only to be awakened by laughter as her husband, brother-in-law, and their guest came out of the dining room. She tucked her lace ribbon in the book to mark her place and put it aside to stand and extend a farewell to Mr. Harper.

He looked her directly in the eye and shook her hand warmly, as though she were a long-lost friend of his.

"My thanks to you, Mrs. Morgan, for a fine meal, although I must skedaddle now. May I ask how little Susanna is faring?"

"Your restorative worked wonders, sir. She sleeps like the dead."

"With whom you are well acquainted. I would be most interested in hearing tales about your profession one day, should your husband see fit to invite me over again. I'd also like to meet Susanna."

Graham's broad grin suggested that Mr. Harper could move in as far as he was concerned.

"It would be our honor to have you for dinner again, Mr. Harper."

The tips of Harper's ears were tinged with red. "I will look forward to your invitation. Good evening, ma'am."

After Mr. Harper's departure, Graham and Fletcher retreated back to the dining room for more discussion. Graham firmly pulled shut the draperies between the dining room and drawing room, an unmistakable commentary on Violet's undesirability in their conversation. Refusing to stay up waiting for her husband another moment, she put her book back on its shelf and headed out the drawing room's rear door toward the stairs, but her attention was piqued by the brothers' muffled, but raised, voices in the dining room. What were they arguing about? Risking Graham's ire, she unbuttoned her boots and walked as quietly as possible in her stockinged feet to the dining room wall. It was no easy task, for even though their wood floors were new, they creaked under any weight not buffered by carpets.

She put her ear to the wall, ashamed of what she was doing but too curious to do anything else. Violet had never spied on Graham—or on anyone, for that matter—before. She felt like she was in a Wilkie Collins novel.

"—will not do, Graham. If we're to fully profit from this venture, we cannot be supplying top quality."

"I purchased this last batch at an excellent price."

"A price you'll never receive again. Think, brother, not like an undertaker, but as a new sort of businessman."

"Don't condescend to me, Fletcher. Remember that I have invested far more money in this little venture than you have."

"I do remember." Fletcher's voice was soothing now. "And with Mr. Harper's generosity, we're on the verge of great success. I just want that success to be far greater than anything we could have ever imagined. Remember your own personal aspirations in this, too."

"As though I could forget. By the way, did you bring the—"

"Of course. Here."

There was a rustling noise Violet couldn't identify.

Graham's laugh was low and throaty. "Excellent work, brother."

"I always keep my promises, don't I?"

"When it suits you." More rustling and the laughter of collusion ensued.

Violet's stomach sank. Graham was up to something very, very troubling. What kind of disaster would it bring upon their house? Upon poor little Susanna, sleeping downstairs and relying on Violet to erase the specter of tragedy from her life?

No. I won't allow this.

"—must be going now. Remember Mr. Harper wants to . . ."

At the sound of their footsteps, Violet raced upstairs in her stockinged feet, tossed her boots under the bed, and hurriedly changed into her nightclothes while Graham said good-bye to Fletcher. Without bothering with a brush, she stuffed her hair under a nightcap and jumped into bed.

She hardly had time to arrange the covers and prop up the pillows behind her when Graham entered the bedroom, whistling.

"You're still awake, good. Tonight was a resounding success, don't you think, despite the child's crying? Harper was enthusiastic about purchasing our goods, and Mrs. Porter's meal was perfection. I doubt they eat so well in Virginia."

"Mr. Harper's remedy worked wonders for Susanna."

Graham examined his face in Violet's vanity mirror while loosening his cravat. "Do you think I could carry off Harper's long side whiskers?"

"No. Tell me, did Fletcher have anything of interest to say after Mr. Harper left?"

"Not really." His cravat discarded and his shirt loosened beneath his jacket, Graham came and sat on the edge of the bed next to Violet.

"I see. Is there a point at which you will give me insight into what, exactly, all of these business arrangements are, Graham?"

"You already know. We're shipping funerary supplies to the Southern American states. Coffins, wreath stands, and the like. Mr. Harper is our intermediary with the Confederate government. We'll be rich, and I can have the satisfaction—" He stopped.

"The satisfaction of what?"

"The satisfaction of knowing that Morgan Undertaking has become an international concern." He looked away as he said this.

Violet climbed her way out of the opposite side of the bed and stood, arms crossed and glaring. She knew she looked absolutely ridiculous going on the attack in her filmy nightgown, but she was beyond caring.

Graham stood as well. The bed lay between them like a battlefield.

"Graham Morgan, you are a liar. Somehow I suspect you are a cheat, too; I just don't know how."

"Mind your business, Violet. This is no concern of yours. Your only worry will be new frocks and hats. You can even buy them for the girl."

"My only worry right now is Susanna. The child has been through enough, not that you've asked about her enough to know that her mother probably died before her eyes, and that she—"

"That's enough. There's no need to waste my time on her tale of woe."

"Right. Anything that doesn't concern you and your highly suspect business dealings is an utter waste of time. Are you planning some sort of high seas adventure with Fletcher? Intend to plunder the Caribbean like a couple of pirates on your way to Virginia?"

"You know nothing, and I'm nearly at the end of my patience with you. Why can't you be a good wife? I just want a home that can be a source of pride and a wife who admires her husband. What do I have instead? A shrew who cares more about a grimy street urchin than her husband, and who couldn't keep a servant if her life depended upon it doing so, and who doesn't understand proper dinner conversation. Your only competence is in funerals, something I can hardly brag about to friends and neighbors."

"Perhaps you've forgotten how much you once appreciated my talent in undertaking. You told me I was your idea of perfection because I understood the delicacy of this business and could work side by side with you forever."

"I was younger then, and much more foolish. Mother warned me about you being too independent-minded, and she was right.

If I had the opportunity to do it over, I would *never* have chosen you."

Violet froze, overcome by a chill at Graham's words. Even Graham himself seemed shocked by what he'd just said. He had the good grace to redden in embarrassment.

"I believe we've said enough to one another," he said quietly.

Violet nodded, still unable to speak.

He removed his jacket, tucked it over one arm, and headed for the door.

"Will you be sleeping in your study again?"

"I think it's for the best, don't you?"

Yes, indeed.

As her husband walked out of the bedroom without a backward glance, she knew with a certainty that he would never seek to reenter it again. She gasped as her heart split completely in half, with no less force than the rending of the temple in Jerusalem after Christ's death.

God help me, what now?

Samuel breathed in the night air. It was no cleaner than the day air, and he coughed at the dirt irritating his throat. He decided to walk part of the way back to his hotel before hailing a hack, in order to clear his mind.

Discussions with the Morgan brothers had been successful, beyond his wildest dreams. Their deal should be concluded soon and matters could go from there. His superiors would be pleased with how quickly and easily he had accomplished his mission.

Mrs. Morgan, however, was a different story, and a disconcerting one. There was trouble between her and her husband, for certain. Her eyes had blazed with undisguised fury at Graham Morgan, despite her best efforts to hide her feelings.

Samuel's grandmother would have called her an unbroken Arabian mare. Samuel would agree. Violet Morgan was slim, long-legged, and spirited, with a bold disposition and an intelligence that outweighed all of those other traits.

Graham Morgan, though, was a horse's rear. How could he treat a woman like that with such contempt?

Moreover, did Samuel's dealings with Mrs. Morgan's husband mean that he, too, resembled a horse's posterior? She obviously knew nothing about what they were doing, yet the potential ramifications . . . well, Violet Morgan would not escape any resulting danger.

A twinge of regret crept its way into his mind, an unusual reaction for this lawyer who knew no fear and had happily accepted this assignment from his government.

He found a hack to take him the rest of the way to his hotel. He wondered whether perhaps he should be pulling the carriage himself.

At the hotel, Samuel tossed restlessly in bed. Giving up on the idea of slumber, he decided to finish some correspondence.

> . . . I expect the first shipment of goods to be ready
> within the month. My contacts here are confident in their
> abilities. As discussed, my intent is to see if they will also
> use their ship as a commerce raider. First, of course, I will
> ask to see and inspect it, to determine its worthiness for
> such an operation. . . .

Samuel's loyalty was unwavering and he knew that his work here was justified. If he could just get the picture of Violet Morgan's exquisite face out of his mind, he might actually be able to sleep.

Violet never dreamed that her marriage would crumble into a stony silence, although it was preferable to the bickering and accusations.

Ironically, Susanna's silence was of comfort. The girl followed Violet everywhere, even refusing to be left behind when Violet went to visit customers or work at the shop. Because she was so quiet and reticent, most people hardly noticed her. Violet found herself chatting one-sidedly with Susanna, discussing funeral arrangements with her as if she were speaking to another adult, albeit a silent one. The girl nodded, shrugged, and motioned with her hands enough that it became a good replication of actual speech.

Susanna had a natural affinity for the dead, an odd quality for the normal public, but quite gratifying to Violet. Susanna studied deceased faces, at first with wonder in her large eyes, and eventually with an understanding that Violet couldn't quite fathom. Sometimes she would even pat the hands of the dead, as though to comfort them.

Violet and Graham managed to coordinate funerals together, also with no spoken communication, merely leaving notes for one another on pertinent details for various upcoming funerals. At least she had no worries that Graham would attempt to bar her from the business. Much as he resented her unconventional wifely manners, he couldn't possibly run this business without her. And finding someone else who would be as skilled as she was would be nearly impossible.

At home, Mr. and Mrs. Porter went about their duties, pretending there was nothing wrong in the Morgan household. Violet took to eating in the kitchen with Susanna and the Porters, while Graham continued to use the dining room. It was a symbol of his disregard that he made no comment that his wife was dining with servants.

Mr. Porter, already a bluff and hearty man, was exaggeratedly so around Susanna, always trying to charm a smile from her and expressing the hope that one day she would speak to him. Mrs. Porter loved everyone through the liberal applications of pastries and pies. If Violet wasn't careful, she'd be visiting Mary for a new wardrobe herself.

Mary was a frequent guest in the Morgan kitchens, now, too, enjoying the camaraderie that went on long into the night. Mrs. Softpaws, now growing and becoming ganglier by the week, romped and skittered through the basement, happily chasing bugs and feet before tiring and jumping onto Susanna's lap for a quick nap before starting over.

Even the periodic odd smells from the toilet—a convenience that fascinated Susanna, who couldn't flush it frequently enough while gaping at its operation—weren't sufficient to dampen the exuberance belowstairs. It was easy for Violet to forget Graham's sour countenance and cutting words when surrounded by others who loved her.

Violet's London family was now an odd mix of servants, undertaker, best friend, and mute orphan. However, as much as she was growing attached to them, the situation caused her to miss her parents dreadfully.

It was time to visit them in Brighton.

Charles Francis and his son sat across the table from Russell and Palmerston, gratified by the uncomfortable expressions on the British lords' faces.

"You say you've intercepted correspondence to support your assertion?" Lord Palmerston's face was ashen.

Charles Francis pushed the open document over for the two men to examine. Palmerston slowly scratched one side of his sideburns, the longest and curliest Charles Francis had ever seen, literally starting from the top of his head and combed forward apart from the rest of his hair. How did this man develop such a reputation with ladies?

A look passed between Palmerston and Russell that Charles Francis couldn't interpret. Russell spoke up first. "Naturally, our position of neutrality doesn't enable us to overlook criminal activity. We will have this seen to immediately, and pick up all of the parties for questioning."

Charles Francis pulled the letter back. "Actually, my lords, we wish to proceed on this ourselves, with your kind permission, thus leaving your hands clean and giving us the satisfaction of stopping these wretched criminals working to destroy the United States."

Charles Francis saw another look between the two men, but this one was obviously relief. For certain, it would be better for Palmerston's government if the matter could be cleared up quietly and without British intervention.

"Of course. Obviously, we wish to be kept well informed."

"And the queen and prince consort?"

Lord Russell answered this time. "The prince is occupied with other, more pressing matters, so perhaps it is best if our accord is maintained privately. Are we agreed?"

"Yes, my lord. My son and I understand your position perfectly." Next to him, Henry nodded solemnly.

As they left Palmerston's offices, Charles Francis clapped his son on the back. "The noose is tightening, son, and our enemies aren't even aware of it. Now to see whether we can have them all sent back to the United States to punishment there."

"Will the prime minister allow it?"

"If not, perhaps we can see to a swift and subtle punishment conducted here."

Brighton
August 1861

As surprised as they were to see Violet trailing along a young girl, the Sinclairs welcomed Susanna as though she were a long-lost grandchild. Which she may as well have been, given that there was likely to be no issue between Violet and Graham.

Violet stayed secreted with her mother for hours on end, finally unburdening herself in the ageless confines of a mother-daughter relationship. Eliza Sinclair provided the embraces and murmuring words of comfort that Violet needed.

Meanwhile, Arthur Sinclair took Susanna out to run and play in a way that she couldn't enjoy within the restrictions of London life. The girl's face was practically ruddy with joy after her first visit to a bathing hut, which gave her a taste of plunging into the English Channel in a bathing costume. Violet's father insisted that she had even laughed aloud when he presented her with a stick of candy floss, the spun-sugar treat sold by street vendors and at fairs. He took it upon himself to teach Susanna her sums, contending then that her quick progress proved the girl was naturally brilliant, since she was learning without uttering a word.

Mr. Sinclair himself seemed to drop years from his face in the presence of the mute girl. Susanna did have that effect on most people.

As a foursome they sauntered through the streets of Brighton, rambling past the Royal Pavilion, the sprawling Moorish concoction built by George IV nearly half a century ago. Its spires and turrets rose above the gleaming white Bath stone, reminding Violet of an exotically decorated cake.

They also promenaded out onto Chain Pier, as well as strolling past landmarks like the Bedford Hotel and the new Brighton School of Art. German oompah bands and traveling minstrels provided entertainment aplenty. Brighton was expanding and developing at a breathtaking pace.

After two weeks of complete isolation from her normal life in London—two weeks without a single communication from Graham—Violet finally decided it was time to take the early-morning excursion train from Brighton back to London. The excursion trains ran on a faster schedule than ordinary trains, and Violet was anxious to return home. It was time to return home to her normal world. Truthfully, she missed the work of helping the grieving say good-bye to their loved ones. She hadn't held a length of black crape in far too long.

Susanna didn't resist their departure that Sunday morning, but merely stood in the room they shared, single tears rolling down each cheek, as Violet tried fruitlessly to repack their things, a collection of items nearly doubled thanks to her father's purchases of dolls, toys, and primer books for Susanna.

The Italianate-style train station was built on an awkward site on the northern edge of Brighton, at least seventy feet above the shore. The unfortunate siting of the station meant there were only a limited number of platforms for the trains. The growing volume of traffic from popular Brighton was poorly handled by the station, evidenced by the crowds jamming the platforms even at eight o'clock in the morning.

Susanna was unfazed by the hum of the crowds and the acrid smoke emanating from the coal-powered trains, obsessed as she was with the curly-haired doll Violet's father had given her as a going-away present. Violet made a mental note to visit a doll shop in London for more playthings for Susanna.

The station was run by finely uniformed men whose jackets and hats were trimmed in a confusing array of gold braid and brass buttons, each pattern denoting the man's position with the railway, whether a luggage porter, lamp porter, station clerk, booking clerk, ticket collector, dining car attendant, fireman, or any other of dozens of railway positions. At least some men wore embroidered patches on their collars identifying them.

Standing next to their heavy luggage that the driver of the railway-operated taxi had unceremoniously heaped inside the station, Violet looked around among the London and Brighton Railway employees rushing in and about among passengers for someone who could help her.

A man with an embroidered collar patch reading "Guard" approached.

"Excuse me, please, can you help me with my luggage?" she asked.

The man stared at her, aghast. He tapped his collar. "I'm a guard. I don't move bags." Off he went without an offer to find someone to help her.

Another man came by. "Are you a luggage porter?" she asked.

"No, I'm a ticket collector." He was gone.

Finally a porter came by, enabling her to visit the booking office to purchase their fares while he transported luggage behind them. After a long wait in line, she was handed their numbered third-class tickets and they made their way to the correct platform to wait. How Graham would have disapproved of her not spending extra for first-class tickets.

Within a few minutes several trains rushed into the station, quickly spewed passengers and swallowed more, and then raced back out of the station in a cacophony of screeching wheels, high-pitched whistles, and belching clouds of smoke from their coal-powered steam engines.

Finally, though, their train arrived and they settled down in their car, the last one on this particular train except for the guard's van, a small, open carriage containing yet another uniformed man whose job was to look alternately down either side of the train to note any signs that anything was wrong with the train's operation.

Their third-class seats, facing the rear, were comfortable enough despite being wood benches, although the carriage lacked the oil lamps, foot warmers, clerestory windows in the roof, and other amenities of first class. It was mostly like an open-air carriage with a roof covering.

Almost immediately, Susanna curled up across Violet's lap to sleep, while Violet opened a copy of *The Times* she'd purchased at the last minute from the W. H. Smith newsboy.

Against the backdrop of the gently chugging train pulling away from Brighton, neither knew that disaster would overtake them in a few minutes.

All things that we ordained festival,
Turn from their office to black funeral;
Our instruments to melancholy bells,
Our wedding cheer to a sad burial feast,
Our solemn hymns to sullen dirges change,
Our bridal flowers serve for a buried corpse,
And all things change them to the contrary.

—William Shakespeare (1564–1616)
Romeo and Juliet (1592)

A nondescript, middle-aged woman joined Violet on the wood bench opposite her and Susanna. The woman looked pained and exhausted, in the manner of a servant, despite her fashionable clothing.

Since they would be sharing the space for the next couple of hours, Violet folded the paper up and extended a hand in friendship. "Good morning. I am Mrs. Morgan."

The other woman grasped it tentatively. "Yes. I'm Mrs. Wil— Mrs. Barrett."

"Do you live in London, Mrs. Barrett?" Violet asked.

"Yes. No. I've spent many years in London. I lost my husband a few months ago and with nothing left for me in Brighton, I'm headed to Lambeth for a housekeeping position that a friend arranged for me."

The woman was not wearing any phase of mourning clothing, not even a pair of jet earrings or a hair brooch. When in deep mourning, a woman who could afford to do so withdrew from activities for at least a year. During that first year after her husband's death, a widow wore a black dress covered with crape and a widow's cap with a veil, in addition to a full complement of jet ornaments. During the next twelve months, or second mourning, a widow's dress contained less crape and she did away with the cap and jet ornaments. If mourning continued into a third year, it was termed "half-mourning," and gray or purple was added as a color. Mrs. Barrett was probably just running away from an abusive husband, but it was none of her business. "I see. I trust you will have a pleasant journey."

"I wish you a pleasant journey, as well. Is your home in Brighton or London?"

"London. My husband and I are undertakers in Paddington."

Mrs. Barrett reacted like everyone who heard Violet utter those words for the first time, in a mix of disbelief and revulsion, covered over with a falsely bright smile.

"That sounds lovely," she said.

Violet was tempted to laugh but knew she would offend poor Mrs. Barrett's attempt at polite conversation. Instead, she tried another subject. "I've always been impressed by the efficient and complex system of flags and lamps the railway signalmen use to ensure rail traffic moves smoothly and without incident. There must be thousands of miles of track that crisscross the country."

"Yes, very impressive." Which Mrs. Barrett clearly wasn't. Susanna's sleeping form seemed to catch the woman's eye for the first time, and Mrs. Barrett stared curiously at her and back up at Violet. "Surely you aren't her mother?"

Violet started. "I'm sorry, why would you ask such a thing?"

Mrs. Barrett reddened. "Pardon me, it's just . . . you and she look so different. She must resemble her father."

Violet stroked Susanna's curls. How was the child able to sleep through so much noise?

"Perhaps. I'm caring for her in the absence of her mother."

Mrs. Barrett nodded knowingly. "She's a lovely child, though."

"She is, isn't she? Unfortunately, she doesn't speak. I'm not sure if she's mute or simply refuses to talk."

"Is that so? So . . . she's never spoken a single word to you?"

"Never."

Mrs. Barrett sat back, fanning herself in the August heat, which was considerable even at this early hour, and conversation ceased between them. Susanna chose that moment of silence to awaken from her nap. She sat up next to Violet, yawning and rubbing her eyes.

Violet looked at the girl anew. The past few weeks had been good for her. She'd filled out in her face and extremities. Why, she had the look of a girl soon to blossom into womanhood.

It was the expression on Susanna's face, though, that really grabbed Violet's attention. She looked . . . concerned. No, frightened. Of what?

Before she could try to determine what was bothering the girl, the train entered a tunnel and everything went dark, leaving Violet distinctly uncomfortable. Susanna must have realized they were about to enter the tunnel, and that was what made her nervous.

Before Violet could offer the girl a reassuring word, the train slowed to a complete stop inside the tunnel. England's swelling numbers of trains shared tracks and were forever being signaled to stop and wait for other trains to pass by in the opposite direction, but stopping inside a tunnel was a new and unnerving experience.

The forty or so people in the carriage went completely silent, as though the darkness commanded it. For her part, Susanna laid her head on Violet's shoulder and clutched her hand. Violet suddenly wished she'd purchased first-class tickets so that they would have the light of gas lamps.

Suddenly they began to move backward, so that Violet and Susanna were themselves facing in a forward direction, and now Mrs. Barrett, wherever she was in the inky black car, was facing backward.

Violet assumed a signaling mistake had been made and they were now backing out of the tunnel to get out of the way for an oncoming train.

Now she saw light seeping in from the tunnel's end, and as the train curved along a bend in the track, what she saw in the emerging daylight confused her.

It couldn't be.

She raised a hand and pointed, too shocked to even utter a sound, but it was enough to get the attention of other passengers, who gasped and screamed where Violet could say nothing. Their reaction got the attention of the guard, who turned to see what was bothering his passengers.

It was too late for the man to do anything about it.

The Lord is my shepherd, I shall not want, popped unbidden into her mind.

As they came out of the tunnel, another train was hurtling toward theirs from a different track joining it at a point where the guard's van would soon pass. The engine driver must have realized what was happening at the moment Violet did, because suddenly the air was split with the terrible shrieking and squealing of a train attempting to stop in far less space than it was physically possible for it to do.

He maketh me to lie down in green pastures.

"Dear God in heaven!" someone exclaimed from behind her, scrambling out of his seat and running to the front of the car. Others followed him, trying in the space of seconds to rush as far away from the oncoming train as possible. Human nature demanded that they do whatever they could to preserve themselves, yet it was a futile task. The oncoming engine was twice the length of their railway car. They would be obliterated.

As though time had lost its ability to control movement, everything seemed to slow down into motionless frames, like the pictures created by Mr. Laroche.

He leadeth me beside the still waters.

Violet's stomach lurched in a combination of fear and disbelief, while hundreds of thoughts ran simultaneously through her mind. She had to protect Susanna. Were they really to die in a train wreck? She wanted her mother. How badly would it hurt? Surely this wasn't happening. What undertaker would tend to her when she died?

He restoreth my soul.

In a brief moment of clarity, Violet pulled Susanna's face to her chest and wrapped both arms around her, although she knew it was a futile gesture against several tons of iron intent on devouring them.

He leadeth me in the paths of righteousness for his name's sake.

The engine car slammed into the rear of the guard car. The explosive strike of metal against metal and wood, combined with the screeching of a train still attempting to brake, was beyond deafening and overcame the terrified screams of terror in the car. Violet watched in horror as the guard was thrown from the van, his eyes already sightless as he was ejected through the side of his carriage and out of view. The guard van tumbled off the track and down the embankment.

Yea, though I walk through the valley of the shadow of death, I will fear no evil.

Now it was their turn to dance the capricious ballet with death. The engine roared up, still shrieking its desire not to do so, and mounted the rear of their car, pushing the entire train back again toward the tunnel. Violet's head whipped forward and backward, nearly knocking her unconscious, but she wasn't fortunate enough to actually go blank.

She looked up again at the engine, which now resembled a mythical monster overtaking them, given that it was already a big beast and was now hitched on top of the end of her car. It was close enough and twisted at such an angle that Violet could see the engine driver's frantic actions as he stood at the back of the beast he was trying futilely to control.

For thou art with me; thy rod and thy staff they comfort me.

Heat and steam now flooded the car, burning hot like a roasting jack spit. Boiling-hot water was spraying against them all. Violet felt a searing pain rush up her arm, but there was no time to consider it. She attempted to get up from her seat, but with Susanna in her arms and the wet floor beneath her long, heavy skirts, it was impossible to move. She stayed there, bent over Susanna to cover her as best she could while enduring the endless rain of hot water pelting her head, back, and arms. The pain was so severe she cried out, but the sound was lost in the chaos.

Along with the unbearable heat came an odd smell. It was familiar, but what was it?

Thou preparest a table before me in the presence of mine enemies.

Despite her own confusion, she realized that the driver saw something even more fearful than a railway engine climbing on top of defenseless passengers. In an instant, Violet understood the engine driver's panic. The engine, now lifted too high up in the air, collided with the curved arch of the tunnel they had just entered.

The arch stopped the engine, yet underneath the engine still lay part of Violet's car that it had been coercing back into the tunnel. The competing forces were too much for Violet's carriage.

The rear passenger car of the Brighton to London excursion train of the London, Brighton and South Coast Railway split to pieces in a tangle of iron, wood, frightened cries, and flailing limbs. Violet was struck in the face by a child's shoe and out of the corner of her eye saw a man decapitated by a flying piece of metal.

Thou anointest my head with oil; my cup runneth over.

It happened so quickly and the man disappeared from view so fast that she wasn't sure she'd actually witnessed what she thought she had.

There was no time to think on it, for Violet realized that Susanna was no longer in her arms.

Surely goodness and mercy will follow me all the days of my life, and I will dwell in the house of the Lord forever.

Her final registered thought, though, was recognition of what the terrible odor was. She remembered it from the bodies of those who had been in terrible accidents. It was the stench of burning human flesh.

Violet awoke. Rather, she was jerked awake by the sounds of screaming and crying all around her.

Where am I?

She attempted to open her eyes, but only one was functioning. Not that it mattered because the light was so dim. She reached up her left hand. What was smeared all over her face? She put her hand up in front of her good eye. Blood, and a lot of it. She touched around her eye again. Ah, the pain sent shooting stars into her head.

Have I been blinded?

Now gaining enough cognizance to realize she was lying amid gravel and debris next to the track inside the tunnel, Violet pushed herself into a sitting position. The movement nearly caused her to faint.

More realization. There was relentless pain in her right arm. She held it up. The fabric of her dress was charred and molded to her scorched flesh. Despite the number of dead bodies she'd seen in her life, the glimpse of her own burned limb made her ill.

She attempted to work the fingers of her right arm, which sent brilliant lightning flashes of agony up her arm, so she stopped, letting her arm dangle uselessly next to her. *I need help* was her last thought before going unconscious again, a sweet relief from the agony in her arm.

Violet awoke once again and gradually became aware of the world around her. So much crying and moaning. When would it stop? She put her hands over her ears, but it did nothing to stop the piteous cries of those who had been burned or injured far worse than Violet had, and only served to remind her that her right arm could not be moved without a torturous sensation.

She was becoming more alert as she realized she was missing something important.

"Susanna?" she whispered, reaching out into the dark. No answer. Someone stumbled past her, calling out for someone named Jane and kicking up a sharp stone against her shoulder. Violet was still too groggy to even cry out from the impact.

Two swinging pinpoints of light came into focus. She squinted her good eye as they approached. It was a railway worker carrying a pair of lanterns, bending down at intervals, as if inspecting something.

"Hello!" Violet croaked. The lights moved up as the worker held the lamps aloft. In a moment, he was next to her. The lanterns shone on the worker's horror as he gazed into Violet's face.

"Am I that bad?" she asked.

"Er, no, madam, I'm sure it looks worse than it is. Can you stand?" He offered an arm to lift her up. Her blood rushed downward as she stood, and she grasped his arm with her left hand while gaining her balance.

She reached up her hand gingerly once again to inspect her face. Her right eye was completely swollen shut. Well, there was no telling what the real damage was there, and it was of less importance than finding Susanna, anyway.

"May I have one of those?" She indicated his lanterns. "I need to find my daughter."

He looked at her doubtfully, as though he already counted her for dead and didn't want to waste anything valuable on her. "Sorry, madam, I need it to search for the living, although I admit you're the first one I've found."

"But the screaming . . ."

He shrugged. "Most of those are being shepherded along by the Grim Reaper. I'm hoping to find a doctor while we wait for rescue. The signalmen have alerted a nearby hospital and fire department."

"I'm an undertaker, so my best help will be with the dead."

"Sorry?" he said, staring at her in disbelief.

"Nothing. Please, give me one of your lanterns. I can help you search for the living."

The man gave her one, although she could see he had serious misgivings about the wisdom of doing so. *Maybe I will die, sir, but not before I find Susanna.*

She lurched off with the lantern, determined to locate Susanna alive and well. The railway worker went off in another direction to continue his own search. She soon saw multiple lanterns swinging through the tunnel as more workers joined the hunt.

Violet was more than accustomed to death, but heat, noise, and stench inside the tunnel made her feel that she had quite possibly entered a war zone. An image of what Graham's grandfather's experiences must have been flashed through her mind.

Surely it couldn't have been worse than this.

The engine that had demolished her car was still on fire as it remained dangling from the tunnel entrance, although some shouts and a loud hissing told her that firemen were now on the scene, working to put it out. Maybe soon there would be relief from the scorching temperature, although no amount of fire extinguishing would relieve her own scalded arm.

The first victim she came across was missing an ear, part of his scalp, and an arm, and was, thankfully, quite dead. She knelt and studied the young man more closely. He was younger than she was. Someone's husband? A beloved son? Was he headed to London to seek his fortune?

She rose again, once more feeling herself sway ominously. She made her way to the wall of the tunnel and leaned against it, breathing heavily. Holding the lantern out, she looked down at her dress. It was bloodied—whether from her own blood or that of others she couldn't tell—and several buttons were torn off the bodice. It was ripped in multiple places and stained with grease, plant matter, and who knew what else.

But she was alive. And, hopefully, so was Susanna.

The thought of Susanna lying somewhere, desperately injured, or worse, strengthened Violet's resolve. She moved from prone figure to figure, trying to find Susanna as well as fulfilling her mission to discover who might be living. Or living and a doctor. A distant hope, that.

The cries of the dying diminished as she continued on with her gruesome work of inspecting bodies, hoping that one might have a flicker of life. The carnage was revolting, even for her well-trained senses. People were sliced in half, their entrails spread in a horrifying mess around them. Others were bloodied and battered beyond any sort of recognition, with flies already having discovered this fresh buffet tucked away in the brick tunnel. Most of them had massive scalding on their bodies, making Violet realize how fortunate she was. No amount of makeup or prosthesis would ever make these poor people look whole again. They needed immediate burial.

Where is Susanna?

Another woman of indeterminate age came strolling by, singing a baby's lullaby. Violet lifted the lantern to alert the woman to her presence, but she didn't seem to notice Violet, continuing to sing and stare vacantly toward the end of the tunnel.

"Madam, do you need—" At that moment Violet realized the woman needed nothing. Her arm was shredded from who knew what encounter she'd had on the train, with bone and tendon alike dangling openly from her shoulder and blood flowing profusely from her side. Before Violet could offer a word of encouragement, the woman dropped to her knees, then fell facedown in the gravel. Violet went to offer her assistance, but knew it was for naught. The poor woman was gone.

With a mental apology to the railway worker, Violet knew she had to stop inspecting bodies and focus on locating Susanna. Gathering whatever reserve of energy she still had, she called the girl's name out softly as she walked, and called out louder and louder the farther she moved into the tunnel. On the other side of the rail bed, she saw the glow of more lanterns as other people were joining the search on the opposite side of the wreck.

She lifted the lantern again. What was that? A slender, blond-haired girl, lying with her face against the tunnel, her legs twisted at unnatural angles.

No, it can't be. I won't let it be.

Violet felt her insides heaving and tears streamed down her face, even leaking past the swollen knot of her damaged eye. She approached the body, tripping and nearly losing her balance over a twisted chunk of metal. Kneeling down for what felt like the hundredth time, she set the lantern down, took a deep breath, put her left hand on the figure's shoulder, and turned the girl toward her.

She blinked in disbelief.

It wasn't her. It wasn't Susanna. Violet laughed, the demented echo bouncing against the curved walls of the tunnel.

Immediately regretting her instinctive reaction, she whispered to the girl, "You'll be fine. I'll make sure you're given a dignified burial. That's my promise to you."

Violet continued on her search for Susanna, resolving to volunteer to help with preparations for the dead, providing she could find someone with the London, Brighton and South Coast Railway who would accept her help. And providing she could see to the healing of her own injured arm.

What if I am damaged beyond repair? I'll have to give up undertaking altogether. I'd be forced to be the maîtresse de maison *Graham so mightily desires. Or would he simply find a way to divorce me?*

She firmly pushed all of the self-pitying thoughts aside. There would be plenty of time for that later.

A movement inside some of the wreckage on the rail grabbed Violet's attention and she made her way to it, climbing up the raised bed on both knees and ignoring the sharp pain of the stones in the rail bed against them.

She raised the lantern to peer over an overturned bench and nearly burst into tears once again.

It was Susanna, sitting next to the curled-up figure of a woman. Susanna held the woman's right hand in one of her own and gently stroked the woman's matted brown hair with her other hand.

"Oh, child," Violet said, unable to say more. Susanna looked up, as filthy and bedraggled as she was the first day she'd sat up in Violet's coffin, but unhurt and completely unfazed by the horror that had occurred.

"Is this lady dead?" Violet asked, putting the lantern down.

Susanna nodded and returned to stroking the woman's hair.

"You were with her when she died, weren't you?"

She nodded again without looking up.

"Susanna, you did a kind thing by staying with her in her last moments, and I'm proud of you. But listen to me." Susanna stilled. "We have to get help. I promise you we will help her more, but for now we need to get out of this tunnel. Come, take my hand. You'll need to carry this lantern. My other arm is quite useless."

Susanna considered Violet's outstretched hand, looking back and forth between it and the dead woman. Finally, she stopped stroking the blood-soaked hair and pointed at Violet's eye.

"I've been hurt, but I'll be fine, provided I get you home safely."

Susanna patted the woman a final time, grabbed Violet's hand,

and took up the lantern. Together they made their way to the opposite end of the tunnel, where harried policemen, railwaymen, and hospital workers were assembling survivors into some sort of logical groups. As they waited for further instruction, Violet thought of something else.

"Did you ever see Mrs. Barrett after the accident?"

Susanna shook her head. Violet looked, but couldn't find her among the survivors, either.

Another victim of the crash.

Railway taxis waited to take passengers either to the next station to resume their journey back to London, or to the Sussex County Hospital. Violet found a carriage bound for the hospital with room for her and Susanna, but before boarding, Violet went to the stationmaster to offer her services as an undertaker for the victims.

The stationmaster looked at her curiously, but took down the information about Morgan Undertaking.

By the time Violet was declared well enough to return to London, she was certain she had passed through Dante's nine circles of hell. A doctor washed and examined her eye, which he pronounced to have no apparent damage. He then worked tirelessly to mend her arm, but it meant cutting off and peeling away as much of her sleeve as possible, a pain so exquisite she lapsed in and out of consciousness several times during the process, despite his application of salves and ointments to try to loosen the fabric and minimize her torment.

Her now-bloodied arm was washed with a solution that must have contained salt, as she found herself screaming uncontrollably as the doctor pressed on her arm with moistened cloths. Not that it mattered, as her own screams were lost among all of the others in the ward where she lay with dozens of other beds.

The only bright spot was Susanna, who knelt steadfastly next to Violet on the other side of the bed, cooing and stroking her head. The doctor tried several times to shoo her out of the way, but the girl refused to budge. *Thank God for this little mercy.* Violet kept her eyes focused on Susanna's blond curls, a golden halo of hope in the midst of her anguish and distress.

Once the doctor completed his brutal work, he said, "You'll survive and probably regain use of your arm, but it will be forever disfigured. However, you are alive and should be quite grateful," he added before moving on to his next patient.

As tears ran down Violet's face, a mix of relief that he was finished with her, fear over whether he was right about her arm, and discomfort over the continued throbbing from what he had done to help her, Susanna climbed onto the bed and threw an arm around Violet's waist, hugging her tightly.

Now Violet's tears were all gratitude.

The Times
Tuesday, August 27, 1861

THE TERRIBLE ACCIDENT ON THE LONDON AND BRIGHTON RAILWAY.
Latest Particulars.

BRIGHTON, Monday Evening.

The number of deaths by the terrible accident of yesterday has, we regret to say, not been over-estimated. The following are the names of those killed: Mrs. Ellen LOWER of Brighton. Mr. INGLEDE of Brighton. Mr. George WEST-COTT of Brighton. An infant child of the above. Mr. Edward CHARLWOOD, otherwise known as SIMPSON, of Brighton. Mrs. Catherine BARNARD of Brighton. Mrs. TILLETT of Wanstead, Essex. Mrs. Christianna MAINS-THORP of Brighton. Mr. John GREENFIELD, 5, Montpelier-place, Brighton. Mr. John WHEELER of Brighton. Elizabeth WHEELER, wife of the above. David WHEELER, son of the above. Mr. George GARDENER of Pentonville. Miss BARCLAY, recently staying in Brighton. Mrs.

Maria EDWIN of London. Mrs. Jane Elizabeth BEDEN of Brighton. John LOCKSTEAD of London. Agnes PARKER of Brighton. Mary Ann PARKER, sister of Agnes. Mr. William HUB-BARD, lately staying in Brighton. Henry Hay-ward HUBBARD, grandson of Mr. Hubbard.

The body still requiring identification is that of a woman.

With regard to the injured, the latest information obtained by our reporter at the Sussex County Hospital, where they lie, led to the belief that no further deaths would ensue.

This morning, a female child, about three years old, suffering from fracture of both legs and severe scalds and bruises, was recognized by her father, who came from London; and to add to the melancholy character of this case, he identified the body of his wife among the killed. The child is in a very bad state, and but faint hopes are entertained of her recovery. With respect to the other sufferers in the hospital, Mr. J. S. ELLIS, the acting house-surgeon, reports that no serious symptoms have presented themselves.

The railway was fortunate to have aboard an undertaker, Mrs. Violet MORGAN of London, who submitted an offer for caring for the dead at no charge to the families. We are encouraged to see these selfless actions, which may do much to burnish the tarnished reputation of predatory and depraved undertakers.

Poor Mrs. Barrett. She must have been the unidentified woman found.

After Violet's initial excruciating treatment, she continued the gradual healing process on her own. Each night she unwrapped her bandages, applied a mix of noxious ointments, and rewrapped the bandages again. Although the pain dissipated and she slowly recovered use of her arm, it was clear that the doctor was right. Her arm was a railway map of scars and ridges that would never go away.

Graham's initial concern over her was tremendous, making Violet doubt her years of trepidation.

"My God, darling, what if I'd lost you?" he moaned, pulling him to her in the privacy of her dressing room for kisses and caresses. "I couldn't bear it. What would life be without you?"

Yet Violet couldn't help but notice the look of revulsion on his face when he finally saw what was beneath the bandages on her arm. A look that wasn't replaced with tenderness and concern. Nevertheless, they seemed to have another brief truce, and Violet used it to move Susanna into one of their guest rooms. Graham didn't object, even if he pretended Susanna didn't exist, and for a while husband and wife regained a semblance of harmony between them.

Mrs. Porter fussed over Violet and Susanna with a constant stream of pastries and treats, whereas Mr. Porter could hardly stand to have Susanna leave the house to go on undertaking rounds with Violet.

Mary Overfelt clutched Violet and Susanna in suffocating embraces, promising to immediately make dresses as replacements for all of their clothing lost in the crash.

Mr. and Mrs. Sinclair wrote, volunteering to return to London to help their daughter, but Violet demurred. She wanted life to get back to normal quickly, or back to whatever normal was with her husband and with the doe-eyed Susanna, who wasn't her daughter but occupied a bizarre, daughter-like role in her life.

It was all strange, but when had Violet's life not been strange, since the day she'd first picked up her undertaking bag?

The next few weeks went by in a blur for Violet. As skeptical as the stationmaster was, he did indeed have Violet summoned to Victoria station after some of the recovered bodies were brought to London for examination, sorting, and return to families after an initial stop in Sussex to drop off those deceased persons who had already been identified as having lived south of London. For those remaining victims whose families lived in London, Violet offered her services for free.

Violet relished the work, which enabled her to forget about her eye, which was healing at an agonizingly slow pace, although thankfully without any apparent permanent damage. It also gave her an opportunity to uphold her promise to those who perished in the crash.

News of the crash spread through England with a speed that beat any train. A highly publicized inquest was held, revealing that a first train had cleared the Clayton Tunnel just before Violet's train entered the tunnel. There was confusion between the two signalmen, one of whom thought the "all clear" signal meant that Violet's train had already passed through the tunnel as well, even though it hadn't, and he therefore gave the clear for the impact train. Violet's train stopped when the engineer then assumed the first train was still in the tunnel, then further signal confusion caused it to back up, directly into the great steaming beast that had run over the rear end of Violet's car.

The final count was twenty-three dead, most of them from Violet's carriage. She shuddered, remembering once again the engine car ramping up on the rear of the carriage, and the look of terror in other passengers' eyes, the howls of agony around her, and the awful heat.

What a miracle that she and Susanna were spared. Violet's every glimpse at the girl who had stayed attached to her side throughout her hospital ordeal resulted in a tiny swelling of her heart. Soon it would burst through her chest.

Withdrawn and subdued at first, Susanna conveyed her own struggle over the train wreck with her eyes, as Violet could almost see Susanna replaying the entire incident over and over in the depths of her blue orbs. Soon, though, Susanna compensated for her restraint by clinging fiercely to Violet, refusing to let her surrogate mother out of her sight except to sleep.

"I know," Violet whispered to Susanna one evening as she hugged the girl prior to bed. "But we have to make the best of what has happened to us and look for the blessing in it. I know what my blessing was."

Susanna wrapped her arms around Violet, who felt hot tears against the front of her nightgown. Sometimes Susanna carried herself with the dignity of a mature woman, and sometimes Violet was starkly reminded that Susanna was still only a girl who had suffered a greater share of tragedy than most women did in a lifetime.

Mrs. Porter let Violet know privately that Mr. Morgan had invited that Mr. Harper over again for the evening, so Violet was prepared when he arrived, sweeping down the stairs to greet him before Graham could do so.

Mr. Harper lit up noticeably at the sight of her, removing his hat and handing it to Mrs. Porter, who disappeared with it. "Mr. Harper, welcome back," she said, offering him her hand. Fortunately, her disfigurement didn't extend to her fingers, and with Mary's help she'd added dresses to her wardrobe with poufed sleeves reaching below her wrist, completely covering the evidence of the train wreck. "I presume you and my husband have further business to discuss?"

He had the good grace to redden. "It was the source of your husband's invitation, but I confess I have been concerned about your well-being since hearing about the Clayton crash. However, you look as radiant as ever, Mrs. Morgan, so my worries were misplaced. May I inquire as to Miss Susanna's health?"

Like an apparition who has been summoned at the sound of her name, Susanna entered the room unbidden, standing safely next to Violet but studying the visitor.

Mr. Harper nodded his head. "Miss Susanna, I am Samuel Harper. It is a pleasure to make your acquaintance."

Susanna smiled and turned her face to Violet, something unfathomable in her eyes.

"Mr. Harper had the remedy for your digestive pains when you first arrived. Do you remember how it cured you?"

Susanna nodded.

"I'm gratified that it brought you to the bloom of health, Miss Susanna," Mr. Harper said. "I trust the train accident had no lasting effect on you, either?"

Susanna put her head on Violet's shoulder. How had she shot up in such a short time?

"Forgive Susanna, Mr. Harper, she is very quiet these days."

Graham entered the room at that moment, preventing Violet from asking any one of the thousand questions that filled her mind. Susanna fled to the servants' stairs.

Graham greeted Mr. Harper and invited him to the dining room to share a bottle of port and discuss business. Violet understood this was her cue to depart. "Mr. Harper, good evening." She retreated toward the main staircase without a glance at Graham. As her foot touched the bottom stair, Mr. Harper called out, "Mrs. Morgan?"

She turned back. "Yes?"

"It was indeed a delight to see you this evening. To see you feeling well, that is. I trust I might have the pleasure of another dinner invitation soon?"

Violet glanced at Graham. "Perhaps, Mr. Harper, depending upon my husband's schedule and inclinations, of course. Good night."

October 1861

Where was Susanna?

Violet had slipped into the back room for a mere fifteen minutes or so. "Susanna?" she called into the shop. Nothing.

How curious. Susanna typically stayed molded to her side as tight as a piece of boning. It wasn't like her to wander off.

Where would she go, anyway? Perhaps she'd just gone down to the candy seller for a piece of licorice. Violet would reprimand her when she returned.

She sat down to make a list of tasks. Her arm had healed to the point that writing caused only minor discomfort. She needed to send a note canceling one of the professional mourners for the Griffin funeral. Oh, and Will really needed to thoroughly scrub the small glass carriage again. It was covered in smuts and not acceptable for a society funeral. She continued filling out her considerable list.

. . . Visit Messers. Hooper & Co in Covent Garden
   about their wreaths and wreath cases.
New draperies for interior of society carriage. New color?
Write to Whitby Jet Works for more stock of earrings.
See to memorial cards for Mrs. Watson, Mr. Watson
   wishes angel with weeping willow design.
Look through mourning stationery for samples of most recent styles.

Which reminded her, she needed to inventory their closets. She went first to the chemicals closet, where Morgan Undertaking kept not only embalming preparations, but fragrances, makeup, clean brushes, and cleaning supplies, as well as other miscellaneous items. She opened the door to examine the shelves, making counts against a chart she kept tacked behind the door, enabling her to know when they were running low on anything to ensure she reordered long before anything ran out. It would never do to tell a family that a funeral couldn't proceed for lack of medium beige number four.

She glanced at a clock on a table outside the closet. Another half hour Susanna had been gone. What was she up to?

I'll wait fifteen more minutes, then go into the street and search for her myself.

Her attention was diverted by what was on the shelves. Or, rather, what wasn't on them. She distinctly remembered storing a selection of coffin samples on this lower shelf. Only two were left. Where were the others?

Coffinmakers frequently provided undertakers with miniature versions of their wares, replete with whatever linings, handles, and brass commemorative plates would be included. Shelley & May, a large and reputable manufacturer in Birmingham, had recently sent a collection of new designs, so Violet stored the previous styles in the linen closet, thinking they might have some other use one day.

Had she found a use for them and forgotten about it in all of the tumult of the train crash and caring for Susanna?

Maybe.

She moved next to the linen closet to inspect their store of fabrics. Hmm, this was curious, too. Violet was certain she'd ordered a considerable amount of winding sheet linen, as well as some fine white silk for pall cloths that would be used on children's coffins. Children's funerals were always white, as opposed to the severe black used for adults. She'd only coordinated a handful of children's funerals lately, including that of the poor child in the tunnel. Not enough to have decimated their stock.

She flipped to the page in her chart detailing their fabric holdings. There should be at least twenty yards of white silk in here.

Did the train crash completely addle my mind?

She decided to ask Graham about it at the first opportunity.

Violet was distracted by the sound of someone entering the shop. Quickly returning her chart back to its place, she went out to the front of the shop. Susanna had Mrs. Softpaws in her arms, but her fur was filthy and matted.

"Susanna! Where in the world have you been?"

The girl shrugged.

"Did you go to the candy store? To see Mrs. Overfelt? Somewhere else?"

Another shrug.

"Perhaps you and Mrs. Softpaws were somewhere you shouldn't have been? Like playing in street puddles?"

Susanna lowered her head, slowly nodding it once.

For the first time, Violet was irritated by Susanna's inability to talk. "I'll not have you acting like a hoyden. It's dangerous for a young woman to traipse the streets of London alone, and who could possibly know if you were in distress, since you can't shout for help? Do not *ever* run off like that again, do you understand me?"

Susanna set her lips in a stubborn line, her eyes narrowed, but she nodded.

Violet took a breath. "I'm sorry. I keep forgetting that you were in that horrible wreck, too, and surely you were more affected than I was. However, I can't be made to worry myself into a deranged state because you want to go off somewhere alone to play. You'll have to find your amusements with Mrs. Softpaws at home."

Susanna acknowledged nothing, but put the cat down and started straightening up the mourning card samples kept in a silver tray on the counter.

Violet had no idea children could be so frustrating. More so than husbands, except that she found she couldn't *stay* mad at Susanna. Her heart wouldn't allow it.

Much as she detested household work, the experience with Mrs. Scrope had taught Violet not to let the silver out of her sight. So when it showed a desperate need for polishing, she knew that, despite her growing trust in the Porters, she would have to be involved in the cleaning.

She and Mr. Porter washed the silver together in the scullery with Susanna helping while Mrs. Porter was busy in the kitchen with the week's laundry. After sifting through the stored pieces to pull out those that were tarnished, Violet and Walter Porter sat at the long table in the scullery with the silver heaped in the center of it and several basins before them.

Susanna sorted through the pile and pulled pieces to be cleaned, starting with the largest pieces first. She would hand a bowl or carafe to Mr. Porter, who dipped it into his bowl of potash water and washed it, then dipped it into a secondary tub of clean water to rinse it. He then handed the piece off to Violet, who immersed it in her own solution of salt, alum, saltpeter, and water for several minutes to remove tarnish. She then returned the piece to Susanna, who polished it dry with a piece of chamois leather.

They worked their way through a variety of bowls, candelabra, serving pieces and, finally, silverware. As they neared the end of their task, everyone's hands were chapped and sore. They took a cup of tea with Mrs. Porter in the kitchen, then carried the cleaned silver inside crates back up to the dining room.

Violet was replacing a decorative punch bowl when Graham burst into the house, brandishing a newspaper. Perhaps now she could ask him about the missing coffins and fabric, provided he would speak to her.

"Graham, did you—"

"Have you seen *The Times* today?"

"No, the household has been busy polish—"

He held up a hand. "Mr. Porter, can you see to my jacket? It has a stain here on the lapel."

"Of course, Mr. Morgan, right away." Mr. Porter helped Graham out of the offending coat and left the room, Susanna trailing behind him.

Graham resumed what he was saying. "Today's headline proves what I've been saying about the Americans all along. Look."

Violet took the paper and studied the article he stabbed at with his finger. All thought of missing supplies fled as she read the news.

> It requires a strong effort of self-restraint to discuss with coolness the intelligence we publish today. An English mail steamer, sailing under the British flag, and carrying letters and passengers from a Spanish port to England, has been stopped on the high seas and overhauled. Four of the passengers have been taken out and carried off as prisoners, claiming and vainly claiming, as they were being forced away, the protection of the flag of Great Britain. These are the naked facts.
>
> . . . When such tremendous interests are at stake we feel deeply the responsibility of discussing a question like this. Our first duty is to calm—certainly not to inflame—the general indignation which will be felt in these islands as the news is told. We cannot yet believe, although the evidence is strong, that it is the fixed determination of the Government of the Northern States to force a quarrel upon the Powers of Europe. We hope therefore that our people will not meet this provocation with an outburst of passion, or rush to resentment without full consideration of

> all the bearings of the case. On the other hand,
> we appeal to reasonable men of the Federal
> States—and they have some reasonable men
> among them—not to provoke war by such acts
> as these. . . .

She looked up. "I don't understand. Isn't Britain neutral in the American war? Why would they stop a British ship? Does it say whether . . . let's see, was the ship taken by the Northerners or the Confederacy?"

"The North. There's another article farther inside that explains the situation. One of the North's frigates, the USS *San Jacinto*, intercepted the RMS *Trent*, had the audacity to storm it, and removed two Confederate diplomats, Messrs. James Mason and John Slidell, whom the ship picked up to bring back to England for some sort of diplomatic discussions. Now they rot in jail in Boston."

"And the reason you are angry that two Americans are in jail is . . . ?"

"Honestly, Violet, you understand nothing about politics. Britain is not neutral in just this war; we have always been neutral in waters all over the world. This Northern aggression is intolerable. Why, it's a declaration of war upon us. Mark my words, Parliament will demand an apology, and if they don't get one, you can count on Her Majesty's navy sailing across the Atlantic to put them in their place."

Violet shuddered at his words. A third war with the United States? Truly? Even more disturbing was Graham's relish at the prospect.

"How will this impact your dealings with Mr. Harper?"

"Our dealings with Mr. Harper will flourish no matter what."

Now, what did that mean?

Parliament did indeed demand an apology for the *Trent* incident, which the North was disinclined to give, then moved to strengthen Great Britain's military forces in Canada and in the Atlantic. Graham talked of nothing else, perpetually turning the pages of newspapers and angrily circling editorials and penning his own comments in the margins. At least he hadn't extended his anger outside their home. To share his views with their customers would destroy their business. An undertaker must be viewed as concerned with spiritual matters only, much like a man of the cloth. Any acknowledgment of, much less an expressed opinion about, the world's events would tarnish their reputation permanently.

Mr. Harper and Fletcher stopped by on two separate occasions for discussions with Graham behind locked doors. Graham did not proffer an additional dinner invitation to his brother and business partner, although both made it a point to seek Violet out for greeting and farewell during their visits.

Her concern for whatever Graham might be doing was obscured by her discovery that another undertaking shop in London was going out of business. The moment she had free time, she took Susanna along with her to visit this shop, knowing they would be divesting themselves of supplies and fixtures.

She wasn't disappointed. Hargrove Brothers possessed an admirable selection of funerary goods. Martin Hargrove, the eldest of the brothers, thin and pinched-looking, explained that they were moving their business out to Bristol where their parents lived, and found it easier to reequip a new shop than attempt to have everything transferred there.

Violet purchased a quantity of coffin inscription plates in a range of metals to accommodate all levels of funerals, from pure silver plates for the most elegant of funerals to brass, lead, and, finally, tin plates for modest services. She also bought their stock of German metal plates, which looked like silver but were inexpensive, for those of her customers who wished to add an elegant touch to a humble coffin.

Hargrove Brothers also had an interesting assortment of wares that catered to funeral fashions inspired by the rise in spiritualism occurring over the past decade. Most popular now were safety coffins with corded bells, intended so that a person accidentally buried alive could communicate with the outside world. These safety coffins had multiple designs, including some with air tubes, installed windows, and communication "trumpets."

There was increasing fear in Britain of being buried alive, a fear that escalated after outbreaks of fevers and choleras, which could carry someone off swiftly. Violet recalled Admiral Herbert's widow in a dither over her husband not having a finger bell to signal the outside world if he awoke from his death slumber.

She purchased a few samples of safety coffins to meet the growing demand for them, despite her serious misgivings of their worth.

Violet ignored the Hargroves' mawkishly sentimental selection of postcards of such scenes as a child in a roomful of mourners holding her hands upward toward an angelic view of a woman, presumably her mother, with a poem to the deceased inscribed below. Such items diverted from death's great dignity, in Violet's estimation, and she never suggested them to her customers.

Of greatest interest was the ornately carved walnut counter at the rear of the shop. It wasn't made in mahogany, which was all the rage in England these days. Just that distinction made it unique, even before its detailed design. "Is this for sale as well?"

"Certainly. Actually, this counter was here when we moved in nearly thirty years ago. I believe this was originally a draper's shop, hence all of the storage drawers and cabinets behind it."

Violet stepped behind the counter and pulled on the various knobs and handles attached to drawers, compartments, and doors. A brass plate, discreetly nailed inside the side of one drawer, read "Boyce and Sons Cabinetmakers."

"It has a secret compartment, too." Mr. Hargrove joined Violet behind the counter and knelt down, pressing along a nearly invisible seam in the wood. When he reached the right point, a door popped open as if from nowhere. Inside was a shelf containing nothing but a few curled scraps of paper.

"Believe it or not, my brother found a couple of lead balls and some lint cloths in here. Someone must have used it as a hiding place for an old flintlock pistol."

It was spectacular. Violet had to have it, no matter the cost. Already she was mentally arranging her own supplies in it.

Susanna's expression reflected how impressed even she was with the walnut counter.

"Shall I buy this?" Violet asked with a smile.

Susanna patted the top of it and nodded.

After finalizing all of her purchases and payment with Mr. Hargrove, Violet and Susanna left, stopping for a quick meal before arranging with a delivery company to have everything transported to Morgan Undertaking.

Violet offered her old counter to Mary Overfelt, who accepted it happily, and had the delivery men take it to her after installing her own new counter. It was an extraordinary addition to their shop and Graham had no complaint over it. Actually, he hardly noticed it.

Once Violet and Susanna put all of their new supplies away and restocked the new counter, Violet stood back to survey the shop.

Something was wrong.

Susanna pointed at the counter and made a sweeping motion with her hand.

"I agree with you completely," Violet said. "We need an extension of the counter to form an 'L' around the wall, don't we?"

Yes.

"Perhaps we can go to the original cabinetmaker to see about having it made; what do you think?"

Yes.

"It seems to me we need window draperies worthy of this elegant new counter. Perhaps Mrs. Overfelt can help us."

Yes, yes.

She and Susanna set off on making more arrangements, first stopping to see Mary to order new draperies to frame the shop's front window, then on to Boyce and Sons Cabinetmakers on Curtain Road inside the old city of London to discuss having an identical counter made to one they had made so many years ago for a draper's shop. Exquisite samples of clocks, chairs, and musical instruments lined the walls.

Mr. Putnam Boyce, a spry, elderly man, chuckled softly as Violet described the counter and where she'd bought it. "Of course I remember it. I made it for my wife about forty years ago. My lovely Belle owned Stirling Drapers. But she sold it to her assistant when we married and she joined me here to do upholstery. Sounds like undertakers took over the shop later."

"Might I meet your wife?"

The old man's eyes misted over. "Ah, now that wouldn't be possible, would it? I lost her in the cholera epidemic of forty-nine."

"That was a terrible time for London. I'm so sorry for your loss."

He wiped his eyes with the back of his hands. "Anyway, I have two strapping sons to remind me of her each and every day, and I would be happy to make this counter a second time, Mrs. Morgan. 'Twould be a way to take myself back to happier days."

"I look forward to it. Tell me, Mr. Boyce, do you make coffins?"

"When I'm asked. It's good business in slow times."

Violet reached out and caressed a grandfather clock case. "If you invest just part of the love and care into a coffin that you do into your furniture, I'd say you probably create very fine resting places. I'd like to hire you as one of my coffin suppliers."

"I am indeed flattered, Mrs. Morgan. Do you want me to make some pine boxes up and deliver them to you along with the counter?"

"No. Just make up one sample in pine, and I'll order others as I need them. It's best to have fresh-sawn wood for coffins, for . . . indelicate smells. I'm sure you understand."

The old man's eyes crinkled as he smiled. "I do. There's nothing quite like the aroma of newly shaved pine to fill a room, is there?"

"Thank you, Mr. Boyce. I do believe you and I will work well together."

The elder Mr. Boyce and his sons delivered the new counter, a perfect match to the original, in a few weeks' time. They arranged it in place to created the desired "L" configuration, and the entire arrangement looked as though it had been built for her shop.

Violet and Susanna worked quickly to fill the counter and place display trays of mourning brooches, jet jewelry, mourning cards, and coffin plates. Atop the counter Violet placed her cabinet cards and samples of mourning gloves, hats, and other accoutrements from Mary's shop as samples of the Overfelt work for customers to see and feel. Many of them either ordered accessories through Violet, or, if they needed complicated wardrobes, she gave them Mary's card and sent them there.

As Violet surveyed her renovated shop with Susanna at her side, she said, "It seems to me that all of my talents in life are confined here, and do not extend to anything outside these four walls."

Susanna shook her head and patted her own chest.

Violet smiled. "Thank you, sweetheart. I must admit, you do give me comfort."

Windsor Castle
November 13, 1861

The queen was worried about her husband's comfort as he paced back and forth in front of her. Their son Bertie, the Prince of Wales, was utterly incorrigible and their greatest worry. How could they ever rest, knowing that England's future lay in the hands of that wastrel?

Of more immediate concern was Albert's health, which was deteriorating quickly, thanks to Bertie. Her husband's eyes were deep-sunken and his complexion ashen.

He needed a short rest. Perhaps she'd suggest that they spend some time at Osborne House. Albert had personally designed the house on their thousand-acre estate on the Isle of Wight. His love for architecture and design was unparalleled. It was their favorite retreat, and they'd spent many a Christmas there with their large brood of children.

One member of which was causing her husband no end of distress.

She stood and put her arms around his waist to calm him. After twenty-two years of marriage, Victoria was drawn to her husband with a passion and desire she didn't believe was possible between a man and woman. Even now, as he ranted about Bertie's latest escapade, her mind drifted off to more intimate thoughts.

Albert gently removed her arms so he could continue pacing and seething about his eldest son.

"I received confirmation that Bertie has indeed formed a liaison with that actress, that frequenter of dance halls, Miss Clifden. He's even had her here, to Windsor. She's already going by the nickname of 'the Princess of Wales.' She'll probably get with child, and of course our son will be the reputed father."

Albert was working himself into a fine lather. Perhaps Victoria should stop him now before he hurt himself. But Albert was not to be stopped.

"If this happens, and he tries to deny it, she'll drag him into a court of law to force him to own it, and right there in the witness box, she'll be able to give the greedy multitudes the salacious details of their relationship for the sake of convincing the jury. Imagine the Prince of Wales being cross-examined by an attorney and hooted and yelled at by a lawless mob!"

Albert was sweating, the droplets on his forehead making him look even more sickly.

"There's more, of course. I cannot share with you the disgusting details of his profligacy. What a horrible prospect, which this young woman has in her power, to break our hearts, Victoria." He finally stopped, panting.

Victoria sighed heavily. "Oh, that boy. Much as I pity him, I never can or shall look at him without a shudder."

"I must write to him now," Albert said.

Victoria watched over her husband's shoulder as he poured out his grievances against his son on paper. The task exhausted him and he sat back, shivering. "I've lost faith and hope for our son, and with it I believe I am losing interest in life."

Now it was Victoria's turn to shiver. "What are you saying? I'll not listen to such talk. I'm sure your letter will shock Bertie into taking more responsibility for himself and his actions. It was most strongly worded."

"Perhaps, perhaps."

"You should focus on your other duties. Don't you have plans to visit Sandhurst next week? You've taken such interest there."

"Yes, to inspect the buildings for the new staff college and military academy."

She kissed his sweat-beaded forehead. "It will be good for you, my love. It will take your mind away from our son's behavior. You have nights of such great worry and sorrow. It makes you weak and tired."

Albert went to Sandhurst, but it had little good effect on his health. The day of his visit it poured rain and he returned to Windsor drenched and complaining of exhaustion and rheumatic pains. He went to bed, and Victoria sat by his side for a day until he felt better.

So much better did he feel, that he decided to visit the Prince of Wales at Madingley, Bertie's residence at Cambridge University, for a personal interview as a follow-up to his unanswered letter. The day of his visit was chilly and stormy, yet father and son took a long walk together for private discussion away from prying eyes and ears.

Back at Windsor, Albert grew worse, complaining of pains in his back and legs, weariness, and weakness. He had to take frequent rests.

"Don't worry, my love," Victoria told him. "I've sent for Dr. Clark. He'll make you well again."

She had complete confidence that this would be so. Victoria's commands were always followed.

Henry Adams reported the latest news from home to his father. "Everyone at home is jubilant over this situation regarding the *Trent* Affair. Every newspaper I can find applauds it, the House of Representatives passed a resolution commending the captain of the USS *San Jacinto,* and worse, Navy Secretary Welles called the captain a hero."

"Have anyone in the British government read about this?"

"Presumably so."

Charles Francis turned to the window inside the study of his rented residence and peered down at the busy traffic scene below. Horses and carriages competed with pedestrians and street vendors in a chaotic melee that would put New York to shame. London was a bustling, frenzied city, full of paradoxes. Relief societies worked tirelessly to cure hunger and homelessness, while crime and prostitution went on unchecked in parts of London. Yet she was a fiercely proud city. News of his country's apparent hostility would not be taken well by a country used to being in command of the high seas.

When Lords Russell and Palmerston discovered the North's perfidy, what would happen to their accommodation of his stealthy stalking of commerce raider builders? They might find themselves dispatched on a fishing trawler to find their own way home.

Charles Francis sighed. Nothing ever occurred simply or as expected in matters of diplomacy. "Is there anything else?"

"Just a letter from Uncle Henry." His son handed him the envelope.

If Charles Francis hoped to be encouraged by a friendly missive from his brother, he was sorely mistaken. The letter was no enthusiastic cheer over a perceived Northern victory in the capture of Mason and Slidell, the Confederate diplomats taken from *Trent* and jailed. Instead, it was a rant over what he saw as a criminal act by the United States. Seizing the two men was, in his opinion, no better than the search and impressment that the British Navy had always conducted—a practice that the United States had opposed since its founding.

Worse, he thought Charles Francis was complicit in the whole thing.

> *Good God, what's got into you all? What in Hell do you mean by deserting now the great principles of our fathers; by returning to the vomit of that dog Great Britain? What do you mean by asserting now principles against which every Adams yet has protested and resisted? You're mad, all of you.*

"Surely our government will release the men and issue an apology to Britain, Father. If for no reason than a recognition of long-standing international law."

"I'm not so sure, son. Britons can be stubbornly proud, and we are even worse. If my brother's opinion is that our actions constituted an act of impressment and were dishonorable, then American minds will be changed over it. If we continue to crow and beat our chests over it, I believe we are in for a very difficult situation with Britain."

"Are you suggesting they might want to go to war with us?"

"It's a possibility, yes."

Henry blanched before him, and Charles Francis was certain his own face was the same shade of white.

"Father, how can we ever hope to win our war with the South if Britain sends her warships to our shores to do battle with us?"

"We can't. We'll be lost and the nation divided forever, each side ripe for the plucking by other predatory nations."

Henry picked up writing supplies from a desk and poised himself, as if ready to go to battle with pen and paper. "What shall we do, then?"

"We'll have to seek royal interference, I believe."

"The prince is laid low by illness right now."

"I'm afraid that in this case, the prince will have to rally himself out of bed. Britain's security—and ours—depends upon it."

> *Dearest diary, I see that my recent entries have been few and far between. I've had much to occupy my waking moments as of late, and little time to share my deep thoughts.*
>
> *They say the prince consort is ill, although the newspapers don't report it. How do I know? Someone like me can be both inconspicuous and fawning. Some might call me a toady if they didn't know my real self. And, of course, they don't. I move among all classes of people, and because they don't know me, they say any foolish thing in front of me. I try never to discard anything*

*I learn, for you never know when some meaningless piece
of information will later lead to your fortune.*

*'Twould be an interesting development if the prince
died. I wonder what it would be like to kill someone
so famous and important. I suspect most would find it
difficult, but my own method has proven nearly
undetectable.*

*To kill the prince would be enthralling for sure, but of
no value. What can the prince consort possibly offer me?
However, there are others closer to me who can offer much
more in their demises. . . .*

❧ 10 ❦

The rich man in his castle,
The poor man at his gate,
God made them, high or lowly,
And ordered their estate.

—Mrs. Cecil Frances Alexander (1818–1895)
"All Things Bright and Beautiful" (1848)

Accepting Mary's invitation to go shopping along Oxford Street, Violet and Susanna walked to the dressmaker's shop, and together they walked to their destination, spending an afternoon in and out of different shops. Violet noticed signs tacked up on buildings and in windows, reading, "Outrage on the British Flag!" and "Release Mason and Slidell!"

The papers were whipping up public enthusiasm for an attack on the United States for its unprovoked harassment against Britain by boarding one of its ships. Between *The Times* and Graham, she was sick to death of the entire subject.

Mary purchased several pairs of scissors at an ironmonger's, while Violet finally visited a doll shop to browse for more playthings for Susanna. Sometimes the girl was so much older than her age, and at other times she reverted back to a mere child. Since the train accident, Susanna had been a quiet, reserved adult. Today, Violet planned to bring out the child.

The C. Laurent Fashion Dolls shop was run by a tall, elderly woman with an almost regal bearing, as if selling dolls were the equivalent of hosting a diplomatic reception.

That bearing, though, belied her very gentle, soft-spoken nature. "How may I help you?"

"Are you Mrs. Laurent?"

"No, that was my mother. She passed away about twenty-five years ago. I'm Elizabeth Greycliffe Peters. Pleased to meet you." The women shook hands.

"It looks as though your daughter is quite enamored with the dollhouse in the window." Susanna was poking around inside a miniature house that reminded Violet of the sparkling stone Regency townhomes of Brighton. "That's our Barclay House model, and we have many furniture pieces that will fit it, as well as a set of dolls in society clothing that are appropriate to the model."

Susanna's face was so suffused with joy over the assortment of sofas, tables, beds, and lamps she could move around from room to room and floor to floor that Violet was powerless to keep from buying the house, the doll family, and every stick of furniture the shop owner recommended. Mrs. Peters promised to deliver everything the following day.

They left the doll shop and stopped for tea. They nibbled on sweets and sipped cups of Earl Grey at their table next to a window overlooking the street. Violet and Mary discussed the purchases of the day, while Susanna was entirely preoccupied with her almond scone.

They were not to be left in peace, however, as a group of old jacktars—notable by their leathery, wrinkled skin that had surely seen too many years of sun while at sea—marched past their restaurant, shouting obscenities and waving fists in a fury over the slight the Royal Navy had suffered because of the U.S. boarding of *Trent*. Their ages made no difference to their physiques, as most of them were still barrel-chested and powerfully built from years of climbing up masts. They all wore their uniforms of white pants, shirt, and cap, with dark kerchiefs tied around their shoulders.

One of the men, even more intimidating than the rest with a shock of snow white hair on his head, stopped the others and pointed at the restaurant before parting from his mates and entering the establishment. The maitre d' hurried to the front of the restaurant to confront the sailor. A muted argument ensued, with the sailor pointing out to his friends and back to the restaurant, and the maitre d' waving his hands "no" in front of the man.

Finally throwing up his hands in disgust, the sailor stomped out of the restaurant to rejoin his compatriots.

Violet breathed a sigh of relief. At least there would be no violent altercations to ruin their meal.

Moments later, glass exploded next to them as a brick came hurtling through a nearby window. It missed Susanna's head by mere inches as it found its landing spot on an empty table near them.

Violet jumped up, trembling, as she brushed shards out of her hair and off her dress. "Mary, Susanna, are you all right?" They both nodded, their eyes wide in shock. The restaurant was pandemonium as patrons rose, shouting and pointing as they fled through the rear of the building. The maitre d' was helpless in controlling the situation.

Violet felt bile rising in her throat.

Enough.

Enough of men brutishly throwing tantrums. Enough of the flying fur over what the Americans were doing.

Especially enough where it concerned any harm coming to Susanna.

"Excuse me," she said to the still-dazed Mary and Susanna.

Violet marched through the chaos of the restaurant and out the front door, where the sailors were laughing at what they'd done. She didn't stop until she was eye to eye with the grizzled man who had earlier barged into the restaurant.

Rather, she stood eye to chest with him. He was taller and wider than he'd seemed from inside the restaurant. She was too angry to care.

"How dare you. You and your, your *friends*. You think your outrage over some perceived slight against Her Majesty's Navy, your pride, or your oafish ideals entitles you to attack innocent women—"

"Madam, we didn't mean it against you—"

"—and children who are peaceably minding—"

"We just wanted the owner to be patriotic and offer a few old tars a meal—"

"—their own business. Sir, you are a bully and a disgrace to Her Majesty's Navy."

"Madam, we are not—"

"So I suggest that you and your fellow tars mind your own business, stop worrying about other countries, and retire to your own tavern wherever it is that you live."

Violet knew she was causing a worse scene than the jack-tars were, but it was too late to do anything about it. Honestly, all of this posturing about what was happening across the Atlantic was ridiculous.

The sailor and his friends gaped at her for several seconds, nonplussed at the unexpected outrage from a restaurant patron, but Violet maintained her hard stare at the man who could have killed Susanna with his recklessness. Two near misses were all she would tolerate.

The man swallowed and blinked. "We meant no offense, madam. Good day." He nodded at her and shuffled off with his friends.

She rejoined Mary and Susanna back inside the restaurant, where they stood, open-mouthed at her exchange with the sailors. Before they left, the maitre d' approached them, inviting madam back for a complimentary meal at any time of her choosing.

The trio returned home silently, each lost in her own thoughts about the day's events, the dollhouse forgotten.

Henry was right about the prince, Charles Francis thought, observing the man's gray pallor. He was also subject to bouts of sweating, which he attempted to ignore by casually pouring glasses of water from a carafe, but a servant was refilling the carafe with alarming frequency.

Charles Francis had to admire Prince Albert, though, for his dedication to his work. A true servant to his country, the man was. Albert sat behind a desk inside Windsor Castle with Charles Francis, Henry, and Lord Russell gathered around to discuss the British reaction to the *Trent* Affair.

"Palmerston is beside himself," Lord Russell said. "He assembled his cabinet and told us, 'You may stand for this, but damned if I will!' which drew cheers from many. I must tell you, gentlemen, that he asked me to draft a message to Lord Lyons, our minister to the United States, directing him to demand an apology from the Lincoln administration for its violation of international law, as well as to demand the immediate release of Mason and Slidell to British custody."

"Or else . . . ?" Charles Francis asked.

Lord Russell casually poured his own glass of water from the carafe on the desk. "Or else Britain will cut off diplomatic ties with the United States."

Henry's glance surely reflected his own disappointment in things.

"I see," Charles Francis said, waiting to see if there was more. There was.

"In addition, our Atlantic fleet has been put on alert, and plans are being made to send eight thousand troops to Canada. I'm afraid we may have war between our countries."

The worst of news.

Prince Albert spoke, his voice quiet but commanding. "However, at my behest, the queen included in the dispatch her hope that the captain of the USS San *Jacinto* acted without the knowledge or approval of your government or military superiors, and that she presumed the United States had not intended to insult us."

Charles Francis sat back in his leather chair and crossed one leg over the other. "Thereby giving us the opportunity to apologize for the misunderstanding, while saving face diplomatically."

"Precisely. I can also inform you that Prime Minister Palmerston accepted these changes, despite his great anger. I believe a more softened position will benefit both of our nations." The prince opened a desk drawer and pulled out a packet, withdrawing a letter from it. "This is the final letter, and we would like your endorsement by writing a separate letter to accompany it to President Lincoln, expressing your support for this solution."

Charles Francis addressed his next statement to Lord Russell. "Presumably my other activities will not be interfered with as a result of my cooperation."

"What activities are those?" Russell asked.

"Your discretion is appreciated, sir."

They agreed that Henry would draft his father's dictation that very day, to ensure quick dispatch of Britain's official position on the *Trent* Affair.

The prince downed a final glass of water. "And now, I believe I shall take a small rest. Negotiations can be quite exhausting." Albert rose, signaling that their meeting was over.

Charles Francis smiled. He would have sent such a letter without the implied threat, for he, too, wanted all to remain well between their countries. An assurance that he would be left alone to pursue commerce raiders was a sweet extra.

"Those swanky new steam-powered ships have nothing on a good sail when the wind is right, eh?" Fletcher grinned through the rivulets of sweat coursing down his face despite the cool fall weather. "And they have to constantly stop for re-coaling."

Graham grunted as he shoved a coffin farther inside the hold. "You may be faster under a brisk wind, but it's of no advantage if the wind dies down for even an hour. Nor if you run into a recently re-coaled steam ship. Let's just hope our sample run works."

"It will, brother, it will."

Graham hoped so. They were loading coffins and a variety of other funerary supplies aboard *Lillian Rose*. One coffin, made easily accessible, was filled with muslin wrapped tightly around a wax figure obtained from Madame Tussauds. The remaining coffins were stacked tightly together, in hopes that, if stopped, authorities would find it too onerous to check the remaining boxes.

"What do you hear from Mr. Harper?" Graham asked.

"Nothing much."

Graham rapped his knuckles in frustration against the side of a coffin. "Doesn't it strike you as a bit strange that Mr. Harper seems to be avoiding us? It's taking too long for this deal to come to conclusion."

"I couldn't disagree more. He's understandably cautious, since he's representing a fledgling country. I believe he trusts us, though. We just need to be patient."

"Patient! The man is incomprehensible, and my patience with him would impress Job himself. Do I have to erupt in boils all over my body before Harper makes a decision?"

"Peace, brother. Dealings like this aren't the same as a family relying on you to see a body committed to the ground in three days' time. It takes time and a building of trust. All will be well, I assure you."

Fletcher then changed the subject. "Has Violet made any further inquiries into our work?"

"No."

"She's not the least bit curious? She's always struck me as bright and inquisitive."

"Don't worry about my wife."

"Of course I'm not worried, just wondering—"

Graham gritted his teeth. "As you say, 'peace, brother.' Can we speak of other things? Such as how you intend to explain a wax figure if someone stops your ship and does more than a cursory inspection of the cargo?"

Fletcher grinned. "I'll think of something. I crave such challenges and hope to have such an encounter at some point. A whole herd of Yankees are no match for wits with even one of Her Majesty's humble subjects."

"Fletcher, sometimes I wonder how an idiot like you was born my brother."

"And I wonder how a prig such as yourself ever became mine. Peace, Brother?" He stuck out his hand.

Graham shook it. "Peace. Against my better judgment."

In Graham's judgment, they needed more sources than Samuel Harper. If Fletcher didn't think so, very well, but it wouldn't stop Graham from moving plans forward while Fletcher took this trial cargo across the Atlantic.

❧ 11 ❧

The glories of our blood and state
Are shadows, not substantial things;
There is no armor against Fate,
Death lays his icy hand on kings . . .

—James Shirley (1596–1666)
The Contention of Ajax and Ulysses (1659)

Fletcher hadn't agreed with the idea no matter how many times Graham proposed it, but Graham Morgan was going ahead with it. Fletcher claimed not to be solely focused on profit, but when Graham suggested any alteration to their plans that might benefit Graham's personal plans against America, Fletcher always balked.

If they were partners, why was everything Fletcher's decision?

Mr. Harper, for all of his enthusiasm, had yet to produce a single shilling as a good-faith deposit for their risky work. Fletcher continued imploring Graham to be patient, since Mr. Harper would have many arrangements to make to ensure their transactions were unnoticeable.

Graham pulled his hat farther down on his head as he waited irritably on the bench outside Mr. Adams's office. Some clerk told him to please wait while he went to see if the minister was available.

Available? For an irresistible offer to provide great assistance to the United States? From a reliable trader already known for importing sugar to Boston? To be sure, Americans from either side were unable to act in their own best interests, Mr. Harper with his delaying tactics, and now the Northerner not sure if he had time for Graham.

The door opened and the clerk motioned him inside. They were in an anteroom, sparsely furnished with a couple of chairs, a table with a lamp on it, and a small correspondence desk heaped high with sorted papers on it tucked away in a corner. The door leading to what must be the minister's office was tightly shut.

The clerk sat down in one of the chairs, inviting Graham to join him. The man's fingers were heavily blackened with ink. The minister must have him writing letters night and day. "Now, Mr. Morgan, you say you have an opportunity for Mr. Adams?"

What, now he had to explain it again? Well, he wouldn't, not without the man himself in attendance.

"I do. Will he be joining us presently?"

"Perhaps. He is very busy on diplomatic calls, as you can imagine. If I could assist you . . ."

"No, I'll speak directly to the minister."

The clerk tapped his ink-stained fingers together. "I am not entirely without the resources to respond to your request, Mr. Morgan."

Graham had had enough of intermediaries. "Sir, I will wait here until next week if necessary, but I will present my proposal only to Mr. Adams."

Graham didn't like the smirk on the other man's face.

At that moment, a distinguished, balding man with a chin curtain beard cut thin and close and looking like a horseshoe draped under the chin from one ear to the other entered the room, unbuttoning his frock coat as he tossed some more papers on the correspondence desk.

Graham jumped up. "Your Excellency, I've been waiting to speak to you, sir, I—"

Without a glance at Graham, the man spoke to his clerk. "Henry, please step into my office when you're finished here, as I have an important letter to dictate."

"Right away, sir."

The minister ignored Graham's outstretched hand and entered his office, shutting the door behind him.

Of all the cheek . . .

Aflame with embarrassment, Graham let his hand drop to his side. How dare the man ignore his good English manners in such a blatant way. Obviously Mr. Harper was an exception to American rudeness. The rest were like Minister Adams and perfectly fit the description his grandfather had painted for him so many years ago.

Suddenly, the combined plagues of Violet's nagging, Mr. Harper's reluctance to finalize their deal, Fletcher's inability to join Graham's cause, and the strain of their financial difficulties coalesced into a single ball of wrath in his abdomen.

I will *have things go my way.*

He nodded curtly to the clerk and departed without another word.

As Graham left the building, Charles Francis came back out of his office. "Is he the one?"

"He's one of the two Morgan brothers."

"Daring of him to seek an audience with me."

"Criminals usually are, Father, when they believe they have a foolproof enterprise."

December 3, 1861

The queen rubbed her hands together nervously. "What is it, Sir James?" she asked as the doctor exited Windsor's Blue Room to meet with her. The Blue Room was Albert's favorite room in the castle, and he spent more and more time there now.

The aging physician held up his hands. "I'm honestly not quite sure yet. The prince consort displays a variety of symptoms that could mean any number of illnesses. I shall take a wait-and-see approach."

This was becoming a tiresome answer. Victoria had been distressed by the brown color and dryness of her husband's tongue two nights ago. He'd had a restless sleep that night, too, though his tongue was much improved the next morning. They sent for Sir James Clark, the royal physician-in-ordinary and their principal doctor for over twenty years. Albert had other doctors in attendance as well, but Victoria had always placed utmost faith in Dr. Clark. However, Albert's ongoing illness was worrisome. She wasn't sure a "wait-and-see" attitude was correct in this case.

"Has the apothecary brought more of his elixir? It relieves him so."

"Yes, madam, we gave the prince some ether and Hoffman's drops, and the apothecary will be back again in the morning to see if His Highness requires any other medicines. In addition, I will confer with Dr. Jenner over his condition."

William Jenner had been hired on in February as a physician extraordinary. Unlike the queen's highly esteemed physicians-in-ordinary, he was a second-tier doctor and would hope to one day be promoted to physician-in-ordinary. Dr. Clark's manner had always been so reassuring, so kind, but Dr. Jenner was also a competent and sympathetic physician. Yes, it might be time for his additional opinion.

First, though, she had to address a particularly grating letter from Lord Palmerston, who insisted that His Royal Highness have additional medical advice from a Dr. Watson, as well as from Sir Henry Holland, another physician-in-ordinary, whom she didn't trust as much as she did Clark and Jenner. Not because Palmerston cared about her darling Albert, of course, but because he had all of that pesky business with the Americans he wanted the prince involved in. Could Lord Palmerston not understand that her dearest heart was suffering? That his constitution was weak and she had to protect him at all costs from further doctors, who would simply convince him he was dying?

The man had no decorum.

She checked once more on Albert, who was sprawled listlessly on a sofa in his dressing gown. She whispered, "Take some soup and a little brown bread, will you, darling?" before kissing him and heading off to put Lord Palmerston firmly in his place, certain that she'd left the room before Albert saw the tears running down her face.

December 5, 1861

"So, Mr. Harper, you've seen our ship, you've inspected our proposed goods, and you've met with us repeatedly. Are you finally ready to conclude our negotiations?" Graham saw Fletcher's cautionary look, but he was beyond caring. The three men sat inside the Three Hulls, speaking in low tones over port glasses while a chilly rain drilled against the roof and slid along the windows in sheets.

"Actually, Mr. Morgan, I do have a few more questions." Samuel Harper removed a small pad and pencil from his jacket pocket. "My superiors are, of course, concerned that these shipments not be discovered by any passing ship protecting the blockade. No sense in spending a spectacular fortune in merchandise only to have it fall into your enemy's hands."

Graham clenched his teeth. Now what?

"Can you describe for me what your exact routing is for your ship, and at what point you can slip past the North's blockade? Obviously, we are having a terrible time of it."

"Yet you made it here, Mr. Harper," Graham said.

Fletcher spoke up so smoothly that Graham barely caught the warning note in his voice. "For which we are most grateful. And if you would like us to create a nautical chart of our routes, we are happy to do so. I assume this is the final concern you have?"

Mr. Harper put away his pencil and paper. "Why, yes, I think such a map would conclude our negotiations. In fact, it is my hope that we can see our first shipment delivered before Christmas, which would be a fine present for President Davis."

"Then you won't mind committing to a specific purchase today, contingent on providing you with a shipping map?" Graham asked.

"Surely you understand that although I have given you the highest recommendation, it is imperative that I prove that you are a discreet, experienced operation."

Fletcher broke in again. "We are happy to accommodate you in this, Mr. Harper. Shall we meet again in, say, a week's time to finalize everything?"

"That would be fine." The three stood up to shake hands—why, Graham would never know, since it never meant they were agreed on anything—when Mr. Harper paused, as though a thought had just occurred to him.

"One more thing, how is your wife coming along since her accident?" he said to Graham.

"Violet? She's well. Fully immersed back into undertaking."

"And the girl, Susanna? She was growing into quite the young lady the last time I visited."

Graham shrugged.

"Well, then, please extend my Christmas felicitations to Mrs. Morgan and Susanna." Mr. Harper put on his hat and they all braced themselves to face the dreary weather as they went on their separate ways.

It was an innocent enough statement, but it struck Graham that if Mr. Harper was not planning to be honorable in his dealings with the Morgan brothers, then he might not be so honorable in his intentions toward Violet. The tips of the man's ears went suspiciously red when mentioning Violet's name, too.

It would bear watching.

Violet wrinkled her nose at the bundle of evergreen branches in her hand as she surveyed the boxes of dried fruit, pinecones, and ribbons scattered around the drawing room.

"How will we ever turn this into a set of pretty garlands and wreaths, Susanna?" she asked. "Perhaps we should ask—" Graham came through the door at that moment, water sluicing down the back of his jacket. Mr. Porter rushed to the front door to take his hat and coat away.

"Good evening," she said, but Graham appeared too distressed to even notice that his wife had destroyed the interior of their home with all manner of Christmas decorations.

"Is something wrong?"

"No, no, nothing for you to worry about. What does Mrs. Porter have planned for dinner?"

"Roasted pork loin, I think. Here, would you like to help string some popcorn with us?" She offered him a tin of supplies, but he turned away.

"I have serious business concerns and you want me to play with silly bits of greenery and string? Unlikely. Send Mr. Porter for me when my meal is ready." And with that, he went upstairs, presumably to nurse whatever irritation was crawling about under his skin.

Hiding her own irritation that her husband gave no recognition whatsoever of her efforts to decorate their home for the season, Violet smiled and said, "Well, then, I suppose that's all the more popcorn garlands for you and me to make."

While Graham might try to make the atmosphere impossible in their home, Violet intended to try her best to make it a joyful Christmas for Susanna.

December 6, 1861

Lord Palmerston opened the letter, marked "Confidential." The queen had put him off in strong terms, but he had his allies in the palace who reported to him regularly. He scanned it quickly.

> *The Prince is, I hope, decidedly better today—and has taken more food since last night than he had done before since Sunday. After your letter I thought it my duty to keep you informed . . . of the state of H.M.'s health, but everything with the subject requires much management. The Prince himself, when ill, is extremely depressed and low, and the Queen becomes so nervous, and so easily alarmed, that the greatest caution is necessary. The suggestions that it could be desirable to call in another Medical Man would I think frighten the Queen very much, and the Prince already is annoyed with the visits of the three who attend him. Sir J. Clark is here daily, and Dr. Jenner, and the Windsor Apothecary also attends him. . . . I hesitate to act on any suggestion of yours—but I sincerely believe that to ask to call another Doctor would do more harm than good. The mere suggestions the other night upset the Queen and agitated Her dreadfully, and it is very essential to*

> *keep up the spirits both of Her and the Prince. H.R.H. has*
> *never kept his bed, and had several hours of sleep last*
> *night.*

He had hardly finished that missive when a clerk tapped on the door to deliver another one.

> *I am sure that you will be very much disappointed and*
> *grieved to hear that the Prince's illness is declared today to*
> *be a gastric fever . . . the symptoms are all favorable . . .*
> *the illness however must have its course, and it always*
> *lasts a month . . . The Queen is at present perfectly*
> *composed . . . but I must tell you, most confidentially,*
> *that it requires no little management to prevent her from*
> *breaking down altogether. . . .*

A prickle of fear coursed through Palmerston. Gastric fever was typically a euphemism for typhoid fever. Although the doctors appeared to have—finally—diagnosed the prince, it sounded as though the queen was becoming unstable. This was cause for concern in the event the prince did not recover.

God help them all if they lost the prince consort's sure and steady hand over Queen Victoria.

This required a note to Lord Russell to inform him of the latest developments in the prince's illness. Palmerston sat at his desk and filled his fountain pen with ink.

On second thought, he should also write to the American minister. Mr. Adams stood to lose greatly without the prince's support.

Palmerston sighed. May as well pen a note to Mrs. O'Kane. There would be no time for dalliances tonight, and his mistress would not be happy about it.

December 7, 1861

"Now, now, madam, I'll not have this sniffling and crying. You must be your husband's rock of strength."

Victoria folded her handkerchief. "Of course, Dr. Jenner. You're right. What were we thinking? We are so grateful you're here now to help Dr. Clark see the prince consort through this bout of feverish cold."

In the end, Victoria had been forced to allow Dr. Watson to see Albert, but she permitted him to do so once, instructing the physician *not* to be in the way. Naturally, the man was of no use whatsoever, as she expected. Lord Palmerston's demand still rankled. She'd deal with him later, once Albert was better and this irritating illness was behind them.

Jenner pulled off his glasses and tapped them against his nose. "Naturally, madam, I defer to the wisdom of Dr. Clark, given his greater experience and knowledge. But I believe I can make a conclusive diagnosis. As you know, the prince presented a plethora of symptoms—insomnia, fever, shivering, stomach pain, nausea, vomiting, and so on—which made a verdict more than difficult."

Dr. Clark, standing nearby, nodded approvingly.

"However, we must be cognizant of the *feverish* symptoms the prince has. Also, this morning we see that a light rash has appeared, and it is an indication." He perched his glasses back on the end of his nose.

"A rash? From what? What does it signify?"

"It is my assessment, and Dr. Clark agrees, that he suffers from typhoid fever—"

"Typhoid fever! This is all Bertie's fault! He must have contracted it when he went to Madingley to talk some sense into that boy. We'll never forgive him, never."

"Now, now, madam, you mustn't fall apart. Stiffen your shoulders. We shall face this head-on and see our dear prince through it, right?"

The queen sniffed but resisted pulling her handkerchief back to her face. "Yes, yes, we shall see him through it."

"Very good. Now, the rash normally appears between the eighth and twelfth day of typhoid. The overall illness lasts between twenty-one and thirty days, meaning that the prince is already at least a third of the way through these symptoms."

"So he might be healed in just a short time?"

"That is one outcome. It is certainly possible that once the symptoms fade away, he can make a gradual recovery."

"Otherwise?"

Jenner hesitated, as though he was fearful to lay out some sort of brutal truth. When he next spoke, it was in a soft and gentle tone. "Otherwise, I'm afraid he will sink further, until he goes to his reward."

Victoria gasped. "That's not possible!"

"Madam, God gives no one a permanent residency on this planet. The prince is no exception. However, it is my hope that we can seize the day, so to speak, and offer him appropriate medicines now that he is properly diagnosed. God may choose to leave him here a while longer yet."

"Does he know?"

"No, madam, I know it is your express wish that he not be informed of any seriousness in his condition. Although I must say, he would certainly take the news far better than you are. Come, come, you can't go in there with your face blotched and puffed. Pull together so you can offer your husband comfort." Jenner offered her his arm.

Victoria leaned against him gratefully. "Yes, we must be a sturdy wife for our dear Albert. Ah, can anyone else understand our great anxiety?"

"Your Majesty, I have long admired the prince. He is the finest specimen of intellectual and moral and religious greatness I have ever known. Would that I could lie in his place so that he could continue on his noble undertakings for this nation without being laid so low."

"Ah, dear Dr. Jenner, you know our dear Albert so well. You are of such comfort to us. As you have always been, Dr. Clark," she added over her shoulder before they disappeared into the Blue Room to offer Albert encouragement.

December 11, 1861

The four physicians—James Clark, William Jenner, Henry Holland, and Thomas Watson—all conferred and came to an identical conclusion: The prince's condition was deteriorating rapidly. It fell to Sir James to tell the queen, while the others ensured a public bulletin was published for the newspapers, stating that the prince's "symptoms have assumed an unfavorable character during today." Vague enough to provide hope, but truthful enough not to deceive.

The Times printed an editorial after receiving the bulletin, opining that:

> . . . the fever which has attacked him is a wearying but weakening malady, but it is well understood, and the treatment in most cases effectual. The Prince has on his side youth and strength, an unimpaired constitution, and the ablest advice that science can give, and we hope shortly to be able to publish a more cheerful Bulletin than that of today.

England held its breath.

December 13, 1861

Violet and the rest of England were avidly reading every edition of the paper, seeking details of the prince consort's condition. She remembered how pale he had looked the day she met him at Admiral Herbert's home, and was not surprised that he was ailing now. She prayed daily for him, as did everyone else in the country.

Today *The Times* had published three different issues, each with an update on the prince's condition. She read the article, which indicated that four different physicians were now attending the prince.

Surely with that much care His Royal Highness will be cured.

Indeed, the article went on to say that he had shown a slight improvement over the past few hours. London went to sleep that night hopeful that Prince Albert's health would eventually be restored.

December 14, 1861

Victoria was certain she might suffocate. The Blue Room was crowded with family members, servants, and government officials, staring at her poor Albert, who lay there so . . . uncomfortably. His breathing was ragged and uneven, and he drifted in and out of sleep. When he was awake, she was gratified that he recognized her, even rising enough to stroke her face and murmur *"liebes Frauchen," dear woman*, his pet name for her.

Dr. Jenner said it wouldn't be long now, but she still refused to believe that Albert could be taken from her. It was impossible, really. She herself had contracted typhoid fever in her childhood, and here she was, nearly forty years later, alive and well. What had happened with Albert?

In a moment of clarity, Albert sat up and grasped her hands. "Listen to me, *liebling*, darling, you must never erect any effigies to me. No monuments, no statues, no signs to mark my existence. I shall go as quietly as I came, do you understand?"

She nodded and kissed his clammy forehead. He was delirious, of course. There was no need to worry about such a future event. Besides, all of Great Britain would certainly want to see him memorialized.

Bertie had traveled overnight to be at his father's side. Victoria had uttered less than a dozen words to him since his arrival. The boy now sat on a chair crouched over his father, weeping. Victoria was not impressed by Bertie's tears, which surely resulted from an accumulation of too many spirits and undesirable women and not from the grief over having been responsible for his father's condition. A worse future king couldn't be found.

Their daughters Vicky, Alice, and Helena were also there, while the remainder of the younger children were kept away. Vicky, the Princess Royal, was the oldest and had always been her father's favorite child. Victoria allowed herself a fleeting smile. Of course Albert doted on Vicky. Who wouldn't love such a precious girl, so dutiful to her parents and intelligent beyond all imagination? Unlike Bertie, she'd followed her parents' wishes and married as they wanted, and was now the Crown Princess of Prussia at the mere age of twenty-one. Such a good girl.

The real angel in the room was Alice, already eighteen and needing a husband. If only Albert were well enough to discuss an appropriate alliance for her. Alice had nearly taken permanent residence in the Blue Room, and sat reading to him, feeding him beef tea, and talking whenever he wanted to talk. Alice sat next to her father's bedside now, holding his hand and talking to him in low tones. Victoria moved closer to listen.

"I should like some music," Albert said. "A fine chorale, played at a distance."

"Of course, Father," Alice replied, and asked that a piano be brought into the room.

Their daughter played "Ein feste Burg ist unser Gott," *A Mighty Fortress Is Our God,* and several others. Victoria wept to see Albert looking upward with such a sweet expression.

So the long day passed into evening, and the queen left the room periodically to compose herself when her combined anxiety and grief threatened to overtake her. Each time she returned to kneel next to Alice by his bedside and take his hand, it was just a little bit colder and his breathing was a little more labored.

As though a gentle hand passed over Albert's face, his features settled into a calm repose. He drew three long, gentle breaths and then . . . was no more.

Dr. Clark announced the time as ten minutes before the hour of eleven o'clock at night. A servant was summoned to have clocks stopped throughout the palace.

Victoria blinked. It couldn't be.

We've been married twenty-two years. We have nine children, the youngest just four years old. How will we—how will the country—survive without you, my darling?

Even worse, how shall I ever face another day on this cruel earth?

Later, she had a vague recollection of the room shifting and moving in a dozen directions around her, then strong hands coming to support her and escort her from Albert's presence. The doctors were huddled around her darling. She tried to form the words to order them away, to give him air, but her tongue was thick and refused to perform the simplest task. All of a sudden, she was in the Red Room, sitting at the same desk where her beloved Albert had so recently written his missive to Bertie.

Left completely alone, she gave herself over to weeping, as noisily and anguished as her heart could bear. Normally a queen of great decorum, she was grateful to be in private, even if she could be heard from outside the door.

For now, she didn't care what anyone thought.

Victoria wailed, heaped curses on God, and bitterly declaimed her bleak future. She pulled at her hair, threw an inkwell, and beat her breast. She paced, prayed on her knees, and considered flinging herself from a window.

After hours of unleashed grief, she finally sat down at Albert's desk, caressing it like an old friend. Albert loved this desk, and they'd spent many an hour here, discussing all manner of things, important and inane.

She sniffled and opened the top drawer, taking out a pen. Ah, Albert always complained about the nib on this pen. It had too fine a point for his taste. She put her lips to the pen and tucked it back inside. Victoria's hand wandered over the contents of the drawer, seeking connection to her husband.

She touched a card and pulled it out.

It was the *carte-de-visite* from that undertaking woman Albert mentioned after the funeral of Admiral Herbert.

"Graham and Violet Morgan," it read. *So that is what a woman who plans funerals looks like.* Albert had been impressed with her, hadn't he? In fact . . . didn't he ask Victoria to remember Mrs. Morgan when he passed on?

She shuddered at the memory. How could Albert have been so prescient? He was always prognosticating his own death, but she'd never paid attention. The thought sent her into a fresh round of sobbing.

Exhausted, she looked at the clock. No servant had dared enter here to stop its movement. It was nearly six o'clock in the morning. Plans would have to be made to have her darling interred. She picked up the card again.

"Truly?" she whispered. "You actually want a woman in attendance upon you, my love? So unseemly. Ah, but what wouldn't I do for you, even in death? Very well, I'll send for her."

December 15, 1861

The bells at St. Paul's Cathedral tolled intermittently all day, speaking in doleful tones the sad news that Francis Albert Augustus Charles Emmanuel, a prince of the House of Saxe-Coburg and Gotha and prince consort to Queen Victoria of the United Kingdom of Great Britain and Ireland, was dead at the age of forty-two.

Streams of citizens crowded outside St. Paul's, anxious to go in and find spiritual comfort over so great a national loss. Clutching Susanna's hand, Violet joined the throngs waiting outside to attend one of the church's daily services.

She felt little comfort afterward as she returned to the shop.

How ironic that I am hardly on speaking terms with Graham, yet we continue to live on together, but the queen's great love for her husband was not enough to keep him in this world.

The poor queen.

The front doorbell tinkled as a man wearing Hanoverian livery of scarlet and blue entered Morgan Undertaking.

"Good afternoon, sir, how may I help you?" she asked.

"Madam, are you Mrs. Morgan, the proprietress?"

"I am."

"I've been instructed to fetch you, madam. The queen wishes to see you at Windsor Castle."

"Susanna . . ." she began, looking at where the girl was cutting newly arrived black ribbons into lengths suitable for embellishing gloves, fans, and bonnets.

"I can drop your daughter off at your home on our way. You'll need to pack for several days. Quickly, the queen awaits."

With Susanna in tow, Violet left the shop in the hands of Will and Harry, her mind whirling with confusion over why the Queen of England wanted to see a lowly London undertaker.

❧ 12 ❧

He is dead and gone, lady,
He is dead and gone;
At his head a grass-green turf,
At his heels a stone.

—William Shakespeare
Hamlet (ca. 1599)

Violet could hardly believe she was being escorted to Windsor
Castle.

Besides Osborne House on the Isle of Wight, Windsor was reputed to be the queen's favorite residence. It was no wonder. The
long approach to the castle's entrance revealed the majesty and
beauty of the castle's perimeter, set in a figure eight around the
center motte, known as the Round Tower.

Built originally by William the Conqueror as part of a ring of cas-
tles established to fortify London, it had long ago been split into
two uses, the Lower Ward at the bottom of the figure eight for
state occasions, and private apartments in the Upper Ward.

Violet was led down a series of hallways into the castle, marveling at the splendor of the paneled walls, priceless objets d'art,
gleaming furniture, and magnificent ceiling decorations.

It was clear she was being led through state rooms and into the
private apartments of the castle.

This was an honor, yet she had no idea why it was being be-
stowed upon her. The queen's servants hadn't been helpful when
questioned, either.

The servant leading her down corridors wore a black crape arm-
band. He paused in front of a door. Raising a finger to his lips, he

whispered, "The queen is in great grief, as we all are. It is best to talk in low tones."

"I am an undertaker and fully understand the grief that family members endure."

He looked at her in surprise. "Yes, of course, madam."

Knocking softly, he opened the door and announced Violet. The queen sat before a desk, and two elegantly dressed gentlemen were in deep conversation with her. All talking stopped as Violet entered.

Violet dropped into a curtsy upon seeing Victoria. The queen's eyes were red-rimmed and swollen as she sat before a desk, working a lace hanky through her fingers. She had a pronounced overbite that made her look vulnerable yet appealing. The queen also looked unkempt, as though she hadn't changed clothes in a few days. She waved at Violet to sit down.

Poor lady. These first few days of shock and disbelief wreaked havoc on a devoted spouse's appearance.

"Mrs. Morgan?" the queen asked, her voice raw.

"Yes, Your Majesty. May I express my deepest sorrow at the loss of the prince consort? All of London mourns with you. St. Paul's was so crowded today that there were extra services planned."

Victoria said nothing, merely staring off at some distant point in the room.

Violet spoke again. "I am deeply honored by your request to see me, although I admit I am puzzled."

Victoria ignored this. "Lord Palmerston, Lord Russell, may we present to you Mrs. Morgan, an undertaker to whom our husband was partial?"

Lord Palmerston was an elderly man with a gleam in his eye that made him seem much younger. "An absolute delight, Mrs. Morgan. You are brightening up an otherwise very sad, somber occasion."

"Lord Palmerston," Victoria said. "Perhaps you might refrain from flirting with married women for at least one day while we are in deep mourning."

"Your Majesty, my apologies. I mean no offense." His voice had no hint of regret.

Lord Russell, who maintained a serious but not stern gaze, appraised her. "Morgan? Where have I heard that name before?"

"I can't imagine, sir. My husband and I have a shop in Paddington and live in Kentish Town. I'm afraid we don't move in illustrious circles."

"Nevertheless . . . well, no matter, I suppose. An undertaker, you say? How odd."

The queen broke in again. "Yet quite favored by our husband. So although we don't approve of women training outside the home, we will make an exception for her. Now, gentlemen, you may be excused, for we have business with Mrs. Morgan."

Lords Palmerston and Russell departed, but not before Palmerston offered Violet a sly wink on the way out.

The queen looked at Violet as though she were examining a new species of furry insect, curious yet revolted.

Violet resisted the urge to squirm like a child under the scrutiny, but the combination of a royal summons, her first walk inside a palace, and now the queen's observation was nerve-wracking.

Finally, the queen spoke. "We understand you were acquainted with our husband?"

"Slightly, Your Majesty. I had the pleasure of meeting the prince consort during the funeral arrangement for Admiral Herbert."

"Yes, so our husband said. He told us you were a most competent undertaker. Is it true that you embalmed the man?"

"Yes, madam, I—"

"Most assuredly, our husband will not be embalmed. The thought of our dear Albert being injected with some noxious concoction of chemicals is beyond bearing."

"Yes, madam." Violet was confused by the queen's outburst, but those who grieved did not always make sense. She sat still while the queen pondered her next statement.

"Our husband . . ." Victoria began, opening a drawer and pulling out a card, Violet's own *carte-de-visite*. The prince had actually kept it. "Expressed a desire for us to call on you in the event of his . . . in case he . . ." Victoria's chin was quivering.

"Your Majesty, I understand perfectly what you are saying, and I am most grateful and flattered by His Majesty's confidence in me. But surely there is a royal undertaker . . . ?"

"Of course there is, Mrs. Morgan. A dignified and experienced *man* who will take the utmost care with our Albert."

Violet was silent. Why was she here?

The queen sighed as she put her lips to the *carte-de-visite* and returned it to the drawer. "Yet, our husband mentioned you by name, so we must honor him. He would be so disappointed otherwise."

Victoria whisked away an errant tear with her forefinger. "Therefore, Mrs. Morgan, we give you leave to participate in the arrangements for the prince consort's funeral."

A royal funeral? Morgan Undertaking involved in a royal funeral? Violet was too shocked to respond.

"Naturally, the royal undertaker will still be in charge, and you will be merely an assistant. His staff knows what to do, which most certainly does not include embalming."

"Yes, Your Majesty." Violet's mind was swirling. First the admiral, now this. It was overwhelming.

"As we've told Mr. Rowland, we want the deepest possible court mourning and expect all persons to put themselves in decent mourning clothing. We've also ordered the building of a new mausoleum at Frogmore, and our husband will be transferred there when it is completed." The queen tinkled a bell on the desk, and instantly a uniformed servant glided in.

"Yes, ma'am?" he asked in a hushed tone.

"Bring Dr. Jenner in."

"Very good, ma'am." The man glided back out soundlessly.

"Dr. Jenner is one of our husband's physicians. Very skillful and most comforting. It was he who made the conclusive diagnosis on our darling—ah, Dr. Jenner, you've come!"

"Had you a doubt I wouldn't leave the halls of Windsor until I had you at rights again? Come now, madam, surely you know better. Who is your friend?" Dr. Jenner's voice boomed inside the room.

Violet was taken aback by how forward the doctor was, yet the queen merely smiled at him.

"Dr. Jenner, this is Mrs. Violet Morgan, the undertaker we spoke to you about."

"Yes, I remember. What is her purpose here today in Your Majesty's presence?"

"Surely you recall that our dear prince wished her services in the sorry case of his . . . if he were to unfortunately . . ." The queen couldn't continue.

"Madam, I didn't think you intended this seriously. We are of the same opinion about women partaking in the professions, especially anything medical."

"Yes, Dr. Jenner, but our opinion of the prince overrides our own personal feelings. Would you please be so kind as to guide her to the chapel?"

"As you wish, madam."

Violet's interview was over. She rose and said to the queen, "Your Majesty, I promise to be as gentle and respectful with the prince consort as is possible."

"He thought you would be, so we have to trust him." The queen turned her back to them as she was engulfed by sobs. Violet attempted to go around the desk to comfort her, as was her habit with grieving families, but Dr. Jenner pulled her away, shaking his head.

They walked together outside the royal apartments, down through the Middle Ward containing the Round Tower, and into the Lower Ward, where St. George's Chapel, a Gothic-designed church, stood proudly to their right.

"It's spectacular," Violet said. "Who would expect such a magnificent cathedral inside the walls of a medieval castle?"

Dr. Jenner looked at her quizzically. "Surely you know that most of the castle was renovated into its consistent medieval look by the prince consort, don't you? The chapel, however, is mostly as it has been for centuries."

He led her down along one buttressed side of the chapel and in through a doorway in the south transept, the center part of the church that formed the wings that made any Gothic church resemble a cross.

Inside, the nave was bustling with feverish, if completely hushed, activity. Already Violet saw a line of black velvet ropes being erected, where the funeral cortege would enter through the rear, western end of the chapel and proceed to the burial place, presumably in either a memorial crypt off one of the side aisles, or a tomb behind the apse.

Dr. Jenner interrupted her imagining of how the funeral would take place.

"I'll take you to meet Mr. Rowland, who is overseeing all of the arrangements," he said, guiding her toward the east end of the chapel.

A short man with a nose the size of an eagle's beak was emerging out of a minor side chapel along the south aisle, as though measuring with his feet. He scowled as he pulled a small notepad from his pocket and jotted something down.

"Mr. Rowland," Dr. Jenner said, his voice ricocheting against the stone walls despite his effort to speak in quiet tones. "The queen commanded that I bring your new assistant to you posthaste. This is Mrs. Morgan."

The man ushered them into the side chapel, which had been converted into an undertaker's workshop with tables heaped with piles of cloth, boxes of candles, and dozens of wreath stands. Beneath the tables lay the flat stone markers in the floor that indicated who was buried beneath.

Mr. Rowland scowled again. "What new assistant?"

"Mrs. Morgan is an undertaker who caught the attention of the prince consort."

"An undertaker? Where is your husband, madam?"

"Managing our shop in London."

"I see." He blinked. Perhaps he was more like an owl than an eagle. He turned back to Dr. Jenner. "What does Her Majesty say my new assistant is to do?"

"Obviously, whatever it is an undertaker's assistant does."

Mr. Rowland grunted. "As busy as we are . . . very well, you may arrange for all of the flowers, and you may be present during the service to help ensure everyone finds his place. Naturally, you will need to remain as discreet as possible."

Naturally.

Dr. Jenner grudgingly helped Violet find temporary quarters within the castle and ensured her luggage, still stored on the carriage, made it to her accommodations.

After sending brief letters to Graham and Mary about her plans at Windsor, she walked the grounds to understand the castle's layout before reentering St. George's Chapel to explore the entire nave, transept, and apse. When she was satisfied that she had memorized the entire surrounds of the funeral, she sought out Mr. Rowland again for further direction.

She was now armed with his instructions for entirely too many lilies and his plans for too little ceremony. She urged Mr. Rowland to increase the number of dignitaries invited, as well as the number of official mourners. His feathers ruffled by her audacity, he merely told her to keep to her tasks and stop bothering him with inane ideas, since it was up to the lord provost to decide such things anyway.

Although she had clearly made an error because she didn't know the intricacies of royal etiquette, it still grated. *Surely I am as competent as Mr. Rowland.* Moreover, she was here at the queen's command, because of the prince consort's specific request. This man's disdain of her was essentially disdain of Victoria and Albert.

How dare he.

"Sir, I am being perfectly civil to you. I understand that this is a trying time for everyone in the country, and you are in a particularly hazardous position in ensuring the prince is laid to rest properly. However, I am here at a royal request, I'm tasked with assisting you, and I intend to do so."

Mr. Rowland blinked his owl eyes again. When he next spoke, he ignored her outburst. "Ahem, the queen plans to send a spray of flowers to the coffin from Osborne House. You may like to know what it will contain so you can plan others accordingly."

"From Osborne House?"

"Yes, she and the children are departing tomorrow. She cannot

The man's guilt was probably oppressive.

It was of no concern to Violet, who merely needed to see the prince consort interred inside St. George's Chapel without anything disastrous occurring. Mr. Rowland had seen to the prince being sealed inside his simple but elegant coffin, which lay nearby on a bier and was draped in a gold-fringed scarlet and blue cloth of state, waiting to be moved to the church. She had had no dealings with laying out the prince, per the queen's direction, but it was obvious from the odor wafting from the coffin that he had been waiting entirely too long for his burial and needed to be interred quickly.

The ongoing chatter and quarrelling meant Violet could not make herself heard to issue instructions. Their self-serving was appalling. Even the clergymen hovering around the group were unable to instill a sense of decorum.

Enough was enough.

She took one man's walking stick from where it was propped against a sofa and thumped it against the floor to get their attention. "Gentlemen!" she said. "I'll not tolerate your misbehavior any longer. Today we are privileged and humbled to witness our beloved prince consort go to his final resting place. It is not only our privilege, but our *duty*, to see it done properly. I'll ask you now to pay close attention so we may begin."

The men were startled enough by her commanding tone to immediately do as she demanded. She quickly reviewed the procession order and nodded that they were in their proper places. Among the royal relatives in attendance were Albert's brother, the duke of Saxe-Coburg and Gotha; the Duke of Cambridge; the Crown Prince of Prussia; Prince Louis of Hesse; and the queen's nephew, the Prince of Leiningen.

Under normal circumstances, Violet might be awed by such distinguished persons in her presence. For now, there was a funeral to run.

The pallbearers lifted the prince up gently, stoically pretending there were no objectionable smells coming from within. The prince's coffin had been resting on a cooling bed with regularly

bear to remain at Windsor during all of the preparations. Her grief is terrible."

Of course it was, and, as the sitting monarch, the queen wouldn't even be able to attend her husband's funeral, much less witness the burial. Still, it was unusual for any widow to completely flee the scene.

"Her Majesty may bear watching, to ensure she doesn't get too overwhelmed in her grief," Violet said.

"The queen has been ruling for nearly a quarter century now. She knows her duty to the country and will soon be back to rights, no doubt."

Violet had some doubt, but dropped it.

The next several days were frenetic. The chapel floors, as well as all of the chapel's exterior steps and walkways, were swept and scrubbed viciously. All furniture was completely removed from the nave, and a bier, draped in black crape, established in the exact center of it. The bier would hold the prince's coffin during his funeral service, now scheduled for December twenty-third.

Violet placed urns of snow white lilies at the four corners of the bier, as well as placing a variety of sprays around the nave and down the marked path to where the prince's coffin would finally be interred.

Mr. Rowland continually edited and re-hung the lord provost's list of guests and dignitaries. The prince consort's eldest son, Bertie, was to be chief mourner, accompanied by his brother, Prince Alfred.

Representatives from Saxe-Coburg and Gotha, Prussia, and Hesse, along with envoys from a dozen other countries, sent notices that they would be in attendance.

The staff serving the state apartments would be overwhelmed.

Each day, Violet found herself meeting with one florist or another to order more replacements for wilted stems or to place wreath orders on behalf of one group or another inside the castle.

Mr. Rowland gradually accepted her presence and, being thoroughly overcome by his own responsibilities, soon relinquished more tasks to her as the funeral date loomed closer. To satisfy the queen's requirement for deep court mourning, miles of black cloth were hung inside the castle, exhausting all the stocks Violet could find and requiring more to be hastily dyed.

The most lavish amount of cloth was hung in the choir near the entrance to the royal vault. Mr. Rowland took her down into the burial location, a long corridor constructed entirely of stone and lined with rows of shelves to the ceiling. Some of the shelves held sarcophagi of long-dead royals.

"The prince will be placed near the entrance," Mr. Rowland said. "As he will be transferred to Frogmore when it is complete, there is no sense in locating His Highness any farther in the vault than that."

"No, of course not."

"Only Reverend Wellesley and the pallbearers will accompany the coffin down here."

Violet nodded her understanding of the solemn task that lay before them.

Windsor
December 23, 1861

The day dawned cold but clear. Violet scurried down to the chapel before anyone was awake other than servants relighting fires, opening draperies, and chasing out vermin that had crept in overnight to get out of the cold.

She did a final check on the nave, straightening the black cloth covering the bier and righting some candles that were leaning atop their tall floor candelabra. Everything else in the nave was in order.

She heard coughing farther inside the chapel. Following the sound, she walked east toward the choir, her own heels echoing loudly against the floor.

At the intersection of the north and south ends of the transept was the start of the choir, consisting of parallel rows of stalls facing each other where worship hymns were sung. The coughing was louder.

"Hello?" she called.

"Mrs. Morgan?" came a tremulous voice. It was Mr. Rowland.

He rose from a seat in the choir. "Thank heavens you're h eyes were bright and his skin scarlet.

"Mr. Rowland, you need a physician. I'll get Dr. Jen away."

"There's no time. The service will start in a few ho managed to finish everything here, but you'll have to g procession. Here are my notes." He weakly picked up a n stuffed with paper scraps and indecipherable scrawls. there."

There was no time to argue with him. Helping the ma feet, she escorted him back to his quarters, calling out to a walking by to fetch Dr. Jenner immediately. After deposit undertaker in his room, she found a quiet alcove and spill Rowland's notebook onto her lap in order to decipher and his funeral notes.

An hour later, she was ready. She had to be.

It was a great pity women weren't allowed to attend royal als, Violet thought, for surely they would have brought som mestic calm and sense to this motley assemblage just insid royal apartments, all preening and seeking favored placeme the walking retinue. Most had arrived just an hour ago via a sp train from London. One ambassador bickered with another his importance to the royal family, while one of the queen's m ters argued relentlessly with whoever would take him up on v would happen to future world events now that the prince con was gone.

She'd had a devil of a time just getting them in their cor order of procession.

The one striking distinction was Edward Albert, or Bertie, t current Prince of Wales, who stood to one side, trying unsucce fully to contain his emotions. It was well known throughout Lo don that he and his father did not get on well, and it was no secr that his father died shortly after returning from a visit with his so He repeatedly dug out a handkerchief from his jacket and wipe his eyes.

changed ice beneath it, yet it hadn't prevented the inevitable results of decay.

With two clergymen in their sweeping white gowns at the head of the procession, they walked out, followed by the coffin, with Bertie and his brother walking along one side of the procession. The poor man kept his eyes averted from his father's coffin.

The group proceeded outside to where a mounted guard of honor from the Grenadiers—of whom Albert had been a colonel— waited next to the funeral carriage, fashioned as a tall, black box with the royal coat of arms emblazoned on both sides. Footmen jumped down and assisted with placement of the coffin inside the carriage, and the entire procession followed the carriage's walking pace through the wards and down to the chapel.

It was chilly and windy up on the knoll where Windsor Castle rested. Even the walls surrounding the castle environs couldn't prevent the brisk December air from seeping through jackets and cloaks.

At least there was no rain.

Violet walked far to one side of the procession, nearly hugging the façade of the castle's wall as she monitored the pace of the funeral convoy.

All was silent now save the creaking of the carriage wheels, the rough clopping of horseshoes, and the occasional wing flapping and chirping of the birds overhead who didn't realize what a tragic day it was for England.

The procession continued down the long south side of the chapel, moving around the corner and through the archway dividing the chapel from a horseshoe-shaped row of buildings before stopping at the expansive west steps that led to the rear of the nave. The huge bank of clerestory windows above the entrance sparkled brightly as though they, too, were unaware of the calamity occurring before them.

Smartly dressed members of the Foot Guard lined the steps up to the entrance, while two rows of Yeomen of the Guard stood at attention between the carriage and the steps.

Few onlookers were present, just a small gathering of invited guests, a couple of reporters, and a few artists attempting to capture the service with pen and paper. The queen had been adamant that in accordance with Albert's wishes, this be a private family funeral, as far as was possible with a public figure. No tickets had been issued and only close personal friends, relations, and those who had worked intimately with the prince were permitted attendance.

Violet signaled to the clergymen, who broke away from the stopped procession and mounted the stairs to the nave while the pallbearers removed the coffin from the carriage to bring it up the stairs, surrounded by the mourners. Violet scurried around to the south entrance to meet the group.

At the side entrance, a member of the Osborne House staff was waiting for her with moss wreaths from each of three of the prince's daughters. Each wreath was ironically woven with violets.

The servant whispered to Violet as they placed the wreaths on waiting stands near the bier, which was already flooded with lilies, "The Princesses Vicky, Alice, and Helena made these themselves." Normally brisk and businesslike during all funerals, Violet found herself blinking away tears as she imagined the girls' grief. What would be Susanna's reaction if something happened to her? What *had* been her reaction when she lost her mother?

The servant also had with him the queen's offering, a bouquet of violets surrounding a single white camellia, which Violet quickly added to another stand before ushering the servant away from the scene and retreating into a darkened part of the nave.

The procession entered and Albert's coffin was placed atop the bier. Once the mourners each paused at the coffin for last respects and moved away, four Grenadiers stepped forward to stand guard at the four corners of the bier.

The Dean of Windsor, Gerald Wellesley, gave a short but solemn service, while the choir offered the hymns "I Am the Resurrection and the Life" and "I Know That My Redeemer Liveth," followed by a reading of the thirty-ninth Psalm to Beethoven's funeral music. Afterward came a reading from First Corinthians 15, followed by three German chorales interspersed by prayers.

When the service was concluded, the coffin was lifted again and carried to the tunnel to the royal vault, with the mourners following behind. Mercifully, the mechanical apparatus worked without a problem, so the coffin lowered quickly, sparing the onlookers a protracted disappearance of the prince's remains into his vault. Reverend Wellesley and the pallbearers went down another entrance to the vault to ensure the coffin was placed properly and so that the reverend could say another prayer.

From there, Albert would await his removal to the Frogmore mausoleum when it was completed.

The air was particularly heavy with smuts and blacks today, Graham thought as he waited outside Mr. Harper's hotel. It had been no easy feat figuring out where the man was staying, but Graham's irritation at the man's dawdling was such that he was willing to pay someone to figure it out.

He pulled his overcoat closer around him as he paced back and forth. The building's windows were swathed in black crape, and most of the carriages on the busy street outside also sported either black crape on doors, ebony plumes on horses, or dark armbands on drivers.

For the hundredth time, Graham wondered how Violet had managed to pull off such a glorious coup as the prince consort's funeral. It didn't seem feasible that it could have happened just because the prince found Violet competent during Admiral Herbert's funeral.

Not that he minded, of course. Once the public knew that Morgan Undertaking had been involved in Prince Albert's funeral, well, there was no telling how their business might expand. They might even become fantastically wealthy from it. Even famous. Combined with what could be accomplished financially and retributively from his alliance with Fletcher, well, there was no telling what neighborhood they might be living in a year from now.

He was just a little prickly over Violet's ability to secure better funerals than he. It didn't seem right, somehow. Was she—

Ah, there was Samuel Harper now, paying the newsboy perched

outside the front door for this morning's copy of *The Times*. Graham caught up to Harper and tugged on his coat sleeve as the man was about to step off the curb into a hack.

"One moment, Mr. Harper, I would speak with you."

Harper turned and frowned at Graham, but waved the hack on. "What is the meaning of this, Morgan?"

"We've important business to discuss."

"Kindly send along a note to set up a place and time, and do not accost me like this."

Graham was tired of Harper's stalling and hedging. "No, sir, we will speak now."

"Where is your brother?"

"Fletcher, unfortunately, doesn't share my concerns about the progress of our agreement."

Harper shook his head—was that disgust?—before grabbing Graham by the shoulder and pulling him into an alleyway next to the hotel. "How may I help you, Mr. Morgan?"

"I don't like the tone of your voice, sir." Graham shook out of Harper's grasp, unwilling to admit the man's grip was powerful and had hurt him.

"That is of no moment to me. What do you want?"

"I want to know when the Confederacy will uphold her end of our bargain. We're ready to ship and I—we—have a lot invested in this venture."

Harper shrugged. "And I have many contacts here in London who are quite anxious to take your place, Morgan, yet I stay the course with you to suit my own purposes."

"Which are?"

"None of your business. Although I will tell you how concerned I am over your rashness. What if a police officer were to walk by? Have you no sense whatsoever? You have always been my greatest worry in this enterprise. You are stupefyingly dim-witted and irritating, and serve as my greatest risk. I can only imagine what Mrs. Morgan must think about her stalwart and audacious husband." Harper stared fiercely at Graham, causing him to flinch inwardly.

"What difference does Violet make?" he asked.

"None. She makes no difference whatsoever."

"You're a strange man, Harper. But then, aren't all Americans?"

Harper said nothing in response, instead maintaining his powerful gaze at Graham.

"Assuredly, she is blissfully unaware of anything I'm doing. It's none of her business."

"See that it remains so." Harper broke off eye contact. "You and your brother can meet me back at the Three Hulls in two days' time. I'll have money for you then."

Graham slouched away, only marginally satisfied.

I slipped away to watch the prince consort's funeral procession. I wasn't permitted to be in attendance, but, diary, I did tell you before that I have a way of being both unseen and quite ingratiating when the need arises. No one noticed me there and no one noticed that I was gone. Even the undertaker, in her tall hat swathed in black crape, walked right past me without observing my uninvited presence.

Even from a distance, the smell of the prince's rotting corpse assailed me. It was quite nauseating, I must say. How did the undertaker stand it? I wonder if she saw the prince's face contorted in the throes of death. Of course, she wouldn't have been present at that final moment, would she? That crystallizing moment where realization dawns in a pair of terrified eyes. No, she wouldn't have seen it. Yet others near her have seen it, haven't they?

Back to more immediate matters. I see clearly now that it is time to bring about a certain person's demise. Can't say as it isn't deserved. After all, I'm running out of both money and patience once again. The only question is whether to use my earlier method, or perhaps employ something a bit more . . . ostentatious. I think the punishment should fit the crime, don't you, dear diary?

❧ 13 ❦

Die when I may, I want it said of me by those who knew me best,
that I always plucked a thistle and planted a flower where I
thought a flower would grow.

—Abraham Lincoln (1809–1865)
American President (1861–1865)

Morgan House
December 1861

Violet was relieved to be home for Christmas, not the least reason being the way Susanna propelled herself into her arms.
After so much depression surrounding her at Windsor, it was good
to draw strength from Susanna's innate warmth.

The remainder of her time at Windsor had been nerve-wracking.
The Grenadiers standing guard by the prince consort's coffin had to
be relieved every hour, as they were complaining that the overwhelming fragrance of the lilies was making them light-headed. In
fact, one Grenadier had indeed fainted. Violet knew they were too
polite to state what was really bothering them.

The queen had indeed fled to Osborne House, refusing to stay
at Windsor for Christmas and refusing to tell her closest advisors
when she planned to return from her sanctuary.

The entire household, including Graham, sat enthralled as Violet discussed what had happened in the days leading up to the
royal funeral. Graham was certain it would lead to more distinguished clientele using Morgan Undertaking's services, and Violet
agreed.

As jolly as Violet's news made him, Graham still slipped out of the house early Christmas evening, claiming he had business to conduct.

"How could you possibly have anything to do today that can't wait?" she asked.

"I just do. Don't wait up for me. Mr. Porter, I'll want my brown suit for tomorrow."

"Of course, sir."

And like that, he was gone into the black night.

Violet refused to let Graham make the household Christmas miserable. "Mrs. Porter, let's have some Lambs Wool to drink. Mr. Porter, please fetch Mrs. Overfelt. She loves to sing carols. What do you think, Susanna?"

The girl looked up from where she was playing with her doll-house—Graham had been appalled that Violet allowed the child to play with it in the drawing room—and smiled broadly.

Mrs. Porter swept open the curtains covering the entry between the drawing and dining rooms so they could easily move between the piano and the dining table.

Once Mr. Porter and Mary had returned and everyone had a cup of Lambs Wool, Mary sat down to the piano and played a rousing rendition of "The Holly and the Ivy" while the rest sang and Susanna clapped her hands.

> The holly and the ivy, when they are both full grown,
> Of all the trees that are in the wood, the holly bears the crown.
> Oh, the rising of the sun and the running of the deer,
> The playing of the merry organ, sweet singing in the choir.
> The holly bears a blossom as white as lily flower,
> And Mary bore sweet Jesus Christ to be our sweet savior.

Mary looked particularly radiant tonight. Violet pulled her away from the piano and into the dining room as Mr. Porter boomed out a version of "God Rest Ye Merry Gentlemen" while leading Susanna in a silly dance. Mrs. Softpaws was perched atop the fireplace mantel, watching the proceedings warily.

"You are positively glowing, my friend," Violet said. "I had no idea cold weather agreed with you so well."

Mary's cheeks reddened. "Oh, it's not the cold. You've been so busy lately that I haven't had a chance to tell you, but—"

"Mrs. Morgan, Mrs. Overfelt, will you join us for 'O Christmas Tree'?" asked Mr. Porter, who still held Susanna by the hand.

"In honor of the prince consort, a lovely idea," Violet said. It was a very old melody, but had been rewritten a few decades ago by German composer Ernst Anschütz and was now popular in England.

Mary was also enthusiastic. "Of course. Susanna, I can't let you think Mr. Porter is the only baritone in the room."

As Mary returned to the piano, she deepened her voice and comically portrayed a man singing, with Violet joining them with an equally silly deep voice. They were interrupted during the chorus of "We Three Kings of Orient Are" by a rap at the door. The room went silent.

"Who could that be so late?" Violet said.

Mr. Porter left to admit the visitor, whom he ushered into the dining room.

What was Samuel Harper doing here?

"Mrs. Morgan," he said in greeting, sweeping his hat from his head.

"Mr. Harper, to what do we owe this unexpected visit?" She entered the dining room to greet him.

"I see that I'm interrupting your festivities; my apologies, although I heard your fine rendition of our American tune. Is your husband at home?"

"No, he left some time ago on business. I assumed it was with you."

"Hmm." Violet didn't like the way Mr. Harper's eyes surveyed the room. Did he not approve of her surroundings? Was she cavorting too much with servants?

He tapped his hat against his leg and looked at her thoughtfully. "Have you room for a tenor? I've sung my fair share of choruses in church back home, although I cannot promise to successfully carry too many notes to a pleasant conclusion. I'm a man far from home tonight, and would appreciate some friendly company."

Susanna approached Mr. Harper and stood in front of him, staring up at him intently. Violet was about to admonish the girl, when, to her surprise, Susanna took his hand and led him over to the piano. Given how much the girl avoided Graham, Violet was surprised by her behavior with this veritable stranger.

"Mr. Harper, I believe you've made a friend in this household. You may of course stay to sing carols with us. Would you like a cup of Lambs Wool?"

He smiled at Violet in gratitude. "Certainly. What is it?"

"It's a hot punch made from apples, cider, wine, and cinnamon. You'll enjoy it."

They sang carols for another hour, drank more punch, sampled Mrs. Porter's macaroons and plum pudding, and Susanna showed off her dollhouse to Mr. Harper, who inspected it as though he were considering the purchase of it as his residence. Susanna was animated over the man's interest in her toys.

How peculiar.

Violet escorted Mr. Harper to the door herself as he was ready to leave. He paused before exiting into the wintry air, turning back to thank her yet again for such a memorable evening. He started out the door once more, and again turned back. "Mrs. Morgan, you should know that your husb—that I do not . . . that is, you may find that—"

"Yes, Mr. Harper?"

He shook his head. "Good night, Mrs. Morgan. Happy Christmas, and may God forgive me." With that, he was gone.

Before shutting the door, she sensed something was wrong outside. She ventured out onto the stoop. Why, what was this? All of the garlands she'd so carefully assembled and hung over the door had been torn down and lay scattered on the ground. A delinquent hooligan, no doubt. She'd clean it up and hang new garlands in the morning.

Washington City, D.C.

The president wished for Christmas to be one day he could spend alone with his family, but it was not to be. Too much was at stake with the rising tension between the United States and Britain. The entire situation was ridiculous, and if he didn't know the facts of the case, he might almost think the Confederates had manufactured the entire affair to destroy the relationship between the two countries.

So here he was this Christmas day, meeting with his cabinet to discuss the diplomatic crisis that had been provoked.

Partisans on both sides of the issue railed on about what to do. Charles Sumner, the senator from Massachusetts as well as chairman of the Senate Foreign Relations Committee, read aloud letters from the leading British and French supporters of the United States. They all urged release of Mason and Slidell.

Attorney General Edward Bates also argued that war with Britain would effectively end their chances of suppressing the Southern rebellion.

Others disputed this, firm in their belief that they should not allow themselves to be bullied by Britain. Hosting the two Confederate diplomats aboard *Trent* was a clear demonstration of hostility toward the North, and deserving of punishment. A show of strength against both the South and their neighbors across the Atlantic was what was needed.

The president himself was having serious doubts about the wisdom of holding Messrs. Mason and Slidell. It would be dangerous to have a war on two fronts. Already the South was demonstrating more force than had been anticipated. If the North had been unable to crush the South's ambitions thus far, how would war with Britain further erode their strength? No, Mr. Bates and Senator Sumner were correct in their assessments of the situation.

If only he'd been able to put Sumner in as Minister Plenipotentiary to the Court of St. James instead of the colorless Adams, perhaps he could have intervened successfully and smoothed everything out before it reached this point, where the queen herself had to send correspondence on the matter.

Instead, Adams was mostly concerned with intercepting commerce raiders. An admirable enterprise, to be sure, but hardly the most critical activity given the state of things. To his credit, Adams had at least reported on the *Trent* situation, informing the president that Britain fully believed that it was the intent of the U.S. government to drive both countries into war, but little had he done to diffuse the situation.

If it be possible, as much as it lieth in you, live peaceably with all men, Lincoln remembered from the previous Sunday's sermon. *Yes, peace is what we need wherever it can be ascribed.*

He cleared his throat. "Gentlemen, I believe we have reached an overall consensus—with apologies to those still in disagreement—that it is best to release the two men and patch things up with Britain as quickly as possible. Besides, with Britain in mourning over the death of the prince consort, they might be in a more conciliatory mood.

"Mr. Seward," he addressed the secretary of state, "I leave it to you to finesse the details without offending our friends in Congress, nor American public opinion."

Seward took on the job with relish. His formal reply to the British government did not include an official apology, which would have outraged those whose American pride had been grievously wounded, but did state that Captain Wilkes of USS *San Jacinto* had violated international law by not taking *Trent* to an international prize court to determine the fate of both the ship and its passengers. Seward furthermore stated that Mason and Slidell would be "cheerfully liberated," and that the British would be permitted to carry them to the British Virgin Islands for pickup by a commercial vessel headed back to Europe.

Lincoln was pleased with Seward's efforts. Now they could get on with the work of bringing the South to heel. Might that the peaceful resolution of the *Trent* Affair dash the South's hopes of diplomatic recognition by Britain.

For this evening, though, there was a Christmas party to host.

Portland Place, London

Charles Francis Adams enjoyed a subdued, private family meal on Christmas. The goose was succulent and the sweet potato pudding a perfect accompaniment. After dinner, the family retired to the drawing room and parents exchanged gifts with children. As soon as was practical, Charles Francis signaled to his wife that they should leave the merriment to the children, who were laughing at ridiculous stories Henry was inventing and acting out.

They retired to their bedroom, where he gave Abigail a gift for which he'd searched all of London to find: a perfect cameo necklace. Abigail's eyes sparkled their excitement over her husband's gift, causing Charles Francis a pang of guilt as he draped it over her neck. His wife had uprooted herself to follow him to this godforsaken place and never complained about anything. She deserved a hundred necklaces for her devotion.

Tonight he would show her his deep appreciation for her loving fidelity.

Osborne House, Isle of Wight

The queen stared sightlessly at what went on around her. Osborne House had been decorated with pine boughs and festive ribbons, but the minute she swept in, she demanded that it all be taken down immediately and replaced with black crape. Servants were instructed to speak as infrequently as possible, and all of her children were sent to other parts of the residence to quietly contemplate their sadness. Presumably Bertie, who chose to go to Sandringham instead of joining his mother here, was also grieving properly.

It was an insult to dear Albert, not yet two days in the ground, that anyone even suggest there was to be any sort of celebration. Christ's birth, indeed. What of her saintly Albert's death?

Victoria couldn't get comfortable anywhere. She tried to walk down to the seaside, where they and the children had spent so many joyous days splashing about in the water. The sight of the bathing machines, standing upright in the cold winter air as a promise of warm days ahead, made her nauseous.

Inside Osborne House, she refused to eat at the dining room table. Merely sitting at her usual spot and looking over to Albert's empty chair was enough to completely eradicate her already diminished appetite.

Every other part of the house, so lovingly designed by Albert, had the misfortune of having his personality indelibly stamped on it. She loved being here because she felt like she was near him, yet she hated being here for the overwhelming grief.

She spent Christmas Day locked in her rooms, refusing to see even her youngest child, Princess Beatrice. Still in her nightgown and wrapper, not having bothered to dress, she paced back and forth, stopping only to stare listlessly out the window at the gardeners fussing with the removal of some dead shrubbery.

Victoria wondered how long she could stay sequestered here at Osborne House. Eventually her ministers would expect something from her, but what did they know about tragic loss? How was she supposed to make decisions without Albert's wisdom and guidance? How would marriage alliances be formed for their children? Who else would craft such cleverly written missives to international friends and enemies alike?

It was too much to bear.

She trailed throughout her apartment, picking up and holding porcelain figurines, carved boxes, and other trinkets. Each one held a memory of some sort, whether it had been a loving gift between spouses or something Albert had specifically ordered for Osborne House. She paused by each painting in the room, putting her fingertips to the frames. Albert had a hand in every little detail of this home, his labor of love.

She collapsed into an upholstered rocking chair and let the movement soothe her. It was of comfort for about five minutes. The table next to the chair contained another assortment of objets d'art. Her gaze caught a highly polished mahogany jewel casket. Albert gave it to her on their eleventh wedding anniversary and had placed a necklace of plump alabaster pearls inside. She reached for the casket and opened it. Ah yes, the necklace had long since been removed and placed in safekeeping with her other jewelry.

Victoria closed the lid and ran her hand down the length of it. Was this what Albert's coffin looked like? So smooth and perfectly carved, with a padded interior. Did he rest there in St. George's Chapel, wearing an angelic smile to outshine any of the priceless jewels in her collection?

She sighed and replaced the casket on the table. What had transpired at Albert's funeral? Did it go well? No one at Windsor had sent any reports about it, and Bertie was resolutely silent on the matter. Arthur was too young to have anything intelligent to say.

Would knowing the details of her husband's funeral help her? Would she rest easier knowing that Albert rested peacefully? Clutching to the idea like one of the tattered life preservers dangling from the sides of the bathing machines, she scrawled off a note to be delivered right away to Mr. Rowland.

The King's Arms, London

Finding his hotel room stuffy and claustrophobic after several hours of song and merriment with Violet Morgan, Samuel retreated to a nearby public house to nurse his unease over a pint of bitters at a table in the rear of the taproom.

He found British ale stronger than the beer favored in America, but at least it was plentiful here. The armies of both sides were already purchasing the stuff by barrels to use as an inexpensive but soothing tonic for soldiers far from home. The more they consumed, the cheaper the quality would undoubtedly become.

He took a long draw from his glass and returned to the letter he was writing to his father.

> *. . . I have written separately to Frank Merrill about several pending matters in our law practice. I am anxious to conclude my business here so that I may return to it, although I suspect the longer the conflict drags on, the more likely I am to be dragged into it. Had hoped that my business here would suffice as service, but perhaps not. In any case, my speech gets me strange looks from the English, and sometimes I wonder if I might find myself gang-*

pressed into their navy just so they can ship me home. How
fares the farm? Still problems getting milk from the new
Holstein you purchased from Mr. Chenery?

Samuel finished his pint and ordered another as he contemplated whether to tell his father what was really on his mind.

As you know, Father, I've never doubted the nature of
my business here as a patriotic boon to the States, although
I confess my dealings have placed me in the path of a
certain innocent party who is sure to be ruined if I make
any missteps. It is making me overly cautious and worried
about overplaying my hand. I cannot understand why I
am permitting my thoughts to drift off to the impossible
and impractical where this particular person is concerned.
It threatens to destroy everything I am working toward.
My brain is addled from too much British ale, I guess, as
well as the smothering fogs of the city. It's enough to rattle
anyone's mind. When I return home, I'll help you repair
the hay barn roof, unless it needs to be tended to right now,
in which case see Merrill for funds to cover it.

Samuel folded the letter and slipped it into his jacket for posting the next day. What a soft old fool he was becoming, allowing a woman—and a married one, at that—to affect his good sense. No grit to him at all.

Christmas was a torturous affair for Graham. After leaving home, he'd sought out Fletcher, who was otherwise occupied at his home with some giggling redheaded woman. As his brother was disinclined to leave his snug and entertaining surroundings, Graham prowled about awhile, then, cold and bored, walked home. As he was about to cross the street to the Morgan residence, he looked up at the bright light shining out from the dining room.

What he saw heated his skin in a slow, fiery burn as though he were tied to a stake. Why was Mr. Harper carrying on with his wife like that? The two of them were laughing and singing, with the servants no less. Graham recognized the look in Harper's eyes, and it wasn't that of a disinterested visitor.

Did Violet share the man's feelings? Was she encouraging him? The flames licked a little higher. Was Mr. Harper dragging out their negotiations in order to have time to seduce his wife? Treacherous American. Graham should have known something like this was possible. He'd warned Fletcher, hadn't he? Americans were the scourge of the earth and couldn't be trusted under any circumstances.

The heat rose higher, the flames encircling his heart and causing it to pound erratically. He should burst in right now and roundly thump the man before Violet's eyes. It would teach them both. Yet Graham stayed rooted to his spot, unable to tear his eyes away from the cozy domestic scene going on inside. Violet offered the man a cup, which Harper took with a subtle touch of her hand. The little brat was taking Harper's hand and dragging him to see something. She'd never taken Graham's hand before. He'd given her a roof over her head, and now the spoilt girl was showing preference for this stranger?

The stranger who wouldn't commit to their contract with even a pittance of silver.

Yes, he would fling open the door and physically throw Harper onto the cold, dirty pavement, then deal with Violet.

Of course, it would mean the end of their deal. Mr. Harper would report back to the Confederate government, and they would move on to another merchant. Not only would Fletcher be furious, but everything Graham had worked for would be for naught. Ignoring the tiny voice that wondered if this trade was worth losing his wife, Graham knew that he had to remain silent as to what he saw playing out before him.

The thought paralyzed him, permitting the fire to consume Graham's entire body. He fought the urge to thrash wildly in the street. Wouldn't do for any neighbors to happen to peer outside and witness him; he'd be permanently ostracized from what little advancement he'd made in society.

He had to do something. In his fit of anger, he ran to the front door and ripped down the garlands that Violet had so painstakingly hung around it. He remembered the look in her eyes when she'd shown them to him. She'd wanted approval for her domestic efforts, and for certain he was glad now that he hadn't given it to her.

Graham ripped apart the branches and tore off the spruce needles, their pungent scent filling his head with memories of a Christmas at some time in the past, he couldn't remember when, that he'd actually been happy. Having destroyed the garlands beyond recognition, he stomped on the debris several times, knowing he was behaving like a child whose toy horse has been taken away, but too far gone in rage to care.

His meager revenge complete, he slid into the shadows to wait for Harper's departure. Once he knew the invader had left his home, he planned to spend the night elsewhere. Let Violet wonder where he was. The door finally opened, but Harper seemed to have difficulty leaving the little nest he'd created. Graham burned once again, but was mollified when, after Harper moved on into the night, Violet saw his handiwork.

The look of dismay on her face was well worth it.

In the spirit of celebrating our Lord's birth, I've decided to delay my plans momentarily. Let it not be said, diary, that I am not charitable. Somehow it seems wrong to conduct an act of deep personal and financial satisfaction on a day when we are supposed to commemorate the supreme act of selflessness. My restraint will be my own act of selflessness.

In fact, I may spend time reconsidering exactly how to go about things. Some confusion here, a little intrigue there, and soon everyone in London will be baffled by what I've done. What exquisite joy will be mine.

A pity my intended will never understand how much my self-control has benefitted her.

❧ 14 ❦

To be, or not to be: that is the question:
Whether 'tis nobler in the mind to suffer
The slings and arrows of outrageous fortune,
Or to take arms against a sea of troubles,
And by opposing end them?

—William Shakespeare
Hamlet

Mrs. Porter had already swept away the garland debris the next morning, and asked Violet over breakfast whether she wanted to replace them.

"No, I think not. If there's a ruffian in the neighborhood, he'll just tear it down again."

"I noticed that it was only the garlands on this house that were torn down, Mrs. Morgan."

"Yes, well, who can understand the mind of a brute? Susanna, please use a knife on your sausage, don't cut it with a spoon. Where was I? Anyway, what time did Mr. Morgan return last night?"

"Can't say as I know, ma'am. Mr. Porter laid out his brown suit, but it's still there. His bedclothes are still in place."

Violet was nearly beyond caring how Graham spent his time, except that his actions were so utterly disrespectful of her and he was neglecting his duties at the shop. Bless Mrs. Porter for her studied oblivion about what was happening between husband and wife.

"Very well, thank you. Susanna, dear, come, we must hurry or we'll be late opening the shop."

Almost immediately upon entering the shop, Violet was immersed in problems surrounding the transport of a body from

Cambridge back to London—the railroad having misplaced it somewhere between Royston and Stevenage—and she promptly forgot about Graham and his wanderings.

Maybe if she spent every waking moment at Morgan Undertaking, she might forget he even existed.

Samuel was just exiting the Langham one morning when Morgan accosted him once again.

"Harper!" the man said sharply. Morgan was unshaven and his eyes were red and rheumy. Samuel made the mistake of breathing in, and was overwhelmed by the fumes of liquor wafting off the man.

"Morgan," he replied evenly. "I trust you had a pleasant Christmas."

"It's none of your business. No doubt you had a delightful one."

"I did. I came by your home to see you, but you weren't there, yet your charming wife allowed a poor bachelor to linger and sing carols with the family."

"A woman, two servants, and a vagrant child hardly make a family."

"For a lonely man they do, Morgan. You would be wise to appreciate what you have." How had this man ever secured Mrs. Morgan's affections?

"I know what I *don't* have, and that is a commitment from you." Graham held up a hand. "Wait, before you assault me with more excuses, I have news for you. Your compatriots, Mason and Slidell, have finally made it to London. I read about it in this morning's paper."

"And?"

"*And* presumably they now carry great esteem and clout since their public abduction by the Northern miscreants. They're here to negotiate Confederate recognition, aren't they? What better than to demonstrate our commitment to helping the South by providing valuable goods that will slip past the blockade at great risk to British souls? I want you to set up a meeting with them to discuss it. Perhaps those gentlemen have a little more authority than the man originally designated to handle things."

This was something Samuel never expected Morgan would attempt. The man bordered on derangement, but he was clever. How should he get a handle on this? Pretend to set up a meeting? It would enrage Morgan further, and who knew what he might do in retaliation? Samuel had little fear for himself—Morgan was no more than a roaring black bear like the ones he'd captured and killed many times in the forest behind his father's farm—but it did give him pause to think that Morgan could be dangerous to others in his household.

For an animal like Graham Morgan, it was best to be aggressive right back. "Although a sound idea, my friend, I'm afraid I have some bad news for you. I've just had word from Virginia that the Confederacy has decided to obtain its merchandise elsewhere." Samuel opened his jacket and pulled out the letter he'd been holding for some time.

Morgan snatched the letter before Samuel had a chance to open it. He snapped it open and read, his bloodshot eyes quickly scanning the pages. He crumpled it up and threw it to the ground.

"Elsewhere?" Graham didn't so much shout as explode. "How could they possibly know of anywhere else to go? Haven't you been their agent, working exclusively with my brother and me?"

Samuel shrugged. "It appears they hired other agents to work in London."

"I don't believe you. I haven't heard of any other agents seeking traders, and I make it a point to stay informed."

"You're obviously not that well informed, Mr. Morgan."

"I know what I'm talking about. You've been rolling a ball of string before my brother and me, just out of paws' reach, in order to suit your own nefarious purposes, haven't you? What is it that you *really* intend to do?"

"You're a madman, Morgan."

"And you're a no-good, lying coward, not worth a shilling of horse dung."

"Watch yourself," Samuel growled.

"Watch myself? All I've done for weeks, no, for months, is watch, watch, watch and wait while you stumble about making promises and agreements you don't intend to keep. You're a feckless braggart, Harper, and I know you have designs on my wife, making you a conniving trickster, as well."

"That's enough," Samuel roared. Without a care as to who witnessed it, he pulled back and punched Graham in the face. The man flew backward onto the filthy, slushy pavement and slid along the ice. Samuel followed him. Graham put a hand to his nose, but blood was already pouring out between his fingers.

"If it weren't illegal, I'd call you out," he mumbled from behind his hand.

"I'd accept, legal or not."

"That just proves that everything I've said about you is true," Graham said.

"No," Samuel replied, bending over to speak quietly in Graham's ear. "It just proves that you're a shyster playing in a game whose rules you do not understand."

"What happened to you?" Fletcher asked when he opened the door.

"Shut up," Graham said as he brushed past his brother. "I need some rags and a basin of water."

After cleaning up and assuring himself in a mirror that his nose was not broken, he told his brother what had transpired between himself and Samuel Harper. Instead of the rage he expected from a sympathetic brother, Fletcher merely pursed his lips, as though considering things.

Why did every confounded person in his life have to behave in a totally unexpected—and abominable—manner?

"Well, I suppose that ends our dream of quick riches through Mr. Harper, doesn't it? I'm disappointed, of course, but it's not wholly unexpected. I'm sure we can find something else. For tonight, let's head over to the Three Hulls and drown our sorrows. Then tomorrow we can—"

"Have you lost your sense, Fletcher? This is not a temporary setback; we're ruined. Everything I've invested, gone. Oh, right, you don't have as much invested as I do, so it's of little matter to you, isn't it?"

"You're wrong, Graham. I made the trial run at my own expense, remember? Your problem is that you think every setback is a personal affront to your dignity. Perhaps Mr. Harper lost his backing and didn't want to admit it. Perhaps he's holding out for more favorable terms. In any case, standing around quarreling about it doesn't move us toward another profitable enterprise. We're best served to forget him and make new plans."

"New plans? After months sacrificed on this one? You're the one who assured me this was a perfect scheme because it would help me avenge Grandfather's death as well as bring us untold wealth. It would catapult me further up into society, you said. Now you casually shrug your shoulders as though you've merely lost a pair of theater tickets."

"No, Graham, I am a realist who understands that in any great undertaking, there are many steps along the way. Some will be successful, some won't. We don't know that Mr. Harper is no longer useful to us, just that a single door has closed. There are plenty of other ways to profit from the American war—and provide you with your precious revenge—if we just sit down and consider it. Instead, you run in here like a madman."

"That's the second time today I've been called that. I tolerated it from Harper, but I won't tolerate it from my brother."

"All right, I'm sorry. We have to discuss this rationally, Graham. There's no sense in—"

"You're a fool, Fletcher, but I'm not. While you've been waiting for Harper like a lovesick calf, I've been making my own inquiries. He's not the only man willing to help us. Trust me, brother, I will have satisfaction out of this."

Graham waited again for Harper, this time inside a public house across the street. As soon as he saw Harper step outside and head south, he threw down some coins to pay for his drink and went outside to follow him. It was time to discover who Harper was meeting with and what London contacts he had.

Graham followed him on a circuitous route down to Oxford Street, then west a few blocks and back north and around Cavendish Square. Harper turned east on Cavendish Place, strolling along as though he hadn't a care in the world.

You'll care once I'm finished with you, Graham thought.

Another left and they were back at Portland Place. Where was he headed? Graham's quarry stopped at an elegant residence and rang the bell. A uniformed servant answered, listened to instruction from Harper, then retreated back inside. When the door opened again, Graham was struck by the familiarity of the man standing there.

Where had he seen him before? Perhaps he'd not seen the man himself, but an ambrotype or an engraving of him. But where? Who was he?

In a sickening rush, Graham realized everything. He remembered where he'd seen the man before, and who he was. Moreover, he understood Harper's relationship with the man and exactly what game Harper was playing.

And Graham knew what he had to do.

"Sorry to force you to the door," Samuel said, "but my little English friend has been following me, and I decided it was time to take care of him once and for all."

"So you wanted him to see me, eh?"

"Yes. I also brought him here circuitously, in order to confuse him a bit as to whom I was seeing."

"The game is afoot, then? Care to stay for some port until we go out to our meeting? I've just purchased a case of fine—"

"No need to convince me. I'd be happy to drink your port."

"You always were a good sport, Mr. Harper."

Graham rushed home blindly, his rage rendering him incapable of complete thought as he stumbled and shoved his way past people in the street. The interior of the house was dark and he called out, "Violet? Mr. Porter? Mrs. Porter?"

No one home. Violet must be at the shop with the girl, and the servants were on some kind of errands, he supposed. He was blessedly alone.

He took the staircase two steps at a time up to his study. He yanked open a drawer of his desk. The steel contraption lay there, its oiled barrel gleaming and seductive. For one moment, he reflected back to the time that Violet stood here next to him, consoling him over his sorrow for his grandfather. He'd felt then as though she really loved him. Maybe she still did. What he was about to do might have grave consequences for her, but there was no time to think about it now.

The image of the treacherous Samuel Harper loomed up in his mind once more, and he realized he was a fool if he thought Violet cared anymore. No longer caring a whit about what might happen to Violet, he searched another drawer for ammunition, tucked everything back into his coat pocket, and rushed back out of his house to Portland Place.

To wait.

When Violet and Susanna returned home from the shop, the house was dark. She'd given the Porters the day off, and naturally Graham was nowhere to be found.

After finding adequate leftovers in the kitchen, she and Susanna shared supper, then Violet suggested they play with the dollhouse together. The house was still in the drawing room where Violet had allowed it to sit since before Christmas. Perhaps she should leave it there, since it was becoming its own piece of furniture and Susanna loved it so. It was a joy to watch the girl rearrange the rooms of furniture.

With their skirts spread out around them, they opened up the front of the white Regency-style dollhouse. Violet went to work on the dining room, turning the scale-sized table at a ninety-degree angle, and rearranging the chairs and other room furniture to go with it, while Susanna began rearranging one of the other living areas into an approximate replica of the Morgan house drawing room. Soon there were as many pieces on the floor around them as there were in the dollhouse. Mrs. Softpaws stepped daintily through them, occasionally batting one over.

So absorbed were they in their play that they both jumped in terror when Graham burst through the front door.

"Graham, honestly, must you be so noisy? We were just—"

"Come with me," he said, grabbing Violet by the hand and

pulling her up. She heard a piece of miniature furniture snap beneath her shoe as she struggled to gain her balance.

"What's gotten into you?" she asked. "Let go. You're hurting me."

"No time. Get upstairs." He pushed her along in front of him.

Violet saw fear on Susanna's face, but called to her from the stairs, "Don't worry, I'll be right back."

Graham jostled her all the way up to their bedroom, or, rather, her bedroom, as it had been for several months. What was his intent? Surely he didn't plan to . . .

He thrust her onto the bed and slammed the door. She sat rigid, her mind whirling as to what she would do if he attempted to force her to anything.

She quickly realized that was not in his mind. Graham paced back and forth in the room, still wearing his overcoat. His face was flushed, despite how cold it was outside, and his hair was wildly mussed. Beneath the flush his nose was swollen and bruised.

"What happened to you?" she asked.

"There's no time for that. Listen to me, Violet. Something terrible has happened. I've done something very bad. I'm going to swing, I know it."

"What are you talking about?"

"I shot and killed a man today. Just now."

Violet felt a distant hum in her ears. Surely she hadn't just heard that her husband committed murder. "What are you talking about? What on earth would possess you to do such a thing?"

Graham stopped long enough to pass a hand over his eyes as if to rub away whatever visions he was having. "I did what was necessary. I avenged Grandfather, taught a man a lesson, and ruined your lover's hopes and dreams."

"My what? What was necessary? Graham, you're making no sense whatsoever. Shall I ask Mrs. Porter to get you a pot of—"

"There's no time. I won't be here long enough for tea. Pay attention, woman. I just shot Charles Francis Adams, the Minister Plenipotentiary to the Court of St. James."

"I'm sorry?" Surely Graham hadn't just said he'd murdered an

American diplomat. "Who is Mr. Adams to you? How do you even know who he is?"

"I've seen his likeness in the newspapers with regard to the whole *Trent* Affair. Harper is from the *United States*, Violet, not the Confederacy. He was never with the South. Don't you understand?"

"Not a bit. All this fuss over funeral supplies? Why would you accuse the minister of being my lover? I've never even met the man. What has gotten into you?" She had so much to ask it was hard to know exactly where to begin, so questions were tumbling out. It didn't matter, for Graham was paying her little heed.

"Please be quiet, Violet. I can't think. I may have acted a bit rashly—"

"A bit?"

"—but what's done is done. He deserved it for his perfidy, and I know Pap sleeps well tonight. Naturally, I can't stay here. Where do we have a traveling bag?"

"We have one in the armoire, but the latch doesn't work well."

Graham went to the armoire and pulled the traveling case out, leaving the room without another word to her. She followed him to his study, where he began scooping up clothes that were in the folded piles on chairs that he now favored over maintaining his wardrobe in Violet's room. He reached into a drawer of his desk and pulled out a jingling sack that he thrust into the bag as well before trying to lock it. He struggled with it for several moments before giving up in disgust.

"I'm on my way to meet Fletcher at *Lillian Rose*. We're headed for Martinique or Guadeloupe, I'm not sure which. I'll write to you. I'll send papers to turn over the shop to you, although you probably don't deserve it. At least I know you'll carry on with it, whereas Fletcher would just sell it."

"Graham, you are behaving like an utter fool. Whatever you've done can be reckoned with. Cease this nonsense."

"When they come to question you, say nothing about my whereabouts. I have enough money to last awhile, plus the coffin cargo on *Lillian Rose* should fetch good money depending on where we land."

Coffin cargo? Did he mean the funerary supplies? She couldn't give it more thought because her husband was moving again, this time down the stairs.

"Graham, wait," she said from the top of the staircase. "I don't understand any of this. Please stay and discuss it."

"Fletcher's waiting." He opened the front door and turned back to her. "My final word to you is this: Stay away from Samuel Harper."

With that, he disappeared out the door and into the busy street. Violet looked to where Susanna still sat with her dollhouse. The girl held a red velvet upholstered chair midair as she stared back at Violet, eyes wide and mouth agape. Mrs. Softpaws, too, was stunned nearly senseless, her play with the furniture forgotten.

Violet shook her head. "I don't know what just happened, either, Susanna, although I don't think I can return to playing with a mere dollhouse, as Morgan House seems to be in complete chaos."

Tell me not, in mournful numbers,
Life is but an empty dream!
For the soul is dead that slumbers,
and things are not what they seem.
Life is real! Life is earnest!
And the grave is not its goal;
Dust thou art; to dust returnest,
Was not spoken of the soul.

—Henry Wadsworth Longfellow (1807–1882),
American poet and educator

Violet took Graham's place in pacing back and forth in her bedroom. She had to do something, but summoning the police against her husband seemed so . . . unfaithful. A betrayal. Yet if he had truly murdered someone, justice must be had.

Violet had just concluded that she would seek Mary's advice when the doorbell rang. It rang again a few moments later, making her realize that the Porters had not yet returned. She went down and answered the door herself.

"Mr. Harper," she said flatly.

"Is your husband here?"

"No."

"Where is he?"

"He's gone. I don't know where."

"You must have more information than that."

She shrugged and folded her arms in front of her, as much to protect her from the chill of fear overcoming her as to put distance between her and the mysterious Samuel Harper. "I don't."

"Mrs. Morgan, please don't lie. Graham Morgan is in serious trouble, and if you withhold information, you could be, as well. There are men far more dangerous than I who are looking for him. You are his wife; you must know where he is."

"Sir, I don't know who you believe you are, but this is my home you've just barged into, demanding answers to which you are not entitled. I won't say a single word until you tell me precisely what is happening here. I do mean every detail, Mr. Harper."

He nodded. "Yes, you deserve that. May we sit down?"

She sat down on a sofa in the drawing room, assuming he would take the chair across from her, but unexpectedly he sat down next to her. Susanna remained, her attention back to her dollhouse and Mrs. Softpaws. Violet turned to face him, and he stared at her with an intensity that was white-hot. She felt the urge to look away, but was determined not to wilt.

When he next spoke, she was startled by his voice. Gone was the lilting accent he said was from his native Virginia, replaced with something flatter, more even. It wasn't unpleasant, just completely different.

"My name is Samuel Edwin Harper. I am from Massachusetts, and I am a lawyer by trade, although my family has been farmers for generations. It is through my trade that I became acquainted with Mr. Adams, who himself was a lawyer before entering politics and the U.S. House of Representatives, and now serving as Minister Plenipotentiary to the Court of St. James.

"Adams had a specific mission to accomplish here, Mrs. Morgan, which was to prevent the building and running of commerce raiders. Because I am someone he respects, as well as a bachelor with no wife or children to hinder me, he asked that I join him here on this project.

"I posed as a Southerner directed by the Confederacy to find these potential commerce raiders and blockade runners, to learn of their plans and routes, in order for the United States to successfully intercept them on the high seas before they could reach ports like the one in Hampton Roads, Virginia.

"After I dropped some open hints in London, your brother-in-law approached me, and soon I was meeting with him and your husband. They were eagerly seeking a contact in the Confederacy to whom they could sell weapons, and I was more than eager to deal with them, in order to foil their plans."

Small things were clicking together in Violet's mind. Graham's secret conversations with Fletcher. Graham's desire to do the Americans harm. The coffin cargo. She dreaded what she would learn next.

"I believe there was some disagreement between the brothers as to their goals in the enterprise, but it wasn't relevant to my own purposes."

Violet slowly nodded. "Yes, my husband has always been obsessed with seeking some bizarre sort of revenge against Americans on behalf of his deceased grandfather. He hates your countrymen, you know."

Samuel smiled. "That mutual distrust has long been a staple of our countries, hasn't it? I, however, find much to admire in England. Ahem, anyway, Mr. Adams and I were slowly drawing a net around the Morgan brothers, and I'm sorry to say that Adams wanted to include you in the catch. Having met you, and having, ah, understood your innocence in it all, I told him that you were never, ever to be harmed in the operation.

"I must apologize, though, for despite my efforts, it is clear that I couldn't avoid being responsible for great pain for you."

Strangely enough, though, Violet didn't feel hurt, even though she knew she should be destructively angry at Mr. Harper's deception. There was an extraordinary feeling of relief in just finally hearing the truth, both about Graham and all of the bizarre occurrences over the past few months.

"I am an undertaker, Mr. Harper. It is my job to be impervious to pain and grief. Please continue." Violet relaxed her arms, folding her hands into her lap.

"Unfortunately, my desire to protect you resulted in my dangling your husband and brother-in-law along much longer than anticipated. I should have simply given them some money once they showed me their travel route, sent them on their way, and let the authorities pick them up en route to our shores. All of this might not have happened otherwise."

"What is 'all of this'?"

"Your husband threatened me on more than one occasion, and yesterday I had to be more forceful than usual in rebuffing him. I made sure he wasn't too badly injured."

Another detail clicked into place.

"Later, I caught your husband following me and decided to give him what he wanted. I led him to Mr. Adams's residence in Portland Place. When Mr. Morgan saw the two of us together, I'm sure he put it together quickly. My hope was that it would anger him enough to do something foolish and out in the open, but I didn't expect it would result in what he actually did."

"Which was to kill Mr. Adams."

"What? No, he didn't kill him. Didn't even hit him. I'm afraid your husband is a lousy shot. I went with Adams and his son, Henry, to a meeting with Lord Palmerston to tell him what our progress was in ferreting out commerce raiders. The British government doesn't much care for us, but they also don't want to go to war with us, no matter how much posturing they do. Hence they have given Mr. Adams free rein in his work here.

"Conversely, they are never going to recognize the Confederate government, despite the best efforts of Mason and Slidell to plead and persuade. Regardless, Morgan lay in wait for us, and when we returned to Mr. Adams's residence, he took a couple of shots at us before fleeing. Henry pushed his father to the ground to protect him, which is probably why Morgan believed he had killed him. I caught sight of him as he left the scene, and after ascertaining no one was hurt and settling both men back indoors and talking to the police, I came here."

"I'm surprised the police didn't arrive before you."

"The police don't yet know it was your husband who attempted to kill Adams."

"You didn't tell them?"

"No, I didn't want you subjected to an invasion of police officers, and asked Mr. Adams to give me an opportunity to apprehend Morgan before saying anything to them. I thought it was better to come here first myself to see if I could get him to surrender."

"He was here but moments. I believe he's gone for good."

Mr. Harper nodded. "Do you know where he went?"

Violet heaved a sigh and bit her lip. What husband puts his wife in such a precarious position, no matter what the nature of their relationship? When was the last time Graham had considered anyone other than himself and his own selfish desires?

She suddenly had her own selfish desire, to scurry back to the shop and immerse herself in the world of undertaking, where all was peace and calm for her. Alas, it was not to be. Graham's misfortune was now hers, and she had to face it. However, if Graham ever dared enter her presence again . . .

Once again, with her uncanny ability to sense the thoughts of others, Susanna rose from where she was playing and came to Violet, putting her arms around her shoulders and kissing her cheek. Such actions nearly always melted Violet's heart like a spring thaw.

"You are a sweet girl, aren't you? Have you heard what Mr. Harper told me?"

Yes.

"I believe we have some difficult times ahead of us. Are you afraid?"

No.

"Then neither am I. We will stare this down like a workhouse matron, right?"

Yes!

Mr. Harper looked puzzled, but Violet didn't explain, instead squeezing the girl's hands and saying, "I think I heard the basement door open. Why don't you go see what Mr. and Mrs. Porter have brought back for supper?"

"She's a clever girl even though she doesn't speak," Mr. Harper said, watching her flounce out to the rear stairs.

"Yes, she is." Had Graham even once acknowledged anything about Susanna? Her sweet nature or her desire to help others around her? Her bright smile that perpetually shone like a thousand suns despite all that must have happened to her? Yet this man who had been near Susanna just a few times recognized all that Violet did.

To her own amazement, she felt a hot tear running down her cheek. She quickly brushed it away.

"Mrs. Morgan, please forgive me if I've upset you."

She laughed unsteadily. "Actually, in a bizarre way, you've said something rather nice and brought me a little joy in the midst of what I'm realizing is a never-ending nightmare. I am probably a fool for suggesting this to the one person I should consider my mortal enemy, but would you care to stay for dinner? I'll tell you all I know about Graham's whereabouts, and in return I insist that you play dominoes afterward with Susanna."

"A double pleasure for me, Mrs. Morgan. Truly it is. Now that I see your husband isn't here, I must return to the minister's residence so he can engage the police in the search. I'll be back in a jiffy."

Violet tossed about fitfully all night, between anxiety over what might happen to Graham, and the unwanted but oddly pleasing air of ease and charm Mr. Harper had brought into her home last night. He'd insisted that she call him Samuel, or even Sam, but she refused. It wasn't right to be on such intimate terms with the man who intended to have her husband—curse his misguided soul—arrested.

Mrs. Porter was her usual discreet self, not even raising an eyebrow when Violet told her that Mr. Harper would be returning for dinner, but instead adding another potato to her boiling pot and taking another cod filet out of the icebox.

Susanna was overjoyed at Mr. Harper's attentions. The two of them played bonesticks, or dominoes, in the drawing room until Violet, sitting in a corner reading a book, could no longer keep her eyes open. Mr. Harper noticed her drifting off and ended his play with Susanna.

As he departed, he warned Violet that he had no choice but to tell the authorities what he knew. Violet merely nodded in tired resignation. He promised to keep her informed as to what was happening and left.

Now she was completely unable to sleep, as thoughts swirled around in her mind like the first spin of snowflakes prior to a blizzard. From odd thoughts of Graham as he used to be in the early days of their marriage, she turned toward his increasing paranoia and dismissal of her role as *maîtresse de la maison*. As she considered all that had happened since his involvement in the trading scheme—his move out of their bedroom, the Clayton Tunnel wreck, and the prince consort's funeral—her thoughts became a jumbled mix of images, blowing hard and fast through her mind to the point that she felt she might be buried in the drifts.

Violet rose in the morning, exhausted. She needed to talk to someone. She needed Mary.

Violet waited in a corner of Mary's shop while the dressmaker finished taking measurements of a woman and her young son. Afterward, Mary greeted her warmly and invited her to sit down.

"I'm so glad to see you, Violet," she said, crossing the floor to bolt the door to the shop. "I've been anxious to talk to you."

"But your customers—" Violet said, not intending for Mary to actually close the shop for the day on her account.

"Can wait. We shouldn't be intruded upon. How are you, dear?"

"Not very well, I confess."

"You must tell me what's wrong."

Violet did. On and on she went, from Graham's shocking outburst followed by his abrupt departure from Morgan House, to Mr. Harper's admission about who he really was and his relationship with Graham, Fletcher, and Charles Francis Adams, the minister plenipotentiary.

"How awful for you that Graham abandoned you this way. I'm not surprised Mr. Harper turned out to be so noble."

"I'm not sure he's *noble*, Mary, but I suppose he's not the scoundrel I initially thought him to be."

"He's very handsome, though."

"Why, Mary Overfelt, do you still have a crush on Mr. Harper?"

"Not at all. I'm just aware of an attractive man's presence. Which is what I've been meaning to tell you about. Oh, I can hardly believe it myself." She patted the side of her great pouf of hair.

"What is it?"

Mary dropped her voice to a whisper, as if afraid the walls might eavesdrop on her secret. "I've met someone."

"And?" They met people all day long in their respective professions.

"A special someone. A very nice gentleman named George Cooke."

Violet was rendered nearly speechless. In the years she'd known Mary, not once had the other woman expressed an interest in leaving her widowed state. "That's delightful. Tell me about him."

"I don't know Mr. Cooke all that well yet, but he's a watchmaker whose family came to England from Amsterdam—or was it somewhere in Germany?—in the seventeenth century."

"How did you meet him?"

"Strangely enough, he was entering the same draper's shop where I had gone to buy some fabrics, held the door open for me, and we struck up a conversation. He's a widower and understands me."

Violet leaned over and took her friend's hand. "How very happy I am for you. I hope I can meet Mr. Cooke soon."

How ironic that she and Mary had very nearly traded places. Mary was in the thrill of new love, as Violet had been so many years ago, and now Violet was like an aging widow, with little to live for other than her business.

Violet rejoiced for her friend, but thought the winter inside her heart might go on forever. At least there was Susanna.

Violet and Susanna were returning home from the shop one day with Violet's mind awhirl with plans. Perhaps it was time to make Susanna a formal apprentice. Her muteness created certain difficulties—how would she ever communicate with the families of the deceased?—but the girl had such an aptitude that it somehow seemed wrong not to formally train her as she had Will and Harry. Just today, Susanna had rearranged the greenery in a wreath delivered from the florist. Violet shook her head when she compared that maturity with the girl who still loved her dollhouse.

As they approached the front door, Susanna tugged at her skirt and pointed to the street. Mr. Harper was crossing over to them, carrying a wrapped box with a frilly bow on it.

"Mrs. Morgan, Miss Susanna, I trust you are doing well today. Quite blustery out, isn't it? I have some news for you, if I might come in for a moment?"

Violet knew she really shouldn't permit it. Thus far, none of her neighbors had noticed Graham's absence since he'd been keeping odd hours for months, anyway, but Mr. Harper was becoming a regular visitor, and it was Violet seeing him to the door each time. Yet he had information, presumably about Graham's whereabouts.

"Certainly. I'll have Mrs. Porter prepare some tea."

Once again, Mr. Harper joined her on the sofa. It wasn't quite so uncomfortable this time. Over steaming cups of Earl Grey and gooseberry scones, Mr. Harper shared his news, which was far more disturbing than Violet expected.

"You are to be summoned to Parliament for special questioning about your husband's disappearance."

"Me? Why? I've told you everything I know."

"Yes, but now that everything is patched up between the United States and Britain, Parliament wants to make a good show that they are aggressively rooting out our enemies. You may be their sacrificial lamb if we can't apprehend Morgan quickly enough."

"Are you suggesting that they will try to hang me in Graham's place? Good Lord."

"No, I believe they will strut and posture like a bunch of roosters, nipping at you with their big beaks until they've drawn blood, then they will declare themselves satisfied and return to their own yard, so to speak. I'd hoped to have Morgan found before he got on the open seas, but he and his brother slipped away."

So Graham had not only abandoned her with only a cursory explanation, he was now leaving her to take the blame for everything he'd done. What would Susanna now think of her? How would her business be hurt? Violet thought her heart had hardened greatly toward her husband, but in that moment, she realized it had just a little further to go, and now it was as black and shiny and unbreakable as the finest piece of jet.

Maybe it was time to leave this house and everything associated with Graham altogether.

"Mr. Adams and I will be in attendance, so you'll have sympathetic friends there. I'm terribly sorry, Mrs. Morgan."

"It isn't your fault, sir. I don't suppose the package at your feet is a peace offering for me, is it?"

Samuel reddened. "Actually, no. It's for Miss Susanna."

Susanna eagerly took the box and opened it. Inside was a family of dolls, sized for a dollhouse.

Still blushing furiously, Samuel said, "I saw from the plate on the rear of the dollhouse that it came from a shop on Oxford Street, so I went and made a purchase to thank Miss Susanna for a very challenging game of dominoes."

Susanna picked out the father doll, who wore a severe black suit and carried a wooden cane. "That," Mr. Harper said, pointing, "is Mr. Ebenezer Orange Peel. That is his wife, Matilda Orange Peel, and their two children, Pomegranate and Plum Pudding. And don't forget the new baby, Huckleberry."

Susanna grinned, delighted with her gift. She lay the open box in Violet's lap so that Violet could view the entire family. The girl then took one of Mr. Harper's hands and said, "Thank you for my lovely present, sir."

Violet dropped her half-full teacup to the floor, where it splattered tea on the carpet and on her gown, but thankfully didn't break. It didn't matter.

"What did you just say?" Even Mr. Harper was staring openmouthed at the girl.

Now it was Susanna's turn to blush, and she went silent, still holding Mr. Harper's hand. He covered it with his other hand, stood, and gently guided Susanna to take his place next to Violet.

He knelt before the girl, still encasing her hand between both of his own, while Violet picked up her cup and saucer and set them on the tea table next to her.

"Miss Susanna, I do believe that the sound of your voice is better than a Sunday choir to Mrs. Morgan, do you know that?"

Susanna nodded.

"I imagine there are lots of things she'd like to know about you. Would you be willing to talk some more to her?"

"Yes."

He nodded at Violet and moved away to sit on the chair across from the sofa, while Violet took over.

"Susanna, dear, where do I begin? Why did you choose to speak just now?"

The girl shrugged. "Speaking gets you in trouble."

"What trouble? You've lived here for months and I've never raised a hand to you."

"Yes, but I'm safe now." Susanna stole a glance back at Mr. Harper.

Oh dear.

"Tell me about the day I found you in the shop. How did you get there?"

"I ran away from the workhouse. I took some cheese and sausages with me, but they ran out. After a few days, I was tired of sleeping on doorsteps, and when I found your shop with no one in it, and the coffin there was just like a nice bed, I fell asleep."

"Why were you in the workhouse in the first place?"

"My mama died. A neighbor took me there to protect me."

"What about your father? Where is he?"

Another shrug. "Never knew him much, he was always gone. Mother said he was a railwayman and got killed in the Lewisham crash." So Susanna's father had just died four years ago, in the sort of accident that had nearly taken Susanna's life.

"And then you yourself were—never mind, tell me about your mother? What was she like?"

Susanna considered this. "She smelled good."

"What happened to her?"

"She died."

"Yes, but how?"

"They said she ate tainted meat."

Tainted meat? That would have made her ill, but probably wouldn't be fatal, unless the woman was sickly to begin with or she'd eaten a great quantity of it.

"Do you have any brothers or sisters?"

She shook her head no. Just like Violet, the girl had no siblings with whom to confide and share life's experiences. Violet dropped the subject and hugged Susanna. "Thank you," she whispered in the girl's ear. Releasing her, she turned to Mr. Harper. "Well, I think at this point you may as well stay for dinner again, if you've no other plans. I'll need advice on what to do during my questioning."

Mr. Harper stayed long past dinner and Susanna's bedtime, advising Violet in the manner of all lawyers, peppering her with every question he could conceive of and analyzing her answers. Violet was thoroughly exhausted by the time the clock chimed one o'clock in the morning. She covered a yawn with her hand.

"My apologies. I've long overstayed my welcome."

"Not at all. You've been very helpful. It's just been a very eventful day."

"Send word to me at my hotel the moment you receive your summons. I'll accompany you." He pulled a piece of hotel stationery from his jacket and handed it to her.

She walked him to the door. "You've performed the miraculous here today, and I'm grateful to you . . . Samuel."

His grin nearly split his face in half. "I've done nothing, but I'm happy to accept your undeserved praise anytime, Mrs. Morgan."

"Please, call me Violet."

"Violet." He sounded as though he was about to start singing her name.

She shut the door behind him. Every day was dawning with multitudes of surprises, some dreadful, and others delightful.

She turned to find Susanna standing at the bottom of the staircase, holding Mrs. Softpaws.

"Why are you up?"

"Mrs. Softpaws was having a dream and woke me up."

"I see. Do you think she might be ready to go back to sleep now?"

"I think so. She might sleep better if she had another one of Mrs. Porter's gooseberry scones."

Violet shook her head. "All right, go downstairs and get one. But just one."

"Thank you, Mama," Susanna said as she cradled the cat and headed toward the back stairs.

Violet watched her depart. *Mama*, Susanna had said. How was it that this young girl had filled Violet's heart near to bursting? Yes, some surprises were dreadful, but the more memorable ones were positively delightful. Violet slept dreamlessly all night.

The dreaded summons arrived, making Violet both fearful and relieved to be done with it. Graham hadn't been captured, nor had he written her, so she assumed he was hiding somewhere, only who knew where? Portugal? America? The Caribbean? Canada? He could be anywhere. He said he was heading for Martinique or Guadeloupe, but who knew where circumstances may have taken him?

She dressed in one of her finest gowns, a brown skirt edged with a Greek key pattern in copper, and a gathered linen bodice with billowy sleeves buttoned at the wrist, topped with a copper-colored Zouave jacket, its wide-open sleeves permitting her sleeves to show. She angled a small brown hat on her head and completed the ensemble with tan kid leather gloves.

She'd even had Mrs. Porter come and assist her with her corset, ensuring the tightest closure possible to emphasize her small waist. Usually she laced her own corset, which meant she couldn't pull it as tight as someone standing behind her. However, her daily work did not require impressing anyone. Besides, some of the lifting and bending she did made a tight corset nearly impossible to manage, although she did appreciate how it forced a good posture.

Violet guessed Mrs. Porter's cinching of her waist brought it down to about nineteen inches. Breathing was tricky, but she could survive for a few hours until she returned home.

If Samuel's eyes were any indicator when he arrived to escort her, she was ready to impress Parliament.

Much to Violet's relief, her appearance wasn't before the entire body of Parliament, nor in front of the House of Lords or the House of Commons. Instead, they went to an antechamber inside Westminster, where about a half dozen gentlemen were present, including two men, one older and one about her age, who sat off to one side. They were dressed in attire similar to Samuel's, so she assumed they must be Mr. Adams and his son. Behind Minister Adams sat two other men, notebooks and pencils in hand. They were either secretaries or, heaven forbid, reporters. Even worse, they might be political cartoonists.

Also present were Lord Russell, the foreign secretary, and Lord Palmerston, the prime minister.

Courage, Violet. Remember, you faced Queen Victoria in that woman's hour of great grief. You can easily withstand a few questions from a couple of pompous old men.

Lord Palmerston cupped his hands behind his back and paced in front of Violet as she sat on an uncomfortably hard wooden chair. "Tell us, Mrs. Morgan, about your husband. Where is he?"

"I don't know."

"Come now, a wife doesn't know where her husband is? How can that be possible?"

She raised an eyebrow. "Does *your* wife know where you are every minute of the evening, my lord?"

This elicited chuckles in the room, and even Palmerston himself gave her a thin smile. "Well done, Mrs. Morgan. Yet we'll remain focused on the subject, which is your knowledge of your husband's activities. Did your husband not inform you that he attempted to kill His Excellency?" Palmerston motioned to Adams.

"Yes, after the fact, but obviously he was unsuccessful."

"Obviously. What is less obvious is whether he informed you of where he was going when he chose to flee the country like a coward with his brother. Perhaps you can enlighten us?"

Sam nodded at her in encouragement.

"He . . . he said they were going to sail to one of the French

Caribbean islands, but he had no firm plans. After all, he thought he'd just murdered the American minister plenipotentiary. I doubt he was quite altogether sane."

"A point on which we can definitely agree, Mrs. Morgan." More laughter.

From there, Lord Russell took over the questioning, quizzing her in depth about Morgan Undertaking's practices as if to somehow suggest that she was among the unscrupulous sort which would prove that she was not above concealing her husband's whereabouts or misdeeds.

Violet bristled at the insinuation and let Lord Russell know so in direct, unmistakable terms.

"I am an honest woman, my lord. I have always traded fairly and in a Christian manner. I'll not have my reputation impugned by two lords and one faithless husband. I'll ask you, sir, to address me respectfully."

Russell was stunned into silence, so Palmerston continued the questioning, looking at his pocket watch every so often, as if to ensure he was spending enough time on the interrogation.

Meanwhile, the men in the back were scribbling furiously.

Thankfully, after nearly three hours of questioning, Violet was permitted to leave. She needed to return home immediately and get out of her corset, as she hadn't been breathing in more than short gasps all day. The boning was probably permanently imprinted on her skin.

"You performed admirably, Mrs. Morgan, my congratulations," Samuel said as he handed her into the hackney before stepping up inside to join her.

"I had excellent preparation from my American solicitor," she replied.

He laughed. "I suspect lawyers are the same the world over and your resilience and sturdy exterior would have gotten you through it, no matter what lawyer prepared you."

"Speaking of my sturdy exterior, I find that I look forward to arriving home so that I can—"

"May I interest you in an ice from the confectioner's before taking you home?"

"In the middle of winter?"

"I'm a man of few needs, Violet, but an ice cream cornet, I'm afraid, is a year-round requirement."

"I could freeze to death while eating it."

"If you could take on Lords Russell and Palmerston, I've no doubt you could quickly and easily conquer a small wafer filled with cream and sugar."

"If you say so."

"I do say so. I insist. In fact, I am willing to place a bet on it."

"Are you proposing a wager, sir?" It was highly inappropriate to be flirting with him, but how long had it been since she'd had a lighthearted moment like this? Her restrictive corset was forgotten.

"I am. Let's see, I propose that if you are able to finish your ice cream, you will then have to accompany me on a sleigh ride through Hyde Park."

"But that's an activity for society members. Besides, I'm married and you're not my husband. It isn't done."

"Yes, it would be absolutely scandalous."

His eyes were dancing with humor. Very well, she could play this game, too. "Fine, I accept. Now, if I *cannot* eat my ice cream in its entirety, you, sir, will have to teach Susanna another game."

"Accepted. I win either way. Now come, I know a place that doles out the tiniest of servings."

Violet was quite happy when she lost the wager. She found herself breathing quite easily the rest of the afternoon.

Osborne House
February 1862

"Lord Palmerston, ma'am." The servant bowed as he let in her visitor. Was this someone else wanting to urge her back to work? Queen Victoria sighed. She supposed he was yet another minister she'd have to toss out on his ear.

She remained seated and offered him her hand. "Lord Palmerston, how good to see you," she said in a voice that conveyed how displeased she was at the interruption.

"Thank you, Your Majesty. I have news for you, important

enough that I thought it wise to come to Osborne House and deliver it myself."

"What is it?"

"You recall that the prince consort was instrumental in crafting a letter to the United States, advising their government of Britain's position on the *Trent* Affair? It probably saved us from being dragged into a war with them."

"Yes, we remember our dear Albert's fine work with that."

"In our ongoing effort to maintain friendly relations with both sides, Lord Russell and I gave Minister Adams permission to seek out any commerce raiders here in Great Britain, despite my misgivings about anything having to do with the Americans. The news here is mixed: He caught the trail of a pair of brothers seeking an opportunity to sell arms to the Confederacy, but one of them attempted to assassinate Adams."

Why was it that men continued to find reason to intrigue, conspire, and do harm to one another when the entire country was in the depths of darkest mourning? Had they no sense of decency?

"No one was actually hurt—thank goodness, for it saved another diplomatic incident—but the pair of men slipped away to sea before they could be caught. The brothers' names are Fletcher and Graham Morgan."

Morgan? Where had she heard that name before? Oh, of course, the undertaker.

"One of our dear Albert's undertakers was a woman named Mrs. Morgan."

"Yes, ma'am, that's the odd thing. She's Graham Morgan's wife."

Albert's undertaker was married to a common criminal? Impossible.

"Was she part of their conspiracy?"

"No, Your Majesty. We have questioned her thoroughly and believe she had no knowledge of her husband's schemes."

"Naturally she was innocent. Albert wouldn't have selected her otherwise."

"Your Majesty?"

"Never mind. How is Mrs. Morgan?"

"Doing well, I suppose, madam." Lord Palmerston's face was puzzled.

Let him be so.

"We have questioned Mrs. Morgan at length, madam, about whether she was involved in her husband's activities. We concluded that she knew nothing, but have not issued a formal statement exonerating her, so as not to alienate the North."

Victoria's mind wandered as the prime minister rattled on about the state of things between Britain and both the United States and the Confederacy, especially now that Messrs. Mason and Slidell were in London.

Perhaps she'd been too hasty in her assessment of Mrs. Morgan. After all, dearest Albert had been impressed with her, and she had quickly and efficiently taken over much of Albert's funeral service when Mr. Rowland came down ill. Victoria had only learned of the change in directors when she'd invited Mr. Rowland to Osborne House to give her every imaginable detail about her husband's funeral.

He was of no use, since he'd ultimately missed it all as he lay shivering in bed. He'd sent Mrs. Morgan in his stead, and claimed she'd performed admirably. Victoria had forgotten about the funeral itself as she wrapped herself up in ordering scads of first-year mourning dresses, fans, and ornaments, certain that a grief as large as hers could never be overcome.

However, Lord Palmerston's mention of the name again reminded Victoria that she had never obtained the details she desired. Perhaps it was time to summon Mrs. Morgan. Surely another woman would understand her terrible sorrow and want to discuss it. Yes, she'd send a note today.

"Do you seek our signature for something, Lord Palmerston?"

"No, madam, I merely wanted you to hear from me about the state of things, especially since the criminals were related to the woman who—"

Victoria waved a hand. "Yes, yes, thank you. We're tired now and wish to sleep."

Palmerston hastily stood and bowed before leaving.

Victoria reached for a bell. She needed writing paper.

* * *

Far from removing herself from Graham's skullduggery, Violet was being drawn further and further into it. First there was the grand inquisition by Lord Palmerston, which she'd sailed through thanks to Sam. Today, however, she opened the latest copy of *Punch* during breakfast, only to find an unflattering account and engraving of her questioning. The John Tenniel engraving depicted her as a harpy swooping over the heads of Palmerston, Russell, and Adams, plucking their heads off with her claws. The article inside *The Times* was even worse.

> . . . As we have frequently stated—and today confirm—the untrustworthiness of Americans cannot be overstated. The same is true for those who AID and GIVE SUPPORT to American false dealings. Today we learn that even a WIFE, that tenderhearted and most gentle sex of our society, can be as dark and evil as any conniving husband. As such we will carefully watch Mrs. MORGAN, whom we admit acquitted herself well under questioning, but can any wife be too far removed from her husband's activities?

Violet crumpled the paper up and added it to the pile of them next to the fireplace, which Mrs. Porter would eventually twist into spills for lighting fires.

"What's the matter, Mama? Are you angry with me?" Susanna asked.

"Of course not. The newspaper is full of nonsense today is all. Why would you think I'm angry with you?"

"You said you would teach me to read from the newspaper."

"And I will. Just not from today's paper. No pouting, Susanna, it's unbecoming of a girl your age."

After breakfast, she left with Susanna to head to the shop, stopping first at the bookseller's for something new to read.

Susanna had picked up the odd habit of taking Mrs. Softpaws

for walks on a lead. The cat didn't seem to mind unless she saw a tasty mouse or another cat with whom to do battle, in which case Mrs. Softpaws struggled as though she were being led to her own hanging.

Violet realized she probably looked like the most eccentric woman in England walking London's streets—an undertaker in her tall black hat accompanying a child and a leashed cat.

Graham would have much to say about their chances of entering society with *that* kind of odd behavior.

Worrying over Graham and his whereabouts had consumed great quantities of time, despite the fact that she'd not received the briefest of notes from him, but she was now resolved to cease her worries, which gave her more time to read.

The bookseller, however, was less than friendly.

"Yes?" he asked, his glasses far down on his nose.

"Good morning, Mr. Hatchard, I'm looking for a novel to read. Do you have anything new?"

"You could write your own lurid novel, I'm sure, Mrs. Morgan."

Violet felt heat rush to her face. "Excuse me?"

"I didn't realize I've been selling merchandise to such a bad piece all these years."

She saw the newspaper lying open on the counter behind him. So years of patronage meant nothing as compared to a garish piece in *The Times*.

"Mr. Hatchard, perhaps you don't realize I have a young girl with me. Kindly mind your manners."

"She looks old enough to me. Presumably you didn't realize you had a young girl with you when you entered into your husband's mischief."

Violet's heart pounded so noisily she barely heard her own next words. "I see you are the most gullible of men. My mother often warned me of simpletons who believe the baldest lie published by scurrilous newspapers seeking to sell copies. I'd once thought you were a man of taste, Mr. Hatchard, given your selection of fine books and the discerning clientele you attract, but I see now that you are just a common fool. Susanna, come, there are more respectable shops to visit."

From the bookshop, she and Susanna went to the chemist's, as Violet was nearly out of tooth powder. She received an equally frosty reception there with the owner, a man she'd patronized for years, who nearly refused to help and accepted her payment with complete disdain.

Once outside in the street, Violet took a deep breath. *This is dreadful,* she thought. *What if everyone in London is reading and believing this tripe? My business will shrivel up overnight. I cannot permit it. How ironic that I am found innocent before the government, but guilty, guilty, guilty in the court of public opinion.*

She stood still in the middle of the noise and congestion around her, lost in contemplation over what to do about her situation, which did nothing but grow worse. Finally, Susanna squeezed her hand. "Are we going to open the shop for today?"

Violet then realized what she had to do. "Indeed we are. In fact, we're going to open up everything."

Violet took the advertisement she had written to Mary to ask her opinion.

"Oh, my dear, you've had such hardship lately. If you need someone strong to intervene for you, I can ask George to—"

"That's quite all right. I intend to take care of this myself."

"If you're sure . . ." Mary proceeded to proffer advice on how to more strongly word her advertisement, which Violet planned to place in *The Times, The Illustrated London News, Punch,* and whatever other periodical she could find.

Violet was proud of the final published advertisement, which cost her a small fortune and took up a half page in several newspapers. It would be worth the money, if it stopped the libelous attacks against her.

Morgan Undertaking offers complete
and professional funeral services
to SOCIETY, the TRADES,
and those of LESSER MEANS.
All work overseen by Mrs. Morgan,
assistant undertaker to the recent burial of

His Highness, the PRINCE CONSORT.
Competent, honest, PATRIOTIC
Let any man who can claim otherwise provide proof.
Funeral inquiries can be made on premises
at Queen's Road in PADDINGTON.

Violet and Susanna were alone in the shop together, while Will and Harry were out hanging black crape on the family home of a local theater actor who had just passed on. Violet, meanwhile, was busy preparing his obituary notice. At least all of her business hadn't dried up. She reviewed her notes as she wrote:

Departed this life February eighteenth, at his residence in Covent Garden, Mr. Herbert Goodwyn, husband to Lucy Goodwyn, in the 50th year of his age. In recording the death of this truly estimable gentleman, we are forcibly reminded of the seeming truth of the sentiment, "Death loves a shining mark." By his uniform kindness and amiability, and his superlative performances upon the stage, he won the esteem and affection of all who knew him, and lastingly endeared himself to those with whom he was more intimately connected.

Mr. Goodwyn had been ravaged by an illness and required extensive cosmetics, which reminded her that she needed to purchase more—

The bell jangled, distracting both her and Susanna, who was unpacking a box of mourning fans and arranging them in a pretty display. It was Samuel Harper.

"Why, Sam, is it true that I have still have a friend left in London?"

He entered, one hand behind his back. "I can't speak for any other faithless scoundrels, but I am—and always will be—your devoted friend."

"It would seem that my friends now live across the Atlantic Ocean."

"Except your friend Mary."

"Except her. And my family."

"Yet, if it is true that I am your only other friend, you'll find none truer."

"Thank you, Sam. Is today's visit intended solely to boost my wounded pride?"

"Er, no, I, um, was wondering if you've received any word from Mr. Morgan."

"Ah, speaking of scoundrels. No, he hasn't contacted me. I've no idea if he's on a remote island somewhere, was lost at sea, or picked up by pirates."

"You're remarkably calm over it."

"I've decided that my tears are better spent elsewhere."

"I see." Samuel shifted to one foot. "I brought with me a gift of friendship." He moved his hand out from behind his back. He held a single yellow rose, its petals poised to open, and promising to be a luscious bloom when it did so.

"How lovely, Sam. Yellow is indeed the color of friendship, isn't it?"

Samuel's earlobes turned red again. "Yes, I came for another reason, though. I've read the salvos against you in the papers and saw your rebuttal advertisement, as well. How have you been faring since?"

"I've not seen a disastrous drop in business, even if it isn't what it once was. As for neighboring shops and acquaintances, well, let's just say that if I were a member of society, I would declare myself cut."

Samuel looked puzzled.

"You see, the worst thing that could possibly happen to a society matron is to find herself snubbed in public, or cut. It's really a tragedy beyond compare."

"Ah. It doesn't appear to have you too overwrought."

"Since I don't have the worries of being in society, it isn't terribly devastating. I'm mostly concerned about the drop in business." Violet laid the rose across the papers she was working on.

"You look busy enough."

"Appearances can be deceiving. I still have some clients, but for how long? Reputation is everything in the undertaking business.

After all, we deal with people in their most private moment. A blot on our character is our ruin. I cannot afford a scandal."

"I understand. There was recently such a scandal in America."

"You have unscrupulous funeral men there?"

"Not generally, but the war is, as you can imagine, increasing the need for them. A pair of undertakers, Hutton and Williams, set themselves up to especially care for dead soldiers before they are shipped home by train."

"Your undertakers must be expert embalmers."

"I'm afraid I wouldn't know. However, the two men were recently accused of lifting bodies from the battlefield, embalming them without family permission, then refusing to release the bodies for shipment home until the families paid their outrageous fee for the embalming."

"What were they charging?"

"Something around a hundred dollars."

Violet drew in a sharp breath. "That's an outrageous price."

"The U.S. government thought so, too. Hutton and Williams were arrested and imprisoned, but a sufficient case could not be brought against them and so they were released."

"Reputations ruined, I presume?"

"Time will tell. There's a great need for their services right now, and we don't have quite the penchant for 'cutting' as the British do."

Violet laughed. "Perhaps I'd be much more successful in America, then."

Susanna tossed aside the empty box from which she'd been pulling fans. Nodding in satisfaction at her countertop display, she came to where Violet stood talking to Samuel.

"Good day, Mr. Harper. Do *you* think Mama would be successful in America? I do."

"This does bring me to my point, though, Violet, which is my recommendation that you consider moving—for your and Susanna's protection."

"Moving! Where?"

"To where you and Susanna both recommend yourselves . . . the United States."

"The United States? You're at war! How in heaven's name would that be safe for us? Besides, my entire life is here. My parents are in Brighton, I have a home here, and presumably at some point Graham may be back."

"The war is mostly confined to the South. The capital is safe, your honest services are desperately needed, and, quite frankly, Violet, I doubt Graham will return. Even if he did, you need protection from him as much as from anyone else."

"This is foolish. I'm in no physical danger, from Graham or anyone else. I'm simply in a difficult situation at the moment. Susanna and I will be fine." She stepped over to put a protective arm around the girl, who stood stiffly next to her. It wasn't like Susanna to not immediately lean against Violet.

"I've no doubt about your capability to fend off the average ill-wishers and name-callers, but I'm not as convinced that they are the totality of peril to which you may be subject. I'm sure you're aware of the anti-American sentiment here, and Mr. Morgan's activities ensure those sentiments will extend over your own household."

"It is probably far less than the anti-British sentiment in your country."

"That's not true in Washington City. There are diplomatic corps from many countries living in that city. You would be made welcome there, I'm sure of it."

"You underestimate my ability to defend myself. Have you ever been to Washington City, Sam?"

"Of course. My law practice is situated there."

"I thought you were from Massachusetts?"

"I am, but my law partner's family is from Bladensburg, Maryland, near the capital, and so he is based there, while I spend most of my time in Massachusetts."

Violet had heard details of that city. Wasn't that where Graham's father had fought during the War of 1812? "Mr. Dickens writes that Washington is a city of magnificent intentions, but little else. That it has spacious avenues that begin in nothing and lead to nowhere, and lack only for houses and inhabitants. I cannot believe you would recommend I go to such a place."

Samuel shook his head. "Typical inane British reaction to all things American. You've never set foot in our country, yet you have the notion that we're nothing but rustic savages who traipse about in patched-up clothing, bickering about everything in barely passable English. You Brits know nothing of how modern we are. You stay insulated inside your antiquated notion that we are still one of your humble little colonies with no wherewithal to govern ourselves."

"You obviously have no idea what I really think of Americans."

Samuel plowed forward. "And when I—a humbled American—offer you protective advice, your fur goes flying and your sharpened nails are ready for the attack."

How dare Sam insult her? She'd been minding her shop, not requesting his interference in her personal life, when he strode in, telling her she needed to transplant herself across the ocean, as though he were her father. Or worse, as though he were Graham.

"Mr. Harper, how could you suggest that I flee London like some common criminal scheduled for transportation to a penal colony? In fact, how dare you suggest anything at all? I'm not your wife, we are merely friends, if you recall." Violet picked up the rose and flourished it once before slamming it down on Mr. Goodwyn's unfinished obituary.

"I suggest no such thing. If you don't just beat the Dutch, Mrs. Morgan. I am merely making a recommendation for your future, out of concern for you and Susanna. You've already seen the elephant in your life and I am not suggesting that you do something any worse than you have already experienced."

"Beat the Dutch? See the elephant? I have no idea what you're talking about."

"You never do. Good day to you, madam." Samuel slammed his hat on his head and banged his way out the door. The bells jangled viciously, unlike the sweet tinkle they'd made when he first entered a half hour ago.

Already Violet regretted her harsh words.

Susanna put her head on Violet's shoulder and wrapped her arms around her. "Why are you so unkind to Mr. Harper? I like him. So does Mrs. Softpaws."

Violet sighed. "I suppose that's the problem. Sometimes liking someone means you push them away before your feelings can cause trouble."

"Mama, that makes no sense. It's only words that cause trouble, not feelings."

"I know, but there it is. Why don't we concentrate on some more of your grammar lessons this afternoon, since the shop isn't too busy?"

Later that evening, Violet took the rose home and spread the petals in a bowl on her vanity table, inhaling deeply of their rich fragrance and wishing life weren't so difficult.

Osborne House
March 1, 1862

A new summons to see the queen, this time at Osborne House on the Isle of Wight, erased Violet's misgivings about what had happened with Samuel and replaced them with a new and different fear. What did the queen know about Graham's activities? Had she been properly apprised of Violet's innocence by Lord Palmerston, or had he let the queen believe whatever she read in the press?

If the queen read all of the scurrilous news about her, was this summons intended to rebuke Violet even further? If she was to be chastised by Queen Victoria, all hopes of continuing her business would evaporate, once the foxes and hounds alike were finished devouring her in the press.

Instead of the excitement she'd felt on her first journey in comfortable luxury, the trip to Osborne House filled Violet with terror, the choppy, bitterly cold ferry ride from Portsmouth to the Isle of Wight adding to her trepidation. She felt as though she were seeing the sun, the rolling landscape, and the bouncing waves for the last time on the road to her own execution. All that was missing were bystanders throwing rocks and vegetables at her. As usual, the servants in their scarlet and blue livery were uncommunicative, so Violet didn't even bother trying to get information out of them as to the purpose of the summons.

The queen had changed drastically since the death of her husband. Violet was struck by how puffed and swollen her eyes and cheeks were, as though her tears had run in an endless stream for more than three months. The queen's mourning gown was fashionable, and jet dripped from her neck, ears, wrists, and fingers. In fact, her ensemble threatened to swallow the queen whole in her misery.

Was Dr. Jenner attending to the queen?

Violet curtsied to the queen and sat in the chair Victoria indicated.

"Mrs. Morgan, this is a singular honor for you, as we now live mostly in seclusion here at Osborne House. We join hundreds of thousands of our countrymen in remaining in mourning for the prince consort."

"Yes, Your Majesty."

"We're sure you, as an undertaker, can feel the pall that has blanketed Great Britain. We fear that the lowest bootblack struggles to fulfill his daily duties, so great is our national grief. It is as though we'll never see our way through it, is it not, Mrs. Morgan?"

"Yes, Your Majesty." Violet wondered if Dr. Jenner was on the premises, and, if so, could she find him?

Victoria stared blankly at the wall behind Violet for several moments before continuing. "Yet, you are wondering why we called you here today."

Wondering, and praying she wouldn't have cause to tell Sam he was right.

"To assuage our personal grief, and therefore giving reason for all others to lessen their own, we wish you to tell us about our dear prince's funeral."

"You mean . . . you wish to know about the mourners in attendance, the flowers, that sort of thing?"

"Much more than that, Mrs. Morgan. We especially want to know of the prince consort's repose. Was he peaceful? Was his brow unfurrowed? How was he dressed? Did our son show the proper amount of respect to his father?"

Violet explained in as comprehensive a way as she could, leaving out the more—unpleasant—details. The queen constantly interrupted her with questions and for clarifications. Did the horses have black plumes on their heads? Did Bertie touch his head to his dear father's coffin? Did Dean Wellesley read from the Psalms? How many wreaths were placed on the coffin? Who placed the violet and camellia wreath she had sent from Osborne House?

Violet was exhausted by the end, but comforted by the fact that the queen apparently had no intent of dismissing her from the royal presence and thereby giving the press an even more delectable bit of haunch into which to sink their fanged teeth.

Once the queen was satisfied that she'd wrung every pertinent detail from Violet that she could, her mind wandered to other things.

"We believe we may have told you, Mrs. Morgan, that we have decided to have a new resting place built for my husband at Frogmore, our home about a half mile away from Windsor. A glorious mausoleum is being built there. A private place where he can rest in peace and comfort away from the others buried in Windsor."

"He is right now among the greatest kings and queens that have ruled England, madam."

"Which is entirely unsuitable for our dearest Albert. He needs quiet and calm, not to be placed under the floor where he'll be trod over by millions of feet over the years. It's unthinkable. No, the prince must rest in a place befitting his greatness. It is in this mausoleum that we shall join him one day, to rest in eternal glory together."

"Yes, Your Majesty."

"Which brings us to the second reason for your presence. When the mausoleum is finished, we may require you again to assist. Albert did, after all, mention you by name."

So far from a dismissal, she was to be summoned again for the reinterment. What a fantastic piece of luck. If only she could enjoy so much good fortune until that time.

My dearest diary, I've agreed to a new . . . commission, shall we say. My mark accepted all of my credentials and didn't even ask for my characters. What kind of fool doesn't ask for references for the most important sorts of work? Clearly I was brought here by destiny. I find it fascinating how well I can hide in plain sight.

❧ 16 ❧

It is uncertain where Death will await you;
therefore expect it everywhere.

—Lucius Annaeus Seneca (4 B.C.–65 A.D.)
Epistulae morales ad Lucilium

Morgan Undertaking
March 3, 1862

Violet tried to organize receipts and bills, but she was distracted.

Graham had now been gone two months with no word forthcoming from him. Violet despised the purgatory he'd left her in, still viewed with suspicion by her neighbors and without any idea as to whether she was married, a widow, or simply abandoned.

If Graham came back, perhaps she should ensure her own widowhood.

At least none of her supplies were going missing anymore, which told her exactly who had been stealing them. She imagined he'd used them to hide weapons, to be used by Southerners for killing Northerners. What an incomprehensible use of funerary equipment.

She shook her head. It no longer bore thinking about.

What of Samuel Harper and the cold way they'd parted? Did that bear further thought?

She finished what she was doing and called out to Susanna, who was now flourishing. All of Violet's efforts in teaching her to read, write, and do sums were paying off. Violet would watch, bemused, as the girl painstakingly entered customer names and payments into their giant brown-leather journal. Susanna always frowned in concentration as she struggled to enter everything in without making mistakes.

In fact, it was quite remarkable the advances the girl was making. Violet commented on it once, and Susanna told her that her mother had spent some time teaching her things, but when Violet inquired further, Susanna clamped her lips together and refused to talk about her early home life.

At the moment, Susanna was bent down behind the counter, rearranging empty mourning brooches in their tray, while Will and Harry were off on errands. The girl had an affinity not only for recordkeeping, but for the artful arrangement of the shop's displays. Graham had never appreciated the girl's natural talent for this business. Perhaps tonight she should talk to Susanna about a formal apprenticeship.

Together they closed up the shop and went home, where Violet was startled to find Samuel Harper waiting for her in the drawing room. "Mrs. Porter let me in. I hope you don't mind."

Susanna bounded right over to him as he stood to greet them. "Mr. Harper, you didn't forget us. Have you another present for me?"

"Susanna! You can't speak to our guest that way."

"It's fine, Violet. Actually, Susanna, I'm afraid I only have something small for you." He reached down to the sofa where he'd been sitting. Violet's copy of *Silas Marner* lay open next to another wrapped package. He handed the gift to Susanna, who tore it open to find a miniature carriage and two horses, with a driver behind the reins. It was exquisite.

"The driver is removable, in case you have other work for him to do." Samuel plucked the driver from his seat to demonstrate before giving it back to her. "I thought the empty room in the basement would be perfect for a mews."

Susanna darted over to her dollhouse, which now held a permanent place atop a table in the center of the drawing room. Violet sincerely doubted she'd be hosting any further social events that would make obvious her lack of propriety in domestic matters.

Samuel cleared his throat.

"My primary reason for coming by was to talk to you, Violet. May I still call you Violet?"

She nodded.

"First, I'd like to offer my apologies for what happened last time we met. I'm afraid my temper ran away with me."

"I'm fairly certain it ran away with Graham at least once, too."

His ears turned pink. "Yes, well, I come with a gift of peace." Reaching back over to the sofa, he picked up another gift, cradled in tissue with a tiny golden bow around it. It was a yellow rose.

"I'm sure you cast the other one in the sewer, so I brought you this one in hopes of starting our friendship over. I am truly sorry for suggesting that you flee London and your life here. I'll never ask again."

Violet took the rose and smiled. "I wish I had a gift to offer you in return as an apology. I had no right to shriek like a harpy at you. It made me look exactly as the newspapers have portrayed me." She laid the rose on top of the piano. "Here it can be a reminder of our Christmas sing-along, before life was torn asunder. Do you remember?"

"I do. In fact—" Sam pulled a small tin instrument from his pocket. "I brought this along to share with Miss Susanna. My harmonica always reminds me of home." He cupped the harmonica in his hands and blew against one side of it. It made a wheezy sound. After several puffs he began to sing, once again adopting his false Southern accent.

I came from Alabama, with a banjo on my knee,
I'm gone to Louisiana, My true love for to see.
It rain'd all night the day I left, the weather it was dry,
The sun so hot I froze to death; Susanna, don't you cry.
Oh! Susanna, Oh don't you cry for me,
'cos I've come from Alabama, with my banjo on my knee.

Violet and Susanna clapped along. At the end, Susanna said, "The song is about me!"

"Indeed. Did you enjoy it?"

"Yes, sing it again, Mr. Harper."

He smiled. "Maybe later. I need to talk more with your mother. Which brings up the other reason I'm here," Samuel said, turning his attention back to Violet. "With Mr. Adams's assistance, we've convinced Lord Palmerston that you have been unfairly tormented by Parliament's questioning and the resultant blot on your name, so he agreed to write a letter that formally clears you of any wrongdoing in the case of your husband's criminal activity." He pulled a sealed letter from his jacket for Violet to read.

In flowery language, it apologized for Violet's inconveniences without actually apologizing for Parliament's hostile questioning.

"Are politics in Washington City as scheming as they are in Great Britain?"

"They're probably worse. Just two years ago we were engulfed in a scandal when a congressman from New York shot and killed the district attorney of Washington City when he found out the district attorney was having an affair with his wife. Naturally, he was acquitted of any crime since he was prominent and influential."

"So politicians are the same the world over."

He laughed. "It would seem so."

"Tell me, Sam, have you or Mr. Adams heard anything about Graham?"

"I'm sorry, no. Although I have to be honest, we're beginning to assume he's gone."

"Gone? You mean hidden himself beyond finding?"

"No, Violet, I mean *gone*."

Violet's stomach lurched despite all of her stored anger toward Graham. "That can't be true, can it, Sam?"

He shrugged. "No ship has discovered him on the seas between here and the United States, and agents sent to both French and British holdings in the Caribbean haven't found him, nor has he been found trying to slip past the blockade in Hampton Roads."

She nodded. "I understand. I do believe I will avoid asking about him again."

Susanna reappeared between them to drag Samuel over to the dollhouse to see what she'd done with the horse and carriage. After several minutes of Susanna chattering about the Orange Peel family and their trip to the countryside in their new carriage, Samuel turned back to Violet.

"Now that we've made amends, I must confess that I am having a serious yearning for more ice cream, and was hoping you and Miss Susanna would like to accompany me."

"Ice cream?" Susanna asked.

"Please don't tell me your mother has never treated you to this wonderful concoction of cream and sugar."

Susanna shook her head.

"Impossible! Obviously it has merely slipped her mind that everyone needs a taste of this treat at least once in his lifetime."

The trio went out into the cold, where Samuel hired a hack to take them to the same shop where he and Violet had shared ice cream before. Susanna declared the treat "perfect" and asked if they could return every day. Violet slipped into the comfort of chatting amiably with Samuel, with time passing in such a rush that it was pitch black outside when they were finished.

It didn't seem frightening to go outside with Sam at her side.

It was good to be friends again.

At Samuel's urging, Violet published Lord Palmerston's letter in several newspapers. It had the desired effect, for business almost immediately began to improve; hence she and Susanna were now at the residence of Mrs. Saunders, who ran a boardinghouse in Lambeth. Mrs. Saunders, an elderly woman with bulging eyes and hair an unfortunate shade of red, greeted her at the door, wringing her hands and chattering nervously.

"Thank you, Mrs. Morgan. Mr. Atkinson asked me to take care of this for him and I'm not sure how he expects this to be my responsibility when it's his wife and all, and I've already had so much to endure what with the police and all and I—"

"Excuse me, did you say the police have been here?"

"Yes, but I suppose it's nothing for you to worry over. Poor Mrs. Atkinson passed on, then a thief broke in during the night and robbed her of all her money and jewelry, if you can imagine such an un-Christian and uncharitable thing to do to the poor lady. The scallywag swiped several items from my other boarders while they slept, too. Mrs. Bainbridge lost a tortoiseshell comb that was a gift from her grandmother, and Mr. Devon says his silver-tipped walking cane is missing, and then there's poor Mrs. Wilson, who shared a room with Mrs. Atkinson—they were great friends, you know—and she not only lost her friend but a—"

"So you say the police have investigated the matter?"

"Yes, yes, both the police and Dr. Beasley. The police say they're investigating the matter, although it seems to me that nowhere in London is safe anymore, what with the hooligans hiding in the smoky vapors swirling in the streets and leaving us women open to attacks. I take a kitchen knife with me everywhere these days just so I—"

"A very sad state of affairs, indeed." Violet shook her head in sympathy. "About Dr. Beasley . . ."

"He came to visit poor Mrs. Atkinson, but he said it looked as though she'd died peacefully, perhaps some unknown heart trouble or something. Is your girl going upstairs with you? Doesn't seem proper, does it?"

When Violet ignored the comment, Mrs. Saunders followed her and Susanna up to the third floor where Mrs. Atkinson had lodged, still nattering on.

"I think Mrs. Atkinson and her husband were having troubles, if you understand my meaning, else why would she have come to London from Lincolnshire—or wait, was it Yorkshire—to stay with her friend? Mrs. Wilson is simply devastated, too. She sleeps in my room, won't eat a thing and paces the streets for hours at a time. I tell her it's dangerous to do it, but—"

Violet tapped her undertaker's bag. "I believe we have all we require, Mrs. Saunders. We shan't be long."

"Oh, of course, right. I'll be downstairs if you need me. I'll brew up a nice pot of tea and—"

Violet quietly shut the door to Mrs. Atkinson's room and Mrs. Saunders's voice faded. The room was dark, although Violet could make out the shape of two beds, with one of them containing a prone form.

"Susanna, open the curtains, will you?"

Light flooded the room, despite the fog outside. Without having to be asked, Susanna dragged a chair over to Mrs. Atkinson's bedside, then went to the other side and knelt next to the dead woman.

Violet set her bag on the chair before examining Mrs. Atkinson. She was of indeterminate age—perhaps in her early forties?—and her teeth were grossly stained and pitted, a condition which had carried over to her lips. "Don't you worry, Mrs. Atkinson, I'll take care of putting your lips together so that no one ever need know what's inside. A little tinted salve for your lips will brighten your entire appearance. I know you'll want to look pretty when your husband arrives."

The blanket covering Mrs. Atkinson was entirely too thin for the season and looked as though moths had enjoyed a great feast on it. Was this the best Mrs. Saunders could do?

Susanna was now stroking Mrs. Atkinson's hair, which lay long and loose under her, away from her face. The girl began humming.

Violet continued her inspection of Mrs. Atkinson in order to decide what supplies she would need. The woman's complexion was extremely sallow and would be difficult to improve with her cosmetic massages. If only embalming were more accepted in England, she could bring this woman's features nearly to life.

The unbidden thought of Samuel's suggestion to move to Washington City reared up, and she quickly swatted it away.

Violet ran her hands down the woman's arms, both of which lay outside the blanket. Mrs. Atkinson's right hand had tiny blotches that had been eaten away, almost as if the moths had included the deceased woman in their feast.

But moths aren't carnivorous.

"Susanna, look at this," she said. Susanna gently took the woman's hand from her to view it. With a gasp, she dropped Mrs. Atkinson's arm, which landed on her body with a thump and rolled off to loll listlessly from the side of the bed.

"Susanna, that's no way to treat Mrs. Atkinson. What's wrong with you?" Violet asked of the girl, whose shocked eyes were the only thing visible from where she now cowered in a corner.

"No—nothing."

"There's no need to be frightened. Mrs. Atkinson just had some kind of odd skin condition that we'll have to cover. Come, you can't insult her by sitting there chattering your teeth."

"Mama, I don't feel well. I'll wait here while you finish."

How strange. Susanna had never shirked from a dead body before. Surely a skin disease wasn't enough to frighten the girl. She shook her head. How very little she understood about children.

She lifted Mrs. Atkinson's dangling arm and placed it back on the bed before rolling the moth-eaten blanket down farther. The woman wore a typical ivory nightgown with lace details at the neck and wrists, although it was bunched up around her thighs. There were more of the round, decayed spots farther down on her legs. Was it some kind of unusual rash? Had Mrs. Atkinson scratched the bumps to the point that her nails had broken the skin and dug small holes?

It didn't seem likely. Yet the doctor had seen her and declared nothing out of sorts. If a doctor found a death to have been the result of natural causes, an undertaker was in no position to suggest an autopsy. Dr. Beasley's findings were unquestionable, unless the family requested an autopsy.

Violet continued looking at the round holes on Mrs. Atkinson's legs, trying to puzzle out what they were. At least Susanna's teeth had stopped chattering, and she was sitting quietly in the corner.

She continued puzzling over it while preparing Mrs. Atkinson's body, working as best she could to give the poor woman a flesh-tone color to her skin and arranging her hair into something more fashionable than the long tendrils that were matted under her body. Finally she gave up thinking about it. She was no doctor.

As she and Susanna prepared to leave, the landlady rushed to greet them again and accompany them down the stairs to the door.

"I know we all feel better now that Mrs. Atkinson is ready for visitors. Everyone here will want to pay their respects, and I'm sure Mr. Atkinson will appreciate what you've—"

"Mrs. Saunders, you say Dr. Beasley determined no autopsy was necessary on Mrs. Atkinson?"

"That's right. He said he saw no sign that it was anything other than some unfortunate illness she must have had. He was a very nice gentleman, very kindly with such a gentle manner. If I wasn't still so attached to my Martin, gone all these years but still my one and only—"

Martin had undoubtedly been talked into an early grave. "Thank you, Mrs. Saunders. Mrs. Atkinson is prepared. When will her husband be here? Shall I take possession of her until that time? I can send one of my assistants around with a hearse."

"Oh no, he'll be here tonight and wants to see her himself. Maybe you can return tomorrow to see what arrangements he wants to make?"

"I'll do that." It would be an excellent opportunity to discuss with him what she'd found and recommend that he ask for an autopsy on his poor wife.

It was a wasted trip. When Violet arrived the next day, Mrs. Saunders explained—at great length—that Mr. Atkinson had come in a large carriage in the middle of the night and whisked his wife away to be buried back in York.

How very curious.

☙ 17 ❧

For the wages of sin is death.

—Romans 6:23

Violet stared at the letter in her hand, which had arrived during the morning post as she ate breakfast. Finally Graham had communicated with her, but the contents of his missive made her stomach roil.

> *Lillian Rose, somewhere in the North Atlantic*
> *I haven't much time. We've met up with another ship on its way back to England, and the captain promised to post this for me. You would be shocked to see how my beard has grown. I blend well with the savage Americans, as well as with the pirates who prowl these waters. Fletcher and I have learned enough accents to get us through most encounters. I don't know when I can possibly return to London, but I've decided that it is unsafe for you to continue as you are in London. You may come under suspicion for my actions.*

Really, Graham?

> *I've given it considerable thought and have decided the best thing for you is to sell Morgan Undertaking and return to your parents' home in Brighton. You'll be secure there and the sale should give you enough to live on for*

*some time. You will be more comfortable with the girl
there, too. Do not sell the house, as I'll need a place to stay
whenever I can make it home. Obey my instructions
quickly.*

She reread the letter. There was no inkling of an apology in it.

"So let me understand this, husband," she said aloud to the walls of the drawing room. "You deceive me, abandon me, and leave me to fend for myself, and now you instruct me to further ruin my life? I believe I'll manage quite well on my own, thank you. Nothing will ever, ever make me part with Morgan Undertaking."

With that, she angrily shredded the letter in her hands and threw the pieces into the fireplace, deciding as she did so not to share the fact that she'd received it with anyone.

Not even Sam.

*Osborne House
March 7, 1862*

Violet was surprised to receive yet another summons so soon from the queen. This time, she took Susanna along with her.

The servant who came to escort her looked askance at Susanna. "I'm not sure Her Majesty wished to see both of you."

"The queen has nine children of her own. I imagine she would enjoy meeting a well-behaved girl like Susanna."

The servant seemed doubtful, but permitted it.

Violet should have paid attention to his hesitation, for the queen was not at all pleased that Violet had brought Susanna along.

"Mrs. Morgan, who is this, your daughter?"

"Not exactly. She's an orphan from a workhouse that I found. Or rather, she found me. She's my apprentice now."

"Like *Oliver Twist.*"

"Except that she's like a daughter to me."

"I see." Her tone suggested that she didn't. "Perhaps she would like to play with one of the palace dogs." The queen rang a bell, and a servant appeared to take Susanna away to play with the royal dogs, a ménage of spaniels, terriers, and greyhounds. At the same time, a maid appeared with a tray heaped with sandwiches and cakes, along with a pot of tea and cups. She poured two cups and silently disappeared.

"Help yourself, Mrs. Morgan. Our appetite has not quite recovered yet." Indeed, the queen was still pale and ashen.

Violet nibbled at a smoked salmon sandwich. It was delicious.

"You are probably wondering why we called you back again so soon."

"I am honored to be called, no matter what the reason."

"You sound like one of my ministers, Mrs. Morgan. Come, have we not had frank conversation in the past?"

"Yes, Your Majesty."

"I've been reflecting upon our last conversation, and realized what a sympathetic soul you are. You truly understood our pain, and shared our deep and abiding grief. The prince was correct in his assessment of you."

"Thank you, Your Majesty."

"This is why we knew you would enjoy another opportunity to reflect on the prince consort's passing and the momentous occasion surrounding it."

Oh dear, not again.

Unfortunately for Violet, the queen wished to go over the funeral once more in fine detail, even to the point of asking how well polished the mourners' boots were.

This was going to require more sandwiches in order to maintain fortitude.

After an hour of this, a servant scratched at the door. "Dr. Jenner to see you, ma'am."

"Dr. Jenner, you have an uncanny talent for appearing when Mrs. Morgan is here. Come, we are having the most pleasant *tête-à-tête* about our dear prince. Join us."

Jenner poured himself a cup of tea before sitting down and crossing his legs. "Now, madam, please tell me you've not allowed Mrs. Morgan to disrupt your tranquility. I'll not have it, you know."

Victoria broke into a tremulous smile. "To the contrary, Dr. Jenner, she brings us great peace. We're even considering offering her a place here, to work with Mr. Rowland."

Violet nearly dropped her fourth sandwich. The pleasurable thrill at the thought of a royal appointment was immediately replaced with the terror of what such an appointment would mean. "Your Majesty, I—"

Dr. Jenner interrupted. "What ho, madam, are you reduced to finding comfort in dredging up gloomy doings? In walking in a black cloud? How can our great and noble queen recover her firm constitution by engaging in these conversations?"

"We find Mrs. Morgan to be a woman of gentle spirit. Despite her unladylike profession, she is quite devoted to our prince and her conversation is a balm to our soul."

Jenner focused on Violet. "How long have you been an undertaker?"

"Almost ten years. I joined my husband in his business upon our marriage."

"Have you any children?"

"None of my own, no."

"That's because of your unnatural work outside of your natural sphere of domesticity, my dear. The queen shares my aversion to women usurping the role of men."

Unnatural? "But I don't—"

"We've made an exception for Mrs. Morgan," Victoria said. "Our dear prince respected her." The warning in her tone was unmistakable.

Dr. Jenner, however, seemed to take no offense. "The prince was always insightful and the greatest judge of character, wasn't he, madam? Therefore, I now renounce my previous statement and offer my hearty welcome to our dear Mrs. Morgan."

Was the man being sarcastic, or merely bluff and hearty?

"Thank you," Violet said, unsure what else to say.

"Well, well, then, Mrs. Morgan, tell us more about what you do. Since the prince thought so highly of you, you must not be one of those unscrupulous types who starts a burial club that never pays when needed."

"Of course not. Such practices are blights on my profession."

"You pride yourself, then, on being a paragon among undertakers."

"No, just a respectable tradeswoman."

"Yes, quite. You've been recently involved with an American agent, haven't you? No need to bristle, madam, I am merely wondering if you know whether their funeral practices equal ours."

"Well, one thing I admire is that the Americans are widely using embalming techniques prior to burial. It extends visitation time and enables them to ship their soldiers home across great distances."

"Interesting. Don't you think that it's unnatural, though, to commit a body to the earth when it is saturated in chemicals?"

There he was with that word again.

"Embalming preserves our loved ones. That's all that matters to me."

"Enough!" Victoria said. "Such talk is revolting. We insist that you take it elsewhere. Dr. Jenner, we're sure Mrs. Morgan misses her daughter and would like to be reunited with her."

Taking the queen's direct hint, Jenner escorted Violet back to the reception room where she'd entered, his attitude more congenial now that he wasn't near the queen, protecting her. As they walked, he spoke of his own profession, his investigations into causes of various fevers, and his opinion on how long the prince's condition had existed prior to his diagnosis of it.

"The queen has named me her physician-in-ordinary now that Dr. Clark is retiring. I suspect a title will be forthcoming."

"A singular honor for you, sir."

"Yes, and my singular goal is making the queen well again. Somehow your depressing talk of her husband's death is pleasing to her."

"I don't know how helpful it is to her, though, Dr. Jenner. Does it seem to you that the queen is overly . . . obsessed . . . with her husband's death and funeral?"

"She was deeply in love with him."

Violet tamped down her impatience. Did the man think an undertaker had never witnessed a widow passionately committed to her recently deceased husband? "I know the queen and the prince consort were very devoted to one another, but most widows return to some form of a normal life within a couple of months, no matter how deep the mourning. The queen seems mired in an unhealthy way, don't you think?"

"I think you have no concern in the matter, Mrs. Morgan. I have the queen well in hand."

The subject was closed with the finality of one of Mr. Dickens's thick books slamming shut. Dr. Jenner left her in the reception room to wait for Susanna.

When Susanna was brought to her, she carried a new doll—a gift from one of the attendants who had watched over her—while a yipping pack of puppies followed at her feet. Susanna was entranced by her visit to the castle and talked at Mrs. Saunders speed about everything she'd done at the castle, finishing up with a plea for a dog.

"Susanna, what would Mrs. Softpaws think?"

This caused the girl consternation and she ceased that line of thought, returning instead to a monologue about the sandwiches and cakes she'd had during their visit, a topic in which Violet could happily participate.

Off Sewell's Point, near Hampton Roads, Virginia
March 9, 1862

Controlling his great desire to shiver in the frigid air, Graham peered through the twin telescope lenses at the darkening scene in Sewell's Point before handing the brass and copper telescope to Fletcher. "It's been two hours since the final cannon firing. I think it's over for good."

Fletcher looked through the lenses at the place where a sea battle had been raging just a few hours earlier. "What do you think? Is it the North or the South that's won?"

"Hard to tell." Graham and Fletcher had kept *Lillian Rose* hidden from the fracas, which had started earlier the previous day, but watched everything from the deck through their telescope. An ironclad ram, CSS *Virginia*, accompanied by several wooden ships, entered Hampton Roads, which connected Virginia's James River with the Chesapeake Bay, in an obvious intent to smash through the blockade. The air was soon filled with smoke, shouting, and a never-ending barrage of cannon fire. The brothers and their crew had rocked gently in the water as they watched chaos and destruction from a distance, the rhythmic slapping of water against the hull punctuated by tremors as each combatant fired upon its enemy. Even with the telescope, the smoke had prevented them from seeing much.

Surely it was as blazing hot in the battle as it was bitterly cold from their vantage point, especially now that the sun had set.

After the debacle with Samuel Harper, and with Queen Victoria's recent prohibition against the export of armaments to the United States, Graham and Fletcher decided to stick to what Fletcher knew, which was liquor. They off-loaded most of their original cargo of weapons on several passing commerce raiders, then sailed to Jamaica with their profits to buy sugar to exchange for rum in Boston, then sailed down to Hampton Roads to sell the rum to the Confederate army, since there was no safe way to return to England with it, not with the government succumbing to the Americans' demand to hunt them down like they were rabid dogs. The brothers had originally planned to slip through the blockade themselves after dark with their load of rum they'd picked up in Massachusetts, but the unexpected battle caused them to give the area a wide berth and hide to the east side of the fracas. Now the crew slept below while Graham and Fletcher kept watch.

Thus far in their adventures, they'd eluded any sort of notice on the seas, and now assumed that the British government had forgotten all about them.

Or perhaps they were simply too clever to be captured.

Graham gripped the rail tightly as he thought of his wife for the hundredth time that day. Had Violet received his letter? Had she done as he instructed and sold Morgan Undertaking? Was she back in Brighton with her parents?

With his free hand he scratched at his full beard. It had grown in quickly, and both it and his hair already had gray streaks in them.

Living a clandestine life took its toll on a man. Not that Fletcher seemed disadvantaged at all. Not a line on his face nor a wisp of silver anywhere.

Graham's mind continued wandering over familiar territory. What would he do over again? Probably nothing. Things might have turned out differently if Fletcher hadn't put his trust in Samuel Harper. Who could trust an American? And Violet's carping over every little thing was enough to drive a man to Bedlam. If she'd been a better wife, maybe Graham wouldn't have felt a need to actively involve himself in the affairs of North and South.

Surely his great misfortunes were Violet's fault, weren't they?

He wasn't sure anymore. Living this scraggly, flea-infested, *ungentlemanly* life made him pause.

Was this all a little bit my own fault?

Fletcher elbowed him and pointed. "*Virginia* hasn't fired in over an hour. I think she might be done."

Graham took up the glass again. "Are the North's ships fleeing?"

"Hard to tell, it's too dark. Everyone is extinguishing their lanterns. I don't see any floating munitions batteries left, so if they've retreated, we know the ships can't re-arm."

"What do we do?"

Fletcher considered. "I say we wait another hour. If there's no further activity, we'll wake the crew and slip in, unload as quickly as possible, then get back out before dawn. If we can make it down around Old Point Comfort, it should then be a quick jaunt up to Hampton. Should be quite fun."

"Yes, positively exhilarating," Graham said.

All was silent for the next hour, so they woke the crew, pulled anchor, and quickly sluiced through the waters around the edges of where a fierce sea battle had raged just hours before. Fletcher forbade the crew from lighting any lamps or using any voice signals. They would travel by instinct and moonlight.

The crew steered *Lillian Rose* so that she made a wide berth to the north, bringing the ship to a slow crawl. No need to alert anyone of their presence through wave motion.

Almost there. As they neared the coast, Fletcher commanded a hard turn to port so they could hug the shoreline on their way into Hampton Roads harbor. It was risky, for they still had to stay five hundred yards out to avoid running aground.

The men aboard *Lillian Rose* were silent, hardly daring to breathe as they crept their way past both Northern and Southern warships toward Old Point Comfort and an escape into the harbor.

Graham could hardly contemplate the danger in getting back out.

The men were all focused on the shore as they inexorably floated to the point. Slowly, slowly now. They were almost there. Yes, just a bit farther and—

A light came on at their port side. What the . . . ?

"Identify yourself," came a voice from near the swinging lantern.

"Who are you to demand my identity?" Fletcher called back toward the light.

"I am Lieutenant John Worden, commander of USS *Monitor*. You sound British, sir, and you are in dangerous waters. What is your purpose here?"

"I am Fletcher Morgan and this is my brother, Graham. We are undertakers delivering much-needed supplies to all of the Confederate soldiers you are dispatching faster than the spin of a screw propeller."

"Surely, sir, you understand there is a blockade in force against the Confederacy?"

"And surely, sir, you understand that we are on a humanitarian mission, as willing to help fallen brethren in the North as well as the South."

Graham lit his own lantern and peered over the side of *Lillian Rose*. If he thought *Virginia* looked strange, this . . . contraption . . . was otherworldly. There was hardly more than the deck of the ship riding above the water line. A half dozen men stood on the deck, next to a round turret anchored down to it. Surely there were more crew members for the ship, which must have been nearly two hundred feet long, as long as *Lillian Rose*, but prowling along the water line like one of the crocodiles he'd seen in Jamaica. Were they all on decks below what was visible? How was it possible for a ship to maneuver through the seas like that without sinking, especially since the exposed sides were clearly ironclad?

Graham held his breath as Lt. Worden conferred with his own

men. He expelled it in disbelief when *Monitor*'s commander stated that he was sending a boarding party onto *Lillian Rose* for a search.

"Don't worry," Fletcher muttered before going to assist some of *Monitor*'s crew in boarding. "We still have plenty of weaponry hidden in this old girl to scare them off."

Graham wasn't so sure. *Lillian Rose*'s wood hull was no match for this monstrosity and its turret, which had several cannon pointed menacingly through openings in the turret. What if the hull below water decided to ram *Lillian Rose*? They'd be splintered to pieces. They were also thoroughly outnumbered and had no authority to be in these waters.

The crew of *Monitor* threw up two rope ladders, which *Lillian Rose*'s men deftly caught and held to allow Lt. Worden's men to board.

Graham was nervous, yet Fletcher appeared unconcerned. "Are there more than just a few whiskey barrels keeping that thing afloat?" he called down to *Monitor*'s commander.

Fool! Graham thought bitterly. What was it about sea life that turned some men into arrogant imbeciles?

As expected, Lt. Worden took offense. "Sir, I'll have you know this ship is new, nearly indestructible, and far more formidable than your leaky wooden bucket."

Fletcher laughed. "I suppose you back up such words with the little whirlabout you have there."

Graham was certain Lt. Worden would not hesitate to back up his words.

"Quiet," he hissed to his brother, but the damage was done. The best Graham could hope for was that their cargo would not be seized. At worst, their ship would be taken as a prize and the entire crew made to fend its own way back to England.

Lt. Worden's voice was now frosty. "*Monitor* may only have two eleven-inch cannon aboard her, but they hold thirty-pound charges and rotate around quickly in our steam-powered—what did you call it?—whirlabout. Your rowboat will be decimated in seconds should I call for it."

"Ah, but you won't, sir," Fletcher said. "For you were not present at the battle earlier today, so I suspect your arrival now is intended to be a secret from the Confederates. Why would you reveal your stealthy approach over a couple of innocent undertakers?"

Lt. Worden ignored Fletcher, instead calling out to the men he sent aboard *Lillian Rose*, "Be thorough."

Graham was now tamping down full-fledged panic as Worden's men scrambled down the stairs belowdecks and into the hold.

"Fletcher," Graham said quietly, pulling his brother aside. "It may be time to start negotiating with Lt. Worden. Offer him something to let us pass."

Fletcher lifted a shoulder. "Why give up what little gold we have? It's not as though the Americans have the desire to do anything against a British ship, not after the humiliating apology they had to make over the whole *Trent* incident. Perhaps I should remind Lt. Worden of that as well." He moved as if to return to his taunting spot next to the rail.

Graham grabbed his brother by the arm. "I don't think you realize how much trouble we're in."

Fletcher shrugged him off. "I don't think you realize how enormously hen-hearted you are." Yet he stayed where he was and no longer engaged *Monitor*'s commander.

The minutes ticked by inexorably as they waited to see what Worden's men would find. Graham's thoughts drifted back to Violet. It was early dawn back home; surely she was in deep slumber. Alone. The image of Samuel Harper rose in his mind like a hideous specter. Violet wouldn't dare cuckold her husband. Not after all Graham had done to improve their status, even now risking his life so that she might move about as a society matron one day. The mental image of Harper was replaced by the cursed minister, Charles Francis Adams, who was hopefully lying in some unmarked grave. Both men were equally responsible for Graham's misery.

This whole rotten episode was initiated by Graham's desire to fulfill Pap's final wishes and Fletcher's assurances that he could do so. He remembered their discussion when Fletcher had first proposed smuggling guns to the South. "Why would you want to help them? Either side?" Graham had asked.

"I don't care about helping them. I only care about helping me.

I mean us. First, envision how thoroughly you could avenge Pap by having the Americans kill themselves with abandon. Now think how much money either side would be willing to pay to restock their armaments. I imagine we could make a sizable fortune in a very short period. A fortune you could use to expand your funeral services, furnish your home, attire Violet in elegant gowns, and elevate your status."

"And what would you use a fortune on?"

"Refitting my ship, possibly buying another one. Acquiring a small country estate somewhere south of London."

Graham had narrowed his eyes. "And why do you propose inviting me into this scheme of yours, rather than keeping all the profits for yourself?"

"Simple. I need cover for my shipments. What customs inspector is going to open up funerary supplies to look for goods being transported illegally? And a man's coffin would hold a rifle just perfectly. Also, there is the little matter of financing."

"Meaning?"

Fletcher spread his hands. "Those who would profit from this bountiful enterprise should be expected to invest in it, right? I need a little seed money before I meet with my contacts so that I can make a good-faith deposit on my first order."

"Hmm, I'm not sure I like the idea of providing the Americans with quality English goods, even if it's for profit, and even if they will use them to slaughter each other."

"Ah, now, brother." Fletcher clasped an arm around Graham's shoulders. "Who said anything about the goods being of quality?"

Graham had signed on to Fletcher's plans, but now everything was ruined.

If he could make it back to London one day, he would set things right. First, he would restart Morgan Undertaking but leave Violet out of it so she could concentrate on their home and having children. It wasn't too late for them to have a son. She'd be much happier at home, too, in her proper place. It had been a mistake to let her do men's work. Conversely, he would forget his dream of avenging Pap's death and just be a husband and a businessman.

Meanwhile, he had to survive this inspection as well as Fletcher's conceit.

Monitor's sailors emerged from belowdecks, their faces grim. One went to the rail, calling out "Lieutenant!" and making indecipherable hand signals.

In moments, Lt. Worden and at least ten more men had clambered up the ladder his own men now held, brandishing pistols and swords.

Graham turned to Fletcher, who had scurried to the other end of the deck and was unlocking a chest.

"What are you doing there?" Lt. Worden demanded.

Fletcher spun around, holding a pistol in one hand and an old saber in the other. He was no longer his sunny, affable self, and instead wore the dripping sweat of a terrified man.

"I'm doing what any self-respecting ship's captain does—protecting my ship and crew. Men, there are more weapons in the chest, help yourself."

His crew was paralyzed, eyeing both the chest and *Monitor*'s well-armed crew nervously. Was it wise to risk spilling your own blood when it wasn't for queen and country?

"Oh, all right then," Fletcher said. "I'll defend us all myself." He brandished the saber at Lt. Worden. "Fancy a fight between blades? No? Then what if I simply place a large hole in your heart with this?" He held up the pistol and waved it back and forth.

In the dim lantern light it looked as though Fletcher was aiming the pistol directly at Lt. Worden. It probably wouldn't fire anyway, given the lousy imitation Tranter revolvers they had purchased for trade. Not that Lt. Worden understood that.

Barking a shout of alarm at Fletcher's presumable aim at him, Lt. Worden didn't hesitate. He raised his own pistol and fired.

Fletcher looked down in great surprise at the dark stain spreading across his chest. His gaze sought his brother's, which shook Graham out of his own disbelief and sent him running to Fletcher's side.

Fletcher fell to the deck and was sightless before Graham reached him.

First Pap, then Father, Mother, and now Fletcher. It wasn't possible. How had life gone so abominably wrong in such a short period of time? *Why does everyone persecute and work against me?*

His frustration, anger, and grief welled up in one surging ball of red-hot fury, releasing itself in a tortured, animalistic howl as he crouched over his brother's body. As he sought to find his balance and stand up once again, his hand instinctively closed around his brother's pistol, which he picked up.

Graham stood and looked at Lt. Worden, who was already crossing the deck to inspect Fletcher's body. Graham lifted the pistol and realized rather too late that there was actually a third outcome to the evening's events, one he regretted more than everything that had happened with Violet.

❧ 18 ❦

Dishonor will not trouble me once I am dead.

—Euripedes (ca. 490–406 B.C.)

Portland Place, London
March 23, 1862

Charles Francis Adams digested the correspondence Henry laid before him. President Lincoln had issued an order reorganizing the Army of Virginia under Major General John Pope and relieving General McClellan of supreme command.

"I guess now the president is too busy with his latest crisis to send missives chastising my own work," he said to his son.

Henry nodded. "Keep reading, there's more."

Charles Francis read the rest of the report. Two weeks ago, the first naval engagement between ironclad ships occurred. Confederate engineers converted USS *Merrimac*, a scuttled Union frigate—curse their ingenuity—into an iron-sided vessel rechristened CSS *Virginia*. The ship went into Hampton Roads, near the point where the James River meets the Chesapeake Bay.

Now an ironclad ram, *Virginia* destroyed two ships of the federal flotilla and was about to attack a third ship, USS *Minnesota*, which had run aground when darkness and falling tide halted action. *Virginia* retreated overnight to repair her minimal battle damage.

The following morning, on March 9, *Virginia* returned to the fray to finish off *Minnesota*, but was caught unawares by the ironclad USS *Monitor*, which had taken a defensive position during the night to protect the other wounded ship.

The two ironclads fought viciously for about three hours, with neither side able to inflict significant damage on the other. Eventually, both ships retreated, but the blockade was still in place—a victory for the North, as far as Charles Francis was concerned.

"This is excellent news, Henry. No further blockade running will be possible with ships like *Monitor* guarding Southern ports."

Henry's face split into an unusual grin. "Would you believe there's even better news? We've also just received a secret report from Secretary of State Seward that during the night, between battles, *Monitor* happened upon a stray British ship, circling suspiciously around the fray. They stopped her, and guess what ship it was? *Lillian Rose.*"

Charles Francis shook his head. "Should I know of it?"

"You might be more familiar with her owner, Fletcher Morgan, who was aboard with his brother."

"We finally captured them?"

"Not exactly. The commander of *Monitor* boarded *Lillian Rose* to determine whether she was a blockade runner and found the brothers had hidden a large cache of rum inside coffins in the hold."

Charles Francis shook his head. "So they gave up arms smuggling to ply the liquor trade inside coffins. Daring."

"More than you know. They had a wax figure in one of the most accessible coffins, more than likely in hopes that it would scare off anyone in the exact circumstances they found themselves in. Or would at least make authorities believe they were what they claimed to be—innocent undertakers. Fortunately for us, the commander of *Monitor* was the suspicious type."

"Where are the Morgan brothers?"

"A meal for Neptune, I'm afraid. Fletcher Morgan drew a pistol on *Monitor*'s commander, Lt. Worden, and was promptly shot. His brother pretended to grieve, using his prone state to grab Fletcher's gun. Lt. Worden was hesitant to shoot two brothers in succession and tried to reason with him. The man was demented and charged Worden, shouting the craziest things. Finally, Worden had no choice but to shoot him as well. Both bodies were tossed overboard, the crew transferred to *Monitor* to be moved to a mail steamer bound for England, then they towed *Lillian Rose* to shore near *Minnesota*. After the final battle, *Monitor* fired on *Lillian Rose* and destroyed her."

"A fitting end for all concerned, including the ship. Tell me, what was Graham Morgan shouting?"

"It was the oddest thing, Father. Lt. Worden swears he was yelling, 'All for Pap! All for Pap!' over and over."

"Bizarre. What did it mean?"

"I don't know. Just the rantings of a deranged criminal."

"I'm sure you're right, son. At least we've put this ugly situation behind us and can quit spending time on tracking down the Morgan brothers."

"What about Mr. Harper?"

"Yes, he'll be gratified to know our quarry was brought to justice. I do believe he would prefer to bring the sad news of her husband's death to the widow Morgan himself. Now that his work is complete, the fortunate man can go home to Massachusetts."

"What do you plan to tell Lords Palmerston and Russell?"

"I think that after the dustup over the *Trent* Affair, it might be better to cover up this incident of Englishmen smuggling goods to the South, thus alleviating Great Britain of any further ill will with the North."

Henry smiled. "Well said, Father. I'm sure they'll agree. You say you aren't a diplomat, but I think you are quite the statesman."

Negotiating with Palmerston and Russell was simple. It was Samuel Harper who caused no end of grief.

"Our work is hardly done here, Mr. Adams," Harper said. "Surely there are more weapons smugglers in England eager to get their wares to the Confederacy."

"There have been none that you've found."

"Naturally, the Morgans occupied a great deal of my time."

"You mean Mrs. Morgan occupied your time."

Harper had the good grace to redden at Charles Francis's barb.

"Come, Sam, what more do you really expect to discover?"

"I think my presence will be helpful for the next six months or so, until the South is completely beaten back. I'll keep a constant watch out for commerce raiders being built around Isle of Dogs and ports around London. There will be many more to take the Morgans' place."

Charles Francis frowned. "You think we have six months of war left?"

"At least."

"I can imagine it. I'll authorize another two months of your expenses, then you're free to return home."

Harper inclined his head. "As you wish."

Violet shut the door behind Sam, her mind and stomach swirling in disbelief. Without a word to anyone else, she picked up her skirts and ran to her room, locking herself inside and collapsing on her bed, face up to the ceiling.

The builder had attempted some decorative detailing on it, but it was a hodgepodge of uneven plaster trimwork. Graham disliked it and once threatened to scrape it all down himself, except his other obsessions took priority, so nothing ever happened. And now never would.

Violet threw an arm across her eyes, blocking the light filtering in through a crack in the draperies and waiting for the tears to course bitterly down her cheeks.

Sam's visit had left her speechless. According to his account of events, Graham and Fletcher were smuggling rum past the U.S. blockade in Virginia when they were stopped by a U.S. ironclad ship. Fletcher foolishly taunted the Americans, and Graham died defending his brother. Fletcher had always been too sure of himself, but Violet never thought of Graham as a great protector. It gave her comfort to think of him this way now.

Was that why tears refused to flow? Or was she just completely spent of them over the last few years of her marriage?

Sam said Fletcher and Graham were given respectful burials at sea, so there were no bodies for her to bury. Like Graham with his mother, Violet didn't think she had the stomach for tending to her husband's funeral. Yet . . . shouldn't he have a ceremony? Fletcher, too. Surely she could do this for both men.

Even the thought of a memorial service wasn't springing tears to her eyes. What in heaven's name was wrong with her?

She rose from her bed and went into the corridor. A large window at one end overlooked the street below. She went to it, slipping inside the draperies as if she were a mere caterpillar wrapped in a cocoon. Resting her elbows on the sill, she gazed down at the activity below.

The street was full of the typical bustle of daily London life. Newspapers were hawked, wares were sold, and women's skirts were muddied in the noxious mixture of road dust and horse dung that was the hallmark of most streets. No one saw conspiracy at every corner, nor felt a special calling to avenge the dead.

Despite the sorrows and gut-wrenching heartaches every human being endures, Violet imagined that the men, women, and children she watched down in the street at least lived a normal sort of life inside Her Majesty's kingdom, notwithstanding the poverty endured by those like Susanna and her mother.

Violet wanted normalcy again, the simple life she had as a child. Would it ever be hers?

She stood motionless a while longer, gazing down on the world below. As her eye caught the paperboy once more, the thought occurred to her: Was Graham's death in today's news?

Startled out of her reverie, she scrambled out of the draperies, nearly tripping in the process. She fluttered down the staircase and out into the street to buy a copy of the evening edition of *The Times*.

She secreted herself in the dining room, dropping the drapes that closed it off from the hallway and sitting down to scan the paper.

Nothing. Not a single word about Graham's misfortune at sea.

Impossible. The press had gobbled up the story of his treasonous activities not long ago. Why would they ignore this?

It was a relief, really. Violet wouldn't have to defend her reputation in the public eye again.

Give yourself over to grief, then. Have a good cry.

She sat at the table, her elbows propped impolitely on the pages of the paper. They'd certainly be black with newsprint later, since she'd not taken the time to ask Mrs. Porter to iron the printed sheets.

A clock on the mantelpiece ticked and tocked in its usual endless manner. Violet normally paid it no mind, but willing herself to sadness made the room go stark, and the clock's gentle noise was deafening, as though it were loudly reminding her that it needed to be stopped now that Graham was gone.

"Oh, for heaven's sake," she said aloud. She pushed the newspaper aside, got her gloves and hat, and called for Susanna, who came bounding down the stairs holding Mrs. Orange Peel.

"Do you want to go to the shop with me? I'll teach you how I enter customers into the ledger that's been used by Morgan Undertaking since the business was started."

Susanna wrinkled her nose. "Where is Mr. Harper? Isn't he staying for supper?"

"No, he stopped by because he needed to deliver a message is all."

"Oh. Aren't we done at the shop for the day?"

"Yes, but—no, I find I need to return there to busy myself."

Susanna nodded with the wisdom of an eighty-year-old. "It will be fine, Mama, whatever it is that troubles you."

That's the entire problem. I'm not troubled at all.

Violet only told Susanna, Mary, the Porters, Will, and Harry of Graham's and Fletcher's deaths, in addition to sending an invitation to her parents to attend the memorial service. The black bunting draped across the windows of the shop and their home would tell their neighbors and customers all they needed to know.

Will and Harry did a commendable job of handling most matters so Violet could play the grieving widow.

Is that what I'm doing? Acting in a role?

She ordered coffins from Mr. Boyce, asking that he stain them as dark as possible. She also visited the chapel at Kensal Green to talk to the clergyman there about the unusual memorial service she planned to hold, replete with all elements of a funeral except for the bodies. Most everything else she left to her employees while she assembled the widow's weeds she would now wear for the next year. Black dresses, hats, gloves, and jewelry.

To Violet's great surprise, Mr. Boyce and his two sons attended the service, the old man's eyes misty once again as he lamented that "there's just no happy outcome to any marriage, is there, Mrs. Morgan?"

Violet put framed ambrotypes of Graham and Fletcher in each of their coffins, as well as their *cartes-de-visites*. That way, should their coffins ever be removed in the future, the world would know who the men were who belonged in the empty coffins.

The day after the memorial service, Violet received a package from Sam. Inside was a watch, its case intricately filigreed, with an unusual opening mechanism shaped like a small bird. When the watch opened, it played a snatch of a melodious tune. Sam's enclosed note expressed his sympathy over Violet's loss, as well as his hope that the watch, a Margaret Fleming–made piece crafted during Charles II's reign, would help her look back fondly through time.

What a sweet gesture. He must have scoured London's antique shops for it.

Graham's brief will left his estate to any issue from his marriage. If there were no children, it was to be divided between his wife and brother. Therefore, his entire estate—the shop and its contents and the possessions of their home—was Violet's.

Violet's parents stayed on a mercifully brief time before returning to Brighton, sensing their daughter wanted to throw herself back into her strange world of work.

It suited Violet to be consumed with work, which was preferable to being preoccupied with guilt over not mourning Graham properly. It conflicted with the extraordinary sense of—not just relief, but *freedom*—she now felt. As though she'd been buried alive, but someone dug her up in time before she used up all of the oxygen in the coffin.

She was breathing easily once again now that her husband was gone. Was Graham correct in saying she was a poor excuse for a wife?

*   *   *

Violet resumed work, puzzled each day as to why the papers made no mention of Graham's and Fletcher's deaths. The next time Sam came round with a gift for Susanna—a miniature but ornate gold-leafed mirror to hang in the Orange Peels' dining room— as well as a yellow rose for Violet, she asked him about it, but he had no explanation. Instead, he suggested that they leave Susanna with the Porters and make a trip to the British Museum together.

"I've heard much about it, and we have nothing to rival it back in the States."

"Must we be rivals?" she asked.

"No, it's just that we pride ourselves on all of our advancements, and having a place that chronicles how far we've—oh, you're teasing me."

"Only a bit. I've never been there myself, although I hear the Reading Room is simply magnificent."

"We shall make a point of seeing it."

"I'm afraid we can't. It belongs to the British Library, and one must have a researcher's credentials to enter."

Sam smiled. "Surely being a member of His Excellency's diplomatic corps will enable us that privilege."

The museum was all Violet could have imagined and more. Wide, sweeping staircases took visitors to upper floors, full of priceless treasures from ancient Greece, Rome, and Egypt. The museum's collections were vast and overwhelming. For the first time, Violet saw the famed Elgin Marbles brought back from Greece, as well as the Rosetta Stone, which Napoleon's army had uncovered.

Sam was right about gaining entry to the Reading Room. Although the attendant on duty frowned at Sam's papers and made them wait while he conferred with a superior, they were permitted inside. The circular Reading Room, immense and spanning all four stories of the museum, was lined all around with bookshelves containing titles in English and Latin.

Violet ran her hand across a row of leather-bound books on English flora. "Imagine having all of this to read at your leisure," she said.

Sam pointed up. "Don't you want to visit those before making your decision?"

She laughed, garnering a hard stare from a patron who then scowled upon noticing Violet's mourning dress.

"Now you're the one making fun at my expense," she said before heading up to the metalwork catwalk surrounding an additional story of filled bookshelves lining the massive library. While up there, Violet randomly selected a volume regarding the cultivation of American ferns in England and returned downstairs to take a seat at one of the long tables radiating out from the center of the room. Her Grafton Terrace neighbor, Mr. Marx, sat nearby and gave her a cursory nod of recognition before returning to his studies and furious scribblings.

It was almost like reading a novel, so transported was she by the book she'd selected. Violet whiled away nearly an hour flipping through the pages of ferns artistically pressed down on each page, accompanied by a notation of their Latin names and where the specimens were found, until Sam's gentle "ahem" brought her back to the present.

He leaned toward her conspiratorially. "I must tell you, I noticed a confectionary on our way here, and I think it imperative to stop for a bowl of sweet frozen delight."

Violet shut the book. "Oh dear, what of Susanna? She'll never forgive me for having ice cream without her."

Sam winked. "Shall we keep it our secret? If you'll permit me, I can stop by another day to escort you both for ice cream."

"I wouldn't like to put you to such trouble."

"It's a pleasure, Violet, on many counts."

London
April 1862

The deceased was an elderly widower of some means, living as he did in a fine home almost in Marylebone and possessing a collection of Limoges snuffboxes that adorned every square inch of available space on tables, credenzas, and mantelpieces.

He'd been discovered that morning by one of his maids, who

had found him unresponsive when she brought up his breakfast tray.

In the way of overly staffed homes, the maid told the housekeeper, who then informed the butler, who sent another maid to awaken Mr. Young's live-in nurse, who dressed and went to fetch the doctor.

How did anything ever get accomplished in society?

According to the butler, who summoned Morgan Undertaking's services at the request of Mr. Young's son, the doctor pronounced himself satisfied that Mr. Young had died of natural causes and was ready for burial.

Violet and Susanna arrived for preparation of the body. Violet ignored the butler's frown of disapproval at seeing Susanna at her side. She was used to the sidelong glances and hostile stares her profession and Graham's shenanigans heaped upon her and mentally brushed the butler aside, much as a horse would an irritating but harmless fly.

They went upstairs to Mr. Young's rooms to prepare him for his funeral. Violet recalled his son as someone in attendance at Admiral Herbert's funeral. Perhaps he had some sort of high commission in the Royal Navy? No matter. Mr. Young's son was coming into London from his home in Greenwich later in the day to meet with Violet over arrangements.

Violet was struck by Mr. Young's agonized expression. Some people died with expressions of utter calm and composure, even smiling at the end, whereas others died with fearful looks on their faces, as if they had peeked beyond the veil and were unpleasantly surprised by what the afterlife had in store for them.

Mr. Young, however, appeared to have been personally escorted by Satan to dance in the fiery depths. His mouth was contorted in anguish and his partially open eyes shouted in horror. One hand was clutching the edge of the bedcovers as if Mr. Young was protecting himself from something. It was most unusual.

Violet shut the man's eyelids and put a hand on either side of his jaws to soften his appearance, but his skin was not obedient. Rigor mortis was setting in.

"Our job will be difficult today."

Susanna nodded in understanding. With effort, Violet removed the twisted covers from Mr. Young's clutches and unrolled them to expose his arms and torso, which were covered with his nightshirt. What was this? She straightened the shirt sleeve that was not bent from his grip on the bedclothing.

"Susanna, bring the lamp closer." Susanna did as she was told, lighting a nearby oil lamp and bringing it to Violet's side for closer examination of the body.

She gasped. Mr. Young had the same worn-away—no, eaten—spots on his nightshirt that Violet had witnessed on Mrs. Atkinson. She pushed up the sleeve. His bare arm was covered with a spattering of decaying spots.

"Sir, what kind of disease do you have? And for heaven's sake, why didn't the doctor call for an autopsy? You deserve one, sir." Violet shook her head. "It's outrageous. What sort of incompetent physician attends you? Of course, I run the risk of total censure if I dare question a doctor's judgment. Still, there's no excuse for his having overlooked—Susanna, what's the matter with you?"

The girl still held the lamp aloft but was backing away from where Violet was working, her blue eyes now little round globes of horror. Susanna put the lamp back in its place and stood near the door, refusing to come closer.

"Child, whatever is wrong?"

"I can't help you with Mr. Young, Mama," she said. Her voice was tremulous.

"Susanna, you did the same thing when we visited Mrs. Atkinson. Why won't you tell me what bothers you so?"

Silence.

"All right then." Violet pulled the covers back over Mr. Young, pushed the table back, and picked up her bag. "Let's go find Mr. Young's doctor and have a chat with him, shall we?"

That drew Susanna out from her hiding place.

Downstairs, Violet sought out the butler again. "Kindly tell me who Mr. Young's physician was."

"Of course. He left his calling card when he was here earlier."

The butler found it in a silver tray of other cards and handed it to Violet. "It's not Mr. Young's regular doctor, who has been away on the Continent for several weeks."

She looked down at the card. It couldn't be. *Dr. William Beasley, Aldersgate Street, near St. Bartholomew's Hospital.* The same doctor who signed Mrs. Atkinson's death certificate also tended to Mr. Young? Both bodies had mysterious flesh markings, and in neither case did the doctor see reason for an autopsy? Either the man was a quack or he was seriously inept.

"I see. Please tell Mr. Young's son that I'll return this evening to discuss his father's funeral."

Violet grabbed Susanna's hand and they marched off to Aldersgate Street.

"How dare you inquire as to my findings?" Dr. Beasley said, his languid voice hiding the irritation that flashed in his eyes. He threaded his hairy, sausage-like fingers together across his waistcoat, from which dangled a silver watch. Expensive to demonstrate prosperity, but not gold and thereby offensive to his more prosperous clients. He wore a black wool frock coat trimmed on the lapels with velvet. Dr. Beasley was the perfect picture of a respectable doctor, sitting across his desk from Violet and a still-trembling Susanna.

Except that Violet was fairly certain he wasn't, and she was determined to figure out how Dr. Beasley was managing to overlook a condition so obvious on at least two of his patients.

"I may be merely an undertaker and not of your august stature, Dr. Beasley, but it does seem curious to me that you didn't notice the peculiar wasted spots on both Mrs. Atkinson and Mr. Young."

He unlaced his fingers and spread his hands wide. "Come, Mrs. Morgan. Mrs. Atkinson was of a lower class and her habits were none too clean. She'd had many ailments and complaints of nonexistent ailments. Some rash or skin infection was certainly not the cause of death."

Mrs. Saunders never mentioned Mrs. Atkinson's complaints. At least Violet couldn't recall so from the haze of the woman's chattering. Nor did she remember Mrs. Atkinson looking particularly dirty.

"But Mr. Young was from the upper crust. Did he have a variety of complaints as well?"

"Mrs. Morgan, you're trifling with me over two different people who happened to have similar skin conditions. It is my professional judgment that Mrs. Atkinson died of a sudden heart ailment and Mr. Young simply expired from old age, although yes, he had been suffering some sort of ague prior to his death. Now, if there are no further questions, I have patients to see." He stood, ending the interview.

That evening, after visiting Mr. Young's son to discuss his father's funeral, Violet left Susanna at home and went out to supper with Mary to share with her all that had happened and to ask her friend's advice.

Over rich dishes of baked apple custards, Mary asked, "So the doctor thinks it's nothing to worry over?"

"Yes."

"Then," she said, popping a spoonful of dessert in her mouth, "it seems as though you should forget about it, my dear, lest it get you into trouble."

"Into trouble? Why would concern for the dead get me into trouble? Oh, you mean should the physician begin to spread rumors about me."

"Yes, that's what I mean. Mmm, that was delicious. Shall we have cups of chocolate? It's a bit too indulgent for my waistline, but George says he likes me a bit filled out. He's such a dear. Perhaps you should talk it over with him, Violet. I know you aren't very well acquainted with him yet, but he does give very sage advice. Just the other day he made suggestions for moving things around in my shop to best display my new mannequins. Such a help. Reminds me so much of Matthew." Mary sighed. "I suppose that's why I enjoy his company."

"I'm sure he is of great comfort to you, Mary." Violet reached over and squeezed her friend's hand. "But I prefer to keep this between us for now."

"Of course I won't breathe a word. Now, I hear that a new opera, *Love's Triumph*, is at Covent Garden theater. Let's make a plan to go so you can get to know George. Bring Mr. Harper along; he might enjoy our theater."

Violet frowned, causing Mary to apologize. "How insensitive of me! Of course you're in mourning for Graham and have no desire for entertainment."

"It's not that." It was that she'd hardly thought of Graham lately, as her mind was preoccupied with other things. Even donning her black garb each day felt more like ritual than honor of the deceased.

Violet wondered what Sam would think of one of Covent Garden's playhouses. Did she really dare go out to the theater in her initial stages of mourning? With a male escort, no less. Her heart beat wildly at the thought of disobeying rules that were not only well established, but about which she herself had advised scores of grieving women.

"Let me think on it, Mary. I might enjoy such a diversion."

She did, despite the furrowed brows and glove-covered whispers she encountered at Covent Garden theater. The comic opera about Adolphe, employed at the court of the Princess de Valois and in love with a woman named Therese, who was not only bound to be married to another man but also closely resembled the princess, with much confusion and cross purposes resulting, had them all laughing uproariously.

Afterward, Sam enthused over the elaborate sets and costumes as the four of them headed over to a confectionary for a treat.

"Do you find our playhouses as unusual as our museums?" Violet asked.

"Not at all. You should see Ford's Theatre in Washington City. It rivals Covent Garden theater any day."

Violet gently squeezed his right arm, where her hand was lightly resting, as they strolled with Mary and George behind them.

"There you are again with your competitive talk. Do all Americans approach life as though it is a horse race at Newmarket to be won?"

Sam laughed and covered her hand with his free one, which immediately elicited stares of consternation from passersby.

Drat all of this black crape and jet. I just want to have a pleasant evening.

"I can see I have to tone down my aggressive spirit around you, Violet," he said.

"On the contrary, I like spirit."

"As do I," Sam said, giving her hand another gentle squeeze before dropping his arm to open the door to the confectionary, which was already crowded with other theater patrons.

They sat down to exquisite Neapolitan cups, presented to them on a footed silver tray. The individual treats shaped like handled cups were made of molded ice and filled with ice cream and topped with fancifully colored sorbets.

"I must warn you both," Violet said to Mary and George, "that Sam is a great ice cream lover and we must hurry if we expect to have more than a couple of bites of what's before us before he steals them from under our eyes."

"You like ice cream?" George asked, overstating the obvious for the hundredth time that evening. A plain, even-tempered man who clearly doted on Mary, he nonetheless irritated Violet with his dull-witted statements. Surely Mary couldn't be enamored with such a companion?

Mary looked adoringly at George and fed him from her spoon. Some of the ice cream spilled down George's ginger-colored beard and he laughingly licked at it, allowing Mary to daub his facial hair with her cloth napkin.

Perhaps George was pretending to simplicity in front of Mary's friends to hide his real genius, so as not to make Violet feel dim-witted. Or so that he avoided any hint of arrogance.

Surely that was it. Otherwise, Violet couldn't fathom Mary's affection for the short, pig-eyed George Cooke of indeterminate age and even more mysterious background.

"Here and there," he responded when Sam asked where he was from. His occupation was cloudy, too. First he claimed to be a clockmaker.

"Oh, then you'll be interested in seeing my watch, made by Margaret Fleming," Violet said, unpinning it from where it dangled from her collar and handing it to George across the nearly devoured ice cream sculpture.

He hardly gave the timepiece a glance. "Yes, very nice," he said, returning it.

Violet and Sam exchanged looks. How could a clockmaker not recognize the importance of her mid-seventeenth-century watch?

Mary's new beau was a very curious man. Disturbingly curious.

❧ 19 ❧

Vive memor let; fugit hora (Live mindful of Death; the hour flies).

—Aulus Persius Flaccus (A.D. 34–62)
The Satires

*Dearest diary, I grow irritated at the thought that my
well-crafted veneer may be falling apart. For so long I've
been viewed as innocuous that I fear I've become too bold
in my invisibility. Even more irritating—or frightening,
although I don't allow myself such weak thoughts—is the
undertaker's growing awareness of me. How is it possible
that such a benign slip of a woman should give me such
gastric disturbance?*

*She doesn't know specifically who I am yet, I'm sure
of it. Yet I am firmly convinced that I shall have to
remove her before she becomes too much of an impediment.
A pity, really, because she hasn't truly offended me like
the others. In fact, in other circumstances I might enjoy
her company.*

*But now I've left a rather unfortunate trail of bread
crumbs that the pigeon is now following. If she discovers
the reasons behind all of my activities, then I'll be exposed
for certain.*

*Too bad her husband's death didn't preoccupy her a bit
longer. I might have been done by then and fled the country.
Alas, she recovered remarkably well for a grieving widow.*

*So, diary, a riddle for you: Who undertakes for the
undertaker? Why, the deep sea creatures, of course.*

"Well, Mrs. Morgan, can't say as we're surprised, though deeply saddened we are." Mrs. Porter dabbed at a corner of one eye with her apron.

Standing behind her in the kitchen, Mr. Porter patted his wife's shoulder. " 'Twas a pleasure working for you, ma'am, but we understand you wanting to move to smaller quarters, what with Mr. Morgan gone and all, and you rattling around in this house with Miss Susanna."

Graham's death was only part of the reason. Violet really just didn't want the worry of a home anymore, with the myriad of concerns such as how much coal for eight fireplaces would cost this winter, or whether it was the flushing commode causing the smells in the basement. The house on Grafton Terrace was Graham's love, not hers.

Hence she'd made the decision to re-let it and move Susanna and herself into smaller lodgings.

Once the decision was made, she'd had this discussion with the Porters. Now it was time to see an estate agent to have someone else assume her lease.

"Mama, I'll come with you to see the agent," Susanna said.

Ever since their encounter with Dr. Beasley, Susanna insisted on accompanying Violet nearly everywhere, as though she thought Violet needed protection. From what? Stupid medical men marauding the streets?

Yet Susanna was a determined girl and wouldn't hear of being left behind unless Violet was in Sam's company.

"Of course, sweetheart. Afterward we'll go back to the doll shop to see what Mrs. Peters has that's new. What do you say?"

Violet arranged to have her home advertised and inquired as to smaller places to let in Paddington, closer to Morgan Undertaking. The estate agent, Mr. James, opened his portfolio book, full of engraved drawings of properties and their descriptions. Violet chose two that looked acceptable and arranged to meet Mr. James the following day to view them.

Already feeling as though an oppressive weight had been plucked from her shoulders, Violet returned to the shop with Susanna, bursting with renewed energy for her work and for discovering what was killing completely unrelated persons of London.

Charles Francis paused as he sat at his desk making a diary entry. His assumption that Lincoln would be too preoccupied by the progress of the war to pay attention to his Minister Plenipotentiary to the Court of St. James was wrong. The president was making constant inquiries—without asking Adams directly—as to what diplomatic progress the minister was making with the British now that the U.S. had apologized over the *Trent* Affair.

Charles Francis was equally wrong in his assumption that any sort of congratulations would be in order for his ferreting out of the Morgan brothers. Although the crew of *Monitor* had ultimately seen to their demise, hadn't Charles Francis smoked them out and caused them to act foolishly?

He passed a hand across his forehead. When had his skin gotten so leathery and wrinkled?

This coal-choked, pestilent hole doesn't agree with me, he thought.

No, the Morgan brothers should have been a great glory, but between the agreement to keep it secret with the British and his own government's disdain for his work, there seemed little purpose to his presence in London. Lord Russell, in his great endeavor to keep Britain neutral, hardly received him anymore.

Which brought him round to Samuel Harper. Although the man had made some more contacts with possible blockade raiders, things were moving too slowly there. Maybe there weren't as many of them in Great Britain as Charles Francis had thought. Maybe it was time to send Mr. Harper home.

In the meantime, Charles Francis needed something else, something dramatic, upon which to hang his diplomatic career.

The kidnapping of a famous American in London, in which the Adams men solve the crime and see the victim returned to his homeland. Or perhaps he might intervene in some notorious legal case involving an American abroad. Yes, that would be much more in keeping with his talent for the law.

Regardless, something had to occur soon to save his reputation and that of the Adams legacy.

*   *   *

To share her good news, Violet met Mary out for tea. She had arranged for new lodgings near Morgan Undertaking in Paddington. It was a narrower townhome of only a basement and two levels, not four as she'd had before. It also had a far less grand staircase, but because it was newly built it did have one of Mr. Crapper's wooden toilets in it, a convenience to which she'd become accustomed.

With a kitchen in the basement, small dining and drawing rooms on the first floor, and Violet's and Susanna's bedrooms on the second, with the toilet room off the landing between the first and second floors, it was ideal for Violet's purposes.

The neighborhood was more modest, so hopefully her new neighbors would be less concerned with how often she entertained, whether or not she sent out her laundry or had it done at home, and whether she had both a parlormaid and a housemaid, or just a maid of all work.

"I plan to just hire day help," she said to Mary. "So much less fuss."

"My dear, I'm delighted. You'll be so near to me. I can keep a close eye on you."

"Sorry?"

"To keep an eye on you and Susanna, of course. Have I shown you what George just bought me? Look at this." From her bag, she pulled out a small enameled box with a pastoral scene of a young girl in a swing painted on top.

"George says he had it made for me by a watchmaker friend of his who also makes these boxes. George says his friend is quite renowned for his metalworking skills. Isn't it wonderful?"

"Very pretty," Violet said, discreetly turning the piece over. Although the painting on top of the box was well done and would fool most people, the undercarriage was brass and the legs were glued on sloppily. It reminded her of the work of a shoddy coffinmaker. At best, the piece was a cheap import from the Far East, just like the blue-and-white porcelain Graham had collected and that she planned to sell.

She handed it back to Mary. "Are you contemplating marriage to George?"

Mary blushed. "I don't know. Who could take the place of Matthew? Yet George is so kind and thoughtful, isn't he? And prosperous. Although he has no interest in mourning fashions, he encourages me in my success."

No doubt.

"Do you know where George was born? Where his family is?" Violet said.

"I think he's originally from Northumbria. No, wait, or is it Cumbria? He's been to Germany, you know. He says many famous watchmakers migrated to London from there; that's how London became so renowned for its timepieces."

Mary waxed on enthusiastically about George Cooke. It was so heartwarming to see her friend enjoy a nibble from the buffet table of happiness that eluded so many—including Violet—that it was impossible to express her doubts about the man's honesty.

"Oh, and, Violet dear, I hope you don't mind, but I accidentally mentioned your concerns about the customers you recently prepared. He's such a kind-hearted man, he expressed great sympathy over their situations and wanted to know everything you observed about them. You aren't angry, are you? He has such a trustworthy manner about him that I just want to confide everything in him."

"It's fine," Violet said, trying not to clench her teeth. She shouldn't be talking about her customers under any circumstances, and this was a good reminder why.

I guess my only confidant from now on will be a twelve-year-old girl.

The estate agent came to Morgan House to inventory the furniture Violet planned to leave behind. It was a poorly timed visit, as the basement odors were stronger than usual.

"I don't know what it is," Violet said to Mr. James, a quiet man with a brisk, competent air about him. "I believe it to be the flushing toilet, but I can't be sure."

The estate agent walked from room to room, sniffing the air. Violet was mortified. He pointed to the servants' staircase leading down to the kitchen. "May I?" he said.

Violet followed him down, where they found Mrs. Porter furiously rolling out a pie crust, a light dusting of flour on her apron and on her cap. Chopped apples lay heaped in a nearby bowl. Mr. James ignored her as he continued his olfactory testing of the air. He dropped to his hands and knees, sniffing along the baseboard.

Mrs. Porter stopped her attack on the dough, aghast at what the man was doing. "Sir, I assure you I keep a very proper home for Mrs. Morgan."

He arose, rearranging his jacket sleeves and trousers. "Mrs. Morgan, I believe I understand what the problem is. Do you have a shovel?"

Violet had no idea if she possessed a shovel, but Mr. Porter came in at that moment and was able to produce one from elsewhere in the basement.

"If you would be so kind as to . . ." Mr. James motioned to a section of the hard-packed earthen floor.

Mr. Porter looked at Violet uncertainly.

"Go ahead, Mr. Porter, let's see what Mr. James thinks is causing these odors."

Mr. Porter drove the pointed end of the shovel into the ground repeatedly until he was able to break up some of the dirt. By the time he was able to actually dig up a shovelful of dirt he was sweating profusely. Mr. Porter removed scoop after scoop of dirt and piled it where he could. Mrs. Porter quietly gathered up her pie-making ingredients and fled the kitchen.

Once he was down about a foot, Mr. James stopped him and dropped to his knees to inspect the hole. "As I thought," he said.

Violet stood over his shoulder to peer down. "What is it?"

Mr. James reached down and pulled out an old animal carcass, a rat by the look of it.

"A dead rodent has been causing foul smells on and off for the past year?"

"No, madam. The rat is just the beginning. Many of these new neighborhoods surrounding the city are being built hastily. Instead of properly building foundations, many developers are hauling in refuse and using it as fill underneath basements. I'm afraid yours is one of these properties. I suspect your neighbors have the same problem but are as embarrassed as you are to admit it."

"I thought it had something to do with the toilet pipes. I cannot believe the reason is trash. What can I do about it?"

"Not to worry, Mrs. Morgan, I know a contractor who can dig out your basement and replace it with proper dirt."

Violet arranged to have this done with Mr. James, the irony not lost on her that not only had her marriage been built on falsehoods and illusions, so had her house.

❧ 20 ❧

For everything there is a season,
And a time for every matter under heaven:
A time to be born, and a time to die . . .

—Ecclesiastes 3:1–2

Samuel Harper was displeased with the results of his meeting with the minister. So angered was he by Adams's pronouncement and frustrated by his inability to gainsay him that Samuel merely muttered courtesies and left the ambassadorial residence, jamming his hat on his head as he headed into another dreary, drizzly London day.

The good thing about the city's short-lived but frequent rains was that they at least helped dispel some of the acrid, choking air.

Drown or suffocate, what a choice, he thought, his mood growing blacker as he strode off to nowhere in particular.

Adams was well within his rights to send home anyone attached to his delegation. However, the man seemed more intent on not falling on his own sword than in serving the public good. It took extraordinary amounts of time, money, and guile to ferret out each commerce raider, and there were many more pearls being nurtured in their shells, just waiting to be discovered at the right moment to create a neckpiece of glory. They would not be ready for harvest early just to assuage the minister's doubts about his own position.

The comment about Violet rankled, too. As though Samuel was somehow derelict in his duties because he had formed a . . . friendship. That was all it was. Violet had never expressed an interest in anything more, even since her husband's death. Or maybe because of it. In some ways she flouted convention; in others she was as modest as a novice in a convent.

Samuel suddenly found himself outside the British Museum. It was raining harder now, so he went inside to wait out the weather. He was unconsciously drawn back to the Reading Room, where he was once again permitted entry. He climbed the stairs to the catwalk and went in search of the book on flora that had entranced Violet. Samuel scanned the shelves. Ah, there it was. He pulled out the tome, surprised by its heavy weight, and retreated down to the reading tables.

He opened the book, hardly noticing the difference between *dennstaedtia punctilobula* and *pteridium aquilinum*, but running his hands where Violet had placed hers over the dried fern leaves that were trimmed before being glued into place.

Was he being selfish? Had the chestnut-haired woman in Kentish Town—soon to be in Paddington—lulled his common sense into a drunken stupor? Perhaps it *was* time to return home. His law partner had been managing on his own for over a year, and letters flying back and forth did little to help his father manage the family farm.

Moreover, and probably more importantly, what about the thousands of men signing up to join the U.S. Army in order to cease the South's insurrection? Even one of Adams's sons had joined.

Am I derelict in my duty twice over? he wondered. The thought pained him.

Samuel flipped through a few more pages of the book before shutting it with a firmer hand than he intended. The resulting thud elicited a stern look from a nearby uniformed attendant.

Samuel returned the book to its proper place, his innards decidedly heavier than when he'd climbed the stairs earlier. He'd not been enamored of London when he first arrived; now the thought of saying good-bye was sickening.

My most dearest diary, I suddenly feel lighthearted
again. As you know, my plan was to eliminate our friend

the undertaker, although I'd not quite yet decided the means by which to do so.

Yes, I know you're thinking that I should use my usual means of removing those that either hamper my methods of acquiring money or who are just plain annoying, but for some reason the undertaker is special to me. I suppose it's the fact that she is the very first person—and a woman, no less!—to have some awareness of my activities. Or perhaps it is the fact that she knows me, but doesn't realize she knows me.

Am I the cat, lying patiently in the cool grass as my little mouse sniffs and wriggles her way to me before I, aha, pounce?

You are laughing, diary, at my pretense of patience. You know otherwise. Waiting has never been a virtue of mine.

Which brings me back to what has made me so happy today. I have decided, my dearest, to embark upon another tactic against the undertaker. It is a wonderfully clever plan, sure to evoke great pain in my subject, and that excruciating pain will force her to cease investigation of the dead that are simply none of her business.

I still hear you laughing, diary, and I must insist you stop. You are thinking that anything not resulting in the undertaker's immediate death is useless. I must disagree with you. She is special to me and must be handled in a unique way.

*Morgan Undertaking
June 1862*

Violet was exhausted after seeing to the burial of a young child inside his family's mausoleum. The poor boy, aged nine, had suffered a head injury while away at Harrow School, struck by a ball while learning cricket.

Even worse than the tragedy of the boy's loss were his parents, more overcome than any Violet had seen before. The boy was the fourth of their six children they'd lost, each due to bizarre circumstances: a drowning, a freak carriage accident, a fall while climbing an oak on the family's country estate, and now this.

Death recognized no privilege of social station.

The parents were inconsolable and clung to Violet as though she might somehow bring their boy back through magical means.

All funerals had elements of grief, sometimes great and sometimes minor, but children's funerals—no matter how many of them she arranged—were always the worst.

Not only did they break the natural order of parents dying before their offspring, they were frequently sudden—accidents and virulent disease overcame children in an instant. Hence the family had no time to prepare by starting a scrapbook or sitting at the bedside for hours on end, recording their loved one's final days.

The grief must have made the parents want to fling themselves in the path of an overdue mail coach.

After Will had returned the funeral carriage to the mews and Violet removed the ostrich feathers and black bunting from its exterior, she made one of her last trips back to Kentish Town. Soon she would walk only a few blocks home.

As soon as she entered the front door she called for Susanna, whom she'd left behind for the day, as Violet didn't like Susanna witnessing the funerals of young children. The girl was learning fast, but she wasn't ready for this yet.

Susanna launched into Violet's arms as though they'd been apart for weeks. "Mama! I mean, Mother, I thought you'd never return."

Susanna was filling out and, with her sudden onset of physical maturity, was trying out a more sophisticated tongue, too. Maybe soon she'd be ready to witness death in all of its ugly forms, although the train crash had probably given her more exposure to it than any thousand funerals could.

"I'm here now, although it has been a trying day. We've nothing pressing tomorrow, so why don't we go to the London Exposition?"

"Yes, I'd like that. Is Mr. Harper going with us?"

Violet hadn't heard from Sam in a week, but had been so preoccupied with other business that she hadn't given him much thought.

She put a hand to the jet beads around her neck. Thinking any thoughts of Sam whatsoever was inappropriate anyway.

"Probably not. We can have fun, just the two of us, can't we?"

Susanna frowned. "Yes, I suppose."

Did Susanna's newfound maturity mean she was also developing crushes?

After dinner, Violet retired upstairs to pack up some of her personal belongings. She intended to leave behind most of the furniture for the next tenant, since the same was being done in her new location.

She'd hardly started, having opened a drawer in Graham's desk in his study, when a double rap on the door signaled the arrival of the mail. Mr. Porter appeared momentarily. "A letter for you, ma'am."

It was from the estate agent. The new tenants for Violet's house were newly married and seeking their first servants. Knowing that Violet had no plans to take the Porters along with her, might he recommend them to the new tenants?

"I have delightful news for you, Mr. Porter. It looks like you can stay on here with the couple taking over my lease."

Mr. Porter tried to hide his grin behind an air of mock severity. "It's what Mrs. Porter and I have been praying for, ma'am, so I'm not surprised at all."

He left to go inform his wife, and Violet returned to cleaning out Graham's desk. What an awful hodgepodge of bills, receipts, cigar stubs, pencil shavings, and old editions of newspapers. She began dividing everything into piles for rubbish and for keeping, with most of it destined for the trash heap.

She made her way down through the desk drawers on her knees, eventually finding herself on her rear as she pawed through a drawer at the bottom of the ebonized desk. This drawer didn't seem as deep as the others—why not?

Violet removed its contents and pressed along the bottom of the drawer. The wood had give to it. She realized that it was some sort of trapdoor. Pressing harder on it now, she finally found the spring mechanism. With a final push against it, the trapdoor popped up.

What lay underneath astounded her.

A tattered, yellowed envelope with Graham's name scrawled upon it lay atop some sort of old blanket. She set aside the envelope and pulled out the blanket. No, it was a fur. A mangled-up fur made of at least three different animals, although half of it seemed to be missing. It was just a rag now.

A section of it fell back into the drawer as Violet brought it to her nose, gently sniffing it. She imagined this was what a buried animal carcass smelled like—extremely disagreeable but not as oppressive as human death.

"So your Pap bequeathed his mangy old coat to you, Graham. I stood right behind you at this desk while you told me the story, yet you never showed it to me. Why not?"

She dropped the remnant back into the drawer and fingered the envelope. It was the old-fashioned type, where the sender wrote on all but one part of the page, then folded it up so that only the blank space showed for an address. Pap must have handed this to Graham, for only his first name was on it.

Brittle remnants of scarlet sealing wax remained. She brushed them away and unfolded the letter. It was brief and written in a spidery hand that slanted down the right side of the page.

> *My Grandson—*
>
> *I am enclosing this letter with my will, so the family solicitor will give it to you when I am gone to see your grandmama.*
>
> *I can say here in the privacy of these pages that you have always been my favorite grandchild, a boy I would have wished to have as my own son, were it possible. Fletcher is too sure of himself, and as for all of your cousins—fah, they're worthless, the lot of them.*
>
> *Only you, my boy, have ever listened to your elders and taken seriously what I had to say. Therefore, it is only you I can trust now to remember the past, learn from it, and act on it. And act upon it you must.*
>
> *You alone can understand the sins committed against me by the Americans. They think themselves morally superior because they so rudely threw off their king, but I*

*tell you they are morally bereft. Spineless. Cowards. No
better than disease-ridden dogs. I know of what I speak, as
I have had many years to sit and dwell on what those ill-
mannered, foul-tempered canines did to me and other
good, honest, loyal British soldiers.*

*While I was a guest of the Americans they tortured my
mind day and night. They told me they'd reported me
dead. How was I to know they had no way to do so? All I
could imagine was your sweet grandmama's face and what
her anguish was.*

*Then they gave me false reports of the British fleeing the
country in terror, dropping their weapons and pleading
for mercy. How much shame it heaped upon me to think it
true. They told me I was the sole remaining British soldier
in their godforsaken country, and that I was completely
forgotten by king and crown.*

*Each morning they woke me to say I would be executed
before sundown. I eventually wished they would do so, to
at least make your grandmama's grief purposeful.*

*I am leaving you my old war coat as a reminder of my
tragic past at the hands of others. I ask for your promise
from the grave that when an opportunity ever arises where
you can take retribution for me . . . you will do it.*

*Take my charge seriously, my boy. I realize the notion of
any further troubles between crown and colonies—as they
will always be to me—seems remote, yet you never know.*

Promise me.

Your Grandpapa,
Philip Morgan

Violet let the letter drop from her hand. As cruel and sadistic as
what happened to Pap was, why did he think it proper to guilt a
young boy into seeking revenge for it? *Oh, Graham, I'm sorry you
were led astray by this man.*

Violet and Susanna stepped off the omnibus in South Kensington. The Great London Exhibition was easy to locate, with its

massive façade along Cromwell Road. Wings were set at right angles on both ends and a triple-arched entrance in the center of the building openly invited visitors, who now were flowing in and out, chattering noisily about the treasures that lay beyond the doors. The entrance was topped by two crystal domes, rumored to be the largest in the world. Violet smiled, thinking how distressed Sam would be to see them if there wasn't something comparable in America.

Once inside, Susanna gasped at the magnificence of what lay before them, although Violet was merely reminded of her visit to the Crystal Palace Exposition a decade ago. Together they walked through displays of fabrics, rugs, sculpture, furniture, silver, glass, and wallpaper. Mr. William Morris's firm of Morris, Marshall, Faulkner and Co. had a very busy showroom attracting a great deal of attention.

After browsing through the decorative arts, they made their way through the bustling throngs of suited men, corseted women, and awestruck children to other exhibits, including a cotton mill, an analytical machine by a Mr. Charles Babbage, and an ongoing international chess tournament.

Susanna pulled Violet over to an exhibit where a man was barking his wares over the noise of the crowds. He introduced himself as William England of the London Stereoscopic Company, and invited people to gaze inside his wooden stereoscope.

"You will be transported into an amazing world, ladies and gentlemen. The magic lanterns of yesteryear were just the beginning. Feast your eyes on this new invention, which will change entertainment forever."

Violet and Susanna waited patiently for their turn at one of three stereoscopes Mr. England had set up. They were large, upright wood boxes with a pair of eyepieces set in front and a rotating knob on one side. When Violet peered into the eyepieces, she was amazed. It was an image of the exhibition hall they were in, but it had depth to it that couldn't be found in one of Mr. Laroche's ambrotypes. The picture was a scene showing what looked like large pieces of agricultural machinery, evident by bales of hay and containers of threshed wheat around the machines.

She drew her head back a bit. There were actually two images inside the unit, and somehow they combined when her eyes were pressed up against the eyepiece, creating a single wondrous illustration that she felt she could practically step inside of, so realistic was it. Turning the knob brought up a new image, this time the exterior of the exhibition building.

Violet shook her head as Susanna took her place at the eyepieces. What marvels of technology she was witnessing in her lifetime—photography, flushing toilets, and mass production of basic goods. It was extraordinary.

Too bad such advancements didn't include acceptance of her embalming techniques. With so much other progress in the world, maybe Violet would one day find herself embalming as a matter of routine.

Refreshed from her visit to the exhibition, a symbol of optimism in man's future, Violet went back to work with renewed determination to figure out what strange ailment had stricken two Londoners and might affect more. First, though, Violet hired moving men to see her goods over to their new residence. Once the movers had placed the few pieces of furniture she retained from the old house and unloaded all of their worldly goods, it was up to Violet and Susanna to unpack clothes and possessions and see to decoration. It was exhausting work, but Violet loved their cozier surroundings.

She'd hardly had time to get settled in her shop the day after moving into her new quarters when Mary stopped by with a tattered old book to show her.

"I found this in Mr. Hatchard's shop."

"Ah yes, the eminent Mr. Hatchard, who now finds me so distasteful."

Mary closed her hand over Violet's. "Dearest, I'm sure he was simply swept up in the unpleasantness of the time. He didn't mean anything by his curtness toward you. Besides, I told him I was doing some research on diseases for you, and he was quite happy to give me assistance. He even sold me the book at a discounted price."

Violet looked at the title Mary held out: *A Treatise of Known Diseases and Their Origins.*

"I hope you don't mind, but I read through it with George, and together we think we've found the answer."

"I see." Why was Violet distinctly uncomfortable with Mary's enthusiasm on the topic?

Mostly because she can't seem to quit sharing the topic with others, I imagine.

Although it did beg the question of why Violet herself was so obsessed with finding out what had killed Mr. Young and Mrs. Atkinson. It made no sense whatsoever. After all, she was just the undertaker, not a doctor. Her concern was inexplicable.

Yet here she was, determined to discover the truth about their deaths.

Mary flipped through the pages until she reached one that had been folded over to mark it. "See?" she proclaimed, holding it up proudly.

It was a chapter entitled "Chicken Pox." Violet scanned the symptoms of chicken pox, which included skin rash and pockmarks. The only problem was that the condition was only rarely fatal.

"George says this must be what you were seeing. How fortunate we are to have him."

"Mary," Violet began, hoping to find the right words that would not alienate her friend. "Do you remember that I asked you not to repeat what I told you about Mr. Young and Mrs. Atkinson?"

"Yes, but George is the soul of discretion, I assure you."

"That may be, but it would appear that Mr. Hatchard has now joined the circle of confidence."

Mary put her hand to her chest. "I am very sorry. It's just that you didn't seem at all upset that I told George, and when he suggested that we help you by doing some research, well, I just—"

"Mr. Cooke suggested going to the bookseller?"

"Yes. So you see, he's most thoughtful of others around him."

Violet didn't care much to be so deeply in Mr. George Cooke's thoughts, even if the book may have been a good idea.

She laid the book on her counter. It might require further reading later.

"Mary, perhaps we can let go of this subject for now? I'm sure you and Mr. Cooke have better things to discuss than me."

Mary's cheeks flamed. "Of course, of course. I apologize." She brightened immediately. Infatuation had made Mary impervious to more than a few seconds of gloom. "Speaking of better things, I've decided to purchase a new model of Mr. Singer's sewing machine and hire an assistant to use my old one. George thinks I'm ready to expand my business. It's a frightening thought, but a little thrilling, too. Oh, and while I was at the bookshop, I bought a novel called *Lady Audley's Secret*. It's quite scandalous. I'll pass it along to you as soon as George and I finish it. He loves books as much as we do, and especially likes it when I read aloud to him. . . ."

After she'd apprised Violet of all of George's inestimable qualities, Mary finally left. Violet's stomach sank at the realization of feeling relief over her friend's departure.

She and Susanna and your parents are all you have in the world, you ninny.

What of Sam? Wasn't he an important part of her world? No, he was just a friendly acquaintance who would one day return to his homeland.

How will I feel when he leaves?

The thought kept her up far into the night. Eventually eschewing sleep, she picked up the book on diseases. Was there possibly another answer to the puzzle inside?

Violet scanned the pages, looking for a condition that might accurately describe what she'd witnessed with Mrs. Atkinson and Mr. Young.

Dawn's rays were peeking through the curtains before she closed the cover, having gleaned nothing new.

Violet was no closer to an answer than she was before.

21

Because I could not stop for Death,
He kindly stopped for me.
The Carriage held but just ourselves
And Immortality.

—Emily Dickinson (1830–1886), American poet

The day was unusually hot and stifling, leaving Violet soaked after the brief walk from her home to Morgan Undertaking one Monday morning. Even Susanna was visibly limp from the heat.

It was times like these that Violet was glad for the shop's low lighting and heavy draperies, intended to bring a sense of calm and peace to visitors, but which also served to keep the interior air cooler.

Will had left a note. He and Harry were already at the mews, repainting the carriages with black paint before the sun rose too high. It was amazing how solicitous and thoughtful her employees had become since Graham's death. Will and Harry were now perpetually asking what they could do to help and offering suggestions for improving the shop's operation. It was as though they thought they were helping to fill Graham's place since his death.

Regardless, the shop ran efficiently—and peaceably—now.

Violet set Susanna to sweeping and dusting the shop, something Will and Harry never seemed to do well, while she took out her appointment book to determine what preparations she needed to make for the week.

Mr. Boyce wanted to meet with her to discuss a new coffin design on Thursday, so she needed to decide whether to leave Susanna at the shop or take her home first before heading to Curtain Road.

The Kalon man was stopping by to see what cosmetics Violet needed to order, so she had to be sure to take inventory before his arrival on Friday—

The front door opened and banged violently against the wall. Violet jumped, and saw that two men had entered the shop. They looked neither like grieving family members nor like funeral supply salesmen. One was tall with a belly that strained against his ill-fitting, crumpled brown suit. The other was shorter, with a nose so large it practically floated on top of his face. He, too, wore a suit that looked like it belonged to someone else.

"Gentlemen, welcome to Morgan Undertaking. How may I help you?" Violet asked in her most solicitous tone, despite feeling that there was something very wrong with these two, and that they most certainly were not gentlemen.

"Need to talk to you, Mrs. Morgan, about your husband."

Violet sighed inwardly. Was there no end to Graham's dealings?

"Is there perhaps a bill that he was unable to settle before his passing?" She stayed behind the counter, whereas normally she would come out to greet a visitor. She liked having the walnut expanse between them.

As if sensing Violet's wariness, Susanna set aside her dusting rag and joined her behind the counter.

"You could say that. It's a mighty large bill, though. What do you mean, 'his passing'?"

Violet looked down and back up at the man who spoke, the taller one. "Surely you see I am in widow's weeds, Mr. . . . ?"

"Slade."

Violet turned her attention to the behemoth-nosed one. "And you are . . . ?"

"Cubby. Your husband disappointed us, Mrs. Morgan." The man wheezed noisily through his nose. Violet was unpleasantly reminded of Mrs. Scrope, although these two could prove to be far more foul than her previous servant was.

"Well, I cannot defend my late husband's actions, as I am mostly unaware of them. If the bill is reasonable, I am happy enough to settle it for you now."

"You keep saying your husband's dead, Mrs. Morgan," Slade said. "When did he die?"

"In March. His ship sank on crossing to America. His brother died with him."

"We didn't read anything like that in the papers."

Violet doubted they read anything much at all beyond some gossip papers. "It wasn't in the newspapers."

"What? A dirty character like your husband dies and the rags make no mention of it?"

"The government kept it out of the press."

Cubby snorted and rubbed his hands together, like a bull anxiously waiting for someone to gore. "Do you take us for idiots, Mrs. Morgan? The government would have been happy to report on the demise of a traitor. Of course your husband is alive and well, and hasn't bothered to repay us."

Violet tried to keep any fear from flickering in her eyes. "Did my husband borrow some amount from you?"

"I'll say he did. He wanted five hundred pounds. He couldn't get it from any other sources, so I reckon he had to resort to Slade and me." The two men laughed.

"I don't believe you. Mr. Morgan couldn't possibly have borrowed that much money. For what reason did he need it?"

Cubby shrugged. "A business concern with his brother that we naturally know nothing about. We just want repayment. With interest, he owes us six hundred. We know they left in December, so they should both be back by now. We made a visit to Fletcher Morgan's quarters, but he seems to have skipped out on us."

Violet was completely alone in the shop except for Susanna, and her employees probably wouldn't return for hours if they were painting all three carriages with two coats of black paint. She had to get these vile wretches off the premises on her own. She squared her shoulders, figuring that belligerence might startle them enough to get rid of them.

"You're both filthy liars trying to take advantage of a grieving widow. How dare you barge in here with your false accusations against my dead husband and brother-in-law?"

"Your husband ain't dead, though, is he?" Slade said.

"And you furthermore impugn my own reputation by accusing me of pretending to be a widow. Do you think I wear all of this for enjoyment, you clodhoppers? You're nothing but clumsy, godless oafs intent on destroying a respectable woman's livelihood."

"You ain't that respectable," Cubby muttered.

"How dare you!" Violet picked up her appointment book and slammed it on the counter for effect. It worked; both men jumped. Unfortunately, she overturned her inkpot in the process. A trail of black ink made its way down the front of the display case.

"Tell me, gentlemen, do you slither about from shop to shop, accusing helpless women of their husbands' mysterious financial dealings? How much have you managed to collect? How many widows and children have you managed to starve to death?"

Slade was visibly irritated. "Mrs. Morgan, we don't play false and I don't care about all of your female whining and crying. Your husband borrowed a lot of money from us, and we intend to have it back. Now, do you want to pay us now, or should we come back later when Mr. Morgan returns?"

"I tell you, my husband is dead."

Cubby took over. "I'm sure he is. And if that be the case, then I suppose you'll be paying us back."

"No, I will *not* be 'paying you back.' I've nothing but your word that my husband borrowed anything from you in the first place."

"Our word is good as a gold coin, Mrs. Morgan. Which reminds me, you can pay us either in gold coin or the good queen's currency. But pay us you will."

"Leave my premises. Now." The more frightened Violet grew, the angrier her façade became.

Slade stepped up against the counter, his stomach preventing him from getting too close, but his presence emphasizing his towering height over Violet. She refused to give in to her brain, which was rapidly assessing the situation and suggesting she grab Susanna and run.

You've survived a train crash, Violet Morgan. What are two street cretins compared to that?

She realized Susanna was no longer standing next to her. Where had she gone? There was no time to contemplate it, for Slade was leaning over to stare eye level with her. "I've had enough of your foolishness, Mrs. Morgan. Either you'll pay us yourself or you'll tell us where your husband is hiding."

"I'll do neither. I'm not answerable to criminals."

"Ah, now, that hurts, after all the patience we've extended you. I must inform you that we take our business transactions seriously, and there will be consequences if we aren't paid back. We wouldn't be in business long if we permitted customers to walk off without holding up their end of a deal, would we?"

Violet put her hands on her hips. "Since your deal was with my husband and you are convinced that he is still alive, I recommend that you comb the city until you find him. And may you both be bitten by rabid dogs for your efforts. Now, get out before I start screaming."

"She'll scream, Cubby, did you hear that?" Slade turned briefly to his companion and laughed before turning back to Violet, his face transformed into a mask of fury. "Let me tell you what our efforts will be, and this only because I'm feeling generous toward a woman who might not know where her husband is. *Might* not. You'll meet us at the White Hart Inn down the street in three days' time with our money, or you won't much care for what happens next."

"I don't fear you. You're filth." Violet could feel red blotches creeping up her neck to her face, an expression of fear she refused to let come out in her voice or posture.

Slade put out a hand and pinched Violet's cheek. The pain was sharp, but she refused to react. "You're full of hiss and spit. It has been a pleasure doing business with you, Mrs. Morgan, and I look forward to seeing you in three days."

With that, he nodded to Cubby and the two left the shop. Violet came out from behind the counter and sank down onto one of two upholstered chairs meant for anguished visitors. She gave over to her own fear, trembling over what had just taken place.

What had Graham gotten himself into? It was probably no wonder he and Fletcher were dealing with felons to finance their illegal doings. Who would be the next rat emerging from a dark corner to accuse or blame Violet for things out of control? Would she never be safe again?

She needed to tell Sam what happened; he'd know the best thing to do. Before she could act to send him a message, Will and Harry burst through the door with Susanna on their heels.

"Where are they, Mrs. Morgan?" Will asked, dripping both sweat and black paint despite the apron he wore to protect his clothes.

"Don't worry, they're gone," she said, rising to go back behind the counter.

"Which way did they go? We'll go after them."

"No, Will. All is well now. You can return to your duties."

"Miss Susanna says they were threatening you and demanding money. If you won't let us hunt for them, we should at least fetch the police."

Violet shook her head. "It's not necessary. I'll take care of it."

"You don't intend to give in to their demands, do you? Harry and I will scour London for them and they'll wish they'd never set foot inside Morgan Undertaking."

Violet smiled at the man's bravado. "Peace, Will. I won't be giving them any money, and I'm sure there won't be any more trouble from them."

Will gave her a doubtful look. She didn't feel so sure herself.

"You say Graham borrowed money from them?" Sam asked as they sat down together. His mere presence in the shop was a comfort and went a long way to erasing the memory of Slade's and Cubby's visit.

"That's what they claim. Is it possible that once you finally rejected Graham's and Fletcher's smuggling plans, they went elsewhere to get financing?"

"I guess, but why continue pursuing it without a ready buyer in the States?"

Violet thought about the coat remnant that she'd stuffed into a box and moved to her new location, hiding it down in the basement. "I don't know."

Sam rubbed his chin. His brown eyes were full of worry. "You need police help."

She shook her head. "My business is on tenuous enough footing. Imagine the London talk if a bobby was pacing in and out of my shop. I can't risk it."

"Maybe I should go to the White Hart and meet them."

"No, I couldn't allow that. Perhaps they'll forget about it."

"Forget about six hundred pounds? You must be joking."

"Still, I couldn't ask you to place yourself in danger on my behalf."

"Violet, you can't live in fear that two thugs are going to show up at any minute to hurt you. If nothing else, I insist that you stay out of the shop for the next few days."

"I can't. I have work to do, and I never know when someone will call on me for a funeral. Such things can't wait."

Sam blew out an exasperated breath. "Then I presume I'll have to stand guard in front of your shop and new house day and night."

Violet smiled. "That sounds perfect. You wouldn't mind?"

"Well, I guess I could. I'd have to talk it over with the minister and—oh, you're teasing me again."

"Just a little. I'm not sure what to do, Sam. I admit I'm afraid, but I refuse to let them intimidate me."

"Then you must let me meet with them. It's the only answer."

Violet sighed. "Very well," she said, and described what each man looked like. "I'll be very worried about you."

"There's no need to be concerned about me, although I find it a pleasing thought."

* * *

Determined to put it out of her mind and rely on Sam to resolve the men's demands, Violet met with all of her scheduled appointments for the next couple of days, as well as receiving two families with elderly relatives who had passed on and required burial.

Neither of the deceased, both elderly women, had any of the symptoms she'd seen on Mr. Young and Mrs. Atkinson, a good sign. For the first woman, a Mrs. Davis, the family wanted her placed in their dining room for visitation by family members who were coming from a remote area of Wales. The family wanted to wait a week to bury their relative in order to accommodate all of the travel involved. Violet suggested embalming, which was soundly rejected by Mrs. Davis's daughter. Instead, Violet provided a cooling table for Mrs. Davis, which was placed in the center of the dining room after servants removed the family's regular dining table.

The cooling table consisted of a resting slab of metal atop a lead-lined container to be filled with ice. Violet and Will provided the first load of ice and showed the Davis family's housekeeper where the spigot was in the back so that the container could be drained as necessary and then refilled with ice through an opening at the top of the container.

Violet draped the entire table in black crape before she and Will gently carried in a newly coiffed Mrs. Davis, dressed in her finest clothes as laid out by her daughter. Susanna and Harry hauled in four containers of lilies from their carriage while Violet went over final details of the funeral with the family.

From there, they went to see to the second body. This was a much simpler task, as the family was of modest means and merely wanted its matriarch buried with dignity as quickly as possible.

After the three returned to the shop, Harry handed Violet a letter that had arrived while they were gone. The handwriting was unfamiliar. She opened it to find a single line on the page.

This is your final day of happiness.

Violet blinked. What was this supposed to mean? Her three days weren't up until tonight, and surely Slade and Cubby assumed she was paying them. Why were they torturing her further?

"Mrs. Morgan, is everything all right?" Harry asked.

"Yes, yes, of course. Thank you for giving this to me. Susanna, I think it best that we go home for the remainder of the day."

Susanna frowned but didn't argue. Once home, Violet nearly wore holes in the carpets, pacing back and forth through the dining and drawing rooms, not even sure what to worry about the most.

Samuel approached the minister carefully about his idea concerning Violet and the threats she had received. If he played his cards properly, he would be able not only to protect her, but to also continue ferreting out the financiers of blockade runners and commerce raiders. Not only that, it would garner accolades for Adams, which would in turn ensure that the minister extended Samuel's tenure in Great Britain.

To his gratification, it worked. "So, Harper, you're saying that characters in league with the Morgan brothers are stalking a British citizen?"

"Yes, sir, I know this beyond a doubt. I fear they intend Mrs. Morgan great harm. If we can prevent this from happening, you will undoubtedly be held in esteem not only by Lords Russell and Palmerston, but by the queen as well. Mrs. Morgan is a great favorite of Queen Victoria's since the prince's death."

Samuel stood quietly as he watched gears whirling and clicking rapidly behind Adams's eyes. He knew Adams was coming to the same conclusions he already had.

But Adams was not that easily persuaded. "Ironic, isn't it, that of the two million citizens of London, it is Mrs. Morgan who is being so persecuted, eh?"

"It's hardly of relevance to the state of affairs, sir."

"Isn't it?" Adams turned to the window of his office and stared out at some unknown point of interest.

Eventually, Henry Adams cleared his throat. "Father, this might be the situation you seek."

"Yes, yes, I know." Adams turned back around. "The circumstances just irritate me. Honestly, Harper, I wouldn't be surprised if you'd hired the men yourself to intimidate Mrs. Morgan, just so you'd have an excuse to rescue her."

Samuel bristled. "Sir, with all respect, do not impugn my integrity. First, I would never harass any woman, especially one as innocent as Mrs. Morgan. Second, I have been a dedicated servant to the North's cause and am of no mind to get involved in anything that might detract from my mission or bring disgrace to my country. In fact, I've even been thinking it might be time that I—"

Adams waved a hand. "No offense intended, Harper. My son seems to think your goal a worthy one, and he has keen judgment."

Henry looked down modestly at his father's praise.

"So I'll let you pursue these associates of the Morgan brothers. You'll report to me daily and ensure that the United States receives the greatest credit possible for uncovering what other schemes the Morgans may have been involved in. Am I clear?"

"As a spring morning in Boston, sir."

This time, Samuel was pleased with the results of his meeting with the minister. To celebrate his success, he stopped off at the King's Arms nearby for a pint of bitters. As he sat over the foamy brew, he worked out in his mind how to handle Cubby and Slade. He played several scenarios through his head, but all of them concluded with both men unconscious, bloodied, or screaming for mercy.

The minister would be displeased with any of those outcomes.

As he drained his glass, he decided he would simply do whatever his instincts led him to do in the moment. Thus resolved, Samuel went back to his hotel to write a letter to his father before heading out to the prescribed meeting place, where he intended to put an end to this foolishness against Violet.

Night was falling like a gentle blanket, yet the streets of London were as crowded and noisy as ever. It never ceased to amaze Samuel what a complete contradiction London was. The current building craze meant that rows of sturdy new townhomes with gleaming front stoops and freshly painted wrought iron gates stood proudly across the street from dilapidated, old, cramped rooming houses and shops with disintegrating roof tiles, their windows broken if they ever had them at all.

The prosperous, well-dressed residents of the new homes stepped around the impoverished, ragged, starving Londoners who competed for space in the streets. Some of the poor begged for money and food, and pickpockets were common.

Samuel took a deep breath. Sometimes he longed for the open spaces of America, where there might be poverty, but it didn't seem quite so . . . suffocating.

He'd heard there was a powerful evangelical movement sweeping England, much as it had the U.S., which had led to the abolition movement that resulted in his own country's civil war. Thank God slavery was already illegal in Great Britain.

Evidence of these evangelicals was in the street preachers handing out tracts, churches throwing open doors to offer bland but nutritious meals, and the orphanages run by the devout. Samuel hoped that one day all of London would be lifted out of poverty, but history's lessons didn't suggest that it would.

With this on his mind, he nearly walked by an elderly woman standing at the corner of an alley with her hand out. He stopped, reached into his pocket for some coins, and dropped them into the woman's clawing grasp. She grinned at him with a mouth full of rotten teeth, and he realized that she wasn't old at all, despite her hunched back and weathered face.

On impulse, he asked her, "Have you no family? No one to help you?"

"No, sir, my only family is my infant boy. I keep him safe back here." She nodded her head back toward the alley. Was there a child buried in that pile of dirty blankets and cast-off clothing? "Would you like to meet him, sir?"

How could a baby possibly survive in such conditions? From somewhere behind him came a low whistle. Perhaps the police had discovered some miscreant stealing from a shop owner. He approached the heap of materials. There was no movement. He hoped the child hadn't died.

"What's his name?"

"Billy. You can pick him up if you like, sir."

Samuel bent down, searching for the baby in the dark. "I can't find—" he began, but was stopped short by a blinding flash of pain at the back of his head. As he fell forward into the fetid pile of blankets, he felt hands pawing through his pockets. Another blow to the head created a dazzling display of fireworks in his brain. Before losing consciousness, Samuel realized that the only infant here was himself, naïve and now helpless over his situation.

Violet woke in a panic. What had happened? She slowly blinked herself to complete awareness. All was calm around her, although morning light was filtering through the window. And she was still in yesterday's dress. On the sofa.

She sat straight up. She must have fallen asleep waiting for Sam, who had promised to stop by her new townhome after he met with Cubby and Slade. Except he'd never shown up and she must have fallen asleep waiting for him.

Perhaps he finished late and didn't want to disturb me at that hour.

Or perhaps he'd come to harm with those two. A sour taste rose in her throat. What time was it, anyway? She glanced at the watch Sam had given her. It was already past nine o'clock in the morning. It was time to get to the shop, but first she had to make sure Sam was well. She had his hotel address; perhaps she should go there.

She had little time to think about it before Will came banging at her door, wild-eyed and frantic. "Mrs. Morgan, quickly! Harry had an accident with one of the horses."

"What do you mean?"

"After we painted the new funeral carriages, he thought it would be best to buy all new harnesses for the horses, since the old ones were getting shabby."

"Yes, I remember approving the expense."

"Harry decided to try them out this morning. He was in the process of hooking Dilly to the fancy carriage when something spooked her. She raced off and Harry was dragged along between her and the carriage until he could disengage himself from the straps. He's hurt pretty bad, Mrs. Morgan."

"Good Lord, where is he?"

"Someone carried him off to St. Mary's Hospital while I came to get you."

Violet was on the move now, grabbing a bonnet and her reticule. She turned to Susanna, who was standing on the stairs, rubbing the sleep out of her eyes. "Susanna, I have to help Will. Go back to bed and I'll wake you when I return."

Susanna nodded and headed back up to her room.

As Violet and Will raced into the street together, he gave her more details. "Dilly broke free of the carriage, but someone managed to round her up. I put her back in her stable before coming here. I didn't have time to look over the carriage, but just a glance told me it was damaged."

"We'll worry about it later. First let's make sure Harry isn't badly injured." They jumped into a hackney resting at a corner, the original owner's coat of arms still visible through the paint on the carriage doors. Most drivers purchased previously owned broughams for use as hired vehicles. The driver protested that he wasn't taking passengers at the moment, but Violet pulled a handful of coins from her bag and offered them to the man, who nodded and urged his horse forward.

Violet and Will tumbled out of the hackney before it had completely stopped in front of St. Mary's, rushed inside and asked for the accident ward, which turned out to be a cavernous hall with rows and rows of beds and a number of white-capped, white-aproned nurses milling around tending to the patients. It was much larger than the Sussex County Hospital ward where her arm had been cleaned and bandaged.

Poor Harry was bruised and battered but had no serious injuries. He even joked weakly that he planned to make the most of his trauma with all of the girls in his neighborhood. "I might even find me a wife who wants to take care of me," he said, grinning.

Reassured that he would be well in no time, Violet left with Will to inspect the day's other damage. The carriage in question was a block away from the mews and, indeed, the damage was considerable. At least she had no immediate need of the vehicle. Perhaps Mr. Boyce would be willing to repair it, although it might be beneath his dignity as a cabinetmaker to do a carriagemaker's job.

Will offered to bring out one of the other horses to rescue the carriage while Violet checked on Dilly—who was still edgy but not injured—and returned to the shop. Once inside the relative quiet of Morgan Undertaking, she realized that she was completely unwashed from the previous day and still wearing the same clothes, not that mourning clothing changed enough from day to day that anyone would take notice. Violet spent an hour coordinating efforts for Mrs. Davis's funeral before realizing to her complete mortification that in the fuss over Harry and the carriage, she'd completely forgotten about Sam and Susanna.

She decided to visit Sam's hotel first to be sure nothing had happened to him and to find out what happened with Cubby and Slade. Then she'd return home to pick up Susanna, who was more than likely entertaining herself with her dollhouse.

Inside the lobby of the Langham, Violet asked for Mr. Harper and was invited to wait on one of several plush red velvet sofas that sat atop the largest Turkish carpet she'd ever seen. A bellhop was sent to Sam's room to inquire as to whether he was in. Sam came down a few minutes later with a bandage wrapped around his head, grasping the intricately designed brass rail as he limped down the steps.

Violet jumped up and met him as he reached the bottom of the stairs.

"I'm so sorry," they each said in unison.

Sam smiled. "What do you have to be sorry for?"

"You're hurt. Cubby and Slade did this?" Without thinking, Violet reached up to touch the bandage. Sam snapped his head back as though struck by lightning.

"I'm afraid I'm still a bit sore. And, no, I'm afraid I have no glorious tale of derring-do for you today. In fact, I completely missed meeting them, for which I must apologize to you."

"What happened?"

"I was just thinking about having some lunch. Why don't you join me?"

Over seasoned fish, Sam told her of his misadventure the previous evening: ". . . and so the young woman I thought was helpless and alone actually had at least one accomplice, and once she tricked me into leaving the safety of the street, it was quite easy to bash my brains in and steal everything I had. I vaguely remember waking up in a mound of trash and stumbling back here to sleep a few hours in my room before deciding I needed a doctor, which the hotel manager summoned for me. Fortunately, he doesn't think there is any grave damage to my head. The same cannot be said for my pride."

"I'm just happy you weren't more badly hurt—or even killed." Tears sprang unbidden into Violet's eyes and she dabbed at them quickly with her napkin.

"Why, Violet Morgan, don't tell me you're weeping for me."

"No, of course not. It has just been a difficult day." She sniffed and launched into telling him what happened with Harry and her carriage.

"How much worse can this day become?" she said.

He closed a hand over hers on the table. "Let's hope we're done with bad news. What I need to concentrate on now is where our criminal friends are hiding out. I'm not sure it's safe for you to be at the shop now that you have ostensibly ignored their demand."

"Oh! That reminds me. I left Susanna at home this morning and promised I'd return later to pick her up. She must be worried to death by now."

Sam quickly settled the bill and they headed back to Violet's townhome. She deposited Sam in the drawing room while she combed all three floors of the house, calling Susanna's name. The girl was nowhere to be found. Susanna's bed was unmade, but that wasn't atypical, although Mrs. Softpaws's incessant pacing back and forth on top of it was. Where had she gone? Surely she hadn't decided to go to the shop on her own.

She returned to the drawing room, where Sam was examining a

recent portrait Violet had had made of Susanna by the eminent Mr. Laroche. Susanna sat on a chair with an impossibly large bow on the back of her hair to match the one at her waist. Mr. Laroche's tinting gave Susanna an impish look even though she was practically on the edge of becoming a young woman.

"She's not here. We should check the shop; maybe she went there."

"On her own?" Sam said.

"She must have done so. Where else could she be?"

For the second time that day, Violet rushed into the streets of London. Poor Sam gallantly kept up with her, even though his head was probably aching beyond belief.

"Susanna!" she called out as soon as she opened the shop door.

Will emerged from the back room. "She's not here, Mrs. Morgan. I thought you left her at home?"

"I did, but . . ." All of a sudden Violet remembered the last note. Fishing it from her reticule, she showed it to Sam while Will disappeared again to whatever task he was performing.

"Who sent this to you?" Sam said.

"I don't know. Cubby and Slade?"

"But why would they send it to you before your planned meeting with them? It makes no sense."

"I don't know, Sam, I don't know." Violet heard the hysterical pitch in her own voice. "My God, do you think they took Susanna once no one met them at the White Hart? How will I find her? What will they do to her? I never should have left her alone; she's not used to being alone. Oh God, oh God, please help me." She sank down on one of the visitor chairs.

Sam crossed the room to the front door and locked it, switching the sign to "Closed" before returning to Violet and dropping to one knee and taking her hands in his.

"Violet, listen to me. This is my fault; I was the one who didn't keep the appointment time."

"But you were—"

"I was taken out by my own stupidity. But hear me, sweetheart, we are going to find Susanna. I won't rest until we do. And she'll be fine. They wouldn't dare harm an innocent child like Susanna." Sam gently lifted her up and put his arms around her.

With that, Violet burst into a flood of tears that refused to cease. She stayed locked in his embrace until she was so weak from weeping that she began shivering. Sam took her home and made sure she had a pot of tea next to her on the sofa before leaving with a promise to return as soon as he could.

22

Cowards die many times before their deaths;
The valiant never taste of death but once.
Of all the wonders that I yet have heard,
It seems to me most strange that men should fear;
Seeing that death, a necessary end,
Will come when it will come.

—William Shakespeare
Julius Caesar (ca. 1598–1600)

Violet crumpled the new note up in her palm and resisted the urge to weep uncontrollably again. After several gulps of air, she smoothed out the paper and read it again.

Tell me what to do,
With a girl whose eyes are blue,
She knows too much,
About my deadly touch,
But I'll exchange her today for YOU.

Violet read it three more times. Were Slade and Cubby asking her to look for them in order to sacrifice herself in exchange for Susanna? She'd do so gladly, but they hadn't provided a single clue as to where they were.

The police had proven less than helpful. After they carefully questioned her about Graham's activities, Susanna's awkward relationship to Violet, and Violet's interactions with an American foreigner, the two officials she and Sam visited at Number Four Whitehall Place suggested that perhaps Violet had a domestic household problem.

Sam was livid over their apathetic response and demanded they do something. Casually informing him that American citizens had no right to demand anything, they dismissed both Sam and Violet with a halfhearted promise to alert other officers about the missing child. Sam was nearly apoplectic by the time they left, vacillating between anger at police incompetence and fury at himself for what he perceived as his own failings.

Knowing the value of the newspapers, Violet took her ambrotype of Susanna to an engraver, who reproduced the likeness for an advertisement Violet placed, offering a reward for anyone with knowledge of Susanna's whereabouts. Meanwhile, she knew Sam was scouring docks, inns, and every conceivable nook and cranny of London he could think of where Graham and Fletcher might have been conducting business. Every turn he made led to nowhere, and he became gloomy and dejected.

Violet was chewing her fingernails ragged, she'd stopped eating entirely, and her eyes were puffed from crying and lack of sleep, but she kept trudging through her days of accommodating customers as best she could.

Mary's response was a predictable outpouring of love and grief over Susanna's disappearance and an offer to do whatever was necessary to help.

Letters flew back and forth between Violet and her parents, as they inquired constantly as to the status of Susanna's disappearance and whether they should take the train up to help Violet search for "our precious girl." Violet advised them to remain in Brighton, wanting to devote every minute to Susanna and not having to worry about hosting her parents, especially now that she lived in smaller quarters.

Even with every ill that had befallen her over the past year—Graham's perfidy, the train crash, her public humiliation, and death all around—how did any of those compare to the loss of sweet little Susanna?

I won't survive if she's taken from me.

* * *

Charles Francis Adams eagerly opened the letter from his son, now a captain in the U.S. Army. Although he wrote frequently to Charles Francis Jr., few letters successfully made the return trip. Today's letter was a treat.

> *July 25, 1862*
> *Dear Father,*
> *It has been a terrible time for Union forces here over the past few weeks during what has become known as the Seven Days' Campaign. General McClellan ran a poor defense against Robert E. Lee's offensive at Glendale, Virginia. Losses on both sides are in the thousands with many more missing. The Army of the Potomac was not defeated, nor did it gain a single inch of ground. I served at Glendale under General George Meade, and if that damned old goggle-eyed snapping turtle of a general be our only hope for salvation in this war, we are in mighty trouble indeed.*
> *Also, you may be interested to know that a provisional measure, the Revenue Act, was enacted on July 1, establishing a Commissioner of Internal Revenue responsible for collecting a graduated income tax on those with incomes over $600 per year. I understand the measure is only temporary and will expire in four years. It also implements an inheritance tax, so you shall have to be very careful with the family estate, lest—God forbid— anything should happen to you before the act expires.*
> *Miss Ogden patiently waits for the day that this wretched war will be over and we can be married. I admit that I share her feelings. I send felicitations to Mother and everyone else.*
> *Your son,*
> *Charles Francis Jr.*

Charles Francis carefully folded the letter and added it to his thin stack of correspondence with his eldest son.

What if the North lost the war and the union of states was no more? It was unthinkable. At least the president was finally too consumed with General McClellan's peninsular campaign to be as concerned with Adams anymore. Secretary of State Seward continued to be his champion back home, too.

They were of one mind, he and Seward, convinced of U.S. sovereignty, at home and abroad, and both just a little suspicious of British statesmen, whom they were sure would never look out for U.S. interests.

Adams's family history, well ingrained in its members, had taught him that liberty from the British nation was always just a minor argument away from being threatened. From the Revolutionary War, to the War of 1812, to the recent scrape over the *Trent* Affair, Adams men were always in the thick of the physical and verbal battles with their English cousins.

Charles Francis glanced at his pocket watch. Almost time for dinner. Abigail had invited over a gaggle of female charity workers to discuss some sort of project, and she wanted her husband there to show his support for whatever it was.

He sighed. His time could be better spent elsewhere. Harper had uncovered some intelligence suggesting that a steamer recently sailed from Liverpool to the Portuguese island of Terceira was to be equipped and armed as a commerce raider. Further rumor indicated that the South already had a name for her, CSS *Alabama.*

Speaking of Harper, it was time he summoned Harper back for a report. The man hadn't been by since he'd reported that Mrs. Morgan's ward had gone missing.

Why was that confounded woman at the center of so many of Adams's troubles these days?

"Did you see this notice in *The Times?*" Lord Russell asked as he sat down to a hastened breakfast of sausages and tomatoes at Lord Palmerston's residence. They were to meet with the queen at Windsor later this morning to discuss the impact of Princess Alice's nuptials to Prince Louis of Hesse, an event that had been conducted with unmitigated doom at Osborne House on July 1.

It had been months since the prince consort's death, and she still stayed sequestered at Windsor, surrounded by her ladies and doing nothing all day but eulogizing her husband to them. At least she'd left Osborne House for a residence closer to London.

He and Palmerston were hoping once again to rekindle the queen's interest in state affairs.

"No, I haven't had a look at the paper yet this morning. What does it say?" Palmerston slathered lemon curd on a thick slab of bread and took a large bite, the crumbs spilling down on the opened paper Russell had laid before him.

Russell pointed to a boxed-in notice about two-thirds of the way down the left-hand page. "Our dear Mrs. Morgan has troubles once again. This is the third placement of this advertisement in as many days."

Palmerston brushed away the crumbs and studied the engraving that accompanied Mrs. Morgan's plea for help finding her ward. "The woman has a black cloud of death trailing her, doesn't she?" he said. "I wonder if Minister Adams knows about this?"

"Actually, my thought was that we could use this to awaken the queen from her stupor."

"You think this will concern her? One missing child among hundreds of others in London?"

"Because the child belongs to Mrs. Morgan, yes. The queen has an unhealthy fascination with the undertaker, in my opinion, but if she thinks Mrs. Morgan is in distress it might force her to look beyond her own pain."

"I see. Well, it's worth a go."

To Lord Russell's gratification, the queen reacted just as he had hoped, despite the fact that Violet Morgan was now not only a working woman, but one without a husband, two things the queen frowned upon.

"Oh, the poor dear. Imagine the horror of having your child taken from you so suddenly for no reason at all. Surely we can do something to help her."

"Yes, Your Majesty. Lord Palmerston and I spoke with the commissioner this morning and he said the police have all been alerted regarding the girl's disappearance and are keeping an eye out for her." He didn't share the commissioner's opinion that there was little hope of the girl being found. In fact, he had the sense that the commissioner had little concern for the case, despite a visit from the prime minister and foreign secretary over it.

"The poor dear," Victoria said again. "She must be nearly out of her mind from the pain of it all. It's not unlike what we have suffered since the death of our beloved prince consort."

Well, the queen's *initial* reaction was as Russell hoped it would be.

For the next hour, she waxed on about Albert's many virtues until the two statesmen were finally able to make excuses and slip away.

"We do believe," Queen Victoria said to the door closing behind them, "that Mrs. Morgan might benefit from a visit to Windsor so we can share our heartaches together."

Violet recognized the sparkling coach with the royal crest on the door. *Not again*, she thought, immediately regretting her momentary disloyalty to the queen.

As expected, the liveried servant emerged from the carriage and presented Violet with the queen's express wish that she come to Windsor on the occasion of her own great tragedy, that she and the queen might console one another.

Violet bit her tongue against a pert response. The queen didn't really care for anyone's company these days. Therefore, she knew it was a singular compliment to be thus invited.

"I'll get my hat," she said, scratching out a quick note for Sam and letting Will know she'd be gone the remainder of the day before plucking her widow's bonnet off its stand and following the man out.

The queen greeted her stoically, as though they shared an identical tragic secret. How easy it might be for an observer to assume this, given that both women now wore black gowns and black gloves, and had jet draped around their necks and wrists. The queen's dress was fuller, of course, and her necklaces lay in greater number around her neck and reached almost to her waist.

Her eyes were less swollen than the last time Violet had seen her, yet she had a pinched expression, as though her corset was too tight. Whereas she'd looked so pale and emaciated just after Albert's death, now she was putting on considerable weight. Her fuller face helped hide her overbite. Violet wondered if she might end up with the same pinched look, which then reminded her of Susanna's disappearance, which nearly brought up tears that were perpetually waiting for release.

It was too unseemly to weep before the Queen of Great Britain and Ireland. Violet sniffed as inconspicuously as she could and focused on the wall behind the queen's head until she felt she was in control of her own nerves.

"Mrs. Morgan, we can only imagine how deep and piercing is your grief. For you had not only lost His Highness Prince Albert— a tragedy we might never be able to speak of again without it grasping our hearts—but then your own husband. We don't hold his villainy against you. Now someone has stolen your ward. What manner of beast has man become? We know your great pain, Mrs. Morgan, for we still suffer, too.

"One rides along in the carriage of life, certain that nothing more than ruts to jostle us and a bit of rain to soak us will ever come along, and then we are faced with an oncoming train that demolishes our carriage and destroys our life's ride irrevocably." Victoria sighed, winded after her long homily.

"Yes, Your Majesty," Violet said dutifully. *Did the queen read about my involvement in the Clayton Tunnel crash?* "One's life changes in a flash into something unrecognizable."

"Yes, yes, a pity. You know, Mrs. Morgan, your visit is quite fortuitous. We were just thinking the other day about our dearly departed Albert." The queen shifted in her chair. "In particular, we were contemplating the new resting place at Frogmore. It will be ready for him soon."

"It will be very befitting of a prince."

"As you must realize, Mrs. Morgan, Albert must be transferred to the Frogmore Mausoleum when it is complete. It is our desire that you assist Mr. Rowland once again in this. You will then be able to share the details of the ceremony with us afterward. We do believe another, even more private, service is in order. Mostly family members. It is a great honor for you to be thus chosen twice."

Violet wasn't sure she could handle this much honor at the moment. "Your Majesty, my little Susanna . . ." she began.

Victoria waved a hand. "Will be found in short order, I'm sure. The prince's services won't be for months. You'll meet with Mr. Rowland straight away to begin planning, won't you?"

"Of course." Yes, it was an honor, but how could she possibly focus with the knowledge that Susanna was in the hands of two filthy creatures who might not be feeding her, or had her locked up in a cramped, dingy basement, or had her living with rats, or . . . It didn't bear thinking about, even though she obsessed on it every night in bed.

"We are glad we've had the opportunity for this discussion. And surely your ward will be discovered soon and all will be well. Children are remarkably hardier than their parents."

Violet's interview with Queen Victoria was concluded. Now she had to figure out how to fit a royal reburial into her life.

It was early morning and the sun was struggling to find its way through an overcast sky. Samuel Harper had hardly slept in days, between searching for Susanna's kidnappers, making reports to Charles Francis Adams—who was growing impatient—and staking places at various times in front of Violet's home and shop in hopes of catching Cubby and Slade somewhere before they had an opportunity to commit any other acts against Violet.

He was currently across the street from Morgan Undertaking. No one had passed by in hours who showed any interest in the shop. Perhaps it was time to return to Violet's home. He could escort her to the shop.

Just as he was about to turn away from the storefront, he saw a gangly legged man with a great paunch saunter up to the shop window. At first, Sam thought the man was peering inside with morbid curiosity, but soon realized he was staring at something in particular. The man was looking at the advertisement Violet had placed in the newspaper. She'd cut it out and placed it in her window in hopes that a passerby with knowledge of Susanna would notice it and stop in.

The sun had finally won its battle with the morning's clouds and was warming the street and spreading its rays across the glass windows of stores and eateries all along the block. The man raised a hand to protect the glass from the sun's reflection as he continued to focus on Violet's notice.

Perhaps he knows something or has seen Susanna.

Samuel casually crossed the street, which was coming alive with foot and coach traffic, and cautiously approached the man.

"Promises to be a fine morning, doesn't it?" Samuel tipped his hat at him.

"Indeed," the man mumbled without turning to acknowledge Samuel.

The man's jacket was stretched tightly across his abdomen and was a peculiar shade of gray, as though it had been laundered too many times. In fact, the man aptly fit Violet's description of Slade. Was it him? Was he waiting for Violet to arrive this morning? Where was his partner? Keeping watch over Susanna?

Samuel felt his blood simmering under the rising heat of the sunshine. "Planning for a funeral?" he asked.

"What?" The man finally turned to face Samuel. "Oh yes, my . . . aunt . . . just died. I need an undertaker. I hear Morgan's is a good place."

"I hear the same thing. You seem interested in the advertisement in the window. What is it?"

"Oh, looks like the proprietor's daughter is a runaway or has been kidnapped. Seems to be happening all the time in London these days, don't it?"

"Not in this neighborhood. I'd say it's most unusual to have happened around here, wouldn't you?"

The man's eyes narrowed. "Do I know you? You sound foreign, and I don't care for your tone. Mind your own business." He turned back to the shop window.

Samuel reciprocated the feeling, now certain he'd met the vile

Mr. Slade. He stepped closer, so that their jackets were touching. Samuel decided to be bold, even aggressive.

"You wouldn't happen to be a blackmailer with the undertaker's child in your possession, would you, you cretinous clod? Or should I call you Mr. Slade?"

The man started, but quickly recovered his composure. He was alarmed enough, though, that Samuel knew he had his quarry.

"As I said, I'm just looking for a funeral man. My aunt and all. Good day to you." He ambled away, pretending a nonchalance that didn't deceive Samuel for even a second.

Samuel waited several moments before following Slade. When Slade jumped onto an omnibus, Samuel scrambled to find a hack to follow the public transport. The driver looked at him like he was a Bedlam escapee—"Why would you want to pay my fare to follow an omnibus you could ride for yourself?"—but did as Samuel asked, staying some distance behind the transport. Slade exited the omnibus at Whitechapel. Samuel quickly paid the driver and stepped out after his prey, who seemed unaware of Samuel's presence.

Samuel was unfamiliar with this neighborhood, but it immediately conveyed that it was seedy and undesirable. A prostitute stepped out from nowhere to offer her wares.

"Shh." Samuel raised a finger to his lips and reached into his pocket for a coin.

Realizing she didn't have to do anything to earn the money, she quickly accepted it and disappeared again.

Slade was still within sight and hadn't noticed what went on behind him. He paused in front of a tavern and contemplated the building, as if wondering whether it was too early for a pint of ale. Thirst won any internal argument over the matter, and he stepped inside.

Samuel stayed back for several minutes, waiting until Slade would have ordered his glass and retreated to a table. Hopefully he was sitting with his back to the door—Samuel needed the element of surprise.

After patiently counting backward from one hundred, Samuel

entered himself. Why were taverns in poor neighborhoods always so dark? Old buildings, lack of glass windows, and insufficient gas lighting, he supposed. It stank of urine inside. After taking a few seconds to adjust his eyes to the darkness, he scanned the room. Even at this early hour, there was no shortage of patrons, none of whom took notice of the tall American lawyer at the door.

Luck was with him. Slade sat in a booth with his back to the entrance. Samuel quietly ordered an ale and carried it over. Sliding into the booth across from Slade, he offered the glass to him.

"What do *you* want?" Slade snarled, any pretense of friendliness having fled now that Samuel had so obviously invaded his own territory.

"I know who you are, Slade."

Slade's eyes widened in surprise. He took the glass Samuel offered and drank it down in several swallows. "What of it?"

"Finish your other ale. I'm Samuel Harper and we're going to talk."

Slade picked up his glass but set it down again right away. "Don't take orders from the likes of you. Now, what is it you want? Before I get angry."

Samuel leaned forward, dropping his voice to nearly a whisper. "You're in no position to be angry. Both the British and U.S. governments are very interested in your whereabouts"—a bit of a stretch, but good enough for his purposes—"so either you're going to produce Susanna or you'll find yourself in a short stay in Newgate before your hanging. If I don't strangle you myself first."

"Don't play the stuffed peacock with me, Mr. Harper. Why would the authorities of two governments be interested in me? I'm not a perfect man, but I'm no murderer or traitor or anything."

"You've blackmailed an innocent woman who is a friend of the queen's, for a large sum of money."

" 'Tisn't blackmail to collect what you're owed."

"Owed for *what*, exactly?"

"That woman's husband needed money for a trading scheme. It sounded illegal to me, and although I'm not one to stand in the way of another man's business, I've got to protect my own interests, don't I? Risky propositions mean I have to take lengths to be sure I get my investment back. Mr. Morgan wanted enough that I didn't even have the total to lend him, so had to bring in a partner. Can't always trust partners.

"When Morgan proved himself unreliable and disappeared off to America without paying his debt, I couldn't sit by, could I? So my partner and I went to collect from his only living relative I could find. She, too, has been quite disagreeable—"

"So you took her child in payment?"

"—Although my partner has gone off somewhere, too, and I don't like going on collection jobs myself and—what? Took a child? The one in the window notice? Why would I do that?"

"In revenge for Mrs. Morgan not responding to your threats."

Slade looked at him incredulously. "What would I do with a brat, and a girl besides? They need food, they cry, they escape. Always thought kidnappers were the stupidest blokes. Sorry, I have far better ways to collect from my customers than to kidnap a child. Again, it's all about risk. Children are too risky."

Although Samuel loathed the man before him, his sense told him that Slade was speaking the truth. Unfortunately. "But if it wasn't you, then who was it?"

Slade shrugged. "There's good business in finding children to work for people who don't particularly want to pay wages." He considered for a moment. "Or . . . I do remember the girl, quite comely. She may have been snatched for a brothel. Many possibilities. Now if you'll pardon me . . ."

Slade moved to exit the booth, but Samuel grasped the man's wrists and pressed down on the veins underneath. Slade slid back into the booth.

"You said your partner has disappeared. Where do you think he went? Might he have Susanna?"

"Cubby? Nah. He wouldn't do anything without my say-so. Dumb as toast, he is. Besides, he's been missing since the day after we visited Mrs. Morgan and the notice said the girl's only been missing a week. He even missed our second collection appointment with Mrs. Morgan, which she also ignored. I've not been as particular about her debt at the moment, since Cubby's gone. You're barking up the wrong tree full of sparrows, Harper. Now I'll be going. Don't follow me again."

Sam let him go, lost in his own thoughts. Slade wasn't lying. Sam's law experiences had made him an expert in knowing when a witness's testimony was false or not.

Yet where did this leave him and Violet in the search for Susanna, when her kidnapper wasn't making any formal demands or providing even a hint as to why the girl had been taken?

The question came to a rest after he saw Violet at the shop. She'd just returned from a visit to Windsor, where the queen had invited her to participate in Albert's reinterment at Frogmore.

"Another great honor for Morgan Undertaking," he said.

"Yes, so the queen informed me. Sam, how can I possibly put my mind to it with Susanna missing?"

"I'm afraid I have both good news and bad news on that score. I found Slade, but I don't think he did it."

Sam relayed his visit with Slade in detail. "I don't believe he was lying, Violet."

"But what does it all mean now? A kidnapper taunting me with no intention of making his desires or Susanna's whereabouts known?"

"My thoughts exactly."

Their conversation was interrupted by the mail carrier's rap on the door and several letters dropping through the slot. Violet picked them up and sorted through them. Her face drained of all color as she let everything else fall except for one letter.

"I know this handwriting. It's him." She offered it to Sam. "I can't bear to read it."

As he opened the envelope Violet said, "Do you realize he knows where I live and where my shop is? He took Susanna from my home, to which I've only recently moved, yet he sends his curious poems here."

Of course I realize it. It's why I'm in front of one place or the other almost constantly.

"We'll find him and Susanna, Violet. She'll be fine. Her abductor, however, may not make it all the way to Newgate, much less his trial and hanging, as my patience is wearing thin."

He read aloud the missive, which had the familiar slanted handwriting like the first one.

> *Roses are red,*
> *Violet is blue,*
> *Her heart filled with dread,*
> *Over what I'm to do.*

He looked up, expecting Violet to be trembling. Instead, her face was mottled with rage. "How dare he hold Susanna's life in his palm like this! She's an innocent child. He never tells us what he wants. It's as though torturing me is the goal."

"Maybe that's it. Maybe his goal is your agony, so he dangles you like a toad over a pot of boiling water. Have you angered any of your customers?"

"Not that I'm aware of. Many of the grieving become angry, but not until after the shock of the funeral wears off, and typically it's family members turning on one another."

"Let's go through your records for the past six months or so and talk about each of your customers and their dead relatives. Maybe it will revive a memory of a dispute with someone."

Violet shook her head. "I can't imagine. Unless Graham angered someone."

"At this point, it's all we've got."

While Violet was engrossed in conversation with Sam over what families she had serviced over the past few months, they were interrupted by the jangle of the door's bells. Mary and George came in. Mary held a handkerchief to her eyes and George comforted her.

"Violet, dear, I've been so worried. I haven't heard from you since Susanna first disappeared. George and I have been so concerned. We were talking about it and he suggested we simply come right over and check on you. Good afternoon, Mr. Harper, you remember Mr. Cooke."

The two men greeted one another.

"You both appear deep in thought," George said.

"We're just puzzling out who may have taken Susanna," Violet said, turning over the notes she and Sam had been working on so George couldn't see them.

"Ah, excellent, we've arrived at a propitious time. Four heads are better than two, as they say. Mary and I would be most pleased to assist you in sorting everything out. Tell us everything you know."

Feeling trapped between her friend and this overly inquisitive man, Violet reluctantly shared the state of things with them both. With many interjections of "Yes, yes, I see" and "Most dastardly," Mr. Cooke used up much of their precious time, while offering no truly helpful suggestions.

Violet hoped she hadn't made a terrible error in talking to him.

Charles Francis felt no need to hide his own impatience. "You now say the girl's kidnapping has nothing to do with the Morgan brothers? The Metropolitan Police seem to feel no urgency regarding the missing girl, and my conversation with Lord Russell leads me to believe he's actually happy the girl is gone because it gives the queen something new to dwell on. How did I ever end up in such a position as this? Son, strike all of that last part."

Henry scratched through several written lines on the page.

"Therefore, I see no need for you to continue pursuit of these kidnappers. I'm sorry for your personal feelings in the matter, Harper, but I need you to focus on commerce raiders and blockade runners."

Several moments ticked by as Harper sat in a chair across the desk from Charles Francis, drumming his fingers on the arm of the leather chair without responding. Was he going to be difficult? His affection for the Morgan woman was making him blind to duty.

But Harper knew what was expected of him.

"I know of a suspicious shipbuilder focusing on small, swift ships," he said grudgingly. "I'll look further into him."

"Excellent. Understand, Harper, that the priority here is to serve the United States, despite our personal discomforts. I no longer see how pursuit of the child serves our government's aims."

"Or yours," Harper muttered. The cheek of the man.

"Report back to me when you know something."

Harper rose to leave, but turned back at the door. "Presumably my free time is still that—free?"

"To do with exactly as you please, yes, so long as you don't embarrass the government."

Harper smiled as he left the room. Why did Charles Francis suspect he'd not heard the last of Violet Morgan's troubles?

"Why, Sam, thank you," Violet said, taking the yellow rose he offered and placing it on a table under Susanna's picture. "It looks lovely there. How was your meeting with the minister?"

"More or less productive. I have an assignment to seek out more Confederate sympathizers working against the United States, but also have time to help you find Susanna."

There was a knock at the door. Violet went downstairs to answer it, and found Harry holding an envelope. He'd recovered nicely from his mishap.

"Some mail came after you left, Mrs. Morgan, and I thought this one might be one of those, er, letters."

Harry handed it over and left before Violet could confirm its contents. Why hadn't he brought along the rest of the mail, as well? She shut the door and examined the envelope as she took it upstairs and held it up.

"Is it . . . ?" Sam asked.

She nodded and opened the envelope.

> *Blood is quite red,*
> *Dead bodies turn blue,*
> *You shouldn't have noticed,*
> *What I didn't want you to.*

Suddenly, a whirl of things began arranging and rearranging themselves in Violet's mind.

"I see," she said.

Sam took the note and read it for himself. "You're remarkably composed, Violet."

"That's because I'm finally beginning to understand what this is all about." At least, what it might be about. She had to think.

There was actually a reason behind all of this, wasn't there? And Susanna wasn't just an innocent bystander, either. What was it the queen had said during Violet's last visit? Something about the carriage of life. It was important, but Violet couldn't quite remember what it was.

"Violet, what is it?" Sam asked.

She sank into the chair next to the table holding her rose. Sam went to one knee and took one of her hands in his.

"Violet?"

Dear, sweet Sam. When my mourning period is over, I should consider him. Perhaps he'd contemplate staying in London.

"Do you remember my talking about the bodies I prepared? The ones with the strange disease?"

"Yes, you worried there might be a possible epidemic starting."

"I believe it's an epidemic, but of murder, not disease."

"What are you saying?"

"Give me the note." Sam handed it to her. "Look at these two lines again. 'You shouldn't have noticed what I didn't want you to.' What I noticed were the peculiar signs of Mr. Young's and Mrs. Atkinson's demises."

Sam frowned. "Even if that's true, why would he kidnap Susanna?"

"It's as you said, his goal is my agony, and so I am the dangling toad."

Sam considered this. "What would you say was the manner of their deaths, then?"

"I think perhaps . . . I think they were poisoned with something caustic. An acid maybe? It could have been mixed inside food and given to the deceased. Both had been ill."

"Who would do such a thing?"

"Well, the same doctor attended both of them and was noticeably detached when I suggested that there was something wrong."

Sam shook his head. "The very idea is repulsive. Why would a man committed to healing people commit such an act? What benefit is there for him?"

"I don't know," Violet said helplessly. "But there's also . . . what about . . ."

"Yes?"

"Sam, I hate to even utter the words, but don't you think George Cooke has been particularly interested in this whole situation? It's almost as though he's trying to figure out what I know."

"You're right. There's also the matter of his background. We know almost nothing about him, although we can be fairly certain he's not the clockmaker he claims to be."

Violet was silent. It was too distressing to even contemplate her besotted friend's reaction should George prove to be a criminal. But if George had Susanna, where was he keeping her?

Oh no. No, no, no.

Her voice dropped to a whisper. "Sam, you don't think . . . ?"

He understood exactly where her thoughts had gone.

"Impossible. Mrs. Overfelt loves you too much, and she's virtuous in the extreme. She would never hide a kidnapped child, especially one belonging to her friend."

Violet's stomach was in somersaults. "But you've seen how enamored she is of Mr. Cooke. She believes anything he says, despite obvious evidence to the contrary. Who knows what he's said about me?"

Sam rose from the floor and sat on a chair across from her, rubbing his chin. "I don't know, Violet, I find it hard to believe Mrs. Overfelt would involve herself, even if George Cooke is responsible. It also doesn't explain why he would want to kidnap Susanna. Distressing you doesn't seem a good enough answer. As Slade said, children are a risky proposition for a criminal."

"But Susanna isn't just any child."

"Of course we know she's a special young sprite, but—"

"No, Sam, it's not that. Susanna has been with me each time I saw one of these victims, and her reaction has been near paralysis. At first I thought she was simply horrified by the eaten flesh, but now I'm wondering if she hadn't seen the condition before."

"Seen it where?"

"I think perhaps on her mother. All we know about Susanna's mother is that she died of some unspecified illness. Could she also have been poisoned?"

"But for what reason? And what do Susanna's mother, Mr. Young, and Mrs. Atkinson all have in common that would make them targets for this murderer?"

Violet was too absorbed in her own train of thought to answer his questions. Her theory tumbled out in a rush.

"Is it possible that Susanna witnessed her own mother's murder—which would certainly explain why she refused to speak at first, poor thing—and during one of our visits we met the murderer or he saw us from afar, recognized Susanna, and decided to silence her? Have I mentioned my findings to the wrong person, and so the murderer is now hinting that he wants me, too?"

Sam nodded. "Of course, this brings us around to George Cooke again, who has been engrossed by your opinion of these deaths, courtesy of Mrs. Overfelt."

Violet closed her eyes and leaned back, trying to sort out what was true or not in her head. "Perhaps his initial interest in Mary was because we were friends. It's all so difficult to believe."

"Do you remember George Cooke at any of the homes you visited?"

"No, but I rarely see the entire family on my visits, and I talk to only a smattering of servants. It would be quite easy for someone to notice Susanna and me without being seen in return."

"What do the victims have in common? Status? Age?"

Violet ticked off attributes on her fingers. "Mrs. Atkinson was middle-aged, Mr. Young was much older. Presumably Susanna's mother was around my age. Mrs. Atkinson lived in a rooming house, Mr. Young had a large home and staff, and we can only assume Susanna's mother was of some sort of lower background. The only commonality I can think of is that all three were sick before they were poisoned."

"You mean they were sick because they were poisoned, correct?"

"No, each had a specific illness—or were at least complaining of various illnesses prior to dying. But from what I've seen, the manner of their deaths suggests their illnesses had nothing to do with their final moments."

Sam shook his head. "That makes no sense. Why would anyone murder someone who is already sick?"

"I don't know. All I know is that Susanna is in evil hands, and I have to figure out how to find her."

"Well, I hate to say this, but I think your most likely suspect is George Cooke, which means our best approach is confronting Mary. At least we can take comfort that she probably wouldn't hurt Susanna. In fact, Susanna probably has tinfuls of chocolates and armfuls of dolls to entertain her."

"Maybe. Sam, I need your help. What do I do?" Without thinking, Violet reached over and touched Sam's knee, a brazen move that sent a flush creeping up his face to his ears. She whisked her hand away, embarrassed by her own forwardness.

He cleared his throat. "We'll go together to see Mrs. Overfelt. You know where she lives?"

"Yes, she has quarters above her shop."

"Then Susanna is probably hidden up there. We'll go now, and hopefully have Susanna home with you in under an hour."

Brighter words were never spoken. Unfortunately, their optimism was misplaced.

❧ 23 ❦

O life as futile, then, as frail!
O for thy voice to soothe and bless!
What hope of answer, or redress?
Behind the veil, behind the veil.

—Alfred, Lord Tennyson (1809–1892)
In Memoriam A.H.H. (1850)

Violet had never actually visited Mary's living spaces before, as they always met more conveniently downstairs in the dressmaker's shop. A set of rickety stairs behind the shop led to her rooms above it. The rear of the building was overgrown with vines, and the windows were smudged with dirt. The scrolled grills protecting the windows were rusted and rotting. Broken flowerpots were strewn about the ground, once-proud lavender and monkshood now reduced to dried up stalks in barren soil.

"I'm surprised Mary would allow her surroundings to deteriorate so much," Violet said. "You'd think Mr. Cooke would help her with improvements."

Sam made no response, merely guiding her to the base of the staircase and urging Violet to watch her step.

Mary's eyes widened in shock when she opened the door to Sam's insistent rapping. She was dressed as though about to go out, with gloves and a fancy hat that managed to tame her unrestrained gray hair well. A long shawl lay on a chair nearby.

"Violet, dear, why didn't you ring at the shop door? I would have let you in that way. Come in." Mary stood aside to let them enter, but remained near the door herself, fidgeting with a handkerchief in her sleeve.

"Are you just out visiting this evening?" she asked.

"Not exactly. Oh, Mary, how could you do it?" Drat the tears that always filled her eyes at the most inopportune moments.

"I'm sorry, dear, do what?"

"Hide Susanna from me."

"Hide Susanna? What a crazy thought. Where did you get such an idea?"

"I think that George is behind the deaths of those people who died with mysterious holes in their skin. I believe he has now kidnapped Susanna and convinced you to hide her on his behalf."

"What? Violet, that is the most ridiculous thing I've ever heard. I love Susanna; why would I do such a thing?"

"Because . . . because you love Mr. Cooke more. I think he fabricated some sort of inventive, believable tale for you, and since you are a woman in love, you eagerly believed it and agreed to help him. Please, Mary, give her back to me."

Mary glanced nervously at the door. "Violet, I really have no idea what this is about, but this isn't the best time for me, dear."

Violet felt Sam place his hand at the small of her back, a warning of some kind.

"Susanna!" she called out. "Susanna, sweetheart, are you here?"

No answer.

Mary shook her head. "I believe your grief has rattled your mind. Susanna is not here, nor has she ever been."

"Then you won't mind if I search for her?"

Mary glanced at the door again. "Dear, I don't know what has possessed you, but I must insist that we discuss this at another time. I'm expecting—"

Someone else was rapping at the door. Mary opened it, her face flushed with embarrassment, or was it relief?

"George, welcome. Violet and Mr. Harper just stopped by for a visit, isn't that lovely?"

George Cooke was dressed as elegantly as Mary. The silk top hat that he swept off his head looked new, and the twinkling cuffs at his wrists were gold.

"Lovely indeed. How go your investigations, Mrs. Morgan?"

Samuel stepped in before Violet could respond. "We believe we're very close to an answer. If you'll excuse us, we can see that you both have an important engagement."

He led Violet to the door. As she passed Mary, the other woman embraced her, whispering, "You don't understand, dear, I think that tonight—"

Violet jerked away from Mary, repulsed by her touch and her excuses. In any case, she was already developing another idea.

Sam agreed with her plan, so they sat in a nearby coffee shop until they saw Mary and George walk past, arm in arm and laughing, on the way to whatever plans they had for the evening.

Violet and Sam returned to the rear of Mary's building and climbed the stairs, and Sam pried away the loose grillwork on the window next to the door. It practically decayed in his hands. He set it down on the stoop and checked the window. They were in luck; there was no interior lock on the window. He climbed in, then helped Violet, who struggled over the jamb in her long skirts and crinoline.

Sam laughed quietly. "You look like a blackened brush being pulled through a dirty flue."

Violet straightened her clothing. "Making you the chimney sweep."

"Quite correct. Now, we must be quick and silent. We don't dare light any lamps. It's one thing to go unnoticed in the alley behind the shop, it's another to flood her lodgings with light that can be seen from the street. You check up here; I'm going to go downstairs and inspect the shop."

With that, Sam was off to find the right door that would open onto a staircase leading directly into Mary's dressmaking shop.

Violet took a deep breath, terrified of what she would find here. "Susanna?" she said, her voice barely above a whisper. "Sweetheart? Mother is here. Where are you? Make a noise for me."

Violet continued to softly call out as she moved through the rooms. Much of the shop's untidiness extended up here. Mary was storing bolts of fabric and boxes of trim in whatever available space she had upstairs. She really did need day help, although someone hiding a child wouldn't want a maid poking around, would she?

Violet opened every door she could find, from armoires to cupboards. There was nothing, not even an indicator that a young girl was living on the premises. A seed of doubt planted itself deep inside her. *Was I wrong?*

Sam's return a few moments later confirmed it. "Violet, there is no one down there, nor does it look like there has ever been a resident in the shop. Except for dressmaking materials, the shop is empty. I even shoved aside a few loose pieces of furniture in the fantastical notion that there might be some kind of trapdoor leading to a basement. I found nothing."

Violet shared her similar findings. "If she isn't here, Sam, then where is she?"

"More importantly, if Mrs. Overfelt isn't involved, can we assume Mr. Cooke isn't either?"

They departed by the same window, with Sam adjusting the grill back into place afterward, and discussed what to do the entire way back to Violet's house. Noticing for the first time Sam's haggard face and bloodshot eyes, Violet invited him to sleep in the drawing room. He refused, unwilling to bring compromise to her already tenuous reputation, but promised to return early in the morning to escort her to the shop.

❧ 24 ❧

It's like a lion at the door;
And when the door begins to crack,
It's like a stick across your back;
And when your back begins to smart,
It's like a penknife in your heart;
And when your heart begins to bleed,
You're dead, and dead, and dead, indeed.

—John Newbery (1713–1767)
Publisher, *Mother Goose's Melody* (1761)

As she struggled to focus on the elderly, grieving husband's words, Violet wondered if she now looked as exhausted and disheveled as Sam did.

". . . my darling wife always loved roses. I'd like to have them on top of the funeral carriage. . . ."

Violet jotted down notes and murmured the appropriate sympathies, yet her thoughts were miles away. The one insidious thought that had crept into her brain and taken residence was that perhaps Susanna was no longer alive. After all, it had been nearly two weeks since her capture, and if she hadn't been fed properly—

"My wife never got on with her sister, so I want to be sure Esmeralda has no seat in any of the funeral coaches."

—she could have withered away by now. Violet clung to the idea that Susanna was a resourceful girl, and had found her way from a workhouse to Morgan Undertaking, so perhaps she'd find a way to escape and return once again.

"Do you know of a good photographer who can create a nice card with my wife's picture on it?" The man was close to tears. Violet snapped back to the present.

"I do, sir, and let me assure you that your dear wife will be the epitome of good health and vitality when I am done with her. You will be most pleased with the results of the ambrotype."

The husband smiled in gratitude, then launched into a tale about his wife's love of border collies, enumerating the five different dogs they'd owned over the course of their marriage.

This was a common reaction Violet had witnessed among the grieving. Some were petrified into stone by the shock, while others, especially older family members more prepared for meeting death, would attempt to share every last detail of the deceased's life, as though the dead person's memory would be locked away in the coffin unless firmly implanted in others.

". . . as many mourners as possible to lament my darling's passing. The world should know what it's lost. . . ."

After visiting the body and preparing it for both the postmortem photography and a subsequent burial, Violet left with a sheaf of notes, knowing that she'd have to turn most of this over to Will and Harry. She'd no sooner explained the arrangements to be made for this funeral when there was the familiar banging on the door, signaling that mail had arrived.

Among the letters and bills were two pieces that caused Violet's heart to jump. First was a note from Mary, requesting to come by later in the day to speak with Violet. Mary had never seen it necessary to make a formal request before, but then, Violet had never accused her of kidnapping before. Violet owed her friend an apology, even though she wasn't convinced George Cooke was innocent.

She asked Harry to run over to Mary's shop and tell her she was welcome to visit anytime this afternoon.

The second piece of mail was another . . . taunt . . . from Susanna's kidnapper. Violet sat down to read it, anxious over its contents, yet hopeful that this time he would make an actual demand. She was finally rewarded.

I hold her in dread,
We're waiting for you,

The lion gets fed,
At a quarter of two.

Don't lose your head,
You know what to do,
Come alone or she's dead,
You're my real goal, it's true.

Susanna was still alive. Violet didn't permit herself even a moment to weep with relief. She needed to figure out what was next, although the answer seemed obvious.

The kidnapper held Susanna at the zoo, or was at least taking her there this afternoon. He planned to lure Violet there to kill her. Susanna's eventual fate was unclear.

Her last experience having to do with the zoo in Regent's Park was her mother-in-law's goring by a rhinoceros. She shuddered. Such a fatal outcome would *not* be in Susanna's future. Nor hers.

Violet glanced at her watch. It was nearly noon. She had to prepare.

She wrote Sam a note and left it for him in an envelope on the counter, assuming he would be by soon for what had become a daily visit. "Will," she said to her assistant as she fastened on her hat and gloves, "I think I know where Susanna is and I'm off to retrieve her. Make sure Mr. Harper gets this note."

"Truly, Mrs. Morgan? Where is she?"

"I don't have time to explain. Just be sure he sees the note when he stops by."

"But—"

Violet didn't stop to listen in her haste to leave. She walked home and prepared herself for what would happen this afternoon, changing into a less restrictive corset to wear under her black dress and choosing sturdy boots to replace her regular heeled shoes.

She packed a bag with a change of clothes for Susanna, a wedge of cheese as a snack for her, and a knife from the kitchen drawer. Violet had no idea if she had the nerve to kill another human being, but if it came down to her or Susanna's kidnapper, or if he threatened Susanna in any way, well, Violet would not be responsible for her ensuing rage.

After kneeling at the foot of Susanna's bed in a quick prayer for success and assuring Mrs. Softpaws, who had hardly left Susanna's bed in days, that Susanna would be home soon, Violet left, taking a hack to Regent's Park. The zoo was on the eastern edge of the park, the grounds of which were once filled with fashionable company promenading through its gardens bursting into showy displays of flowers. Today, though, the average citizen found pleasure in the tastefully laid out parterres and zoological attractions.

Violet paid her fee at the entrance gate, located at the right edge of the zoo, and joined the other patrons in a stroll in and among the animal houses and dens in order to find her bearings throughout the park, which might be critical later.

The zoo reminded her of Kensal Green Cemetery, with its winding paths around the various buildings containing animals, and a spiked iron fence surrounding the entire property.

Violet walked along as nonchalantly as possible. She hoped the crunch of gravel under her feet covered the sound of her hammering heart. The zoo's main path led west back to the bear pit, from the center of which a pole with steps extended up so that the bears could ascend and descend from the pit. A low wall topped with iron rails surrounded the pit. A crowd of visitors were at the spot, offering cakes and fruit to the small black bear that had come up for a look around. An attendant fed the treats to the bear on a long pole, and the bear scooped at them with his paws. Violet imagined it would take little effort for the bear to overcome the wall if he so desired.

Behind the bear pit were buildings for a herd of kangaroos, hyenas with their high-pitched barking and yowls, and raccoons. No lions yet.

The pathway veered off to the south, and Violet found an enclosed area and fountain for aquatic birds, such as geese, pelicans, and swans, to her left and an unusual building on her right that looked almost like a Chinese pagoda. She entered it, struck by the pungent odor inside, and discovered a pair of llamas who were distinctly unimpressed by the gawkers waiting for them to do something amusing. Violet left the llama hut and continued on the path, estimating that she was now about two hundred feet away from the entrance.

The path curved back to the west again, this time to a circular aviary for birds of prey. Violet stopped there briefly, imagining a hawk tearing the flesh from the kidnapper's face. She looked at her watch again. One o'clock; she needed to finish her survey of the zoo.

Beyond the aviary was a tented refreshment stand, with a scattering of white-clothed tables where patrons sat and enjoyed teas and cakes. It was an elegant setting in such malodorous, cacophonous surroundings. Beyond that were a zebra pen, an enclosure for tortoises, and a set of strange little houses on poles that had monkeys shimmying up and down them as they screeched in protest at some unseen transgressor. One of the monkeys had escaped from his habitat and was begging for food from visitors.

Farther back was an expanse of acreage that looked more recently developed. The buildings were newer and the grounds freshly landscaped. At the entry to this area was a camel house. A short clock tower protruded from the center of the camel house's roof. Nearly a quarter past one. Violet continued on through the flow of people to another animal house.

Ah, here were the nearsighted and ferocious rhinoceroses. Violet hurried through this enclosure, unwilling to dwell on Ida Morgan's death. How very dangerous zoos could be.

Further enclosures held other treacherous beasts, including leopards, tigers, and jackals. Finally she reached the place which she had been searching for with trepidation, the lions' den. A fluffy-maned male and several females restlessly paced the barren enclosure, which smelled musky and stale. One of the females bared her teeth at another who passed by too closely. A wrought iron fence separated the restless animals from spectators. Violet was alone in the den; the only sounds were the padding of cats' paws across the dirt and an occasional warning growl.

She didn't like this place one bit, yet she had to remain and study the location. There was only a single doorway in and out of the oval-shaped den, which was larger than most of the zoo's other structures. Gas lamps lined the walls, although they provided little light as compared to the partially glassed roof that admitted not only light but warmth.

The den's interior was divided by a fence, which gave visitors about a ten-foot-wide walking area and left around forty feet across for the animals. A padlocked gate in the middle of the fence provided zookeepers access to the beasts. Signs on posts along the pathway in front of the fencing gave the visitor information about the lions' eating habits, their natural habitat back in Kenya, and how the animals came into the possession of the zoological society.

Other than that, there was nothing else inside the lions' den. The kidnapper couldn't hide anywhere, yet neither could Violet.

Mary arrived at Morgan Undertaking, only to discover that Violet had gone home for the day.

"Didn't you just bring me a message a short while ago that Mrs. Morgan welcomed my visit?"

Will apologized. "Mrs. Morgan said she thought she may have discovered where Miss Susanna is, but left in such a hurry I couldn't really understand what she meant. She left a note for Mr. Harper."

"But not for me?"

"No, Mrs. Overfelt, I'm sorry."

Since she'd already closed her own shop for the day, she decided to seek Violet out at her home. It was important that Mary tell her what had happened.

There was no answer when she rang the bell at Violet's townhome. She rang again and followed it up with several knocks. No sign of life breathed behind the door.

How very curious. First Violet came to her with the most outlandish claims, then she disappeared from her shop with momentous news, yet hardly an explanation.

Had Violet done it intentionally, to force Mary to waste her time coming to Morgan Undertaking and then chasing her down at home?

Perhaps, but the idea didn't sit well. Certainly Violet had been acting strangely, both toward her and George, but since her friend's outburst Mary had come to realize that Violet was simply overwhelmed with grief and worry.

George agreed with her, too. She glanced fondly at the ruby and pearl ring that now adorned her finger. As she'd hoped would happen, George proposed marriage, his romantic gesture marred only by the memory of Violet's visit that night, but she would never forget the moment he slipped the ring—an heirloom he said had passed down through his mother's side of the family from one of James II's mistresses—onto her hand. His subsequent kiss at her acceptance was tender and joyful. George had reawakened feelings in her she'd thought buried forever.

Now she wanted to share her good news with Violet, as well as to try to ascertain how her friend had developed her unfounded suspicions against her and George, but Violet was nowhere to be found. This just wasn't like her. And what was this about Susanna possibly being found?

She looked out into the street below. Nothing but a few nannies walking their charges in perambulators and gossiping with one another. Across the street, an identical row of townhomes faced Violet's. Should she try visiting some of these homes and asking if the occupants had an idea where Violet was? Mary shook her head. It was more likely that Mr. Harper knew of Violet's whereabouts. If only she could remember where Violet had once told her he was staying.

The minister asked Samuel to meet him at his residence to discuss the latest news on commerce raiders. Before Samuel could finish his report, which was that the commerce raiders he was watching had made contact with Mr. Slade, the criminal known for financing illicit sea voyages such as that of the Morgan brothers, Charles Francis Adams interrupted him.

"Harper, you look dreadful. When was the last time you slept?"

Slept in more than random snatches? A lifetime ago.

"I'm fine, sir. I suspect the London air doesn't agree with me."

"Nor does it agree with me, but it would seem the air is practically swallowing you whole. Care to join us for luncheon? We received a fresh batch of clams from Boston. It's being made up into chowder. A fond memory of home, I think."

"I should probably leave after we discuss what to do next about Mr. Slade. I typically stop each afternoon by—"

"Nonsense. No man from the Bay State can resist a bowl of clam chowder. We can talk more over our meal. In fact, you can even tell me of your quest for Mrs. Morgan's kidnapper."

The minister was feeling generous today. Maybe if Sam shared what was happening, Adams would reconsider his involvement. It was worth a try. Of course, Sam was visiting Morgan Undertaking with regularity each afternoon, so Violet was probably expecting him, but surely she wouldn't mind if he was late. In fact, he'd visit her home later in the evening, just to check on her.

"I guess it would be to my own gastric detriment to say no to clam chowder."

"That's settled, then." Adams reached for a bell pull, summoning a servant to let him know to make one extra place for dinner.

Finished with her survey of the lions' den interior, Violet stepped outside in order to walk around the exterior of the building. There was a single, locked zookeeper access door at the rear of the building. A large, stuffed canvas bag marked "Deer—Killed Tuesday" was propped against it. Did the lions have a two o'clock feeding time? Would a zookeeper's arrival scare off Susanna's kidnapper?

Almost half past one. Where was Sam? She needed to finish exploring the area surrounding the lions' den. She resumed her walk along the zoo path, coming to an enclosure of peacocks, both females with their dull markings and males strutting about with their bright plumage on display. One of the males emitted a bloodcurdling shriek that so unnerved Violet, already tense from the situation, that she jumped back and dropped her bag. She bent over to pick it up and, when she rose again, saw a vaguely familiar woman approaching from the opposite direction. Violet frowned. Where had she seen her before? The woman noticed Violet's stare and slowed in recognition, as well.

"Mrs. . . . Morgan, isn't it?" she asked.

"Yes, but forgive me, I can't quite place you . . ."

"I'm Mrs. Barrett. We were in the Clayton Tunnel crash together."

Ah, of course. The widow Violet suspected was merely an abused wife. Mrs. Barrett looked much healthier and happier than she had on the train.

"I'm glad to see you survived. I wondered about it when we didn't see you again."

"We? I take it your daughter is well, too?"

"Yes, thanks be to God she had no real injuries. As for me . . ." Violet held up her arm, unbuttoned her cuff, and pushed up the sleeve.

"Ah, how terrible for you. I should very much enjoy a chat together. Care to join me for some tea at the refreshment stand?"

Violet glanced in the direction of the lions' den. "I'm afraid I don't have time today. I have another engagement shortly."

"Surely you can spare a few minutes. I would think it highly unlikely that we would so fortuitously run into each other again."

Perhaps a hot cup of tea would strengthen Violet's innards for what lay ahead. Besides, Sam had not yet arrived in response to her note, and it was best to have him here for the confrontation to follow.

"A few minutes, then."

They walked back to the refreshment stand. Violet selected a table while Mrs. Barrett ordered steaming cups of tea and brought them back on a tray with sugar cubes, cream, and a couple of pastries.

"I thought you might like something besides your tea," Mrs. Barrett said.

"How very kind of you. Tell me, how are you getting on in your position as—a housekeeper, I believe it was?"

"I'm afraid that particular employment terminated rather early."

Violet selected two sugar cubes with a pair of tongs and dropped them into her tea. The cubes were large and plopped noisily into the cup, splashing some of her tea over the side of the cup and saucer to leave a dark stain on the white tablecloth.

Except it wasn't a dark stain on the white tablecloth. It was the brown wood of the table appearing from beneath the tablecloth as the fabric was unbelievably eaten away before Violet's eyes.

❧ 25 ❧

Death is swallowed up in victory.
O death, where is thy sting?
O grave, where is thy victory?

—1 Corinthians 15:54–55

"Good Lord in heaven," Violet said, looking up at Mrs. Barrett.

A triumphant smile played upon the woman's lips. "Drink up, dear, this tonic is good for you. It's what I give all of my sick patients."

Violet emptied the cup onto the ground and listened to it hiss in protest as it soaked into the gravel.

"Hmm, how very ungrateful you are of my hospitality, Mrs. Morgan."

"I suspect there have been many ungrateful victims of your particular style of hospitality, Mrs. Barrett. At least now I understand how they ended up with holes in their skin and bedclothes. What, pray tell, do you use?"

"It depends. If they are in season, I pulverize the seeds of the colchicum flower. Otherwise, I go to the chemist for some sulfuric acid. Just a bit of either in tea or tonic works nearly instantly."

"But . . . why?"

"Oh, a variety of reasons. For example, let's take you. You've been my greatest find to date because you are the first living being to even catch a whiff of what I was doing. I was almost relieved, I must say, to discover someone with nearly as much wit and daring as my own."

"Where is Susanna?" Violet asked through clenched teeth.

"Yet I've been growing steadily dissatisfied with your performance, little undertaker, and the girl is giving me constant pain—like a dull hypodermic syringe that never pierces the skin. She either stares at me sullenly as though she knows all about me, or else it's endless complaining and carping about what's to happen to me when her mother finds me. So now her mother has uncovered me." Mrs. Barrett leaned forward. "What do you plan to do?"

Violet's mind was whirling. Susanna's kidnapper—and the murderess of at least two people in London—was an innocuous woman with whom she shared a train ride? Inconceivable.

Violet looked around at the other patrons seated near them. Where was Sam?

"If you're considering some silly cry for help, I'm afraid I must advise against it. Your little Susanna is safely tucked away for the moment, but if you do something foolish, you can be sure that her situation will become more perilous. Lions are unpredictable, you know."

Keep calm, Violet. Talk to the woman, see if you can get her to admit where she's keeping Susanna. Sam, where are you?

"I understand," Violet said, casting her eyes down, hoping she looked contrite. "You must understand that I am quite shocked to find that the one I've been seeking, who had the nerve to poison at least two people and then turn around and spirit my daughter away from under my nose, is a woman. A woman I hardly know."

Violet picked up her bag from the ground. How easily could she slip her hand inside and grab her knife?

"I knew it would shock you. But from the day of our train ride together, I knew something had to be done."

"Don't you mean from the time I witnessed the horrific crime you committed against Mrs. Atkinson?"

Mrs. Barrett smiled. "Don't get ahead of yourself, my dear. You initially had no idea what you were witnessing. No, from the moment I saw you with the little brat, I knew there would be trouble."

"With Susanna? I don't understand. How could a thirteen-year-old girl be cause for trouble for you?"

"She never told you? Well, she was sleeping most of the time on the train, wasn't she? That little urchin you refer to as 'daughter' nearly ran me aground once. I accepted a position as nurse to her mother, who was ill with consumption. I wanted that job because during my interview I could see the family had some nice pieces of art, despite their rather low standing. Inherited pieces from her great-grandmother, she said. But Mrs. Sweeney simply dragged on too long in her illness, creating entirely too much work for me. The art stash wasn't worth it. I also wasn't getting anywhere in convincing Mrs. Sweeney to write me into her will.

"But your precious little girl saw me administer the final tonic to her mother. Mrs. Sweeney unfortunately choked a bit of it up—I do have to constantly adjust my dosing depending upon what base I'm using—and Susanna saw it. She ran out of the house before I could catch her, but it did give me a chance to change the bed-clothes and pack up what I wanted before anyone returned. The woman had been sick, so no one believed a stupid girl's preposterous story."

"Are you saying you murdered Susanna's mother for a few trinkets?"

"No, silly. Honestly, I bare my soul and you hardly listen. It was because of the great and terrible burden that was placed upon me by foisting a lingering invalid on me without appropriate . . . recompense. I could hardly be expected to do otherwise, now could I?"

How had Susanna survived in the clutches of this monster? How brave she was. Yet none of this made any sense.

"Mrs. Barrett," Violet said carefully. "I'm still a bit baffled."

"Naturally. You aren't quite as clever as I am."

"Naturally. I met you on a train from Brighton to London. You said you were recently widowed. Yet it was earlier in London that you wreaked havoc on the Sweeney family."

"I'm not permitted a husband, is that it? I'm not permitted to move about the country, either? Jimmy Dixon and I ended up in Brighton after I met and married him. No crime in that, is there?"

"No, no crime in *that*."

"He beat me one time too often is all, as he learned to his own detriment. You should have seen the dramatic show I put on for the doctor to avoid an autopsy, telling him how poor Jimmy had a fear of being cut up and mutilated after death. Then I found out Jimmy hadn't paid rent in nearly two months, and our landlady was a little overly insistent about it. Really, people can be quite a nuisance sometimes."

"So you lied when you said you had a housekeeper's position arranged through a friend."

Mrs. Barrett shook her head. "I most certainly did not. How dare you accuse me of lying? Mrs. Atkinson was a friend of mine from long ago. When she heard that my dear husband died unexpectedly, she invited me to stay with her, to recover from my grief." Mrs. Barrett sighed. "But she asked me too many impertinent questions."

"I suppose Mr. Young was another friend who inquired too often."

"Honestly, dearest, are you not following anything I'm saying to you?" Mrs. Barrett shook her head. "No, Mr. Young was quite well off and needed a nurse in his infirmity. I suited his desire for a mature, middle-aged woman to look after him. His son wasn't particularly attentive, and it was a simple thing to so engage the man's mind so that he revised his will for me."

"Wait. You were the nurse who was sent to find Dr. Beasley?"

"Yes, another dolt who was very easy to convince to skip an autopsy since, I, as Mr. Young's nurse, had been tending to his illness and could certify that he had definitely died from it. Medical men are too busy to be that bothered with an old man's death. Yet for some reason a mere undertaker was focusing on what the doctor could be convinced was simply the illness."

"Mrs. Barrett, you are despicable. And vile. And evil."

"Yes, yes, Mrs. Morgan, your outrage is admirable. However, I'll take great delight in showing you Susanna before I dispose of you both. After all, you two are the only impediments to my future. It has been most enjoyable playing with you, Mrs. Morgan. Now come along."

Mrs. Barrett rose, signaling for Violet to join her. Violet obeyed—what choice did she have? They walked over the crunching gravel back to the lions' den.

Whereas just a few minutes earlier, Violet had been inspecting

the lions' den for an opportunity to catch Susanna's kidnapper unawares, now she was returning as though it was her execution site.

She stopped and asked a question, hoping to delay Mrs. Barrett
long enough to give Violet time to formulate a plan. "You didn't
tell me how you were able to convince Susanna to open the door to
you. What did you do?"

"I didn't need to convince anybody. I know plenty about how to
get into a house when the master or mistress isn't home. I've broken into many a place where I was working. Your house required
almost no effort at all. Now move along; we're wasting the best
part of the day."

They came to the entrance of the lions' quarters. The entry
door was shut, with a sign reading "Closed for Feeding" on it.

"I knew you'd understand the humor," Mrs. Barrett said.

When Violet didn't respond, Mrs. Barrett grabbed her arm and
shook it. "I said, isn't it amusing? 'Closed for Feeding'? Meaning
for feeding Susanna to them."

"What?" Violet wrenched her arm away, bewildered, wondering
what horrific scene Mrs. Barrett had planned for her inside the
den. *If Susanna is hurt—or worse—so help me, I'll . . .*

Mrs. Barrett put her hand on the door's handle and stopped.
"You should be flattered, Mrs. Morgan. I've gone to great lengths
this time to do something unique and spectacular for you. I would
never have let you drink that tea, not when I have so much more
planned for you. You can drink your tonic later."

"I'll kill you first."

Mrs. Barrett laughed, a jagged and uneven sound, as though she
was unpracticed at it. "My dearest, no one has ever gotten to me
first, nor is it likely that you will do so. Now, are you ready for your
grand surprise?"

Violet could never be ready. She held her breath.

Mrs. Barrett threw the door open and stepped back to allow Violet in. At first, Violet saw nothing unusual, just the pride sitting
together, staring collectively at something in the far side of the
cage.

Where was the male?

She moved farther in and heard Mrs. Barrett closing the door behind them. It slammed shut with the finality of a coffin ready for burial.

Would the lion house become Violet's own tomb?

A movement in a far corner of the enclosure caught Violet's attention. She ran to the railing, dropping her bag as she gripped the bars in both hands and tried to see what was in the darkened recess of the lions' living area, which must be what also had the females in a rapt state.

The male was there, his swishing tail facing Violet as he bent his head down, gnawing at what appeared to be a leg. Following the movement of his mane, she saw what he was consuming. At his feet lay a mangled scrap of cloth intertwined with . . . with . . .

"No!" she yelled instinctively, before the scene in front of her could fully register in her mind. In response to her shout, which reverberated against the walls of the den, the lion turned his head her way.

"God, no," Violet whispered, her hands sliding down the railings as she sank to the ground. Blood stained the beast's jaws and snout. He swept his tongue along his jawline, then he shook his head, his fluffy mane a blur as he emitted a low growl of satisfaction and sat down to rest over his quarry.

Violet clenched her eyes shut, willing away what she had just seen. *Please, God, don't take her away from me. I love her more than anyone in the world. She cannot be dead. Cannot. Can. Not. Be. Dead.*

It was only when she felt Mrs. Barrett's hot breath on her neck as the woman whispered in her ear to quiet down that she realized she was rocking back and forth helplessly and moaning. Having Mrs. Barrett that wretchedly close snapped Violet back to reality. Her undertaker's instincts that helped her face death on a daily basis took over her mind and body, serving her in that moment in a way she'd never known before.

She got up and faced Susanna's killer, who said, "My, you must be distraught, Mrs. Morgan. Would you like to save Susanna? Here, I'll help you." Mrs. Barrett had a bronze key in her hand, which she inserted into the gate separating the lions from visitors, swinging the door open enough to let someone in. To Violet's unasked question she said, "I was once very friendly with one of the attendants here. I always thought having a set of keys might come in handy one day. Go ahead, my brave little undertaker. Are you willing to confront a man-eating beast to save your little girl?"

For the moment, Violet could only confront her own constricting throat, which seemed to be paralyzing the rest of her body.

"My, my, don't tell me you don't love Susanna enough to do something for her? Very well, I'll shut the door and instead you can take this now." Mrs. Barrett wagged a stoppered vial in front of Violet's face.

How confident this serial murderess was in her abilities to offer poison as casually as if she were offering a patient a warm cup of milk. Which was undoubtedly one of her methods for her poor, hapless victims.

Violet, though, was finished being victimized by this horrid, brutal woman who deserved an eternity in hell. With a strength she had no idea she possessed, Violet pulled her right hand back and brought it forward with as much power as she could muster, connecting her palm with Mrs. Barrett's face in a loud and satisfying smack. The impact brought back the pain of her scalding injury, but the agreeable sound of her hand striking Mrs. Barrett more than made up for it.

Mrs. Barrett was startled enough to lose her grip on the vial. Violet caught it as it slipped from the other woman's hand. For one second she considered trying to force Mrs. Barrett to drink it herself, but thought the better of it and instead threw it against the wall behind Mrs. Barrett. The glass shattered into countless bits of poisonous spray and sharp pieces.

"How dare you?" Mrs. Barrett sputtered, her face mottled with fury. "You nitwitted little coffin ghoul. This was not part of my plan. Now I'm very angry."

"Oh, I dare, Mrs. Barrett. I dare because I love that girl and you took her away from me. What a shame that you should be angry. And now I plan to get Susanna."

"Hah! Not from inside the lions' cage. They'll tear you to pieces."

"A more honorable death than what you've provided for your victims, is it not?"

Picking up her skirts and grabbing her bag once again, Violet tore through the gate and into the lions' enclosure. With her heart pounding erratically from an abnormal combination of fear and rage, she paused and took a deep breath.

The male had wandered back to his pride, and the females were sniffing his jaw. One female took a tentative lick at him. Hoping they were so preoccupied they wouldn't notice the sound of her heart thumping wildly in her chest, she crept toward Susanna.

I'm coming, sweetheart.

She reached what she thought was Susanna's body and knelt down, miraculously without the lions noticing. Or if they noticed, they were too preoccupied with other things. In a flash Violet realized what her haste had wrought.

This wasn't Susanna. On the ground were the remains from the canvas bag of deer meat. Susanna wasn't here at all. But where was she?

Far behind her, Mrs. Barrett was cackling hysterically. Violet couldn't help it, she sobbed aloud as she stood up in relief. The sound must have alerted the lions, because she heard a low growl across the enclosure.

"Pet the darling kitty, Mrs. Morgan. Let him lick your hand." The murderess's laughter was clanging in Violet's head. Slowly turning, she realized that the male was contemplating a return to see what the disturbance was over his dinner. Violet stood as still as if she were a corpse herself, so as not to alarm him.

Mrs. Barrett continued her shrill laughter. "Aha! You thought you could best me. You should have realized otherwise."

Now shaking from disbelief and joy, Violet was wondering how she was going to make it past a hungry lion and a deranged killer in order to get out of here and find Susanna.

As imperceptibly as she could, Violet began backing slowly toward the fence, with her eye on the pride of lions. Her movements, though, were not imperceptible enough, for Mrs. Barrett screamed at her, "Not another step!"

Violet ignored her, continuing her inexorable creep toward the fencing, but the lion was irritated by the outburst, pacing back and forth in front of his females in contemplation of what to do next.

Mrs. Barrett did not pay attention to the cat's displeasure, instead screeching at her again. "Don't move again. You stay in that cage until the lions have had their fill."

Not likely, Mrs. Barrett.

As Violet continued to ignore the other woman while she focused on her goal of reaching the gate, she slowly slid her hand inside her bag and withdrew her knife. Its blade gleamed even in the low lighting of the den.

The lion was approaching her, sniffing the air like an estate agent ferreting out a basement's bad smells. Violet could see the tension in his swishing tail and taut hips. Even the females shrank back at his anger over Violet's intrusion.

The lion bared his teeth at her from about twenty feet away. Violet nearly started cackling hysterically herself, realizing that her knife was a puny defense against such a great beast.

Not that it mattered, for at that moment, the lion roared with all of his strength, the sound of it erasing all human thought and feeling as it reverberated against every square inch of space such that it felt as though the glass panes of the ceiling might crack and come shattering down upon them. Even Mrs. Barrett was stunned into silence.

As she brought her hands up to cover her ears, Violet dropped her bag and knife—her only weapon, pathetic though it was—to the ground.

I'll be dead in just a few moments. Susanna, I am so sorry. Sam, why didn't you come?

The lion went back to the girls one more time, nuzzling one of them before turning back around. As he poised back on his haunches, his nostrils flaring and his eyes blazing, Violet now knew what was about to happen to her. From the corner of her eye, she saw Mrs. Barrett smirking, as that woman also realized that the lion was about to fulfill her wishes.

With nothing left to do, Violet dropped into a crouched position and threw her hands over her head, shutting her eyes and praying that her death would be instantaneous. Was this what a doe felt like in the moments before she felt a big cat clamp its jaws around her neck, bringing her down with his massive feline paws?

But in that instant, everything happened. She heard the den's main entry door open with a great crash, followed by the sounds of multiple shouts and people entering the den. Mrs. Barrett's terrible shrieking rose above everything.

The fence gate also banged open. It swung open so hard that it collided with the fencing behind it, vibrating noisily. More shouting and a thin wail rising up, then hurried footsteps approaching her.

"Back!" a voice attached to those footsteps bellowed at greater volume than the lion's earlier roar. A popping sound followed by a buzz rent the air.

Still she lived. Where was the lion's hot, blood-tainted breath? His sharp canine teeth? His thick, clawing nails?

"Sweetheart," she heard as she was scooped up in strong arms and carried out of the lions' living area and back to the visitors' area, where she was gently put on her feet.

"Sam," she said, realizing that he had come after all. His expression of worry nearly made her collapse in his arms, but she realized there were others surrounding her—Mary, Susanna, a police officer, and a uniformed zookeeper holding a long-barreled gun. The zookeeper walked to the gate and entered the lions' enclosure. The male lay on his side with a dart in his side. He looked to be sleeping.

Mrs. Barrett was tied to the fence by her wrists, and she alternately muttered and ranted profanities at them.

Everyone receded into the background for the moment except for Susanna. "Susanna, love," Violet said, putting a hand tenderly to the girl's face.

"Mama," Susanna said weakly, reverting to her old reference for Violet. "I was so worried about you."

"*You* were worried about *me?*" Violet said, pulling Susanna close and hugging her as if she might never see her again. "I've been nearly out of my mind over you. Where were you?"

Susanna stepped back. "Mama, I was so scared. That lady killed my mother."

"I know, I know."

"She took me from our house and locked me in a basement. She made me drink something foul and then I went to sleep for a long time. I thought she was doing to me what she did to my mother. But I didn't die, and she came down and talked to me every day to tell me that she was just using me to kill you, Mama. It was so hard to understand her sometimes because my head was always muddled."

Violet nodded. "She kept you drugged."

"I knew who she was on the train, but when we didn't find her again, I just hoped she was dead. I really did. I wanted her to be dead. But then when we prepared those other poor people, I knew she wasn't."

"On the train?" Sam asked.

"She was a passenger with us in the Clayton Tunnel accident," Violet said.

He shook his head. "I don't understand, why would that make her want to kill you?"

"Sam, it's a very long story."

It was Sam's turn to nod. "Susanna," he said. "How did you get away from Mrs. Barrett? How did you know your mother was at the zoo?"

Susanna shrugged. "She told me yesterday that the lions would help 'take care of' Mama today. She also forgot to give me my daily potion yesterday, so my head didn't seem muddled this morning. I found a loose brick in the fire pit and threw it at the window. I got out before Mrs. Barrett knew what I'd done. I'm a little scratched." She held up her arms, which had lost the battle with whatever jagged glass they had encountered in Mrs. Barrett's basement window.

"Now we are a matching pair," Susanna said.

Violet laughed. "Yes, we are."

"What does she mean, 'a matching pair'?" Sam said. "Ah, another long story, I see."

"I knew where the zoo was because my mama—my other mama—brought me here once. When I arrived, Mr. Harper and Mrs. Overfelt were also running through the entrance."

With Susanna safe and Mrs. Barrett under careful watch, Violet felt herself unraveling. She tumbled into Sam's arms, comforting and strong around her, and buried her face in his neck, sobbing as she tangled her fingers in his hair. A widow publicly embracing a man was beyond the pale.

She didn't care.

"My God, sweetheart, what if I'd lost you?" Sam murmured in her ear, words she'd heard from Graham once, before he'd seen her damaged arm. What if Sam saw it? Would he be disgusted, too?

For now, it didn't matter. He was whispering reassurances and it was as if they were alone together, with the stench of animals and the fear of death a lifetime away. Violet felt herself go limp in his arms, willing to let him support her while she digested the enormity of what had nearly happened to her and Susanna. Finally recovering her strength, she pulled away and looked at him.

"Where were you?" Violet asked. "Did you get my note?"

"Only just now, thanks to Mrs. Overfelt. His Excellency invited me to sup with him, so I didn't make my daily visit to the shop. She, however, came by to see you, and when Harry told her you'd gone home, she was suspicious. When she didn't find you at home, either, she decided to seek me out. The woman was tenacious in looking for me at my hotel and nearby confectionaries, and she finally decided to try the minister's residence. The minister gave me his personal vehicle to go to the Metropolitan Police and then we got here as quickly as we could. It was Mary who shouted at a zookeeper to follow us with a tranquilizer gun—a brilliant idea, if I may say so."

Violet turned to Mary, tears pricking her eyes once again. "Oh Mary, I owe you such an apology. How could I have distrusted you? I hope you can forgive me."

Mary grabbed both of Violet's hands. "Think nothing of it. Might I not have done worse in your same position? I'm so relieved you and Susanna are safe." Mary flashed a knowing look. "But now I think you probably need some rest. Mr. Harper, I'll find my own way home. I'll call on you tomorrow, Violet."

With that, Mary left the lions' den. Right behind her, the police officer marched Mrs. Barrett out.

"Is she all right?" Sam asked the man. The officer paused, allowing Violet to see once more the mocking bitterness in Mrs. Barrett's eyes.

"Yes. I had to use rope. Her wrists are too small for handcuffs; she'll slip right out of them. She's not going anywhere now, though. The Metropolitan Police thank you for leading us to her, Mr. Harper."

"The United States government will be glad to know it was able to help Great Britain in this small way."

The officer asked Violet, "Do you think you can come around and make a statement about what happened to you?"

"Of course," Violet said.

Mrs. Barrett snatched her moment of opportunity to spit at Violet, missing completely and then bitterly cursing her ill luck the entire way out the door.

"No wonder she used poison as her weapon," Sam said. "She's a terrible shot."

❧ 26 ❧

Faced with conclusive evidence, Dr. Beasley ordered that Mr. Young and Mrs. Atkinson be exhumed. Both were found to have been poisoned by sulfuric acid. A subsequent exhumation of Susanna's mother revealed the same means of death.

Murder charges were brought against Mrs. Barrett, or, rather, Catherine Wilson, as police later learned was her name. The investigation revealed that Wilson had once before been brought up on charges of attempted murder against a Sarah Carnell. Catherine had come to live with Sarah's family as housekeeper and the two women became close, and in due course Sarah altered her will to make Wilson the chief beneficiary. Soon after, Sarah caught a chill and Catherine offered to look after her, even going to the chemist's shop to purchase a healing tonic for her friend.

Sarah took one sip of the tonic and spat it out because it burned her mouth. She was astounded to find the foul liquid eating through her bedclothes. Catherine fled the house, never to return. She was later arrested and duly appeared before the Old Bailey. Catherine's defense team claimed that there was no proof that Catherine had intentionally done anything, that there may have simply been an error at the chemist's. The jury gave her the benefit of the doubt and she was released to the world to reinvent herself and continue her murderous rampage.

There would be no benefit of the doubt this time.

On September 22, 1862, Catherine stood in the dock at the Old Bailey for a second time, this time before Justice John Barnard Byles. The Old Bailey was a three-story building topped by a dome reminiscent of St. Paul's, except instead of salvation from eternal hellfire, its occupants were hoping to avoid the hangman's noose.

All of London was voraciously reading news about the event surrounding the trial, which Violet, Sam, George, Mary, and the Sinclairs attended. The woman's string of murders was endless, as evidenced by those who came forward to testify against her.

Various witnesses testified to Catherine's suspected involvement in the 1854 death of a seafaring gentleman named Peter Mawer, for whom she had been housekeeper and who had obviously been poisoned. However, Captain Mawer suffered from gout and was taking the dangerous drug colchicum, so his doctor declared that he had taken an accidental overdose. His family never thought so.

Next was the case of Maria Soames, who ran the lodging house where the newly married Jimmy Dixon and Catherine Wilson moved in November 1855. Dixon died suddenly in June 1856, followed mysteriously by Maria in October.

Catherine's trail of carnage continued, as she moved from residence to residence, claiming to be either nurse or housekeeper, depending upon what was necessary to secure employment. After subsequently securing the affection of her employers and seeing their wills rewritten to include her, her employers expired quite suddenly, but always such that it could have been from natural causes. Catherine became quite adept at convincing doctors not to perform autopsies.

Taken together, the evidence was damning, but circumstantial nevertheless. Until Violet was brought forward to provide her own eyewitness testimony. The presses ran day and night, releasing additional details of the foul Catherine Wilson's exploits. All of London was clamoring for justice.

Her pursuit of an undertaker who had already been at the center of an earlier scandal was an irony that set the gossips' tongues wagging at a speed faster than that of any newspaper press.

In an episode much like that of her testimony before Parliament, Violet was once again brought forward to testify. All of London collectively leaned forward to listen.

In painful detail, Violet recounted the condition in which she had found Mr. Young and Mrs. Atkinson and her suspicions of the nature of their deaths. Sam nodded encouragingly at her from his seat as she spoke of innocently meeting Catherine on the train involved in the Clayton Tunnel crash, and later having Susanna snatched away from her because of that brief and tragic interlude. With both fists clenched in her lap, she told the jury of the mocking poetry Catherine had mailed her and of their final clash at the zoo, resulting in Catherine attempting to poison her not once, but twice. Heads shook and tongues clucked at Violet's testimony.

Violet was the last witness to be heard, but her statements were the most incredible. The judge sent the jury off to deliberations with a quick summary: "Gentlemen, if such a state of things as this were allowed to exist, no living person could sit down to a meal in safety."

The outcome was virtually certain. It took the jury three hours to return a verdict of guilty—thereby setting the presses off to a fury once again—and Catherine was sentenced to hang by the neck until dead. At her sentencing, Judge Byles declared Catherine the greatest criminal that ever lived.

Violet couldn't have agreed more.

In summing up its own judgment of the trial, *Harper's Weekly* opined:

> She was as foul in life as bloody in hand, and she seems not to have spared the poison draught even to the partners of her adultery and sensuality. Hers was an undeviating career of the foulest personal vices and the most cold-blooded and systematic murders, as well as deliberate and treacherous robberies.

At eight o'clock in the morning on October 20, 1862, a crowd of nearly twenty thousand gathered outside the debtors' door at Newgate Prison, Violet and Sam among them. Because she was still officially in deep mourning, she chose to wear her blackest dress and accoutrements, but this day wore them as homage to all of the victims who had suffered by Catherine Wilson's hand.

Catherine was brought out, her hair tightly pulled back and her arms bound behind her. She stared straight on as she climbed the stairs to the platform of the scaffolding, and acknowledged none of the catcalls and shouting going on around her, even ignoring a handful of blackberries that was pelted at her, leaving a streaming trail of purple mush on her gray prison dress.

The condemned refused an offer to address the crowd and was dispatched quickly and efficiently. Disappointment rippled through the crowd, who were hoping for a long strangulation, or at the very least for Catherine to be humiliated by soiling herself.

Violet hoped for no such thing. She knew that Catherine would be tossed into the rough pine box waiting for her beneath the trapdoor, then likely buried secretly that night in an unmarked grave. Despite Catherine's grievous crimes, it still offended Violet's sense of propriety for any person to be buried so shamefully. Yet she only dwelt on it briefly, for it was proper that Catherine suffer an ignominious end as retribution for her vile life on earth.

Having thus resolved things in her mind, Violet blew out a breath of relief. Never again would she have to fear this murderous woman and her insane notions of right and wrong. She and Sam left the prison, her heart lifted for the first time in years at the prospect of a hopeful future, perhaps one involving Sam.

Her hopes were to be dashed almost immediately.

❧ 27 ❧

Of comfort no man speak:
Let's talk of graves, of worms, and epitaphs;
Make dust our paper, and with rainy eyes
Write sorrow on the bosom of the earth.
Let's choose executors, and talk of wills.

—William Shakespeare
Richard III (1595)

London
October 22, 1862

"I'm returning to the United States," Sam said, his brown eyes sorrowful as he and Violet sat inside his favorite confectionary.

"I don't believe you."

"I'm sorry, Violet, I truly am, but duty awaits me at home."

"I thought your duty was here, working for the minister." Violet knew she sounded petulant, but her shock left her less than composed.

"Much of that work is complete, as Slade and Cubby have been arrested for their financing of illegal blockade runners, which has dispersed many other ship owners hoping to use their, er, services, to develop their illegal trading schemes."

"I see. Surely there is more diplomatic work for you to do here. It must be dangerous back home for you, with a war raging on." She stared down at the table at the yellow rose he'd given her earlier, its petals of warmth and sunshine now mocking her earlier joy at receiving it.

Sam took her hand and held it between both of his. "That's just it. I'm going home *because* there is a war raging on. My country needs me, and I intend to enlist in an army infantry regiment. They organized in August of last year, but they're in need of men. I've already written to my father and my law partner to expect me before the end of October, although I'll almost immediately be leaving for a place called Falmouth, Virginia."

Violet blinked, unsure what to say. Obviously he didn't belong here and would one day have to return home. She had no hold on Samuel Harper, they were no more than friends. Yet . . .

Yet I hoped for more once everything was . . . resolved.

"I'm almost out of full mourning," she said, pointing to her high collar of gray accenting her black dress. She'd put away all of the jet except for a pair of earrings.

He smiled wanly. "I know. We seem to have frightful timing. What is Longfellow's saying about ships in the night?"

"But . . . Susanna will be inconsolable when she hears this news."

"Is she the only one who will be inconsolable?"

"No, I . . . I believe I—" Violet withdrew her hand from between his. "You know, speaking of Susanna, I really should return home for supper."

Sam nodded, the light going out of his eyes. "Of course. I'll be happy to accompany you back."

Sam asked permission to tell Susanna himself, which Violet granted. The three of them stood in the drawing room while Sam told Susanna that he was shortly leaving for the United States. Susanna's reaction was swifter and more feral than Violet expected.

"No!" she cried, launching herself into Sam's arms. "You can't go! Mr. and Mrs. Orange Peel will hate you. I'll hate you. So will Mrs. Softpaws."

"Susanna!" Violet said.

Sam folded his arms around the girl and kissed the top of her head. "Nothing for you to worry over. It's perfectly understandable that you would hate a Yankee rascal like me."

"When will you be back?" Susanna asked, her voice muffled against his chest.

Sam put Susanna out at arm's length. "I honestly don't know.

We thought this war was just going to last a few weeks or months, but now there seems to be no end in sight."

Susanna rubbed her scarlet nose. "Will you be killed?"

Violet's heart lurched. When had the child ever not known death and destruction? Would this be another instance of it?

Sam laughed. "Do you think a pack of Confederate ditch diggers can whip up on a Northern lawyer? Not likely. Listen to me, Susanna. You'll have to take very good care of your mother. She means the world to both of us, doesn't she?"

Susanna snuffled and nodded.

"And you'll need to concentrate on helping out in the shop, not worrying about me. I'll just be living in tents and slogging through mud, I expect."

"Will you come back?"

"Only God knows that. But I have to know that you'll be looking out for your mother. Promise me that you will."

"I promise," Susanna said, her voice barely a whisper.

"Now, you should probably go share the news with the Orange Peels."

Susanna obediently went upstairs. Sam turned his full focus onto Violet. "Will you write to me?" he said.

"Where?"

"My father's farm. He'll figure out where I am and forward them on to me."

"You don't know where you'll be?"

"Battles have been fought in South Carolina, Virginia, Tennessee, and Louisiana. It's hard to say where the war's front will be."

A vision of Sam lying dead on the battlefield, with a surgeon crouched over him with a bottle of embalming fluid, rose up like a specter, causing Violet to gasp.

"Truly, I promise he will get letters to me somehow through the army," Sam said.

"No, it's not that. I just . . . am worried that you'll be cold as winter sets in. I hear winters are difficult in the North."

He smiled. "Well, I'll be warm enough when I remember that you'll be worried about me." Sam reached out a hand and cupped her face. "I can't imagine life without you, Violet Morgan. There's so much I'd like to say, but it no longer seems appropriate. I hope you find happiness once again, even though it cannot be with me."

"Sam . . ."

He reached his other hand to her waist and pulled her close. He smelled as though he himself was freshly laundered, clean and crisp, with the undertones of a spicy cologne. She closed her eyes to inhale him, to imprint his scent on her memory.

She felt Sam slip his hand from her face to around her neck, and he brought his lips down upon hers, gently and hesitantly. When Violet didn't resist, he drew her right against him and increased the pressure and intensity of the kiss. Suddenly his scent completely enveloped her and she felt dizzy from the delight of it. She circled her arms around his neck, determined to not ever release him.

Had she ever been kissed like this before?

Forget what happened in the past, Violet Morgan, this is the present and it's all you have left with Samuel Harper.

When Sam reluctantly broke off their embrace and held her head against his chest, she heard his heart hammering as violently as hers. With her arms still around his neck, she tangled her fingers into the curls at the nape of his neck. This unleashed an unexpected, primitive reaction in him and he sought her mouth again, this time as though he himself were a caged lion waiting to spring out.

It was delicious and heady and nearly too much for Violet, who had never known such ardor. This time it was she who broke it off, so overwhelmed by it that she feared she might lose all control to him.

"I can hardly bear this," he said, his voice ragged. "What will I do without you?"

No tears, you will not become a blubbering idiot. Say something light.

"I suppose the first item on your list of things to do is to avoid injury, since I won't be there to protect you."

He smiled halfheartedly. "Yes, it will be most difficult without your protection. The rebels would be foolhardy indeed to go up against the ferocious little undertaker."

They stood in silence together, Sam's arms now around her waist as he rocked her gently back and forth. Neither was willing to let go and break the atmosphere of the moment.

When Sam did speak aloud, it was with a sadness that reflected Violet's own splintering heart. "I must leave. The minister wants to have several meetings before I depart, and I need to make a statement at Whitehall Place about Cubby and Slade."

"You'll come back once more before your ship departs?"

"No, I can't bear to part from you again. Good-bye, Violet." With a final kiss to the tip of her nose, he walked away quickly, nearly running down the stairs and out the door before Violet could even catch her breath and protest.

She was standing completely alone in her drawing room, which had felt like paradise five minutes ago and now just seemed tiny, hot, and suffocating.

Violet gradually returned her focus to her work, much to Will's and Harry's relief. Even Susanna expressed delight in joining Violet at the shop again, making Violet realize that the combination of her imprisonment and Sam's departure had created nearly unbearable uncertainty for Susanna.

So even though her heart raced daily across the ocean and back, she learned to be content in her situation, if she couldn't be outright happy. Her plagued thoughts of how things might have turned out differently if she'd heeded Sam's initial call to go to the United States were eventually replaced by a periodic throb of regret. It was nothing that couldn't be managed as she succumbed to the daily routine of body preparation, consoling grieving family members, and arranging tasteful funerals.

Susanna, too, recovered from her ordeal and Sam's loss as Violet handed over to her more tasks that her other assistants didn't care to do, such as writing out orders for various salesmen and checking the orders for accuracy when they were delivered.

How resilient children were.

Violet's only surrender to Sam's memory was the planting of a yellow rosebush in the miniscule patch of garden behind her home. It seemed appropriate to have an explosion of golden exuberance in an otherwise desolate plot of ground, just as her life was colored in shades of gray except for the memory of Sam's presence.

A memory she hoped would dim.

Each morning she went to the bush and clipped a stem, bringing it back inside and placing it in a vase atop her dressing table. She had no idea why she was torturing herself like this, yet she was compelled to keep a single bloom adorning her bedroom.

Ironically, as Violet's heartbeat was ebbing, her business was booming. The public's fascination with Catherine Wilson did not immediately abate after her execution. Instead, people found it even more enthralling that the woman undertaker, so recently under her own cloud of suspicion, was the one to uncover Catherine's deeds. All of fashionable London now sought custom with Violet, to know that their dearly departed ones would be sent off to St. Peter via a funeral arranged personally by Violet Morgan.

Funeral arrangements took on a different tone, as now not only did Violet interview family members about their wishes, but they also peppered her with questions, such as "What is it like to look into the eyes of a female killer?" and "Can you tell me how you managed to escape from the lions' den?" and "Did she truly try to poison you with sulfuric acid?"

Violet and Susanna returned to Newgate one final time when they read that Catherine's death mask had been made. In an alcove near the main entrance were shelves protected by glass. On the shelves were death masks of notorious prisoners who had been executed at Newgate. Among the infamous were John Bellingham, assassin of British prime minister Spencer Perceval in 1812, as well as Arthur Thistlewood, who instigated the 1820 Cato Street Conspiracy. Now Catherine Wilson's mask had joined the infamous display of murderers, robbers, and traitors.

They looked at the plaster-cast mask, which was taken from the body soon after execution and then painted for realism. Violet and Susanna shuddered in unison. Catherine's mocking expression was as evident in death as it had been in life.

* * *

When she found spare time, Violet sat at her dressing table to write Sam letters while letting the fragrance of the day's picked rose waft around her. She wrote about her experiences with the macabre public that now embraced her, trying to keep her tone light, but sometimes she couldn't help injecting her worries at the end.

> . . . *I wonder where you might be as I look at a map. New York? Virginia? Georgia? Tennessee? Even farther west? The United States is vast and I know you could be anywhere. I trust your father can track your whereabouts. I read that your president intends on capturing the Confederate capital in Richmond. I pray daily for your safety.*

After one such gloomy composition, Violet frowned at her letter. Did it sound overly apprehensive? She crumpled it up and took out a new sheet of writing paper. This time she purposefully wrote a happy letter, full of anecdotes about Susanna's ongoing growth, both in that she was nearly as tall as Violet with a coltish awkwardness in her movements as she prepared for womanhood, and in her training at Morgan Undertaking. Susanna was now learning Violet's various formula preparations and had even assisted with a recent embalming.

Sam would be pleased to know Susanna was doing so well.

> *Also you will be interested to hear that Mary Overfelt and George Cooke went to Scotland to be married, like a pair of runaway teenagers. I'll never understand Mary's adoration of him, but she seems happy enough. I know you share my hesitation over him.*

She closed with wishes for his health and safety and her hopes that he would reply soon.

There, that was much better.

Windsor
December 1862

Soon Violet was summoned back to Windsor for Albert's reinterment at Frogmore. Frogmore House was located a half mile east from Windsor Castle, and the newly constructed mausoleum was located across the expansive lawns from the house.

The queen would easily be able to gaze upon her beloved whenever she was here.

Mr. Rowland showed Violet and Susanna the mausoleum, a copper-roofed Gothic structure he said was inspired by one built by Albert's uncle, Prince Leopold of Saxe-Coburg, as a teahouse for his beloved wife, Princess Charlotte, Victoria's cousin. After her untimely death in childbirth at age twenty-one, it became a shrine to her. How appropriate that the queen would copy such a structure to hold her own husband's remains.

They moved carefully through the new plantings surrounding the mausoleum, then went up the wide expanse of steps leading to the entrance, which was marked by three archways. The exterior of the building was granite, which Mr. Rowland observed had been imported from Aberdeen, Devon, Cornwall, and Guernsey, alongside stone from Portland.

Inside the building, workers were furiously working on walls and floors, although they would leave the interior thoroughly cleaned prior to the prince's reinterment. The chipping, tapping, and screeching of hydraulic jacks lifting sheets of carved marble up along the walls was deafening.

"It will be at least five to ten years before the decoration is finished," Mr. Rowland shouted above the noise. "The marbles you see have been imported from all over the world: Italy, Greece, France, Portugal, Africa, and America. The Portuguese red marble is a gift from the King of Portugal, a cousin to both Her Majesty and His Highness."

Even though the interior was largely incomplete, it was obvious what the architect's intent was. The floors and walls were being covered in the red marble, with inlaid decoration provided with all of the other colored marbles, in green, white, yellow, and other light shades. Insets along the walls were obviously intended for future statuary. It was like a colossal Roman mosaic being built on a sumptuous scale the ancients could have never imagined, but without the dark and somber effects of most burial sites.

What was complete, though, was the tomb that lay in the center of the mausoleum, a mammoth structure currently covered by canvas drapings.

"Once the workers are finished today and all of the dust is removed, we'll come back and I'll show you the tomb. Seen enough for now?"

Violet nodded, her hands over her ears.

It was truly the most fantastical mausoleum Violet had ever seen in all her years of undertaking. The prince's mausoleum at St. George's Chapel was like a pauper's grave compared to this.

Mr. Rowland escorted them back to Windsor Castle, where Susanna was once again sent off to play with the royal dogs, to her utter delight, while Violet was ushered into the queen's presence.

"Ah, Mrs. Morgan, we presume you've seen our dear prince's mausoleum?"

"Your Majesty, it is beyond what I could have ever imagined from the newspaper drawings. It is both beautiful and cheerful."

"Yes, we are most pleased with the progress. Now the nation's most illustrious prince will have a resting place befitting his good soul, and we can rest next to him one day."

Violet hoped that once Albert was reinterred, the queen would be less fixated on him. Disturbing newspaper articles reported that even a year after his death, Victoria was taking little interest in the affairs of state, and the public was noticing.

"I am honored to be working with Mr. Rowland again, Your Majesty."

The three of them spent an hour discussing the details of the prince's second funeral. The queen wished an even simpler affair than what occurred at Windsor. No foreign dignitaries whatsoever, just family and a few invited guests.

A question arose as to whether the queen herself could be a member of the procession. Although a sitting monarch was not permitted to attend a funeral, this was not a funeral per se, just a relocation. After debates back and forth over the propriety of the Queen of England riding behind a funeral hearse, the queen finally decided that she wouldn't place herself in the cortege, but that she would arrive in a carriage just after Albert's placement in the tomb, so that she could visit her "darling husband."

Thus agreed, Violet and Mr. Rowland set to work on arrangements while the teams of workers scrubbed the dusty walls and floors to a sparkling condition. Once the cleaning was finished, Mr. Rowland swept the canvas cloth from the tomb, revealing the spectacularly carved effigies of Albert and Victoria in delicate white marble covering the sarcophagus below. Even Susanna gasped at the beauty.

Susanna was a great help to them, willingly running errands and delivering messages as required. Violet would have to remember to tell Sam this in her next letter, although thus far she'd received no replies to any of her correspondence. Surely that was because he was difficult to find, and not because anything had happened to him.

Windsor Chapel's dean, Gerald Wellesley, performed a small ceremony to consecrate the new mausoleum, and the next day the funeral was held. The air was nippy but still and the sun shone bright, as if lending itself to the success of the day. Guards were posted at intervals along the route between Windsor Castle and Frogmore as witnesses to the prince's final journey. Mr. Rowland positioned himself at Windsor Chapel to oversee the removal of the prince from his existing tomb, while Violet was ready for the prince's arrival at Frogmore. The queen awaited a messenger who would be sent galloping at high speed to Windsor Castle the moment the prince was sealed inside his new resting place.

In her tall hat banded in flowing crape, Violet watched from inside Frogmore's entrance as the funeral procession approached. So far, all appeared to be well. The carriage bearing the prince slowed to a stop outside the mausoleum, and pallbearers slid the prince's remains out of the carriage, carrying him carefully up the steps into the mausoleum. Violet intentionally sniffed the air as the coffin went past her to be placed on a cloth-covered bier. Enough decay had occurred in the past year that the odor had been reduced to something mildly unpleasant, like a cigar burning from across the room. She was relieved that this time the lilies inside the mausoleum were merely decorative, not necessary.

Reverend Wellesley gave a homily once again, prayers were said, then everyone was ushered outside while Mr. Rowland saw to the workers, who would use a system of ropes and pulleys to remove the sarcophagus lid, place the coffin inside, then carefully seal the lid down again to await its next occupant one day.

Violet and Susanna slipped outside and down the steps as quickly as possible. Mr. Rowland and Violet had worked out a prearranged signal he would give from that side entrance, from which she would instruct the messenger to go to Windsor. She had no difficulty in finding the messenger, as he was one of few people sitting on horseback. Having secured his location, she and Susanna moved toward the assembly of guests outside, all of whom wanted to wait for the queen to pay their respects to her.

Lords Russell and Palmerston were there and acknowledged Violet with tips of their hats. Surprisingly, the Minister Plenipotentiary to the Court of St. James, Charles Francis Adams, was milling about with his son, Henry, who had the most perpetually ink-stained fingers she'd ever seen.

Dare she break protocol and approach the minister? Maybe he knew something about Sam's whereabouts. Doubtful, she thought— why would he be apprised of individual troop movements?—but worth a try.

"Susanna," she said. "Wait near the messenger and look for Mr. Rowland's signal. You remember it, right? I'll return shortly." Susanna nodded and did as she was told. Violet approached Adams from behind, where he was in a bored conversation with some Member of Parliament.

"Your Excellency?" she asked quietly. Adams turned around and greeted her warmly.

"Ah, the indomitable Mrs. Morgan. No surprise to find you here today, is it?"

"No, sir."

"You remember my son, Henry?"

From the corner of her eye, Violet saw Mr. Rowland appear in the side doorway and wave his hands. Seconds later the messenger was galloping out of Frogmore.

"Yes, sir, a pleasure to meet you again, although it always seems to be under awkward circumstances."

They exchanged pleasantries for several minutes as Violet dredged up the nerve to ask what she really wanted to know. Meanwhile, the queen's own carriage arrived, and the guests parted respectfully to let her walk through. Victoria wore a new dress of ebony with a touch of ivory lace at the collar the only dash of color, topped by a long black cloak. She was draped in her usual strands of jet beads, which clicked together as she climbed the stairs to visit her husband. Once the doors were closed behind the queen, people once again strolled about the lawns and conversations resumed. Everyone would remain until the queen departed.

"I was wondering, Your Excellency, if you've perhaps heard anything from Mr. Harper since he left to join your army. Has he . . . seen battle, to your knowledge?"

Adams frowned. "You don't know? I'm surprised his father hasn't written you."

That familiar knot of dread, such a familiar friend to Violet, started to moan low and deep inside her. "Know what?"

"Harper joined the Twenty-eighth Massachusetts Infantry Regiment and was at the assault on Marye's Heights during the battle of Fredericksburg, Virginia. It was a terrible time for our troops, as the Confederates had a very well-defended position there. What was General Burnside thinking to throw his men into such a slaughterhouse? At least the president fired him as commander of the Army of the Potomac. Anyway, I'm afraid to have to tell you that Harper was among those brave souls who knew what he was up against and still threw himself against the hill."

"Pardon me? What are you saying?"

"Harper was listed among the casualties that day."

"I see." The minister's face was receding from her as she imagined what horrors Sam had endured. And was enduring no longer.

"Mrs. Morgan? Are you quite all right?" Adams asked.

"Yes, yes, I'm fine."

"I'm sorry to be the one to impart such news."

"No, I'm grateful. Thank you, sir, for your trouble." Violet stumbled away from Adams and his son, back up the stairs to the entrance of the mausoleum. Mr. Rowland would severely chastise her later for such a breach in etiquette, but for the moment she wanted to be inside its echoing confines.

How appropriate that she was at a funeral the very day she learned that Samuel was dead. For once, she shared the queen's overwhelming grief. She stood inside the entrance with her back to the door and let tears stream unchecked down her face.

Inside the mausoleum, the queen knelt before the tomb, her back to Violet as she prayed, the words unintelligible from the distance. The queen had been provided two opportunities to formally grieve her husband, first at Windsor and now here at Frogmore.

Meanwhile, Violet had no final resolutions to her anguish. For Graham she only had a memorial service to conclude his memory, and now Sam was gone forever without a chance to say good-bye.

Why so soon, Sam? You've only been away less than two months. How could you be killed so quickly?

"Mrs. Morgan?"

Mortified, Violet realized that the queen had noticed her and was now walking toward her. "Your Majesty, please forgive me, I—"

"Don't worry, we understand your grieving. Your devotion to the prince consort is admirable. It is the reason we esteem you so well. Please, join us at his side." The queen led Violet over to the tomb and urged the undertaker to kneel next to her.

Violet didn't dare explain her real sorrow and instead followed the queen's actions, praying quietly. Soon, though, she gave herself over to the pain of Sam's loss. She folded her arms against Albert's marble legs, put her head down, and sobbed.

"There, there, my dear," the queen said, patting her back. "You must remember that we will all be reunited one day with Albert and live in great happiness together with Christ and His saints."

Violet didn't want to be reunited later; she wanted Sam back *now.*

When she was finally spent, she glanced up in embarrassment at the queen, who was actually genuinely smiling for the first time since Violet had met her. "All better?" Violet's sovereign asked.

"Your Majesty, again I must apologize for my unseemly behavior—"

"Nonsense. Now take this handkerchief. Dry your eyes before you go. Your daughter will be wondering where you are."

"Yes, madam." Violet took the proffered lace-edged cloth with the Hanoverian seal embroidered at one corner. As she left the mausoleum, she hoped that one day far in the future she'd be able to look back fondly that the Queen of England consoled *her* during the prince consort's reburial.

❧ 28 ❦

Follow me; and let the dead bury their dead.

—Matthew 8:22

Paddington, London
July 1863

Violet brushed back a loose tendril of hair that had escaped its comb. She glanced into the mirror above her drawing room fireplace. Were those strands of gray winking at her? She sighed. She was a thirty-year-old widow; what did it matter?

Susanna came bouncing down the stairs from her bedroom, ready to start another day at the shop. She'd left behind her coltish awkwardness and blossomed into a beauty Violet hardly recognized from the pitifully thin orphan she'd discovered two years ago.

Young men noticed Susanna, too, with her dancing blue eyes, ready laugh, and the aura of mystery surrounding her family's profession. If they only knew that Susanna had refused to speak for months upon her arrival in Violet's household and then suffered the horror of a kidnapping. Susanna had somehow found the strength to only look forward and never back, a skill Violet had not quite mastered.

The two never spoke of that wretched time, nor of Samuel Harper, but Violet sometimes felt Susanna's sharp eyes on her from an upper-story window when she went outside to pluck a rose from her bush, which had grown into a wild and tangled mess that she refused to prune.

Susanna also didn't miss Violet's perusals of the newspapers and the way she lingered over any news that came from the United States. Violet avidly tracked the progress of their civil war and reacted with as much delight as the rest of her countrymen when the U.S. president issued his Emancipation Proclamation in January, which declared slaves in rebellious states free. Consequently, Violet and the rest of England were also horrified by the continued carnage. Just in the month of May was a battle in Chancellorsville, Virginia, with more than 30,000 recorded deaths, followed by the start of an ongoing siege campaign in Vicksburg, Mississippi, where the Union General Grant was attempting to starve Confederate forces from that city.

Violet clipped articles on both events and added them to the many others she'd cut out and saved in a scrapbook that she kept under her bed. She didn't think Susanna knew about the scrapbook, although Susanna did watch Violet pensively every time she took her pair of snips out of a drawer.

No, they never visited the past, but instead worked together toward a future. Business had continued thriving after Catherine Wilson's death, and in just a few months Morgan Undertaking took over the empty shop next door, as well as purchasing two more funeral carriages and hiring another young assistant, Benjamin Maddox. Susanna was progressing by leaps and bounds, even though she had several more years of apprenticeship left. There was little Violet didn't trust her to do.

Earlier in the summer, Violet and Susanna took the train to Brighton—avoiding the excursion train—to spend time with her parents. They referred to Susanna as their granddaughter, which always made her eyes sparkle in happiness. It made Violet happy, too, since she was now ending her third decade and it was unlikely that she'd ever marry again and have children.

Enough woolgathering, Violet Morgan.

"So," she said. "Are you ready to face Mrs. Bingham today?" Mrs. Bingham was a particularly difficult customer whose parents had died within hours of each other from cholera. Violet hoped that there wasn't to be an outbreak, and it would only be confined to these two. Mrs. Bingham changed her mind every hour or so on what she wanted done for her parents' joint funeral, and routinely sent messengers around with new instructions.

"We'll face her together, Mother, although I'm thinking of carrying my scalpel on a chatelaine around my waist as a warning to her."

"Susanna!"

Animated laughter spirited around the room. "Mother, you know I'm just teasing. Mrs. Bingham's exterior is made of elephant hide, so my scalpel could never cut through it."

Violet shook her head. How proud Mrs. Sweeney would be to see how her lovely child turned out.

Mrs. Bingham was the least of their problems that day. Two more customers came to the shop with relatives who had also died of cholera. Violet sent Benjamin, her newest assistant, out to alert nearby hospitals that London might be facing an outbreak. She asked Susanna to inventory all supplies on hand and place an order to increase everything five-fold, especially winding cloth, which they would need to thoroughly protect others from those who died of cholera.

"Will, I'm afraid you will have to help me deal with Mrs. Bingham today. Harry, please see to our new customers and take very careful notes." The owner and employees of Morgan Undertaking all went their separate ways to accomplish their tasks, hoping they were not facing an eruption of death.

Unfortunately, they were. Days blended with nights and back into mornings as the five workers at Morgan Undertaking worked constantly to manage the influx of burials needed. Every undertaker in London was overwhelmed by the endless succession of funerals, especially since these bodies needed to be buried quickly. Church bells clanged night and day.

The disease knew no preference, whisking away infants, the elderly, and anyone in between for whom it had an affinity. There was no time to consider whether or not she, Susanna, and their other employees were risking contagion—they simply hoped for the best.

Except for Benjamin. After two weeks of dealing with relentless death, he stalked away, vowing that he'd had enough of the sunken eyes and shriveled skin that resulted from cholera's dehydrating effects. So they were down to four able bodies to do work that required at least a dozen people. Still they continued on, determined not to collapse from exhaustion.

Mary Overfelt, too, was fatigued from both the outbreak and the accompanying rush orders for gowns that flooded her shop. She hired a second assistant, but it was of little help against the tidal wave of work. Poor Mary was further distressed when George disappeared on her, leaving behind a brief note that he was ill-equipped to handle the bedlam in London and was headed across the channel to France to wait it out. Besides, he added, he would just be in Mary's way while she worked.

Violet shook her head, hugged her friend, and murmured a word of sympathy, but there was little time to spend on it.

More people were dying.

The lurking exhaustion at Morgan Undertaking was replaced with utter horror when Benjamin's parents came by, their eyes swollen and red-rimmed. Their Benji, just twenty years old, was a victim of cholera and they needed an undertaker for him.

So it went, day after endless day, until Violet was certain she was losing her grip on sanity. Susanna was pale and lifeless, while Will and Harry were not only unwashed and rumpled, but bickered with each other constantly. When would it all end?

It did end, though, in seemingly a matter of moments. As though the sun had disappeared behind the moon, causing black shadows to fall upon the earth, then reappeared again in full force as though there had never been a dark moment, the cases of cholera completely stopped.

Within another week or so, Morgan Undertaking and other funeral men had concluded whatever funerals were left, and London was left to stand up, dust itself off, and continue in the aftermath of disaster as it had done countless times through the centuries.

How many more times would Violet face disease outbreaks in an inexorable march through her lonely life toward her own death?

Portland Place
July 1863

"Father, momentous news."

Charles Francis Adams looked up from his correspondence as Henry entered the room. "What news?"

"The Union has won a decisive victory at Gettysburg, Pennsylvania. Guess how I know this?" Henry handed his father a letter from Charles Francis Jr. "He was there himself, Father."

Hands shaking from the double announcement that his son had been in a major battle and had also survived, Charles Francis opened the envelope.

> *. . . I have been involved in the Gettysburg campaign for weeks, Father. General Meade replaced General Hooker as commander of the Army of the Potomac, and I must admit he acquitted himself well, except for one important fact. After four days of battle, Lee's army retreated south, but was unable to cross a river swollen from recent rains. Meade moved us close to Lee, but we did not attack, permitting him to escape. Lee's army made it across the river the following day, and, needless to say, the president was furious with Meade's lack of aggression. Had we pursued Lee, we would have finished him off. Instead, Lee is now settled into winter quarters near Fredericksburg.*
>
> *Of lesser note is the fact that I was decorated for fighting with distinction at the Battle of Aldie during the campaign. I've written to Miss Ogden to let her know, and hope that pride in her Charles will sustain her for however much longer this tedious war lasts. . . .*

Charles Francis wiped away a tear as he looked up at Henry. "Perhaps I'm turning into a sappy old man, son, but I have to tell you how proud I am of you and your brother. You've both made your marks on the Adams name, and I hope to do the same in my remaining time as Minister Plenipotentiary to the Court of St.

James. Provided we hold together as a nation and such a position continues to exist."

Washington City
July 1863

Although his ministers in England and France, Charles Francis Adams and William Dayton, were working hard to influence those respective governments in favor of the Union cause, the president felt a need to appeal to the average workingman in Britain. Neither Adams nor Dayton had the proper weight of impact to do so.

No, thought Lincoln, *I'll need to craft messages myself.*

He scrawled out the first of many messages that he hoped would convince Britons of the moral imperative of their struggle. Once understood, surely they would sympathize with the North's cause and pressure their government to turn against the South.

> *. . . Our conflict is a test whether a government,*
> *established on the principles of human freedom, can be*
> *maintained against an effort to build one upon the*
> *exclusive foundation of human bondage. . . . the*
> *fundamental objective of the rebellion is to maintain,*
> *enlarge, and perpetuate human slavery. . . . no such*
> *embryo State should ever be recognized by, or admitted*
> *into, the family of Christian and civilized nations.*

He nodded gravely. A good first endeavor.

His commanders assured him that with the victory at Gettysburg, it was no longer possible for the Confederacy to win the war. The only potential for the Union's defeat lay in the hearts of its people. As long as they remained confident, victory was a certainty. Hopefully his own writings would bring Britain to their side, thus encouraging the people as his commanders suggested.

Lincoln rubbed his chin. His wife, Mary, had complained lately that he wasn't eating enough and that his cheeks were too hollow. Perhaps, perhaps. Maybe he'd find a bigger appetite if he could be confident that the Union was indeed on a solid path to victory and that Great Britain would applaud them with formal recognition of their cause.

Until those things came to pass, he was afraid he would have no stomach for more than the sparsest diet.

Windsor Castle
July 1863

Lords Palmerston and Russell sat before the queen, attempting to draw her into a political conversation with the hope of engaging her once again in the running of her country. Since Albert's death a year and a half ago, she'd shown no interest in being head of state and had only been marginally revived when her son, Bertie, married Alexandra of Denmark back in March.

The country needed its monarch to show her face to the people.

These days she only showed her face to her ladies and to that rough hewn Scot *ghillie*, or outdoor servant, John Brown. The man needed a bath and a set of manners, not necessarily in that order. He was entirely too informal with the queen's person, and his quarters were so close to the queen's it was scandalous.

Palmerston brought up the issue currently bothering him. "You know the Confederacy has expelled all foreign consuls, including our own, for advising subjects to refuse to serve in combat against the United States."

A small yipping dog, belonging to one of the queen's ladies, jumped into Her Majesty's lap, twirling around to get comfortable. "Now, Jasper, you mustn't be so naughty, else we'll send you off to your mistress with no supper whatsoever."

Palmerston sighed. "Again, madam, about the Confederacy. As you know, Britain has adopted—and maintained—a strict policy of neutrality with foreign squabbles, hence all of the dustup with the Americans over the *Trent* Affair a couple of years ago."

"We remember. That was just before our dear Albert died."

"Yes, it was just before that tragic event. We've met informally with the Confederates but have always withheld diplomatic recognition. We've never even sent a formal diplomat to Richmond, whereas we've installed Lord Lyons in Washington City."

"Of course, we remember."

Lord Russell sat forward in his chair to emphasize Palmerston's point. "Yet we've turned a blind eye to some of the Confederacy's illegal activities. For example, we permitted the building of CSS *Alabama,* knowing that she would end up a combatant ship."

The queen blinked as she continued stroking the dog.

"Your Majesty, it seems impertinent of the Confederacy to expel us, given that we have secretly given them aid," Palmerston said.

"Quite impertinent. Is it of such great moment?"

At least she wondered about it. "It is a statement by the Confederacy that they do not respect our international policy of neutrality, and is therefore an insult to our national honor. To permit them to do this is to allow all countries to assume they can trample all over Great Britain. It is why we had to take such a strong position against the United States over the *Trent* Affair. Else we would have been overrun by other nations like a plague epidemic."

"Ah, that reminds us of something. We wonder how our dear Mrs. Morgan is. The cholera outbreak must have kept her busy. Such a dear woman. She was quite inconsolable at Albert's reinterment, you know."

"Yes, madam."

"We read in the papers several months ago that she and an American friend were responsible for capturing that dreadful Catherine Wilson, the woman poisoning all of her employers. Awful to think that a Briton would do such a thing."

"Yes, madam."

"It seems the Americans deserve our thanks for such a thing, doesn't it?"

Finally, something to which Lord Palmerston could grasp with both hands. "Indeed, Your Majesty, I agree. It's not yet politically feasible to formally recognize the United States' position that the Confederacy is illegitimate, yet it appears as though the tide of the war has turned their way, so we want to remain in their good graces. I recommend that we do so implicitly through congratulations over that country's aid in ridding us of a terrible criminal.

Meanwhile, we shall ignore the South and halt all attempts at mediation between the belligerents."

"Do whatever you think is best. And now we feel a bit tired. We should like to have Mr. Brown sent in to read to us."

Lords Palmerston and Russell left from their brief audience with the queen. "What do you say?" Russell asked. "Is the queen coming round?"

"Hardly. I'm afraid the American conflict is in our hands. Pray we can continue our successful maneuvering through it until they're done spilling blood."

Earth to earth, ashes to ashes, dust to dust;
In sure and certain hope of the Resurrection unto eternal life.

—The Book of Common Prayer

September 1865

Violet and Susanna had just finished supper after a long day at the shop and were discussing whether to read quietly together or play a game of dominoes when the bell rang.

"Who could that be?" Violet asked.

"I'll answer it." Susanna leapt to her feet and went downstairs. Violet heard the front door open, then the house was filled with the sound of Susanna's scream.

Violet jumped up and ran to the top of the stairs, fearing that some new criminal had entered their lives to wreak havoc upon them. Her own scream joined Susanna's.

"Of all the greetings I imagined, this was not one of them." At the door stood Samuel Harper. A thinner, nearly gaunt Sam, but him nonetheless. He was clean-shaven now, and had deep lines around his eyes that spoke of untold pain. Was he standing in an awkward position? Violet remained at the top of the flight of stairs, her hand gripping the walnut newel. It was difficult to absorb the idea that he was here and staring up at her.

He broke eye contact when Susanna stopped shouting and launched herself into his arms, nearly toppling him. That was when Violet realized he carried a limp, as he struggled to maintain his balance.

"Mother! Mr. Harper's here. Come in, come in." Susanna pulled him in and shut the door behind him, leading him up the stairs. Violet backed away, still in shock, until she nearly collided with the fireplace mantel.

Sam looked around as if searching for something. "Are you . . . alone here?"

"Yes," was all she managed to squeak out.

"I mean, are you . . . unattached?"

Violet nodded.

He relaxed visibly. "I sort of figured a woman like you would have men lining up in gold-plated carriages for her hand. I'm happy to see you didn't go off with anyone. May I be so bold as to inquire as to whether you are, well, pleased to see me?" Sam almost looked embarrassed. Was that a scar above his right eye, cutting through his eyebrow?

Violet tried to speak. "I thought you were—the minister told me—how did you—I never got responses to my letters, so I assumed—" What was this babble tumbling from her mouth?

"Were you informed of my demise? Yes, government efficiency at its best. I imagine you'd like to know what happened. May we sit down? I find that I can no longer stand for extended periods of time."

The three of them sat, Violet and Sam in the chairs they'd used so often during their discussions over Susanna's kidnapping, and sixteen-year-old Susanna on the settee, her skirts prettily spread around her.

"What did you hear about me?"

"Only that you were killed at the Battle of Fredericksburg while attempting to take a Confederate position," Violet said.

He nodded. "That's almost the truth. There was another fellow named Harper in my regiment, and it was he who was killed, although an army clerk misidentified him as me. Even my father thought I was dead.

"The error remained because I had already been captured and sent to Libby Prison in Richmond. I won't tell you what that was like, except to say that I frequently wished for death, and it nearly came at my guards' hands on more than one occasion. The men who died at Marye's Heights may have had the better end of things."

"We also know about your president's assassination. I am so sorry." She did not express shock, though, as the president had come to the same end as their own King Charles I. Civil wars always seemed to end with the execution of one side's leader.

"Yes, it has been a terrible time, but President Johnson is in charge now and we hope for the best. Lincoln's assassin had intended to kill the vice president at the same time, so I guess we came out lucky."

Lucky indeed. President Lincoln had written many missives to the British people that were widely published in newspapers and had stirred some agitators into calling for universal suffrage for all British men, but his efforts had never coalesced Britons into overwhelming support for the North's cause. Nevertheless, the North had prevailed.

"Were you frightened in prison?" Susanna asked, breathless and fascinated.

"Frightened? I don't know if that is the right word for it. It may be hard for you to understand at your age—although it looks like you're practically a woman now—but living under such dismal conditions with your fellow countrymen and never knowing when the sword might come down, a man has to retreat inside himself in order to survive. He has to find sanctuary in his wishes and dreams. His hopes," he said with a look toward Violet.

"I was released a few months ago and found myself aboard a train for Washington City, where I was taken to Armory Square Hospital. I was in considerable pain from multiple . . . injuries I'd received. Once I'd shown some progress in healing and had put on some weight, I was declared recovered and released from the hospital."

"Are you saying you were thinner than this?" Violet said.

"Yes, and still I was among the lucky because I didn't actually die of starvation."

"His Excellency told me you were dead. Did he know you were really alive?"

"No, it took the army nearly two years just to realize their mistake. I went home to Massachusetts to get my affairs back in order once again and to see my father, who acted as though I were a specter come back to life. I guess I was, in a way."

"I had the same thought when I saw you at the door."

Sam grinned. "My gait hardly qualifies for the gliding around required by ghosts and spirits."

"What happened to your leg?"

Sam glanced at Susanna. "Susanna, leave us for a few moments, will you?" Sam said.

Susanna nodded knowingly and went upstairs.

Sam's smile disappeared. "I'd rather not discuss prison. I'll only say that dissenters like me were taught not to complain about anything."

"Is it a permanent limp?"

"Probably. Tell me, Violet, do you think less of me?" His voice broke, but he took a deep breath and continued. "Is it difficult for you to look at me? I have other scars on me. The limp is the least of it. If that bothers you, you'll be repulsed by the rest of it. Besides, wondering if you were already married or had forgotten me was more torture than what any prison guard could render."

"You're alive, that's all that matters."

"I came all the way across the Atlantic instead of just writing to you because I thought it was important that you know the extent of my injuries." He stood, shrugged out of his jacket, and began unbuttoning his shirt.

"I don't care about your injuries. You're living. Breathing." She got up to retrieve his jacket from the floor, folding it neatly and draping it over the back of his chair. When she faced him again, he was standing bare-chested before her.

His torso looked as though someone had drawn battle plans on it, so scarred and marked with depressions and lumps was it. Violet reached out and gently put a finger on a particularly nasty-looking red welt. "This must have been a terrible moment for you."

He didn't respond, but simply allowed her to examine him. Some of the wounds overlapped one another, and some looked as though they'd been reopened after healing. Sam's eyes were closed and he breathed heavily, but still he didn't touch her. Instead, he turned around. His back was covered with white, jagged stripes.

Violet ran her finger down the center of his spine. "How many times were you lashed?"

"I can't remember."

"Sam." She put her arms around his pitifully thin waist and her cheek against his trampled back. He covered her arms with his own. Together they stood there, each lost in thoughts and memories of the past three years.

"Do you think I'm perfect?" Violet said, unfastening the row of buttons at her wrist. "As long as we are revealing our individual battle wounds, you have a right to see mine." She pushed up the tight-fitting sleeve as far as she could and presented her arm to him.

He nodded in understanding. "The train crash."

"I'm fortunate it wasn't worse. I saw terrible things that day, Sam."

"So we're both war veterans," he said as he dressed himself again while Violet readjusted her sleeve. "I said that I went home to get my affairs in order. I love my country, Violet, but I've decided that I've given enough of myself to the preservation of North and South. I want a new start."

"Does that mean you're moving to London?"

"No. I've decided to leave my law practice entirely in the hands of my partner and start again out in the Colorado Territory. There's a great influx of settlers there, and I believe it will be prosperous."

"You mean in the American West? That's even farther from London than Massachusetts. I've read about it. It's a dangerous frontier, full of lawless criminals."

"So even the newspapers here sensationalize it?" He took one of her hands and kissed it, but didn't let it go. "Some of it is dangerous, yes, but don't you have unsafe places right here in London?"

"Yes, that's true. I'll worry for your safety, though, while you're so far away."

"There's no need for you to fret about me if you're with me. Violet, I once told you I'd never again ask you to move to the United States. I'll hold to that promise, which means you'll have to tell me you want to accompany me, to be my wife and the Colorado Territory's most proficient undertaker."

An undertaker in Colorado? She imagined living in a flea-infested tent and having to scrounge for basic necessities, like food.

"Are there . . . conveniences . . . in Colorado?" she asked.

Sam laughed. "Yes, Violet Morgan. There are conveniences. I'll build you a sturdy brick home, fill it with good furniture, send you to dressmakers, and we can even attend the theater together. What you'll be missing are London's filthy air, ridiculous aristocracy, and its monarch."

No monarch. No Queen Victoria. It seemed impossible to live in a place where all men claimed to be equal, even going so far as to fight a war to prove it.

"But my shop . . ."

"Sell it. I'm sure Will and Harry would be interested in taking it over. Remember, embalming is becoming a common practice in the States. You could put your skills to good use."

Ah, Sam knows my weakness. What an opportunity it would be to practice undertaking the way she believed it should be, preserving loved ones as long as possible to make the grieving process easier. Still, she'd sworn after Graham's perfidy that she'd never give up her business for any reason.

But was moving to America to be an undertaker really giving it up?

Violet said nothing as she contemplated the enormity of the thought. Would her assistants really be interested in purchasing the shop? Probably. How difficult would it be to build her reputation in America the way she'd done here? Of course, that reputation had seen bouts of tarnish, hadn't it?

What of her parents? What would they say about their daughter moving across the ocean? What of Mary Overfelt? George had returned after the cholera crisis was over, but he was sure to cause her more distress and anxiety over time. Eventually he would prove himself to be a mere opportunist, not a successful business-man.

Maybe Mary would then like to emigrate to America and join Violet.

Stop it, you're talking as though you've already decided to do it.

"I'm afraid there's one great impediment."

"Which is?"

"Susanna. She's blossomed into a woman, Sam, and already has suitors. I don't think she'd like to be swept away like that."

"May I suggest that we ask Susanna herself?" He called out for her to join them.

Susanna's eyes lit up upon seeing Violet and Sam hand in hand. "Yes?"

"Miss Susanna, your mother is contemplating whether or not to ask me if the two of you can accompany me back to America, but she's not sure you will approve the idea."

"America? Truly? What about Mrs. Softpaws?"

"I see no reason why she can't travel along."

She frowned. "Will Mother have to stop undertaking?"

"I wouldn't dream of asking her to stop. Colorado needs her skills."

"Colorado? Isn't that in the West? How exciting. I could learn how to ride a horse. But what does it mean for Mother? Will you marry her?"

"I'm waiting for her to tell me to ask her."

Susanna rolled her eyes. "You're both quite ridiculous. So, if you're married, what does that mean for me? Will you be my fa-ther?"

"I'd be honored."

"Then I'm going upstairs to tell Mrs. Softpaws that we have some packing to do. Mother, don't be all night about it. London has never meant anything but pain and misfortune for us both. America just might give us life and happiness."

Susanna wrapped her arms around both Violet and Sam before returning upstairs to give them privacy.

Sam dropped Violet's hand and slid both his arms around her

waist. "Violet Morgan, I want you to give up Morgan Undertaking and start Harper Undertaking."

"Samuel Harper, I want to be your wife. Whither thou goest, I go." His kiss picked up directly where he'd left off three years earlier. Indeed, wherever Sam went meant life and happiness.

The next few weeks were a flurry of activity as Violet prepared to hand over Morgan Undertaking to her assistants, who were giddy at the notion of having it fall into their laps. There was also the sale of most of her personal belongings to manage, and saying farewell to everyone she loved. Eliza and Arthur Sinclair rushed up from Brighton, clutching both Violet and Susanna in their arms, wishing them Godspeed on their journey, and even suggesting following them over to America.

All of Violet's old black mourning dresses went to the charity box, along with any other personal effects that reminded her too much of London. She did keep one of her old calling cards, the one with both her and Graham on it, just so she wouldn't forget him. Despite everything, he deserved to be remembered by someone.

Pap's old coat remnant and letter went into the fireplace.

Their departure day came quickly and Sam picked them up to go to Victoria station for a train to Dover, where they would board a ship bound for New York. From there they would take a train to Quincy, Massachusetts, to meet Sam's father and be married in the church the family had attended for generations. After a short respite in Quincy, the trio would board another train to take them as far as St. Joseph, Missouri, before joining a chain of covered wagons bound for Colorado. Violet had no idea what a covered wagon looked like, but Sam assured her they offered good protection from the sun.

Once in Dover they boarded the ship, Sam carrying Violet's undertaker's bag and Susanna clutching the wicker cage holding Mrs. Softpaws. Susanna was already trying out the word "father" as often as possible. Violet watched amusement play across Sam's face as he listened to "Father, I've never been on a ship before" and "Father, do you think the seas will be rough?" and "Do you think I'll be able to let Mrs. Softpaws out soon, Father?"

Violet smiled, too. There was much the three of them had to look forward to in the strange new place called Colorado.

As the ship pulled away from the chalky white cliffs, most passengers stayed at the rail, waving back at the shore. Violet turned to face the ocean and what lay ahead, never once looking back at the past.

AUTHOR'S NOTE

Embalming is a practice that dates back thousands of years, with plenty of documentation available on how it was practiced by the ancient Egyptians. Although its use in more modern societies is scattered, the technique of embalming by arterial injection was developed in the first half of the seventeenth century. Some groups, like the Jewish people, have never practiced it. The Victorians generally viewed embalming as unseemly, since it meant filling a body with sometimes toxic fluids, then committing the body to the ground, where it should be decomposing naturally.

Interestingly, it was the U.S. Civil War that saw great advancements in the science of embalming. Because soldiers were frequently dying hundreds of miles away from their home state, it would take time for their bodies to be collected, identified, and shipped home via train. Railways began refusing bodies that hadn't been embalmed because of the obvious putrefaction factor.

Initially, it was surgeons—called surgeon-embalmers—who performed this service. At the beginning of the war, surgeon-embalmers might charge up to one hundred dollars per embalming, although later this was reduced to fifty dollars for an officer and twenty-five dollars for an enlisted soldier. It didn't take long before undertakers assumed these duties, since it was more in keeping with funereal duties.

The story I relate about Hutton and Williams, who were holding corpses hostage until their families paid for the men's unrequested services, is true, although they were arrested in 1863, not in 1862 as I portray it in the story.

Undertakers had a variety of formulas they used for embalming, including alcohol, arsenic, bichloride of mercury, creosote, nitrate of potassium, turpentine, and zinc chloride. Arsenic was outlawed in embalming compounds in Europe in the 1840s, but was legal in the United States until the 1870s. Formaldehyde was not discovered until 1867, and its preservative qualities were not recognized until 1888.

Whatever an undertaker's formula was, it was typically considered a trade secret and never shared with anyone. Other trade secrets included cosmetic formulas and techniques for positioning and propping the body. Even today, funeral directors hold close their funerary practices.

Charles Dickens's book *Oliver Twist* did much to malign an already tarnished reputation for undertakers in England. Although many were quite scrupulous, there were others who promoted expensive funerals their customers could not afford, started bogus burial clubs, and used shoddy merchandise in place of promised quality funereal goods. In other words, nothing has changed! It was my intent to present this profession in the capable and caring manner in which I believe most undertakers approached it then and still do today.

By the way, popular folklore claims that phrases such as "saved by the bell," "dead ringer," and "graveyard shift" come from the Victorian era and its obsession with death. Not true: "Saved by the bell" comes from boxing, whereas the other two terms date from the twentieth century and have nothing whatsoever to do with funerals.

Although technically a stalemate with both forces withdrawing, the **Battle of Hampton Roads** (March 8–9, 1862) is significant as the first encounter between two ironclad ships, USS *Monitor* and CSS *Virginia*. Neither *Monitor* nor *Virginia* survived long after the battle, with *Monitor* lost in a storm and *Virginia* scuttled by her own crew when in danger of being captured by the Union navy.

The battle received worldwide attention, and as a result, Great Britain and France halted all further construction of wooden-hulled ships. A great example of an ironclad is HMS *Warrior,* built in 1860 and now at the Portsmouth Historic Dockyard in Hampshire, England.

The major diplomatic goal of the Confederate government during the Civil War was to gain the formal recognition of its independence from European nations, particularly Great Britain and France, both of which were officially neutral. In late 1861, the Confederate government sent James Mason of Virginia and John Slidell of Louisiana as diplomatic representatives to Britain aboard the mail steamer RMS *Trent*, hoping to at least gain financial assistance for their cause, if not diplomatic recognition.

On November 8, Captain Charles Wilkes of USS *San Jacinto*, a fifteen-gun war steamer, overtook *Trent* and ordered it to stop. After the British ship complied, Wilkes's men boarded her and removed Mason and Slidell, who were placed under arrest as prisoners of war. *Trent*—which was a mail packet on its regular route—was permitted to continue its voyage. The capture of the Confederate diplomats precipitated one of the major diplomatic crises of the Civil War, known as the **Trent Affair.**

The immediate public reaction in the North was jubilation, but the British were just a bit hostile toward an action they considered to be a violation of their neutrality rights under international law. Lord Lyon, the British minister to the United States, was directed to demand an apology from the Lincoln administration for its violation of international law and to ensure the prompt release of Mason and Slidell to British custody, or else Britain would cut off diplomatic ties with the United States. Britain's Atlantic fleet was put on alert and plans were made to send 8,000 troops to Canada.

A cooler head, in the form of Prince Albert, intervened even though by this point he was close to dying. He recommended that Queen Victoria send a dispatch including the hope that Wilkes had acted without the knowledge or approval of his superiors and that the United States had not intended to insult the British. Victoria did this, and it provided the United States a way of saving face in the situation, which was moving perilously close to war between the two parties. It is doubtful the Union would have survived a war on two fronts.

It is interesting to note that in reacting to the Trent Affair, the British had been solely interested in upholding their own honor on the international stage, and had no actual concern over aiding the Confederacy's cause.

Discovering a Civil War incident that bore my own last name was just too remarkable and intriguing not to use.

The **Clayton Tunnel Rail Crash** on August 25, 1861, was a horrifying event in British history. Out of a total of 589 passengers, 23 people were killed in this wreck, 21 of them from the passenger car that the engine mounted. A further 176 were injured. A nine-day inquest following the crash revealed the cause to be simple human error: One signalman misunderstood the message of another, and thought the tunnel was clear for the next train. Although various charges of manslaughter were brought, in the end, none of the railway workers were actually convicted. However, an end result of the investigation was reform of the railways, to include a better time interval system for the trains, and to also regulate shorter shifts. One of the signalmen working that day had been on duty a continuous twenty-four hours. It is likely that Charles Dickens based his story "The Signal-Man" on the Clayton Tunnel rail crash, as many particulars are the same. Readers of the Christmas 1866 story would have well remembered the Clayton accident.

In the interest of historical accuracy, I'd like to point out to the reader that there was no outbreak of cholera in London in 1863, although there were multiple outbreaks of this disease between 1831 and 1854.

Queen Victoria (1837–1901) died at Osborne House on January 22, 1901, aged eighty-one, forty years after her husband's death. She was taken to Frogmore Mausoleum, where she was laid to rest next to Albert.

Contrary to popular historical opinion, Victoria generally enjoyed good relationships with her children. Tradition holds that she was insanely jealous of Albert's closeness to their eldest daughter, Vicky, but the volume of correspondence between the queen and her daughter proves their affection.

Victoria fled to Osborne House on the Isle of Wight immediately after Albert's death rather than have Christmas at Windsor without her husband. She remained there for three months and returned for every Christmas and most anniversaries for the next forty years.

Within three days of his death, Victoria had ordered the building of a mausoleum on the grounds of nearby Frogmore House. The building was consecrated in December 1862 and Albert's body was reinterred there, although it would be another nine years before the interior decoration was complete.

Victoria policed mourning within the royal household with great zeal. Royal servants had to wear black armbands for the eight years following Albert's death, and she chastised her eldest daughter, Vicky, the wife of Kaiser Friedrich III, for not putting her five-month-old baby into mourning when the Kaiser's grandmother died. Victoria herself became known as the Widow of Windsor, as she remained in mourning the rest of her life.

Sir William Jenner (1815–1898) was an English physician most famously known for having discovered the distinction between typhus (caused by a parasite) and typhoid fever (a bacterial disease). He attended Prince Albert, becoming first a physician extraordinary in 1861, then a physician-in-ordinary in 1862. Jenner was bluff, good-humored, kindhearted, and at times autocratic, and always spoke his mind, often with great wit. He had the booming voice of a military man and was noted at court for being an entertaining raconteur, a fact that also endeared him to the queen, as did his affable bedside manner, which she found calming. He was an old-school, establishment figure, an arch Tory, and as reactionary as the queen, who concurred with Jenner in his opposition to women's training as doctors. Jenner insisted that the grieving queen should not be overtaxed in her widowhood, which bolstered her stubborn refusal to come out of seclusion for state occasions.

As physician-in-ordinary, **Sir James Clark** (1788–1870) was a trusted advisor to the royal family, although it was Jenner who properly diagnosed Albert. Clark was instrumental in the formation of the Royal College of Chemistry. He is buried at Kensal Green Cemetery.

Charles Francis Adams (1807–1886) and his son, **Henry Adams** (1838–1918), were members of the brilliant Adams family of Massachusetts. Although Lincoln did not want him for the post of Minister Plenipotentiary to the Court of St. James and he had to struggle with his own innate distrust of the British, Adams was nevertheless a success in the job, doing much to stop Confederate commerce raiders from leaving British ports. He remained in Great Britain until 1868.

Henry worked as a journalist and as his father's secretary in Great Britain before later becoming a historian and intellectual in his own right. Most famously, he published the classic work *The Education of Henry Adams* in 1907. Although he produced many scholarly writings on topics as wide-ranging as the second law of thermodynamics and the history of the United States, his legacy is tarnished by a variety of anti-Semitic remarks in many of his writings. Henry suffered a stroke in 1912, possibly brought on by the news of the sinking of the *Titanic,* for which he had purchased tickets for its return trip to England. He died in 1919.

Charles Francis Adams Jr. (1835–1915) was the only one of Charles Francis's sons to volunteer during the war. He rose to the rank of brigadier general (brevet), led one of the first black regiments through Richmond after its fall in April 1865, and was a highly decorated soldier.

Henry John Temple, Viscount Palmerston (1784–1865), served twice as prime minister, as well as holding a variety of offices in his lifetime. He was well known for his affairs with Lady Jersey, the Princess Dorothy de Lieven, and, finally, Lady Emily Cowper, the sister of Lord Melbourne, whom he eventually married after her husband's death in 1839. Palmerston was indeed known as "Lord Cupid," and even served as co-respondent in a divorce case when he was seventy-eight years old.

Popular as he was with most women, the same cannot be said for his association with Queen Victoria. The queen not only objected to his licentious behavior (he tried to seduce one of her ladies-in-waiting while a guest at Windsor Castle), but to his foreign policy. Palmerston believed in increasing Britain's power in the world to include policies that sometimes weakened foreign governments. Victoria and Albert, however, wanted to preserve European royal families against revolutionary groups. The queen and her prime minister had an uneasy relationship.

Interestingly, Palmerston served as foreign secretary while Russell was prime minister, and vice versa.

John Russell, Earl Russell (1792–1878) was born into the highest echelons of the British aristocracy as the third son of the Duke of Bedford, and was then raised to the peerage in his own right as Earl Russell, an impressive accomplishment even among his peers.

He entered the House of Commons in 1813 and enjoyed a series of cabinet positions while leading the more reformist wing of the Whig party, including that of prime minister and foreign secretary. In the never-ending dance between the two men, Russell became prime minister once more after Palmerston's death.

After the death of his eldest son, Russell raised his grandson, Bertrand Russell, who became a mathematician, philosopher, campaigner against nuclear weapons, and eventually the third Earl Russell.

Thomas Herbert (1793–1861), Vice-Admiral of the White, was a much-decorated officer in the Royal Navy. He served in the Napoleonic Wars, the War of 1812, and the First Anglo-Chinese War, then went on to serve as a Member of Parliament for Dartmouth. I have no idea if he was embalmed; more than likely not, since it was not customary at the time, but I wanted to provide the reader a glimpse into the embalming process. The good admiral very conveniently passed away in the time frame I needed to have someone rather famous die, someone to whom the prince consort might reasonably pay respects. However, I will note for the record that he died in August, while I have him dying in July.

Although he is a minor character at best, it is worth noting that the revolutionary socialist **Karl Marx** (1818–1883) moved to London in 1849 with his wife, Jenny, and lived at Grafton Terrace in Kentish Town from 1856 until his death. They did name all of their girls after Jenny. Marx frequented the British Museum's Reading Room during this period of his extensive writing on class struggle. In January 1865, Marx sent President Lincoln a letter on behalf of the "International Working Men's Association," congratulating him on his reelection. Charles Francis Adams was given the duty of a reply, which was extremely tepid and unenthusiastic.

Catherine Wilson (1822–1862) was, in essence, a clumsy serial killer who merely had a run of good luck until, well, her luck ran out. Her first experiment on an unsuspecting victim was with a retired sea captain named Peter Mawer, who lived in Lincolnshire. The captain was so pleased with his new housekeeper's work that he made a will leaving all his money to her. A few weeks later, the man died from colchicum poisoning. Because Mawer had gout and had been taking the drug himself, no one suspected Wilson.

Bolstered by her success, Catherine headed to London with a man named Dixon. It is unclear whether Wilson was married to him, although she did claim Dixon to be her husband. Shortly thereafter, their new landlady, a Mrs. Soames, chastised Catherine for being late with the rent. Dixon himself was not earning enough to suit Catherine. No matter, because in a few short weeks, he and Mrs. Soames were dead. As Wilson's remarkable luck would have it, the doctor missed both Dixon's and the landlady's colchicum poisoning.

Catherine continued moving around and changing jobs, gaining employment with elderly or ill, but wealthy, people, gaining their trust and seeing herself written into their wills, only to finalize everything with a fatal dose of "tonic" full of colchicum or sulfuric acid.

My story of Catherine being discovered by a savvy undertaker is completely fictional. She was really exposed while employed with Mrs. Sarah Carnell, who also made out a will in Catherine's favor. She took some tonic from Catherine, which unfortunately the murderess had loaded up a little too well with acid. Spitting out the revolting medicine, Mrs. Carnell watched in shock as it burned a hole in her bedcovers. Catherine fled the scene, but it wasn't long before she was caught and brought to trial, where she was, unbelievably, acquitted.

Catherine was picked up once again in connection with another woman whose death suggested poisoning. This time, she did not escape her fate.

Catherine Wilson was hanged at Newgate on October 20, 1862, before a crowd of 25,000. She was the last woman to be publicly hanged in London, although four more would suffer the ignominy of a public hanging between 1866 and 1868: one in Chester, one in Exeter, one in Lincoln, and the final public hanging of a woman in Maidstone.

SELECTED BIBLIOGRAPHY

Beeton, Isabella. *Beeton's Book of Household Management* (Facsimile Edition). London: Jonathan Cape Limited, 1968.

Bland, Olivia. *The Royal Way of Death*. London: Constable and Company Ltd, 1986.

Bowman, John S., ed. *The Civil War Day by Day*. Greenwich, CT: Dorset Press, 1989.

Brett, Mary. *Fashionable Mourning Jewelry, Clothing & Customs*. Atglen, PA: Schiffer Publishing Ltd, 2006.

Curl, James Stevens. *The Victorian Celebration of Death*. Phoenix Mill: Sutton Publishing Ltd, 2000.

Eddleston, John J. *Criminal Women: Famous London Cases*. South Yorkshire: Pen and Sword Books Ltd, 2010.

Ferry, Kathryn. *The Victorian Home*. Oxford: Shire Publications, 2010.

Flanders, Judith. *Inside the Victorian Home*. New York: W.W. Norton & Co., 2003.

Foreman, Amanda. *A World on Fire: Britain's Crucial Role in the American Civil War*. New York: Random House, 2010.

Hannavy, John. *The Victorians and Edwardians at Work*. Oxford: Shire Publications, 2009.

Jalland, Pat. *Death in the Victorian Family*. New York: Oxford University Press, 1996.

Longford, Elizabeth. *Victoria R.I.* London: Heron Books, 1964.

Lowry, James W. *Embalming Surgeons of the Civil War*. Ellicott City, MD: Tacitus Publications, 2001.

May, Trevor. *The Victorian Domestic Servant*. Oxford: Shire Publications, 1998.

May, Trevor. *The Victorian Undertaker.* Oxford: Shire Publications, 1996.

May, Trevor. *The Victorian Workhouse.* Oxford: Shire Publications, 1997.

Mitchell, Sally. *Daily Life in Victorian England.* Westport, CT: Greenwood Press, 1996.

Morley, John. *Death, Heaven and the Victorians.* London: Studio Vista, 1971.

Nicholson, Shirley. *A Victorian Household.* London: Barrie & Jenkins, 1994.

Pasierbska, Halina. *Dolls' Houses.* Oxford: Shire Publications, 1991.

Pearson, Lynn F. *Mausoleums.* Buckinghamshire: Shire Books, 2002.

Picard, Liza. *Victorian London: The Tale of a City 1840–1870.* New York: St. Martin's Press, 2005.

Rutherford, Sarah. *The Victorian Cemetery.* Oxford: Shire Publications, 2008.

Sacks, Janet. *Victorian Childhood.* Oxford: Shire Publications, 2010.

Shepherd, Jack. *The Adams Chronicles: Four Generations of Greatness.* Boston: Little, Brown and Company, 1975.

Woodham-Smith, Cecil. *Queen Victoria: From her birth to the death of the prince consort.* New York: Alfred A. Knopf, 1972.

LADY OF ASHES

Christine Trent

ABOUT THIS GUIDE

The suggested questions are included
to enhance your group's reading
of Christine Trent's

LADY OF ASHES.

DISCUSSION QUESTIONS

1. The Victorian era was a period of rapidly changing technology and social hierarchies. What evidence do you find of this in the book?

2. Although every profession has its bad apples, undertaking was a particularly reviled industry in the Victorian era. Why do you think this was so?

3. How did Victorian undertaking practices in England differ from what is done now? Are there Victorian practices that you would like to see performed once again?

4. In Victorian England, it was considered important to journal the final days of a loved one as a memorial and keepsake for posterity. Why do you think this was considered important? Why do you think this has fallen out of favor today?

5. Graham was determined to become a part of society, one of the new "self-made" men who came to enjoy substantial prosperity in Victorian England. Was this a realistic goal to achieve? What were some of the ways Graham sought to rise in society that we still embrace today?

6. How would you describe Violet and Graham's marriage? Would you say it was more or less typical than most marriages of the time? What were some of the challenges Violet faced as she struggled to keep her marriage together?

7. Conversely, consider the marriage between Albert and Victoria. What do you admire about it? What weaknesses lay between them?

8. The workhouse was one of the ways in which the Victorians attempted to address the needs of England's poor. Compare and contrast the workhouse to some of today's social programs. In what ways was the workhouse better or worse?

9. What was your reaction when you read that Violet brought Susanna home to live without first consulting Graham?

10. What surprised you the most about British attitudes toward and involvement in the U.S. Civil War?

11. Was the British government right to be outraged by the taking of two Confederate diplomats, Mason and Slidell, from RMS *Trent?* Was their insistence on neutrality in all waters at all times realistic and/or enforceable?

12. After Albert's death, Victoria remained in mourning for the rest of her life, even choosing to be buried in her wedding veil. Yet she later developed a special attachment for a servant by the name of John Brown, with whom many people claim she had an affair. Do you think Victoria had an affair, or was this purely a platonic relationship?